Ace

Spencer Dunmore: born in London, educated in Yorkshire during World War II, left Britain for Canada in the mid-fifties. He lives at present in Burlington, Ontario, where he is an advertising executive during the day, an author in the evenings and a private pilot at the weekends.

Also by Spencer Dunmore
in Pan Books

Bomb Run
Final Approach
Means of Escape

Ace
Spencer Dunmore

Pan Books
in association with
Heinemann/Peter Davies

First published 1981 by Heinemann/Peter Davies
This edition published 1982 by Pan Books Ltd,
Cavaye Place, London SW10 9PG
in association with Heinemann/Peter Davies
© Spencer Dunmore 1981
ISBN 0 330 26741 8
Printed by Collins, Glasgow

For Derek Priestley
with thanks

December 28, 1944: 15:35 hours

The B–17 is a brute to kill.

You watch the cannon shells sparkling like Christmas lights as they explode the big bomber's metal flanks. God only knows how many times you've hit it. At point-blank range. It's impossible to miss. The monster fills the panel of 50 mm armoured glass before you. A moment ago it deflected a heavy calibre machine gun bullet which left a pretty star-shaped fissure. One of the Fort's engines has stopped: it spews oil in a fine spray. A huge chunk of the rudder has been shot away; you can see bits of the structure wobbling in the wind, like some gallant but forlorn flag. The Fort has lost height and speed; it's a straggler, wounded, despairing, having watched the rest of the American formation heading home to England and warm meals and girls and drinks. There can be little hope left in that metal monster. But still it flies. Still its belly turret and waist guns blaze away at you, the 0.50-inch bullets winking as they speed toward you and hurtle past you at incredible speed to disappear somewhere behind and join all the billions upon billions of bullets and shells and assorted hardware that have fallen on the land in the last five years. Break, for Christ's sake! Madness! But you keep on firing, a fraction of a moment longer. You're so suicidally close to the bomber that you see tiny dents in its metalwork. You look into the eyes of a waist gunner. He scowls, intent on killing.

Even as you dive away from the Fort, it lurches, mortally wounded. A wing tank vomits flame. Quickly, hungrily, the fire spreads. The bomber falls away on one wing. Slowly with a kind of ghastly dignity, the great machine rolls completely over on to its back, trailing a huge plume of oily black smoke. A hatch tumbles free. A man follows, clutching his legs to his body like an acrobatic diver. He somersaults clear of the doomed Fort before pulling his ripcord. Another man follows. Then a third.

An instant later the plunging bomber dissolves in a ball of fire. It disintegrates, scattering itself about the sky in fiery fragments.

Two parachutes open.

What happened to the third man?

No time to wonder. Too many Yankee P–51s about. And any moment now the red fuel warning light will be flickering on your instrument panel. The ammunition counter informs you that you have only a few 20 mm shells left for your two MG 151 cannons. A couple of seconds' fire, if that.

Insurance for the trip home.

God almighty! You were close enough to count the rivets on the Fort; a miracle you didn't hit the thing. You're mad, you tell yourself. You nod; you've heard yourself say it over and over again.

A friendly layer of cloud floats only a few hundred metres below. A handful of seconds to reach it. Hope the P–51s don't spot you. And head you off. And blast you out of the sky. Hasty glances over your shoulder as you plunge, innards complaining as usual.

Christ! Two sleek shapes in pursuit!

Old Friend Fear grabs your guts in icy fingers. And squeezes. Mouth dry. Body soaking. Some parts too hot in the electrically-heated flying suit, other parts frozen solid.

Is this the day your luck finally runs out? You consider the question with equanimity. Foot hard on rudder. Wrench the stick as if you're trying to shove it through the side of the cockpit. Engine howling as you demand every last erg of power. . . .

Continuous fire from the Yanks. Determined cowboys.

But they're just a fraction of an instant too late.

You plunge into the cloud. Greyness streaks past the perspex canopy. The colour of brains, someone had once observed. Someone long dead. You hurl the long-suffering bird into a spiralling turn. Again. Level out now; the cloud's becoming patchy; you catch glimpses of solid earth below. Terra firma. Trim to edge the FW's nose back into the cloud. Now turn again. Head almost due east. And turn again: 180 degrees. The cowboys won't expect you to head toward the Allied lines.

Time to take a breath. Now for a cautious dip beneath the cloud layer. No sign of the P–51s. Another breath. Your own personal angel (a female, with huge blue eyes) has bestowed upon you yet another lease on your mortal existence. You wonder if she is saving you for some especially unkind fate.

You handle the FW with care. God knows what structural damage the Americans' bullets might have done. Turn a trifle too tightly and you might find you've left a wing behind. Pilots who perform victory rolls after combat are asking for trouble. And frequently get it.

Strange, how empty the sky has become. Presumably the battle is still raging, the Forts and their long-range P–51 escorts against the outnumbered, outgunned Luftwaffe fighters. But they have moved off towards the coast, towards England. You look down. Your Fort is somewhere down there, still burning probably, a tangle of scrap metal and broken bodies. The crew's luck had run out. Soon your luck will run out; it has to; it is inevitable. . . .

The familiar twitch has set in. Reaction. Nausea. Utter fatigue. You have to will yourself to steer the fighter for home. Think, man, think! Is there enough fuel? Just about, you calculate. Good. You have no wish to land at some unfamiliar airfield to refuel for the rest of the journey home. Landings and take-offs can be a nightmare these days, with the Yanks and the Tommies always buzzing about at tree-top height looking for things to shoot at.

A flak battery opens up at you.

Stupid bastards! Can't they identify an FW, for God's sake? The morons fire at everything in the air, assuming, apparently, that if it is flying, it belongs to the Allies.

The flak ceases. The gentlemen with the popguns have at last recognized your aircraft as German.

Tranquil countryside, the ground patched with the remnants of the snow that fell before Christmas. Snug little villages, the houses clustered closely together as if for mutual warmth.

Wearily you keep glancing in every direction. Surviving means ceaseless searching, endless watching for the Spitfires, the P–51s, the Thunderbolts that roam the German sky as if it belongs to them. Which you have to admit, it does.

God almighty, you're tired. Will you be sick when you land? You wonder. You never know in advance. For a time you kept score. Over a six month period an average of four and a half vomitings for every ten operational sorties. Why the hell did you bother to count? Who cared, except for dear old Dorsch who had to dispose of the mess?

You brace your arms to kill the trembling of your hand on the control column. You're like a wobbly old man, you tell yourself; you'll be peeing in your pants next. Twenty-five years old; looking like forty, according to Dorsch. You push your Leitz goggles up and finger the flesh around your eyes. You can feel the ridge where the goggles have pressed. You shake your head; your brain feels fuzzy and useless. Fatigue is like a drug taking command of every sense.

Why didn't you let the cowboys in the P–51s shoot you down?

Why not get it over with? It's sure to happen one day soon. Why not today? All worries gone for ever.

Stupid, unanswerable question.

The field materializes in the distance. Wheels down. Flaps at ten degrees. Thank Christ they still work. Ease back on the power. No time for elaborate approach patterns these days. The object of the exercise is simply to get your machine down with the optimum celerity.

Wide turn. Left wing down. The place looks deserted. But isn't. The camouflage boys have done a good job. There are a couple of dozen FWs down there, all parked beneath netting and branches, hidden between trees, half buried in revetments.

Automatically, you nudge the rudder, keeping the nose angled to one side to provide a clear view of the strip that sways toward you. There's a brisk crosswind. A worry for a student pilot, but the very least of your problems; besides, the FW has a magnificently wide undercarriage; it will stay the right way up no matter how rough the conditions. Leafless branches of trees sweep up at you. Past you. Power off . . . now! Haul back on the stick. Right back as far as possible. Nose high. Keep her flying as long as she is willing. Bump . . . clatter. Down. Burst of throttle. Instinctive glances over the shoulder: you're even more vulnerable on the ground than in the air. You open the cockpit ventilator to full. The chilly air is delicious. You breath it in, great, hungry lungfuls of it.

The ground crewmen in their black overalls – some sporting fleece-lined flight jackets that once had belonged to downed Allied airmen – come running out to direct you to your dispersal.

You cut the power. The fourteen-cylinder BMW wheezes into silence; the big three-bladed propeller shudders and is still. Curious, how noisy silence can be.

Faithful Dorsch is already on the wing, helping you with your harness straps.

'Welcome back. I'm glad to see you.'

The two of you speak like equals at such times, although Dorsch is always careful to observe the niceties when others are in earshot. He never takes advantage of the time together. How long is it? How many lifetimes?

'I got a Fort,' you announce, your voice husky. 'And a couple of P–51s damned nearly got me.' You glance down at the bag discreetly poking out of Dorsch's pocket. 'It's all right. I won't be needing it.'

'Good,' says Dorsch matter of factly.

'I think I collected a few holes.'

Dorsch nods, looking the FW over. 'We'll patch her up. Good as new. You need sleep,' he adds, like a doctor to a patient.

You don't argue; you could go to sleep in the cockpit. Are you ill? Did one of the P–51's bullets hit you, numbing you and are you at this moment bleeding to death? Such things happen. In the heat of battle a man could be fatally wounded and be unaware of the fact. You glance down at yourself. No blood stains. All limbs present and accounted for.

Dorsch says, 'The two new men haven't come back. Perhaps they landed at another field.'

'One of them went down,' you tell him. 'I saw him go. A flamer. I can't remember his name.'

'Neither can I,' says Dorsch. 'You look like hell.'

'I'm all right,' you say, pulling yourself out of the narrow seat. 'Don't be a bloody old woman.'

Dorsch shrugs, as if the whole thing is a matter of supreme indifference to him. You clap him on the shoulder as you jump down to the grass, a friendly slap to demonstrate that you don't mean it. A good fellow, Dorsch; you couldn't wish for a better chief mechanic or a more faithful comrade. Dorsch is like a father, although only about ten years separate the two of you.

It is evening already; the shadows lengthening; in an hour it will be dark. Mercifully dark. Another day done with; another day of surviving; another day of impossible odds and hopeless sorties. More youngsters straight from training have come and gone and no one even remembers their names. The statisticians claim that if the tyros manage to come back from their first sortie their chances are twice as good of surviving the next two. In the unholy business of air fighting, experience is one priceless factor. Luck is the other. You have only so much in your personal account. When it is gone, you go too.

Some sketching tonight? Can you be bothered?

The old Opel comes bouncing across the grass, the thin-faced driver, Stuckart, wears a determined expression, perhaps imagining that he's driving a tank against Montgomery. He stops with a squealing of ancient brakes.

You collapse in the rear seat. A quick snack. Then sleep. Hours and hours of sleep. To hell with sketching. Or reading. Or paperwork. Please don't make a noise near here tonight, you silently beg RAF Bomber Command.

Stuckart says, 'Sir, I am to instruct you that you are to see the General at 1900 hours.'

Generalmajor Martin Freisler oozes sincerity. His handshake is firm; the gaze of his pale grey eyes is steady. He indicates a chair; his smile seems to say that there is no one in the world he would rather have sit in it.

'A cup of coffee, my dear Brehme? Or would you prefer something stronger? Cognac perhaps?'

'Coffee, thank you, sir.'

Freisler nods gravely, as if a decision of importance has been made. He pours from a solid silver coffee service. An elegant soldier, the Generalmajor; he likes to surround himself with beautiful things. His desk, encrusted with cherubs and gilt, should be in a museum. Booty from France? A memento of the good old days when the flyers of the Third Reich could do no wrong?

'Cigarette?'

'Thank you, Herr General.'

Lucky Strikes. American cigarettes. Freisler smokes no other, it is said. Does he really maintain his supply by diverting Red Cross parcels as the rumours claim? A wag had suggested writing to the makers of Luckies, offering the Generalmajor as an enthusiastic endorser of the product.

'My congratulations on your latest victory.'

'Thank you, sir.'

'A B–17, wasn't it?'

'Yes, sir.'

'How I wish we had ten thousand more like you, my dear Brehme. Your family is well, I trust.'

'Yes, sir,' you say. And think of Jeanne. And feel guilty.

Freisler examines his fingernails, first the left hand then the right. He looks up and smiles. 'I know these past few months haven't been easy.'

You say nothing; there is nothing to say. Surely to God, Freisler hasn't dragged you all the way over here to tell you how difficult things are. The scar on your cheek – a souvenir of Russia – starts to burn as if the flames are doing their work all over again.

'But I think,' says Freisler, 'we will look back on these times and we will realize that they represented only a brief interlude of darkness. The nadir of our fortunes, you might say. For I can assure you that better days are ahead, my friend. Have you flown the new Messerschmitt jet fighter?'

'Not yet, sir.'

'You will, Brehme, you will. There's nothing in the sky to touch it. Incredibly fast and heavily armed. I tell you, that aircraft and the 163 rocket fighter will revolutionize aerial warfare. At this moment they are being produced in enormous numbers. It won't be long before they are standard equipment for every unit!'

'That's good news,' you say; it is expected. The trouble is, they've been feeding fiction to everyone for so long that no one will know the truth if it materializes. Rumour has it that the new jet fighters could have been in action a year ago had it not been for bungling and vacillation at High Command. On the other hand it is also said that the jets are too hot to handle, a score of test pilots having been killed trying to ready the beasts for squadron use.

'Actually,' Freisler goes on, in his smooth, convincing way, 'the new jet and rocket fighters are only part of the packet of surprises that we'll be opening up for the Yanks and Tommies. Nineteen forty-five will be a thoroughly unpleasant year for them!'

'Splendid,' you say. You sip your coffee. Presumably you are here for the sole purpose of listening to the latest batch of fairy stories. You have, however, been given a decent cup of coffee for your trouble; delicious stuff; you haven't tasted such coffee for years. No Ersatz muck for the Generalmajor.

Freisler says, 'The first thing we will do in the New Year . . .' He places his hands flat on the desk as if bracing himself '. . . is to destroy the American and British air forces in the Netherlands, France and Belgium!'

You stare, wondering if you've dozed for an instant and have missed something. '*Destroy* them?'

Freisler nods, smiling. 'I see I have startled you.'

'Frankly, yes.'

'I'm glad, Brehme. And I can assure you that we will do much more than startle the Allies. I wanted you to come and see me this evening so that I can acquaint you with the plan. I have been discussing it with Reichsmarschall Göring all afternoon. He has a great personal interest in the operation; the original concept is his, you see.'

I can believe it, you think. The fat idiot is determined to throw away the last few fighters he possesses.

'Detailed orders are being drawn up at this moment,' Freisler says. 'It will be a devastating blow. We will strike precisely at dawn on the morning of the first of January while the Yanks and

Tommies are sleeping off their hangovers! We will wipe out their aircraft on the ground; we will decimate them – with an attacking force of three thousand fighters!'

You catch your breath. Have you dozed again? 'Three *thousand* fighters?'

'Possibly more!'

'But,' you enquire, 'where are we going to get three thousand fighters?'

'Don't worry.' Freisler smiles in the manner of a man who has solutions to every problem. 'We have been working on this plan for some time, my dear Brehme. Aircraft have been stored, fuel stock-piled. Everything has been thought out.'

'What about pilots?' There aren't enough pilots to meet day-to-day losses. Have the idiots been holding back airmen?

'Pilots will be available too, I assure you.' Freisler speaks firmly. Say it firmly enough and often enough and it will become truth; that is their credo. 'It has all been organized down to the last detail. We are going to shatter them; I tell you, we will change the course of the air war in one stroke!' He springs to his feet, as if glad to get out of his chair. He tugs on a string; curtains swing aside to reveal a map of Western Europe. A series of red card arrows have been applied to the map, darting from locations in the west of Germany, across the borders to Holland, Belgium and France, to point at a score of major Allied airfields. 'They think they have us *beaten*,' Freisler chuckles. 'They are becoming complacent. The war is as good as over, according to them; they're making plans for going home. They have no idea of the true state of affairs!'

You try to think, try to stir your weary brain. Does it make sense to stockpile fighters and pilots when there are too few on the fighting fronts? Three *thousand* of them?

'Sir, these pilots you've . . . reserved – are they experienced or novices?

'Top quality men, my dear Brehme, I can assure you. You need have no concern on that score. What do you think of what I have told you?'

You choose your words with care. 'Sir, if we are able to attack the Allied airfields with three thousand fighters and if the attack is well coordinated and properly executed, then, I think we would deal the Allies a crippling blow. We would knock them out of action, at least for some time, until they are able to provide replacements. Which I suppose they will be able to do, of course, eventually. . . .'

'And by then, we'll be flying the jets, my friend.' Again that self-satisfied smile. Everything has been worked out; tomorrow will bring glory. Always tomorrow; never today. 'No doubt you are asking yourself why I am telling you about this operation.'

You nod. 'The thought had crossed my mind.'

A lean, knowing finger wags at you.

'The fact of the matter is, my dear Brehme, Reichsmarschall Göring wishes – in fact he told me this personally and mentioned it again today just a few hours ago – he wishes you to be the first operational pilot to know about the plan. For a very good reason, my friend: he wants you to lead it! He wants you to fire the first shot! It's an honour you have earned! The Reichsmarschall regards you very highly, believe me.'

How the hell is one supposed to respond? Why not with the truth for once? But no, you find yourself nodding obediently; it is good of the Reichsmarschall to think of you, you hear yourself say.

Half an hour later you leave Freisler's office. At the door, a guard with rifle snaps to attention. You salute. You make your way along the HQ corridors. Orderlies strut about with their inevitable sheaves of paper, their boots clattering importantly. The place reeks of floor polish.

'Excuse me, Herr Major.'

You pause. A young clerk, bespectacled and earnest, stands rigid.

'What is it?'

'Sir . . . I wonder if I might ask you something.'

'Very well.'

Awkwardly the young man produces a small notebook. 'I would be greatly honoured, sir, if you would be kind enough to sign your name . . .'

You smile. An autograph!

'What is your name?'

'Ebert, Herr Major.'

'Your first name?'

'Franz.'

'Very well.' You take the notebook and hold it against the wall to write. 'Is this all right? "To my friend, Franz Ebert, from Ernst Brehme. Good luck in the New Year." '

You'll need it, you think. We all will.

The clerk grins as if he has been handed an extra month's pay. 'That's very kind of you, sir. Thank you so much. I shall treasure this always. It has been a privilege to speak to you. . . .'

You wish him goodnight. As you step outside you pull up your greatcoat collar. The weather is turning. There could be more snow. You hope so. A good fall of snow could put paid to this grand sortie before it starts. It's yet another of their desperate one-blow solutions to Germany's problems – all of them planned by people who seem to have only the vaguest idea of what is really happening at the front.

Does the Luftwaffe really have three thousand fighters in the west? And pilots to fly them? You shake your head sadly as you walk to your car. There was a time. . . .

Part one

"Fledgling"
August 1940

One

Wolfram tossed his flying jacket and helmet on the desk. He ran a hand through his straight hair.

'Sit down, Brehme.' His voice was gentle, almost inaudible. He rubbed his eyes with both hands; a passer-by might have thought he was shedding tears. He sighed as he sat down on the corner of the desk. It was a weary, long-suffering sigh.

'Brehme, you committed . . .'

Someone decided to run up his engine immediately outside the flight office. The windows rattled in their frames. Wolfram's nostrils flared as if he smelt something offensive. He massaged his nose, stroking it between thumb and forefingers, over the reddish mark left by his oxygen mask. He possessed lean, aristocratic features. An elegant young man, he habitually wore breeches and tunic in the air. Rumour had it that he was related to the Krupps. A second cousin, it was said. The din continued. Wolfram took a cigarette from the packet on his desk. He tapped the cigarette half a dozen times at one end, half a dozen times at the other end. Then he lit it with a gold lighter and blew out smoke in a thin, carefully formed stream.

At last the noise subsided; the Daimler-Benz coughed into silence.

Wolfram looked up at the ceiling as he said, 'You did not do well today, Brehme.'

'I know, sir. I'm sorry.' Ernst's voice sounded as if it belonged to someone else.

'It's not uncommon,' said Wolfram in his precise, oddly bored way, 'for pilots on their first operational missions to make mistakes. It is, however, uncommon for them to disobey orders. . . .'

'Sir, I didn't exactly. . .'

'I called you. Ordered you to rejoin me. Didn't you hear?'

'Yes, I did, sir . . . but I didn't know where you were . . . or where I was.'

'Before we took off, didn't I make it clear that your job was to stay at my side, two hundred metres away. Did I not say that?'

'Yes, sir.'

'And did you stay at my side?'

'No, sir.' He cleared his throat. His hands were clammy; he felt sweat rolling down his side; his shirt was stuck to him like a second skin.

'Why not?'

'Sir, I don't know . . . everything was so different from what I thought it was going to be. . . .' He shook his head. 'I haven't any sensible reason for my actions, sir . . . I think I tried to look everywhere at once . . . then I got lost . . . I suppose I panicked.'

'You did indeed. It's easy to get lost in a fight, Brehme. A couple of turns. A dive or two. Suddenly you don't know where you are.'

'Yes, sir.'

'You became disoriented, don't you?'

'Yes, sir.'

'So you found something out today, didn't you?'

'Yes, sir.'

'Do you realize how lucky you are, Brehme?'

'I think so, sir.'

'It was a miracle you weren't shot down; you wandered around the sky like some student on his first solo.'

'Yes, sir.'

'The nation has invested vast sums in training you, equipping you and providing you with an aeroplane full of fuel and ammunition.'

'Yes, sir.' Agree with him; keep agreeing.

Wolfram stubbed his cigarette in the ash tray; grinding out the glow with economical little movements; he might have been adjusting a knob in his Messerschmitt's cockpit.

'It would have been a pity if you had been killed today,' he said. He turned to Ernst. 'But it would have been an infinitely greater pity if I had been killed – because you failed to carry out my orders.'

'Yes, sir.'

'I am far more valuable than you are, Brehme. I am an officer; you are a cadet. I am experienced. I am a threat to the enemy. You are a threat to us. Is that a reasonably accurate statement, Brehme?'

'Yes,' said Ernst. Keep agreeing.

'I value my life, Brehme, even if you don't value yours. If I have to die I would prefer it to be at the hands of the enemy not at the hands of someone who is supposed to be on our side.'

'But, sir. . .'

Wolfram snapped, 'Your job is to protect my arse, Brehme! That's why we keep you! That's why you exist! You're there to make sure no Tommy attacks me while I'm attacking Tommies. But how the bloody hell can you protect my arse if you're farting about, twenty kilometres away?'

'I don't know . . . I mean, I can't . . .'

'The question is, what are we going to do about it? Wolfram lit another cigarette. His fingers were stained with nicotine. A high-strung individual, Wolfram. He smoked too much. A Messerschmitt taxied by; again the windows shivered; Ernst felt the floor tremble beneath his feet. Noisy beggar, the fellow in the Messerschmitt. But thank God for the diversion he caused. Ernst's stomach still gurgled noisily, as if he had eaten something that disagreed with him.

Now Wolfram was leafing through a file, cogitating over a phrase here, a passage there.

The Messerschmitt taxied away; the windows were still again.

'They rated you Above Average at fighter pilots' school. They thought you were pretty hot stuff, Brehme, that's why you were posted here.'

'Yes, sir.'

Wolfram studied the glowing end of his cigarette. 'Some pilots,' he said, a trace of sadness in his voice, 'are quite brilliant at training school; they love flying; they learn fast; they score splendid marks in all their examinations. One might suppose that such men would make marvellous combat pilots. But the sad fact is, things don't always work out as we expect. Something happens to a man when he finds people shooting at him, doing their level best to kill him.'

Ernst nodded, remembering, his innards freezing again.

Wolfram said, 'Flying an aeroplane is an unnatural business; having people in other aeroplanes shooting at you is even more unnatural. And extremely unpleasant. I know of no one who enjoys it; I most certainly don't. But we have to perform our duties in spite of it.'

'Yes, sir.'

'It isn't easy for anyone. And for some . . .' He shrugged. 'It's impossible!'

Outside, a man laughed; a dirty-joke laugh.

Wolfram puffed at his cigarette. 'I may be making a serious mistake, Brehme; I may in fact be condemning myself to death.

But I'll take another chance on you. We will fly together once more. The same as today. You will be my wingman. I will rely on you and you alone to protect my rear end, a rear end I value enormously.'

Ernst nodded again. Was he glad or sorry? He wasn't sure; however, he thanked Leutnant Wolfram as if a thousand Marks had changed hands.

'But,' said Wolfram, pointing at him, 'if I look around at any time during the trip, Brehme, and if you aren't there, two hundred metres away as instructed, then I shall come and look for you, Brehme, and I shall find you and I shall personally shoot you down! Now go away and think hard and long about what I've said!'

In some weird, confused way he seemed to be detached from himself; he could watch himself, observe his disconsolate figure trudging along the patch, ungainly flying boots crunching on the gravel, shoulders drooping, eyes lowered.

No one spoke to him. With good reason. He was a pariah.

A coward.

Shame stung like an ulcer; it was eating away at his innards, tearing at the very fibre of him. Everything was lost. Everything he had ever hoped for was now unattainable; he had proved himself totally, miserably unworthy. Wolfram's words, so scornful, so contemptuous! And he had deserved them, that was the sickening truth of it. He passed a cluster of mechanics. He didn't look at them. No doubt they were nudging one another behind his back and pointing. 'There goes Brehme. First operating trip today. Made a complete balls of it. Panicked. Wanders all over the bloody place, they say. Lucky as hell he didn't get himself killed.'

Lucky?

Little more than two hours before, he had clambered aboard the Messerschmitt and had settled himself into its narrow cockpit. Yes, he had been nervous. Who wasn't on their first sortie? But his nervousness had been a positive thing, sparked by excitement and eagerness; he had been fine-tuned, keen to prove himself.

He had been supremely – idiotically – confident.

Never had it occurred to him that he might fail in combat. There hadn't been room for such thoughts in a mind bubbling with childish images of heroism and daring.

But then, over the green fields of Southern England, the enemy

22

had swooped. Guns clattered. Engines screamed. Voices bellowed over the R/T. The confusion, the mind-numbing chaos of it all! A sky peppered with darting, diving machines, streaking the sky with powdery gunfire trails. British bullets had slammed into the fuselage of his Messerschmitt, only a few centimetres behind him. Terror-struck, he had flung his aircraft into a wild series of turns and dives. He had reacted mindlessly, driven by naked panic. Hadn't spared a thought for Wolfram. Hadn't considered his duty. Hadn't even tried to attack an enemy aircraft. A Dornier had been blown to smithereens only a hundred metres away from him. The thing had simply vanished. The crew with it. The bombs they had intended for the British had instantly converted them from living, breathing, reasoning human beings into shreds of meat like something the butcher would throw away.

The blast had tossed Ernst's machine, flipping it completely over. The earth had revolved; every sense had gone spinning away on its own; a nightmare of whirling impressions, of deafening noise, of dizzying sights.

What had he expected, for God's sake? A pretty air display? Neat aerobatics? Faultless formation flying? Everyone escaping by parachute? No one dying? No one being burnt alive or converted to offal?

But he had survived. Survived to cringe at every recollection. Survived when better, far better, men hadn't. In spite of it all, Wolfram, the Staffelkapitän, had given him another chance. Youth and inexperience had been the extenuating factors. They had won him the chance of going through it all again. Facing the confusion and the gunfire and the naked, gut-wrenching fear.

It began to rain.

Leutnant Ulrich Wolfram lit another cigarette, his twelfth of the morning. He dragged the smoke deep. His insides felt as if they were turning somersaults. Commanding a squadron was hard on the innards.

Relax, he ordered himself. You handled yourself well. Nothing to worry about. Calm down. You can do it. You've done it before.

He held his hands over the desk before him. Blast! No matter how he tried he couldn't make them steady. Damn Brehme! It was his fault – poor, scared-out-of-his-wits Brehme with his sad blue eyes and his ridiculously handsome features.

The stupid bastard was good looking enough to be a film star. Perfect Aryan type. Finely chiselled features. Blond curly hair. A

23

tragedy that he would undoubtedly be dead in less than a month, perhaps no more than a week.

Wolfram dabbed at the perspiration around his neck and on his brow.

He wondered if he had been too hard on Brehme. Had he, in fact, destroyed the last particles of courage in the boy? But could he be blamed for trying too hard to make a fighter pilot of him? Wasn't that, after all, his job – and didn't he have every reason to believe that he was doing it reasonably well?

He nodded. Yes, you're damned good, he told himself, a master at your craft, respected by one and all.

He sighed. Exhausted.

Two

The airfield had once been the property of the French Air Force, l'Armée de l'Air. Reminders of the vanquished former owners were everywhere – signs, daily orders still flapping on notice boards, equipment, vehicles, a forlorn assembly of derelict Dewoitines, a menu in the Officers' Mess. The Luftwaffe had occupied the field a few days after the June armistice; now the only Frenchmen to be seen on the place were the civilians on the construction gangs still repairing the damage inflicted by the Luftwaffe during the spring attacks.

Clusters of Messerschmitt Bf 109 fighters dotted the field, nearly forty machines in all. They formed a Gruppe, commanded by a Major. The Gruppe itself consisted of three squadrons – or Staffeln – each commanded by a Captain (Hauptmann, in Luftwaffe parlance). The Messerschmitts stood in the open; no attempt had been made to conceal them. Why bother? The hard-pressed RAF was unlikely to mount an attack. Soon Britain would fall, as the other nations had done. It was simply a matter of time. The German fighter pilots were supremely confident. And with good reason. They had met and defeated one air force after another. They were the best in the business and their Messerschmitt 109 ('Emil' to the pilots because it was the 'E' model of the type) was the finest fighter aircraft in the world, a triumph of German design and manufacturing skill. But the Emil could be a tricky mount, unforgiving of errors. Ten days earlier, a nineteen-year-old pilot from Breisach had demonstrated the fact all too graphically. He was taking-off on an air test after repair work on the Emil's FuG 7/a R/T equipment. Tail up, he had almost reached flying speed. Without warning another Messerschmitt came in to land across his path. Startled, the young pilot had tried to leap-frog the interloper. But you could never make an Emil fly before it was ready. In an instant the fighter had snapped over on to its back. A scream of tortured, rending metal, audible over the engine's din. The fighter had careered across the grass, upside down, shedding fragments as it went. The pilot didn't have a chance. It was to be hoped that he was dead or unconscious before the remains erupted in fire and black, bloated billows of smoke. When the rescue crews had tamed the blaze there was nothing but charred fragments of the Emil, the two stalky legs of its under-carriage thrust skyward like arms in a hopeless gesture of supplication.

A shame. But such things happened. The pilot's fault, of course. The man had been trained to know the Emil's idiosyncracies. He should have remembered his lessons. It was his job. Far better to ground-loop and write off your undercarriage than to fry, trapped upside down in your cockpit.

The replacement for the dead pilot arrived the next day. His name was Ernst Brehme.

Walter Dietrich peered at his erection with the critical eye of a mechanic studying a particularly troublesome engine component.

He shrugged at it. Helplessly. Five days to payday, he informed it. I know you want the real thing. I know you're sick of me playing with you. But you'll have to be patient. Absolutely nothing I can do about it, old friend.

That bastard in Sick Quarters now possessed his meagre reserves of Occupation Marks. That hawk-faced observer from Kampfgeschwader 100 with the smile, the thin smile of an executioner. Never ever would he play Siebzehn-und-Vier again. It was a moronical game. No skill. Blind, stupid luck. And his had been all bad. He had suspected that Heinkel observer of cheating, of setting up the pack his own way. The sod had been too pleasant, too damned amiable. His smile had never wavered. Men playing cards for money had no business smiling.

Dietrich glanced at his watch. Still an hour to wait until supper. Odd, ever since that Hurricane's bullet had nicked his thigh, his appetite had been voracious. Dietrich imagined a table laden with

25

food: freshly baked bread and fine game, juicy beef and orange-flavoured chocolate cake. All of it served by nubile creatures with heroic breasts and sensuous underlips. Dietrich had recently developed a keen interest in underlips; they were, he decided, a sadly neglected part of the female anatomy. Underlips said a lot.

The rain beat a monotonous tattoo on the roof.

Dietrich gazed reverently at the ceiling. 'Be a good fellow, God, and make it stop raining while I go to supper. It would be greatly appreciated. Many thanks.'

After supper he would have a chat with everyone. Be welcomed back to the fold. With a bit of luck he might be able to borrow a few Marks until payday – although the lender would undoubtedly insist upon a signed and witnessed receipt. These days too many people were borrowing money and getting themselves killed before paying it back.

Dietrich was twenty-three, a veteran of the Condor Legion that had fielded the Luftwaffe's first aircraft against the Republicans in Spain. Dietrich had shot down a Russian 1–15 near Cuenca. Since September he had destroyed two French aircraft, a Morane fighter and a Potez bomber, plus an RAF Battle over Saarbrucken. Dietrich's face was quizzical, long and angular. His dark hair was usually unruly; he persisted in running his fingers through it whenever he was interested, alarmed or delighted. Or bored. He rarely remembered to get it cut; Schiegl, the adjutant, was obliged to remind him about it, again and again.

Dietrich had returned for duty earlier that afternoon, driven from the base hospital by Vosser – talkative Corporal Vosser who complained incessantly about the vehicles he had to drive. A tiresome character, Vosser, but he had his uses. He could get you anything, a bottle of genuine Scotch whisky ('Haig or Black and White; take your choice.'), a Rubens stolen from the Louvre, a woman, black, white or any shade in between. But you needed cash. Vosser never gave credit.

'You may let the rain start again during the night,' Dietrich advised God. 'And please make it heavy. Torrential. A deluge to cancel any flying. . . .'

The door opened. A blond, quite remarkably handsome young man entered. His blue eyes travelled rapidly, first to Dietrich's nakedness, then to the rest of the room. Clearly he had expected more than one occupant.

'I was talking to Goc,' Dietrich explained.

'Ah. . . .'

The fellow's mouth had dropped open. Poor devil didn't know what to say. Dietrich sighed inwardly. Why couldn't fate send a room-mate of wit and imagination, someone to lock intellectual horns with? Someone who might bring a little levity, an original idea or two, an amusing anecdote to this Spartan accommodation?

'I often talk to God,' Dietrich said. He made no attempt to conceal himself. It pleased him to observe the newcomer's embarrassment. 'As to this,' he said, pointing, 'rain makes me randy as hell. I've always had an intense desire to do it outside in the middle of a thunderstorm. God knows why.'

'Oh. . . .' Soft cheeks a-pinkening.

'You too?'

'No . . . no, I don't think so.'

One might have guessed. They were getting younger and younger, the children they sent out to war these days. This one was so correct, so proper, so well brought up.

And glum.

Definitely down in the mouth. Did he miss his Mutti?

'By the way, my name's Dietrich.'

The glum one looked up. 'Sorry,' he said. He got up, crossed the linoleum floor and shook hands. 'My name's Brehme.'

'So you're my new room-mate.'

'Yes.'

'I've been in Sick Quarters.'

'Yes, they told me. You were wounded.'

'Right here,' said Dietrich, indicating the bandage. 'Bloody Englishman nearly removed my leg.'

'Is it very painful?'

'Excruciating,' Dietrich told him. 'But they said the war couldn't go on without me so here I am back again, ready to do my duty in spite of the agony.'

Brehme cracked a ghost of a smile. It quickly died.

'Where are you from?' Dietrich asked, although the newcomer's Rhineland accent made the question superfluous.

'Köln.'

'My home is Hamburg,' Dietrich announced, as if to answer a question that was sure to be asked. 'How old are you?'

'Twenty.'

'Married?'

'No.'

Dietrich placed his hands upon his stomach. 'I was nearly married once,' he said. 'But when I was out of the country for a

27

few months, she went off with another fellow.'

'Shame.'

Mechanical tone.

'Actually I think she did me a favour.'

'I see.'

Nobody, Dietrich decided, had any right to be that good looking. It was almost obscene. Now what to discuss?

'You're properly settled in?'

A nod. 'Yes, thank you.'

'It's not exactly the Adlon Hotel but it could be worse.'

'Yes.'

A brilliant conversationalist! Such stimulating conversation! God, was he shy, sullen or merely stupid?

Brehme seated himself at the small folding table fastened to the end wall, beneath the framed coloured print of the Loire Valley. He had a leathery writing case with little compartments – every one so neat and tidy; one for paper, one for stamps, one for labels. No doubt an adoring parent had pressed it upon him when he went off to do battle for the Fatherland, urging him to write every day, without fail, no matter how little he had to say. Tiresome business, letter-writing.

'Writing home, are you?'

'No actually I'm writing to a friend.'

'Girl friend?'

'Yes.'

'What's her name?'

'Ilse.'

'Pretty?'

'I think so.'

'Good in bed, is she?'

Splutter, splutter. Cheeks positively glowing now. Brehme really didn't think that was anyone else's business.

'Perhaps you're right,' said Dietrich. 'I'm just interested, that's all. No offence intended. It's just that I'm always interested in girls.'

He smiled. Being outrageous and amusing when you had a foil like Brehme; it was good sport to talk of intimate matters in the way everyone else spoke of the weather or price of schnapps.

'What this air force needs,' he declared, 'is a well trained, superbly equipped corps of whores. Stunningly attractive girls. Eighteen to twenty-one – with perhaps a few older ones thrown in for those who fancy them mature. They'd be smartly dressed in special uniforms – removeable in ten seconds or less. They'd have delicious quarters to welcome us to. Perfumed, seductive as hell, with silk cushions strewn all over the place so that a fellow could loll about a bit after a hard day of being shot at by the bloody British. They'd be an invaluable aid to morale. And efficiency. It's a sad fact but the majority of our pilots are frustrated as hell when they take off! They're always getting erections in the air – and that's damned dangerous, particularly if you have to climb in a hurry! And it's a well known medical fact that randy pilots are lousy shots and suffer particularly severe groin pains when subjected to G-forces in dogfights. So if we make sure every man gets all the sex he needs we will have a far better air force and in no time at all we'll have the British beaten and our glorious victory will be due to the gallant, self-sacrificing corps of whores, the unsung heroines of the Western Front! Isn't that a damned fine idea?'

Again that fragile ghost of a smile.

'An amusing idea.'

'And sensible. The difficulty is to get HQ to see just how eminently sensible it is. All the rules are made by dry old codgers who've forgotten what it's like to be twenty and permanently desperately randy. I tell you, I'll change things when they make me Reichsmarschall. How long since you've seen your girl friend, Ilse?'

'Nearly three months.'

'And no extra-curricular fun to take her place?'

'No . . . no, of course not.'

Heavens, no! Perish the thought!

'Well, that's precisely what I mean. It's downright unhealthy for a fellow. We need regular maintenance, just like our aircraft.'

Brehme went back to his Feldpost form. What was he telling his girlfriend? That he was having a fine time and only wished she could be here to share it with him? No doubt he was assuring her that the local girls were of not the slightest interest to him. And no doubt she was whiling away the lonely hours in bed with some vigorous male.

In Dietrich's experience, good looking women were almost certain to be coaxed into bed if their husbands or boy friends were away long enough. Good looking women received far more than their fair share of compliments and women as a species were quite incapable of resisting compliments.

But it would be unkind to tell Brehme such facts of life. The

29

poor bastard looked low enough already.

'When did you get here?'

'Five days ago.'

'Been over the Channel yet?'

Curt, hurt nod.

'Rough?'

Another shrug.

'It's confusing as hell the first time.'

Brehme put his pen down. He looked at Dietrich. The dam broke. 'Confusing; yes, that's just what it is. I got separated . . . I didn't know where I was. I panicked, I suppose. I heard Wolfram on the R/T . . . but I couldn't rejoin him . . . I couldn't find him.'

Dietrich groaned inwardly. Why, he asked himself, did you have to ask?

'You were Wolfram's wingman?'

'Yes.'

'I suppose he told you if you ever strayed from his side again he'd personally go looking for you and shoot you down.'

Eyebrows up. 'How do you know?'

'He said the same thing to the fellow who had that bed before you. What the hell was his name? Pleasant enough in his own way, but had smelly feet.' Dietrich pulled his knees up to his chest; still naked, he looked as if he was posing for a sculpture. 'Forget about it.'

Eyebrows down. 'Forget about it?'

Impossible demand!

Dietrich ran a hand through his unruly hair. 'Listen, I know what's bothering you. Everyone's been through the same sort of thing. Nothing to worry about. You'll be all right. I promise. At least you got your crate back in one piece. The first time I got into a fight I wrote mine off. Not that it was any loss – one of those crappy old He 51s. In Spain. The Republicans had Russian jobs – Chatos, they called 'em. Bloody things could turn like a one-wheel cycle. I had had three of them on me – the bastards sniffed me out as a novice. God only knows why they didn't get me. Somehow or other I found my way back to the field – but I was so shaken up that I turned the crate over when I landed. Smashed it to hell.'

Lies, all lies. His first trip over the lines near Talavera had been totally without incident. No matter. If lies would do the trick then lies were justified.

'I got confused,' Brehme muttered.

'And you're scared stiff that it'll happen the next time too.'

The shrug was quickly followed by a nod.

'Don't give it a thought,' said Dietrich. 'You'll be perfectly all right the next time. You'll know what to expect.'

Unless of course you get so bloody frightened thinking about it that you make an even worse mess of things than you did the first time. Dietrich remembered the young pilot in Spain who had blown his brains out after his second trip. Was it his way of avoiding going out a third time? Who could tell? Terror did odd things to people.

'To be perfectly honest . . .' Brehme began.

Dietrich sighed. Nothing was worse than people being perfectly honest.

'. . . I don't think I have guts enough for this job.'

'Who the hell has?' replied Dietrich. 'Personally I nearly wet my trousers every time I go near an aeroplane. I've applied for a transfer to the veterinary service, but some clerical bastard keeps delaying it.'

Wan smile from the handsome aviator. 'I'm sorry. I shouldn't be unburdening myself on you.'

No, you shouldn't, Dietrich said silently. He yawned. In the middle of the yawn an idea popped into his mind. He glanced down at himself; at last he had subsided. But perhaps. . . . 'You should get your mind off flying,' he told Brehme. 'Damned important to get your mind off flying now, tonight. If you have any money and wouldn't object to lending me a little, I happen to know just the place. . . .'

He had been there more than an hour before he realized what the establishment *was*! At first he took it to be a private club of some sort. There was a woman called 'Auntie', a hefty, brightly painted creature of indeterminate age, who apparently ran it; she seemed to know Dietrich well. When she opened the door he had planted an enthusiastic kiss on her vivid cheek and said she was as gorgeous as ever. He introduced Ernst; she had declared him to be 'magnifique.' Then she had drifted off. Cognac had arrived – the genuine article, Dietrich said – not the cheap brandy Auntie passed off on undiscerning customers.

'We can look over the merchandise later,' Dietrich said.

'All right,' said Ernst, having not the faintest idea what Dietrich was talking about. They were sitting in a cramped, smoke-filled room. It was packed, the majority of the occupants being German officers: Wehrmacht and Luftwaffe with a scattering of naval specimens here and there.

'A popular place,' Ernst observed.

'That's because it gives good value,' Dietrich told him.

'I can see that,' said Ernst – who could see nothing of the sort. The dense smoke stung his throat and the heat made him sweat.

An attractive girl came into the lounge and crossed to a Wehrmacht captain, a plump, middle-aged, avuncular man. Supple type, no doubt.

'Christ,' hissed Dietrich, 'look at those.'

Those were the girl's breasts, almost toppling out of her low-cut dress as she stooped to converse with the officer.

Dietrich sighed and shook his head. 'What the hell is it that makes tits so appealing? They're nothing but great lumps of fat hanging on to a thorax! Mounds of tissue! Dollops of lard. Ah, but I adore them! Although it's often struck me that they're like hors d'oeuvres: they entice you into the main course – but afterwards you don't want them any more.'

Ernst gulped. He tore his gaze away from the girl. He had the uncomfortable feeling that his eyes were bulging. He blinked as if to set them back in their normal position.

Dietrich watched the captain strutting away, arm in arm with the girl.

'Bastard looks pleased with himself; anyone'd think she'd chosen him for his charm!' He nodded towards Ernst's glass. 'Good stuff, isn't it? Shall we have another?'

'I really don't think. . . .' But it was too late; Dietrich had already summoned the waitress to order more of the fiery muck.

It was towards the end of the second glass – swallowed like medicine – that the world became a pleasanter place. Dietrich was an amusing companion; indeed his remarks became wittier with every swallow of cognac; the parade of girls became more and more delicious, a tantalizing display of thighs and bouncing bosoms. To hell with the problem of the morning; that unpleasantness was all forgotten, something from the dim, distant past. Now everything was going to be all right, *he* was going to be all right.

'Which one do you like?' Dietrich enquired.

'Which one?'

'Which *girl*?'

No hesitation. 'The dark one with the blue eyes.'

'Angélique. Good choice.'

Ernst beamed, the excellence of his taste verified by an expert. What a fine fellow Dietrich was, wise and whimsical. And now the smoke and the heat no longer bothered him. Nothing bothered him. He felt marvellous; on top of the world.

Dietrich was chatting with Auntie. She nodded then drifted away.

Magically another glass of cognac had appeared before him. Odd how the stuff was now slipping down so readily, creating a delicious glow in the region of his solar plexus.

'There's a little matter of thirty Marks,' Dietrich told him apologetically.

'Certainly, old fellow,' Ernst peeled the notes off without another thought; they were merely bits of coloured paper.

It was the most natural thing in the world when Angélique appeared at his side. Smiling. Beckoning. Would he like to come to her room? Yes, he would; indeed he would. Charming mademoiselle. Woops, a little hard to stand upright but no matter . . . a little more concentration and everything would come back into focus . . . the room would undoubtedly stop revolving . . . and then it would be simpler to make one's feet follow Angélique's up the narrow squeaky staircase with the slightly threadbare runner bearing the geometric red, yellow and purple pattern. . . .

But fifteen minutes later Angélique had aged; her features were puffy and punctuated by irritable little lines; her make-up was patchy; she had a sour, used smell.

She sniffed. 'I can't do any more,' she said like a doctor abandoning all hope for the patient.

Ernst felt terrible. He daren't move, for movement would undoubtedly throw off the whole delicate balance of him, with God only knows what awful consequences.

She said, 'I can't waste any more time.'

Her breasts were limp and shapeless. Were they really the same breasts that had looked so fetching in that low-cut dress? Why was he still holding one?

'I don't feel very well,' he muttered.

Angélique muttered something, shaking her head, despairing. 'If you're going to be sick,' she said in the monotonous way of someone who has said the same thing again and again, 'then for Christ's sake don't be sick in here. I'll have to clean it up. Go in the bathroom. Down the hall. Second door on the right. But put your trousers on first.'

Just in time.

A. –B

An agonizing upheaval in the bathroom, pained eyes staring at the V-shaped crack in the porcelain of the lavatory bowl. Then a wash with cold water. Another wash. Feeling slightly better now. Buttoning-up of uniform. Fresh air: an immediate, urgent need. Down the red, yellow and purple staircase. Push through the throng and the smoke. Rapidly. Feeling ill again. Outside. Another ghastly retching and splashing into the gutter. Fervent wish to die there and then, face resting on the cool wet pavement. Then, the sound of footsteps.

'Pig!'

'German bastard!'

He saw the boot an instant before it connected with his abdomen. No time to move. Just watched the boot thud into him. Pain exploded, darting like fire through his body.

'No . . . don't!'

He tried to scramble to his feet. But they kicked him again. Helplessly he slumped back on the pavement, gorge erupting.

He saw the glint of steel in the man's hand.

'God . . . no, please.' Vomit burst into his mouth.

'Bastard!'

The foulness spewed out of him. So did the last vestige of strength. He was helpless, incapable of resistance. He looked into the man's eyes. Dark eyes, full of hatred.

'Hurry . . . for God's sake!'

'Hold him still!'

'Now . . . go on!'

Ernst winced, flesh contracting, already feeling the blade cutting into him, slicing through skin and muscle. Cold damp air flooding into the great gaping wounds. He closed his eyes. Squeezed them shut. Saw his father. Heard him speak. Do it. Quickly. Mercifully.

Shouts. Running, clattering feet. Approaching. Then passing. He was sick again. And again.

'Jesus.'

He managed to lift his head. He opened his eyes.

Dietrich was kneeling beside him. There was a gendarme, pistol drawn, shouting and gesticulating to someone on the other side of the street.

'Are you all right?' Dietrich talking. Odd voice.

'Yes. Think so. Yes.'

'Who were those fellows? Friends of yours?'

Incredibly funny remark. Just like Dietrich. Christ, it was good to be alive when you had abandoned hope, when you had kissed yourself goodbye for ever and ever.

'You look like hell.'

'Thanks.'

'Can you get up?'

'I think so.'

Dietrich helped him to his feet. He clutched a lamp post for support, resting his head against its cool, rough iron.

Dietrich stepped back a couple of paces like a photographer studying his subject.

'All right?'

He nodded, slowly, carefully.

'Good,' said Dietrich. 'Where would you like to go next?'

Three

The Messerschmitt lurched on its narrow undercarriage as the mechanic heaved on the starter handle, spinning the engine's fly-wheel.

Watch the revs. Start switch on. Fuel injection pump primed. Now! Tug at the starter clutch control beside the left knee. Bang! Throaty bellow from the Daimler-Benz. All twelve cylinders firing, the power sending shivers through every spar and former, the joystick vibrating eagerly. Test magnetoes, check fuel pumps, pressures and temperatures, compass, gyro, altimeter, barometric reading. . . .

Head throbbing, skull burning, flesh aching.

Would he ever recover? Would his body stop hurting? His stomach stop writhing? His head pounding? Damn the bloody weather for clearing! Damn the sun for burning a hole in his skull!

The Frenchman should have done it. Stuck the knife in. Ended it all there and then. Killed on active service. Proper military funeral. Honour guard. Consoling letter to his mother saying how bravely he had died in the great cause, what a splendid fellow he was, how everyone admired him. . . .

Difficult to credit that the Frenchman had really tried to stab him. But it *had* happened. It wasn't a bad dream. The Frenchman *hated* him. Actually hated him. Hatred was there, in his eyes. You could see it, identify it. 'You shall be correct in your dealing with the population,' the occupation orders had stated. Did they forget to tell the population the same thing?

All that damned money.

For what?

He had failed with Angélique. Failed miserably. A pathetic performance. Second of the day.

He closed his eyes; the warmth of the tiny cockpit seemed to swallow him; his body felt as if it was expanding, as if it would quickly fill the restricted space like some monstrous concoction in an oven.

He could have reported sick. *Should* have, perhaps. Was he in any condition to fly? Was he in fact adding to the danger for everyone else?

His heart thumped. Throat dry. Mouth vile. His eyes prickled with fatigue. He had slept poorly, turning and twisting, suffering the darting, grinding pains in his stomach, as he listened to Dietrich's contented breathing.

The Obergefreiter, bespectacled and officious, stood to one side of the flight line, red flag in left hand, white flag with green cross in right hand.

Why was he waiting? Had the operation been called off? Please God. If only the rain had lasted a few more hours. If only the mist hadn't cleared. If only, if only.

Wolfram's Messerschmitt squatted, nose-high, a few metres away, propeller turning, airframe trembling as if impatient for flight. Wolfram's helmeted head could be seen behind the little square-framed canopy. He had been crisp and businesslike at briefing. The job of the fighters was to protect the bombers, he had declared. If the bombers didn't get through to their target, the operation was a failure, no matter how many British fighters might be shot down.

The targets were the radar station at a place called Ventnor and airfields at Hawkinge and Lympne. The names were unfamiliar to Ernst; mere dots on the huge chart of southern England that adorned the Operations Room wall.

Wolfram had accorded Ernst a nod on the way out to the aircraft. A friendly greeting? Or simply a reminder of what had passed between them the previous day?

With Wolfram it was hard to tell.

Like countless young warriors before him, Ernst was as afraid of his comrades as of the enemy. Better to be shot down and killed by some Englishman than to fail Wolfram yet again and have to face his anger and scorn – and the disgrace of dismissal from the unit, if not a court martial for cowardice in the face of the enemy. Such things happened. Pilots were stripped of their rank and their flying insignia; they found themselves in the infantry, carrying a rifle. How could one possibly live with oneself?

White flag!

Time to go.

Eager, nervous hands eased throttle levers forward. Wings rocked as wheels began to roll over the bumpy turf. Mechanics waved farewell to their charges and turned away from the howling gales churned up by spinning propellers.

It was always tricky at the beginning of the take-off run; pilots could see little ahead because the Messerschmitts rolled with their tails still on the ground, long noses obscuring the forward view. Right feet pressed firmly on rudder pedals because of the fighters' tendency to swing to the left as they picked up speed.

And they gathered speed quickly, whisked along by the 1100 horses of the DB 601. Up tail! Now the view ahead was clear. The field shimmered in the heat.

Let her fly herself off. Ground dropping away. Undercarriage lever. Grinding of levers and pulleys and the thump of the wheels settling into their wells in the wing. Now the flaps, up in stages, trimming and retrimming, compensating for the loss of lift as they disappeared, leaving the wing clean and efficient.

Hurried glances to the left and right; the sky full of aircraft, rising, sinking, swaying. A pilot who grew careless was liable to find himself battered out of the sky by another aircraft's propwash or bumping wing tips with the man next door.

Climbing, the fighters streaked over the quiet land, the din of their engines rolling like some invisible monster across the fields and along village streets. Countless eyes followed the aircraft, some hard with loathing, others without apparent interest, still others warm with approbation. To the vast majority of French citizens, the Germans were enemies, invaders, detested occupiers of their sacred land. But some accepted the Germans philosophically; they were here; the intelligent thing was to make the best of it. To a minuscule proportion of Frenchmen, the Germans were friends, allies, the strong arm that would protect France from the iniquities of the British and the horrors of the Reds.

★

The aerial armada struck out across the Channel. Six hundred aircraft: Heinkel and Junkers bombers flanked by an equal number of Messerschmitt fighters.

Ernst's head was splitting. He winced with the pain of it, half closing his eyes to shut out a little of the sun's cruel glare. The dark glass of his Nitsche & Günther goggles seemed to be totally ineffective. He had the feeling that his vision was about to snap out of focus; something behind his eyeballs was stretching to breaking point. He had an appalling thirst. Desperate, he tried to suck up sufficient saliva in his mouth to constitute a swallow of liquid.

The one positive aspect of feeling this dreadful was that it blunted the terror of what was to come. Life seemed to consist only of five-minute fragments; the object of the moment was simply to struggle through to the next five-minute segment.

He willed himself to concentrate on the instrument panel. The umpteenth perusal. The studying of the dials and gauges that indicated the pulse and heartbeat of the engine. Revs. Pressures. Temperatures. Now the umpteenth glance at Wolfram and the others around him. Keep station. Adjust power a fraction. Drifting too close to the man in front. No, too much. Back. God, it was beyond him, the ceaseless adjustments and corrections necessary to keep his station in the formation; his brain was too weary, too battered. In a moment he would slide into someone for no better reason than his inability to instruct his hands and feet in time to apply the necessary corrective actions.

He would drift into one of the bombers and everything would be blown into several million minute pieces. The bomber leaders had insisted that the fighters stay close in tight formation, deaf to arguments that it was tactically wiser to permit the fighters to roam ahead, clearing the skies, attacking the enemy before the enemy could attack. The bomber crews wanted to see the Messerschmitts tucked in close, reassuringly close. And what the bomber commanders wanted they invariably got.

A cloudless day. Perfect visibility. The English coastline was there, straight ahead, a few minutes' flying time away.

A wave from a dorsal gunner in a Heinkel.

The poor bastard was in an unenviable position, stuck out in his 'B-Stand' with only a perspex window to shield him from the blast and only a single 7.92 mm MG 17 machine gun with which to fight the eight-gun RAF machines.

Ernst raised a hand, returning the greeting. His reward was a fresh stab of pain across the temples. God, did he deserve to feel *this* dreadful? Somewhere in the distance, over England, the RAF fighters were taking off, climbing, wheeling, setting out to meet the enemy. Hurricanes and Spitfires. The former went for the bombers while the latter engaged the fighters. That was the classic British tactic, according to the experts. The Hurricane was on the slow side and somewhat sluggish, they declared; the Emil outclassed it in almost every respect. The Spitfire was another matter; a nimble dogfighter, dangerous as hell in skilled and determined hands.

'Get in close,' the veterans advised. 'Get in so close that the target fills your gunsight, so bloody close that you couldn't miss even if you tried. Fire. Then run. Don't dogfight with Spitfires below five thousand metres. They can turn inside you. You'll stall out if you try to beat them at it. Then they'll be on your tail before you blink.' But the German pilots possessed one priceless advantage: the fuel injection system with which their Daimler-Benz engines were equipped. The British Merlin that powered the Hurricanes and Spitfires used a conventional carburettor. A sudden dive in one of the RAF fighters meant a temporary cut in the gravity feed of the fuel to the engine. For a few precious moments the Merlin would lose power. But not the Daimler-Benz.

So if in doubt, *dive*.

Yes, yes, he had nodded; yes, he understood all these things. But it was one thing to know them, quite another to be able to think clearly enough during combat to use them. The pilots who survived long enough to accumulate the high scores were the cool professionals, the men with the ability to size up each situation in an instant; calculate the probable intentions of the enemy, then decide upon their strategy – all in a few whirling fragments of moments in which the whole station changed half a dozen times. God knows how they did it.

The British, said the experts, were tough, aggressive adversaries. It was foolish to belittle them. Respect Tommy's abilities, they advised – and thank God for his incredible lack of gunnery skill; he regularly sprayed thousands of bullets around the sky for every hit. 'And thank the Almighty too for the fact that Tommy possesses only one Spitfire for every three Hurricanes.'

He stared into the distance through half-closed eyes. No aircraft ahead. Yet. His stomach contracted; it felt as if it had been tied in knots. He pressed the oxygen mask against his face. He breathed deeply. Whiffs of pure oxygen were said to be good for morning-afters. But it did nothing except to make him thirstier than ever.

Now the English coast was only a few kilometres away. At any moment the enemy would be upon them – unless every RAF squadron was already fully occupied with other elements of the attack. It was possible, wasn't it? The formation might fly straight to their target, drop their bombs and return to France without seeing a single British fighter.

Possible. But highly improbable.

Wishful thinking. Cowardly thinking.

Ernst bit his lip. Hard. Punishing himself. He despised the weakness within him. He wasn't worthy to be here, flying with these men. He had been brought up to admire physical courage. Every childhood hero was fearless; he laughed at danger; he was never dismayed by the odds.

Fear roamed his innards; it was like acid eating away at his vitals. He had been on edge during the outward journey on his first sortie, but that had been the nervousness of the unknown. Now he knew only too well what to expect. No . . . no, damn it, he had to force himself not to remember the first time. Watch Wolfram! Bank with him! Dive with him! Be his shadow! That was all he had to think of.

A Messerschmitt turned out of the formation and sped back toward the French coast, leaving a thin, oily haze in its wake. Lucky bastard. Soon he would be back on the ground, safe. *If* he made it back to the coast. The Channel looked damned cold.

His instrument panel vibrated; the glass of the gauges trembled as if they were as shaky as he was. He placed his hand flat against the cool metal. The vibration ceased. Something needed tightening up.

'Indian ahead!'

Indians were enemy fighters.

'Approximately twenty!'

Two hundred metres. Sun-up. Watch Wolfram. Keep watching.

Switch on Revi reflector sight. Safety catches off. Tug goggles down and adjust them to sit comfortably over the eyes. In the days of open cockpits, goggles had protected the wearers' eyes against the screaming, battering wind. But now pilots sat enclosed in transparent canopies. They needed no further protection from the blast. But in combat they might need protection against fire. Goggles could save a man's sight.

'Dead ahead!'

Little black objects; high against the sun. And still climbing.

A glance at Wolfram. Helmeted head glancing back. Another of those curt, oddly formal nods.

The English coast lay directly below; sunshine shimmered on the water. Deep breaths. Strange with what clarity he observed every detail, every nook and cranny, every rivet, every knob, gauge and lever in the cramped metal cockpit.

'Indians approaching!'

Muscles contracted instinctively. Tongue moistened dry lower lip, contacted sour, rubber taste of oxygen mask.

The Indians peeled off, one after the other, then hurtled down on their prey.

Already some of the bombers' gunners were blazing away at the on-rushing British.

Don't look at the British – only at Wolfram! Break when he breaks . . . *now*! Hurl the machine into a turn . . . swing to avoid the plunging Spitfires. Dry rattle of guns, like someone beating the rim of a drum. A sky full of hurtling, skidding aircraft. Eye on Wolfram's tail – then scanning the sky behind him, for Indians.

Earphones crackled with a hundred voices.

'Look out! Below you!'

'Break right!'

'Yellow Four! Spitfire on your arse!'

'Christ . . . I'm on fire!'

Then the German pilots' yell: 'Horrido!' – after their patron saint, St. Horridus. A yell of victory!

'Help me!'

Indignant voice.

A Hurricane minus one wing cartwheeled across the sky.

Wolfram whipped his Emil into a bank to avoid it. Then he was on the tail of another Hurricane. Snapped into an almost vertical turn. Ernst followed at full throttle, airframe creaking. Another Emil curved in on the left, but quickly vanished from view. Rap-rap-rap-rap of cannon fire. The earth rolled and fell away. Disappeared. Sunlight splashed dazzlingly into the cockpit stinging Ernst's eyes. No time to think about stinging eyes.

Wolfram was on the tail of a Hurricane that was itself on the tail of a Heinkel.

Quickly the distance telescoped.

But not quickly enough.

The Heinkel staggered, under the onslaught of the Hurricane's eight Brownings. Flame suddenly gushed from the bomber's starboard engine. In an instant half the wing was on fire as the one thousand litre fuel tank was punctured by De Wilde incendiary bullets. The metal structure sagged, folding, fracturing in the fury of the wind-tortured blaze. It failed, becoming a flurry of tumbling, spinning, burning fragments. The entire starboard wing ripped away, the propeller still revolving.

The Heinkel whirled earthward. A crewman jumped. And hit the tail. Poor bastard spun, like a rag doll, every bone in his body shattered.

The Hurricane turned, still diving. Wolfram followed. Ernst swung out to cover him. No one else in view. Left rudder and stick. Hard right now. The earth rolled to the vertical then back the other way.

'Indian coming up on your arse. I'm attacking.'

Christ.

'All right?'

'Victor.'

A procession of fighters: Hurricane, Messerschmitt, Spitfire, Messerschmitt. Firing. Missing. Turning. Skidding. Diving. Sweating. Swearing.

Wolfram's target vanished in a sheet of flame.

The explosion threw the procession into confusion. Ernst's Emil shuddered and lurched. A shape flashed past him.

A Spitfire!

Wolfram's voice: 'I'm covering you.'

Full throttle! Airframe shivering. Thumb on cannon button, forefinger on machine gun button. Don't fire yet. Not yet. Not yet. Get closer! Stupid bastard's diving! A Spitfire can't dive as rapidly as a Messerschmitt. Doesn't he know that? Hard rudder. Skid. Slam your way about the sky. Follow him. Get closer! Closer!

Glint of sunlight on the bulbous cockpit canopy. Dull green and brown camouflage pattern on the Spitfire's metal body and wings. Pretty, elliptical wings. Contrails snapping back from their pointed tips.

No time to think of being frightened now. No time to think of failing. Life consisted solely of getting in position to deliver the final burst.

Empty cartridge cases tumbled from the Spitfire's wing chutes as he fired a burst at a stray Dornier. Missing.

Diving now. Straight through the wheeling fighters. Turning, gravity squeezing him down into the seat, doing its best to crush the consciousness out of him. Dim red veil over the eyes. Green camouflage paint on the Spitfire now an odd shade of purple.

Clearing now. Vision returning to normal.

Someone else going down in flames.

A tiny figure swaying beneath a white parachute canopy.

Wolfram's voice: 'That's it! Stick with him! I'm covering you!'

Good God almighty! Almost hit the Englishman! So incredibly close, close enough to read the stencilled lettering near the tail, the serial number and handling directions.

Then the Spitfire snapped into a sudden turn to the left. Displayed pale blue underside, streaks of oil, black powder smears behind machine gun muzzles and cartridge chutes.

Gone!

At the precise instant of pressing on the firing buttons.

No targets. Just empty sky.

'Bad luck.' Wolfram's voice. 'I'm on your right.'

'Yes.'

'Reform.'

'Victor.'

Afterwards it was impossible to remember how long it all took. A minute? An hour? A day? Time ceased to have relevance. Life was simply a sky full of whirling, spitting aircraft, streaks of fire and oily smoke and the din of engines and gunfire, the earth tumbling on to its side then rolling back and, a moment later, over the other way again.

Then, abruptly, it was all over. The Channel lay beneath his wings. Now the coast in the distance was French. The enemy had been met and had been allowed to escape. Another failure.

But he had stayed with Wolfram; that much had to be said for him. He might be accused of poor fighting technique but not cowardice. His nerve had held, albeit somewhat shakily.

I did a little better that time, he told his father.

He pushed the goggles back on to his forehead. He was exhausted; weariness crept up his legs and body like a warm, comforting liquid. He blinked hard. Stared. Hard to stay awake. Had to.

He smiled weakly. He realized something. His hangover had gone, blown away by battle.

He felt the first stirrings of appetite; lunch was a pleasant prospect, a *very* pleasant prospect.

★

'Didn't I tell you?' said Dietrich. 'A disaster the first time; second time no problem at all. Reminds me of my initial dabblings in sex. Took me a couple of tries to get the hang of it.'

Ernst munched a chicken leg. 'But I didn't actually do anything,' he pointed out.

'You got back didn't you?'

'Yes.'

'That should be enough to satisfy anyone.'

'I fired my guns,' Ernst said. 'Strange to think of actually firing your guns at someone.'

'You'll soon get used to the idea,' Dietrich assured him. 'The human being is a marvellously adaptable creature; he can even get used to doing something as mad as going up in the air and shooting at other people just as mad.'

'I wish I'd hit something,' Ernst mused.

'You missed me,' said Dietrich. 'That's all that matters.'

The Mess in which the airmen dined was roomy and comfortable, a high ceiling'd hall with something of the atmosphere of a hunting lodge. On the dark panelled walls hung portraits of commanders of the French units that had once flown from this base. Now the place was occupied by their conquerors. The Luftwaffe pilots were in good spirits; three Hurricanes had been added to the unit's score, and for once the unit had suffered no casualties. It was a moment to relish.

He wrote a long letter to his mother. He was well. He thought of her often; he hoped Maria was behaving herself.

Then he wrote to Ilse, telling her about the battle over Ventnor. 'I shot at a Spitfire,' he told her. 'But I missed. Very annoying. I intend to do better next time.'

The flippant tone of the letter irritated him. It sounded so damnably cocky. The battle was a sort of high-altitude sporting event. A fine time was had by one and all. We won. Three-nothing. Yet how else could he describe the fight? Should he tell her about the confusion and the din, about the jarring manoeuvres, about the gut-wrenching terror of it all? He shook his head as if in response to his silent question. As he did so he sketched a moment in the death of a Hurricane. He had seen the sight that morning. The fighter had been ripped apart by cannon fire, the fuselage fracturing immediately aft of the wing. For a moment the rear fuselage had held but at a weird, comical angle, bent sideways as if the aircraft was made of some soft plastic material; the

44

stricken machine had described a skidding, falling turn, the pilot frantically trying to maintain control. Then the rear of the fuselage had broken away, the tail unit still in place. The wings and nose had tumbled vertically, streaming flame. Did the pilot jump? Was he at this moment safe and sound, drinking tea and chuckling over the experience? Or was he an unspeakable lump of charred pulp, something to shovel out of a field?

Ilse had sent a photograph, taken only a week before in the park behind their houses. The snap was slightly out of focus but charming nonetheless. She was seated on the stone pedestal of the monument to Emperor Charles. Her arms were folded, her shoulders squared, displaying her ample bosom to advantage. She possessed splendid breasts; she loved him to caress them, stroking the nipples until they were hard and erect. Ilse Gebhardt was a beautiful girl, everyone said so. He was as lucky as hell to have her. Everyone said that too. They had known each other since childhood, living less than a kilometre apart, she on the east side of the street, he on the west. Ilse's father was a lawyer, a pedantic, overbearing man whose small almost colourless eyes had a strangely penetrating quality. He managed to give Ernst the uncomfortable feeling that his innermost thoughts were being tapped. Herr Gebhardt seemed to be able to see the lust fermenting there, the sexual hunger, the shameful disgusting desires. You are unworthy of her, those eyes seemed to say; you are vile. Herr Gebhardt was a humourless individual but he occasionally took some small pleasure in demonstrating the range of his vocabulary. He was fond of employing long, obscure words when discussing any subject, the weather, the war, local politics; he would smile knowingly when Ernst admitted ignorance of the word in question, an I-thought-as-much smile. Thank God Ilse took after her mother.

Four

Dietrich was right. A man could learn to adapt to the terrors and trials of aerial combat, accepting them as a sort of weird normality. This was now his life, this business of clambering again and again into a narrow cockpit that smelled of fuel, warm metal and sweat, securing his body with stout straps, breathing oxygen from a mask, battling with the choppy summer air, then battling with the enemy, watching bullets slashing past him, seeing men die, some painlessly, speedily, others horribly. His fears were just as new each time but fear became a familiar companion, to be expected at regular intervals, to be contained just as the onslaughts of nausea and trembling had to be contained. Strange, how one could come to terms with the probability of violent death. It was the price for losing, the price so many of the unit's pilots kept paying. One had to accept that truth; and one did by a slow process, a gradual giving-in, learning not to hope, learning to let the odds take care of the future. It was better that way.

He flew a dozen operational sorties in ten days. By now he was a reliable wingman; he followed Wolfram's every move, protecting his flank and his tail from predatory Englishmen. He saw many aircraft fall; he fired at several targets; as far as he knew he hit none.

On the fifteenth of August the weather was fine and warm; it was a day of maximum effort against RAF Fighter Command fields and radar stations. The British defended the targets energetically, pouncing upon the German formations while they were still over the Channel. The Messerschmitts had to fight a running battle, flying at full throttle, gulping down fuel at almost twice the normal rate.

The order had to be given. Break off! Return to base! If the fighters delayed their return any longer they would end up in the Channel, one by one, their fuel tanks empty.

The Emils waggled their wings in apologetic farewell to the bombers who still had twenty kilometres to go to their target. God only knows what the crewmen in the Heinkels said as they saw the fighters go. It was as well that there was no R/T connection between bombers and their escort. The Heinkels would suffer; it was inevitable; and the suffering would do nothing to improve the already severely-strained relations between the two arms of the Luftwaffe. The bomber leaders claimed that the fighers weren't doing their job; the fighter leaders declared that the bombers expected too much of a force that had never been created for the protection of bomber squadrons. There weren't enough single-engined fighters – and none of the available machines had sufficient range. Long-range drop tanks had been promised for months. But none had arrived at the line squadrons. Why the delay? Where, the pilots asked, were the drop tanks that had once

46

been used on the old He 51 biplane fighters? Didn't anyone at HQ understand their problems?

The Channel lay ahead, sparkling softly beneath the warm haze.

Ernst had fired half his ammunition at a couple of Hurricanes. But the enemy pilots had been good; they had evaded him, leaving him to shoot at the empty sky. He was never fast enough, never in just the right position at the right time. He saw the action again as if watching a newsreel. A Hurricane on Wolfram's tail! A wild, swerving, skidding, screaming chase. Hurtling through the flimsy sky-lines left by the tracers. Engines howling. Viscera lurching, complaining. Blood surging, adrenalin pumping. Thumb pressing on the firing button . . . drilling holes in the air. . . .

Then it was over. Break off! Head home! And hope like hell. Would the wind help or hinder? Fuel gauges indicated rather less than half. But you couldn't rely on them. Only two indicators could be relied upon: first, the red light warning of five minutes' fuel left and second, total silence from up front.

The fighters flew in scattered groups of three or four. The RAF left them alone, only too happy to concentrate on the bombers. There was a little light flak on the way but it hit no one. Fuel was the big problem at the moment, plus the bloody Channel that had already claimed so many lives.

Ernst pushed the goggles up on to his forehead. He opened the panel at his side. The chilly air felt good; it helped to blow away the nausea and the trembling, the familar after-effects of combat. Would he ever get over it, completely?

He resumed his wingman's station, flying slightly behind Wolfram. Wolfram's tail had been peppered. It was as if some British pilot had been determined to obliterate the victory symbols that adorned the lieutenant's rudder.

'You've got several hits in your tail area.'

'I know,' acknowledged Wolfram. 'I felt them. But everything seems to be working so far. Thanks for the report.'

Ernst switched off his transmit button. He scanned the instrument panel. Pressures, temperatures, revs. . . .

Revs!

The needle had slipped. Bubbly shiver down the spine. Was the drop in revs real or just his imagination? A touch more throttle. Better. He was maintaining his position near Wolfram.

He frowned, listening. Was the engine running roughly? Was there a soft grinding note interposed between the normal rhythms of the twelve-cylinder DB? Perhaps it was just nerves. No; he heard it again.

And he *was* falling behind. No question. Another touch of throttle. For the moment it was fine; but now the revs began to drop again.

He swallowed. Perturbation was a heavy lump that settled in his stomach and began to roam.

Instinctively, like every other pilot who has ever had engine trouble in flight, he looked down, searching. It was futile. Stupid waste of time. The formation was already well out to sea. No gentle pastures down there; just the Channel, ready to swallow anything that fell.

Think!

How far to the French coast? Ten minutes' flying time? More? Less? If his engine cut at this moment, how far could he glide?

He scraped his teeth over his lower lip. Alarming, sickening, the prospect of putting an Emil down on the water. If you touched down badly, if a wave happened to catch you, you would dig your nose in and go straight to the bottom, dragged down by the weight of your engine. If you were lucky, the old He 59 biplanes of the Seenotdienst – the Air-Sea Rescue Service – would come and pluck you out of the briny. . . .

Perhaps this is where your luck runs out, he heard himself say, the words sharp and penetrating in his mind. It was as if some complacent bastard without a problem in the world was butting in where he wasn't needed, for the express purpose of creating alarm and despondency. He shook his head as if to shake the voice away. No, he wouldn't listen. He flicked the transmit button.

'Yellow Five to Yellow Three. I've got engine trouble. I'm losing power.' Peculiar tone to the voice.

He saw Wolfram's head turn in his direction.

'No external sign of damage.' Cool, calm Wolfram. 'We'll slow down to your speed.'

The three Emils clustered around the wounded bird, escorting him home. The Schwarm looked after its own.

The coast was a thin, dark line in the heat haze ahead. If the engine cut now he might just reach it. . . .

Now the temperature needle was climbing.

The engine was committing suicide. Soon, inevitably, it had to die. But when would it die and how violent would be its death?

Land looked beautiful. Solid. Reassuring. Every second

brought it closer. He could already pick out dark clusters of buildings, the ribbons that were roads. A few more moments. Keep going, good old faithful DB, ignore your aches and pains.

By now he was perhaps within gliding distance of dry land. But it all depended upon the wind. What was it doing? Which way was it blowing? The damned temperature needle was climbing rapidly now. The end wasn't far off. A glance up. He had slipped slightly below Wolfram and the others. And he was dropping back. The lame duck.

'You're trailing oil now.'

'I'll have to put her down on the beach.'

'Very well,' said Wolfram. 'We'll keep an eye on you. Sorry we can't stay with you.'

He nodded; he understood. Wolfram had no more choice in the matter than did the fighter leader when he ordered his formation to return to base and leave the bombers to their fate. Operational necessity.

'Good luck!'

'We'll have a drink waiting for you! I've called Air-Sea Rescue, just in case. They're on their way.'

Throttle back more. Already he was in what was virtually a powered glide. It would, he calculated, get him to dry land. With luck. Wheels up, he would plop down on the beach; scores of Emil pilots had done it already; only one, to his knowledge, had come to grief. He had bounced on touch-down and had flipped over, knocking himself unconscious. Still strapped in his seat, he had drowned in a couple of metres of water.

The temperature needle was steady. Revs down to 1200. The massive monster up front, with its pistons and cylinders and superchargers, was still functioning. But only just.

Wolfram's voice: 'You'll be all right.'

'Yes. Thanks. See you back at base.'

Carefree voice, but tightening guts. Bastards, Wolfram and the others. Abandoning him. Already they were tiny specks far above.

He looked around, touching the rudder pedals to swing the Emil from side to side as he searched. No sign of any British fighters, thank God. Sometimes they shadowed returning formations, eager to pounce on stragglers.

Temperature needle still climbing.

The feeling of loneliness was acute, almost physically painful. Empty sky above, friends and comrades long gone; below, nothing but the detestable Channel, swelling, swirling in its evil, oily way.

Concentrate! Forget the Channel! Think about the shore! It's not far off!

The details were becoming definite, taking sharper form through the haze. There was a good stretch of beach almost dead ahead. The wind seemed to be from the west. So, simply make a wide turn to the left to line up with the beach, then a direct approach. And hope for the best.

Revs needle steady. Temperature needle too. Oil pressure down.

Gingerly he advanced the throttle lever. Revs up. Temperature still behaving itself. Stick back a little. Hope glowed within him. Perhaps he wouldn't have to land on a beach after all. Straight and level flight! The red warning light still hadn't lit up; he had enough fuel to get home. And, damn it, if the dear old Emil was willing to keep flying, why should he wallop her down on a nasty damp beach. . .?

She *was* holding her height. Groaning and grinding a bit, but unquestionably holding.

Elated, he looked over the side. The shore slid below.

The others had vanished ahead. By now they would be over the base, letting down their wheels in preparation for landing.

He patted the instrument panel. 'Good girl! Well done!'

That was when the engine seized up.

Christ! It was so damnably sudden – even though he had expected the thing to seize up all the way across the Channel.

The big three-bladed propeller shuddered to a halt.

Stick forward. Pick up gliding speed. First lesson in dealing with engine failure. Descent is inevitable but it's infinitely better to descend in a glide than to stall and tumble like so much scrap metal.

Switches off. Weird silence, broken only by the swishing of the air past his cockpit canopy.

Lesson number two: find a place to put down. And find a place that's in front. So forget the beach. To go back to the beach meant a turn. Turns without power meant loss of height. . . .

He was already four or five kilometres inland. Below, little but fields and trees. A narrow road that turned at right angles in the middle of nowhere. He didn't recognize anything. No matter. He was over dry land and within a few kilometres of base. All that mattered was how to find a spot to rest.

Or should he jump?

He grimaced as if he tasted something sour. No one in his right mind would jump unless there was absolutely no choice. Besides, his faithful machine had brought him all this way; he couldn't desert her now.

He trimmed and retrimmed.

Wind coming from *there*, as indicated by the bowing of the trees. So edge her gently to the left and find a field. Plenty of choice, although many were so damned small and hemmed in by trees.

There!

Reasonably long field. Side-slip the rest of the height off. Over that copse beside the stream. Straighten out. Over the little house. Then land. At that spot, in the middle of the field.

He tugged at the lever to jettison the canopy. Nothing happened.

Damned things! They were always failing. Everyone complained. No one did anything about them.

Too fast! Ease back on the stick. Straighten her up. Foot hard on the rudder pedal, to make the Emil skid, to provide a clear view of the house and the field that was swaying, rocking towards him. Use the undercarriage emergency release? No . . . too tricky. Better to belly her in on a surface like this.

Crank the flaps down.

Yank the canopy jettison lever again. Still without result.

Too late to worry about it.

Past the house, close enough to see damaged tiles, a washing line. Nose up. Speed dropping. Grass rushing along below like a never-ending carpet. Stick right back in the belly. Keep her flying until she refuses to fly another centimetre. . . .

Bang! It was as if a cannon shell had slammed into the machine directly beneath him. A giant hand grabbed him and threw him against his harness straps, knocking the air out of his lungs.

It sounded like a factory gone mad. Fantastic, brain-dazing din. Metal ripping, grinding, tearing; great hammers banging the helpless Emil again and again.

He didn't see the gulley until it was too late.

For a crazy instant the Emil was airborne again. Altitude: one metre. A wing fell. Its tip dug in. The wing crumpled and collapsed; the Emil cartwheeled, hesitated, wobbling on its nose, toppled over on to its back.

He heard the impact, the crumpling and grinding of metal as his head thudded against the roof of the canopy. The blow stunned him. Sent him back to ride his bicycle and to have it skid on a wet, cobbled street; he was rising gracefully over the handlebars, turning, falling slowly, gracefully.

He opened his eyes.

And saw an unfamiliar, upside down world.

An uncomfortable world. A world in which harness straps sliced into a fellow's shoulders and pulled on his legs.

Jesus Christ!

He remembered. All too clearly. No wonder it was upside down. *He* was upside down!

And there was a smell. An unmistakeable smell. And a sound. Drip-drip-drip. *Fuel!*

Oh God, no please. Don't let me be burned. Please, I beg. . . .

There was grass only a few centimetres away, pressed flat by the perspex panel of the canopy. Grass, so near yet utterly beyond his reach.

His voice sounded strangely hollow and weak. Could anyone hear him? No one had been in sight as he had glided across the fields to land here. Sweet Jesus, it was possible that he had landed without a solitary soul witnessing it! No one knew he was here! And – chilling thought – even if anyone had seen him come down, who would help him? You're in France, he reminded himself. *France.* They'll be glad to see you burn to death. You're an enemy. He caught his breath; he seemed to see a ring of French people, men and women, children, too, standing around the blazing wreck of his Emil. Laughing. Pointing. Deriving the keenest of pleasure from his agonies. Entertainment for the whole family. . . .

No, please, help. . . .

Then he spotted him. A boy. Short trousers. Glasses. Pale, serious face. He approached cautiously, timorously, as if preparing himself for a terrible sight. His face appeared at the scarred perspex panel.

'Bitte . . .' No, speak French, for God's sake. 'Please help.'

The boy knelt on the grass. He reached out and grasped the twisted, contorted frame of the canopy. He tugged. It wouldn't move.

'There's a hinge on the side,' Ernst said.

The boy nodded. 'I know. I've seen how they open. But you can't open this one because the weight of the whole aircraft is on it. It has no room to move. Do you understand?'

'Yes, yes I understand.'

Still the fuel dripped, the sound echoing in this tiny coffin.

'What do you think I should do?' the boy asked.

'Can you help to move the aircraft?'

The boy nodded, frowning. 'My mother will help,' he said. 'And Dupas. But he's very old.' He sniffed. 'I smell fuel.'

'Do you see any sign of fire?'

He wanted to scream, to fight his way out of the aircraft, but he forced himself to sit motionless, to talk to the boy as if he was merely asking the way to Paris.

'I can see where the fuel is dripping,' the boy announced. 'It's on part of the wing.'

Thank God. 'Not on the engine?'

'No.'

'Good boy.' The small face appeared at the canopy and peered into the cokpit. 'Are you injured, sir?' he enquired.

'No, I don't think so. Please go and find some help.'

'Very well.' The boy stood up. His knees were stained with green. 'I won't be long,' he said. Then he was gone.

The drip-drip-drip was a drum beating in his brain. He imagined the fuel, falling harmlessly on a wing panel. But it had to run somewhere. It travelled along a pathway, a maze of lanes battered into the aircraft's metal skin. The stuff could travel from one end to the other!

To the engine!

He had to get out! In an instant the whole thing would go up. He'd be cooked!

Panic galvanized him into frantic efforts. He heaved against the cockpit roof. He would break through the thing, smash it and lift the Emil bodily so that he could escape.

But he couldn't. He was trapped. Powerless.

Please, please, please . . . don't let me die here, not like this . . . not here, at this place, at this time. . . .

Drip-drip, drip-drip.

The fuel was leaking out more rapidly now. Oh God, the slightest spark would turn the whole thing into a bonfire. . . .

Then – holy miracle! – the boy returned.

'This might help,' he announced. He held a steel fence post in both hands. Ernst stared, heart sinking. Did the stupid little bastard think he could lift an entire aircraft by himself?

'Didn't you get anyone else?'

The boy shook his head. 'My mother isn't at home. I think

she's gone into the village. She often does on Wednesdays. She goes shopping.'

Christ, this was madness, talking about shopping days with a child when at any instant he would become a bonfire!

But the boy seemed unperturbed. He was doing something with the post, applying his weight to it, face reddening, mouth pulled into a strained grin. Ernst could hear a metallic creaking and groaning behind him.

'What the hell are you doing?'

He had to ask the question again. The first time, he had asked it in German.

'I think this will work,' said the boy.

Ernst couldn't see him now. He was out of sight, doing something to the rear of the fuselage. And oh God, he was probably going to set off a spark to send the whole thing sky high. . .

It lurched.

There was a crumpling and groaning of metal.

The whole thing moved as if it had suddenly found life.

The canopy fell open half-way.

The boy tugged at it, moved it a few more centimetres.

'Can you get out now?'

'Yes . . . I think so.'

Gingerly he unfastened his harness, still holding on to the cockpit sides. He had heard of pilots breaking their necks by falling out of aircraft upside down on the ground.

Now! Awkwardly, painfully he half slithered, half tumbled out of the cockpit into the shallow depression. He crawled out from beneath the remains of the Messerschmitt.

He was sore and bruised but otherwise unhurt. He scrambled away from the immediate vicinity of the wreck, still conscious of the danger of fire. But the dripping sound seemed to have stopped. The Emil was a harmless heap of junk, a write-off – scrap metal to be melted down and used again. An inglorious end for a bird which had served him so nobly.

The boy took off his glasses, rubbed the lenses with his shirt sleeve, put the glasses on again and studied the wreck as if seeing it for the first time.

'Thanks very much,' said Ernst inadequately.

The boy shrugged.

'What's your name?'

'Georges.'

'How did you move it, Georges?'

The boy pointed. 'I saw that it was balanced on the edge of the trench,' he said. 'I thought a little push might move it enough. And I was right.' He shrugged again. 'It wasn't hard.'

Ernst felt in his pocket but he had no money, nothing to give this remarkable, heaven-sent creature. He reached inside the cockpit and removed the ignition key.

'A souvenir for you,' he said.

'Thank you, sir.' Very correct, very formal.

Now a cluster of children came running toward the wreck, their faces alive with the delight of the unexpected.

'You were very brave to do what you did. How did you know the thing wouldn't go up in smoke?'

Another shrug. 'I hoped it wouldn't.'

'Where do you live?' Ernst asked him.

The boy pointed to the small house over which Ernst had glided on his landing approach.

'Do you have a telephone there?'

'Not now. But there are telephones in the village.'

'How far is the village?'

'Two kilometres.'

Then he saw the truck approaching. It stopped with a squealing of brakes. Half a dozen Wehrmacht men jumped out, carrying rifles.

'What's your second name, Georges?'

'Goutard, sir.'

'I thank you again, Georges Goutard.'

Solemnly they shook hands.

Five

Wolfram was killed at 0942 hours the next day. He collided with a Spitfire. Head-on. Combined speed of Messerschmitt and Spitfire: approximately 1200 kilometres per hour. Two aircraft became one. For an awful instant the unholy embrace of shattered, tangled metal seemed to hang motionless. Then came the fire; voracious, insatiable. The mess toppled, twisting, rotating, showering blazing fragments, painting a black smear across the brilliant sky. Down, down, down. Hopeless. No one ever got out of a crash like that.

All one could do was stare, hardly believing the evidence of one's eyes. Wolfram, so calm, so efficient. Now dead. Now ground into mincemeat and cremated. One cursed that nasty mental process that insisted on declaring that in some obscene way Wolfram's death increased everyone else's chances of survival. Pity about him. But better him. . . .

The wreckage hit the earth. Dead centre of a large field. A flash of yellow flame. Black smoke billowing. Tiny dots hurrying toward the site, like unspeakable little insects converging on a fallen carcass.

Damn them! Damn everything!

An instant later Ernst heard the dry rattle of guns. As he twisted in his seat he felt the fighter shudder. Bullets slammed into her fragile flanks. Christ! A Hurricane! Angled at him, an eagle swooping in for the kill! He reacted instinctively; adrenalin quickened his heartbeat, injecting extra blood into his brain and muscles. Snapped the Emil on to one wing. Saw another Messerschmitt dive by, dangerously close. A second Hurricane. More gunfire. More hits. Strangely calm. But working like hell to survive. Eight Brownings on a Hurricane, each with 334 rounds, each firing at a rate of 1200 rounds per minute. Five kilos of lead in a three-second burst, fire from the eight guns converging some 200 metres ahead of the aircraft. These facts danced through his brain as his hands and feet worked ferociously, hurling the fighter, twisting, diving. Every atom of his being concentrated on the fight. A good man in that Hurricane. Knew his business. Determined as well. Stand on the wing! Feel the centrifugal force working to push you out through the floor of the cockpit. Engine howling, trying to tear itself free of its mountings. Down! Muck floating up from the cockpit floor. Dangling, weightless. Bits of dried dirt from the field, scraps of paper, a nut dropped by a careless mechanic. Distant horizon at right angles. Ugly little holes abruptly appearing in the wing's upper surface. Did they hit something critical. Slot actuating mechanism? Main spar? Undercarriage? Questions without answers.

More turns. Violent. Punishing. Don't fall apart, Emil old friend. Absorb the stresses, apportion them among your ribs, stringers, spars, longerons and formers.

Jam the stick to the left, to the right. Right rudder pedal, left rudder pedal. Full power. Airframe trembling, threatening to separate into several dozen separate pieces. Out-manoeuvre him! Shake him! If you don't you're dead. Simple as that.

A bullet scarred the perspex canopy beside his head. A glancing memento of the encounter.

Over to the right! Steeper! Earth rotating. Hold on, tail! Now!

Thumb and finger simultaneously squeezed the two firing buttons: one for the Oerlikon cannon, the other for the machine guns. The Emil shuddered; the stink of cordite swept back into the cockpit.

Bullseye! Fragments of the Hurricane's canopy sparkled in the sunlight. A section of the engine cowling broke away. Fire snaked the length of the fuselage. The British fighter fell away on one wing, its nose snapping earthward.

Good God almighty! He had scored! He had actually done it!

He found himself bellowing amid the metallic clatter of the cockpit, telling everyone to look, to witness his triumph. There it was! That Hurricane! That was his! The one describing a neat spiral as it headed earthward, streaming flame and smoke!

A tiny figure detached itself from the doomed fighter, a tiny figure that spun away awkwardly, clumsily, as if possessing no control over its limbs.

Then the parachute opened: a puff of white instantly followed by a great snapping blossoming of the main umbrella. The figure bounced, its plunge arrested. But was the Hurricane pilot alive? It looked like a corpse dangling beneath the flapping, swaying umbrella.

Ernst dived. The parachute swept toward him.

The British pilot saw him coming. He stiffened, alarmed. His hands – one bare, the other gloved – flew to his face, fingers extended.

Ernst's mouth dropped open in astonishment.

The man thought he was going to fire at him! Incredible! No self-respecting fighter pilot would even contemplate such a thing. He banked away, waving. The parachute disappeared from view. Ernst turned for home.

Dietrich was waiting for him, still in flying garb, clutching his helmet and R/T connecting cables. He grinned as Ernst clambered out of the Emil's cockpit.

'The conquering hero! Well done, old fellow! I saw it! A clean victory! We've got to celebrate!'

Ernst managed a smile but there was nothing he felt less like doing than celebrating. His legs were rubbery, his head throbbed, his stomach stirred threateningly. The flight home had been an ordeal, a reliving of every instant of the fight, an endless reminder of how damned nearly he had come to being killed, how nearly he had ended up in some English field – or, at best, in some English prisoner of war camp.

Everyone was congratulating him – mechanics, pilots, clerks; a man's first victory was a major event; he had become a member of one of the world's most exclusive clubs.

Dietrich ran his finger over the bullet holes that peppered Ernst's Messerschmitt. 'Your friend was a fair shot.'

'I was lucky,' Ernst mumbled, wondering if he was going to disgrace himself by vomiting; his nostrils were still full of the stink of fuel and cordite. The worst of it was that he had to smile and say modest things as befitted an aerial victor.

'Damned shame about Wolfram,' someone said.

'Stupid bastard in the Spitfire wasn't looking where he was going.'

'I think he'd been hit. I saw him a moment before they collided. He was out of control, if you ask me.'

'How could you tell?'

'By the way he flew.'

'You always fly like that!'

'Only when my piles are hurting.'

The pilots nodded. They wondered if there was some earnest little fellow in a dusty office in Berlin working out the statistical probabilities of collisions during combat. It seemed likely.

Strobel, Clauser, Krüger, Berthol, Rudat, Staemn, Berger, Stahl, Betz, Dietrich. They were the pilots. Young men of nineteen to twenty-six, of above-average intelligence, education and physique. Casual in their dress by the standards of the other military services; envied for their comfortable billets, their servants, their excellent food. Much of their existence was spent in waiting. For orders, for weather. They wrote letters; they listened to the radio or records; they sat and absorbed the summer sunshine, sprawled in deck chairs. Some read the classics; some read trash. Some were ambitious professionals; most had little concern for the future. Once pilot spent his free time making models of old sailing ships, galleons and windjammers, barquentines and brigantines; another pilot constructed models of modern military aircraft. Several kept pets, mostly large dogs (a nearby unit kept a pet bear as the mascot). One pilot was fond of photography. He spent hours snapping the mechanics at work on the twelve-cylinder DB engines or feeding the guns with endless belts of shining ammunition. He looked for amusing shots: the legs of a service-man protruding from the radio panel in the rear fuselage of an Emil as he sat in the tiny radio compartment; a mechanic, munching a sandwich, using the tailplane of an Emil as a dining table; the concentration of a fitter painting a pilot's personal emblem on the nose of his aircraft.

The pilots were in the main an amiable group, tolerant of one another's shortcomings, as are most individuals who fly. A man's weaknesses were his own affair – as long as they did not endanger the lives of his comrades. The airmen were intensely proud of their unit, and of their country, although they seldom discussed politics. It was enough that their country's cause was just. No one questioned that fact. The war was being fought to right a terrible wrong, to regain the honour and prestige that the Allies had so cruelly snatched away in 1918. Few doubted that most of the trouble in the world was caused by fear of Germany's superiority. It was the reason the Western powers had created a veritable spider's web of treaties around the Third Reich. But German ability, inventiveness and sheer drive had smashed the whole flimsy mess to bits, had sent them all packing, one by one.

Except for Britain.

Soon she would fall like the others. Not one of the airmen doubted it for a moment.

But as the days multiplied, the pilots wondered how long it would take. The battle intensified. Casualties mounted steadily. Betz went down in flames to smash into a village street near Brighton. Strobel vanished in the Channel, his battle-damaged engine failing halfway across. He hit the water, broke up and was gone, all in a matter of seconds. Too many of the casualties were the veterans, the irreplaceable men who had fought in Spain and in Poland, the pilots who were needed to train the new men, to help each one through that early, appallingly dangerous time.

Afterwards it was hard to separate one day from another. They became merged, entangled, the memories tumbling over one another creating a kaleidoscope of sights and sounds and smells, all laced with terror and trepidation, elation, frustration, disappointment, regret. Day after day they flew, climbing, formating, rendezvousing with the bombers, the Heinkels, the Dorniers, the poor bastards who had to keep on flying straight and level while the Spitfires and Hurricanes tore them to shreds. The Bf110s came along too, lumbering twin-engined, two-man fighters. Their original purpose had been to protect the bombers while the 109s took on the fighters. But the 110s suffered such crippling losses in combat that it was decreed that they too should be protected by the Emils. So the protected outnumbered the protectors.

Oberstleutnant Gossner had been an airman for a quarter of a century. During the Great War he had flown two-seaters; in a twenty minute battle with DH 4s, he downed three, for which a grateful Kaiser presented him with the Iron Cross First Class. Gossner participated in the great assault of March 1918, operating with Schlachtstaffel 2 from Grougis. His Halberstadt CL 11 had been shot down near Clery and he had spent the rest of his military service in a British prisoner of war camp. Between the wars, Gossner had worked as an airline pilot, flying Junkers and Dorniers for Lufthansa. Now he was Kommodore of a Geschwader consisting of three Gruppen, with more than a hundred aircraft at his command.

Oberstleutnant Gossner was a worried man. His unit had been badly mauled; its best pilots had been lost; morale was suffering. In Gossner's opinion, too much was being demanded of the unit. The pilots were becoming numbed by exhaustion. There were stupid, needless accidents. During a formation landing, Krüger got sloppy, stuck a wing in, ended up in hospital with a broken back. The Oberstleutnant was furious. He berated the unfortunate Krüger in his hospital bed. Loss of invaluable aircraft because of sheer bloody incompetence. Then, thirty minutes later, the Oberstleutnant returned to apologize. He wished Krüger a speedy recovery. Back in his office, the Oberstleutnant made out his report. Losses. Aircraft, pilots. Achievements, types of enemy aircraft destroyed, times, places and remarks. *Remarks?* God yes, he had plenty of remarks. And questions. How long did the lunatics at High Command think the unit could sustain such losses? Was there no one in authority with the intelligence to realize that the fighters were charged with duties which they couldn't possibly carry out? Had anyone bothered to inform the Reichsmarschall how many fighters were being lost in the Channel because they were always operating at the very limits of their range? Why did the radio broadcasts persist in claiming that the RAF Fighter Command was virtually eliminated when it was all too obvious to the Luftwaffe pilots that it was as strong as ever?

But the Oberstleutnant omitted such observations from his report. He was a professional soldier. It was not his place to question grand strategy; no army could operate if every order was challenged. But, damn it all, something should be done. By someone. It was heart-breaking, seeing his unit decimated. But he continued to obey orders, sending the fighters out day after day. Replacement pilots kept arriving, each batch younger and pinker and more enthusiastic than the last. You could almost predict how long each one would last. One of every three would become a casualty within the first week. It happened again and again, as if there was some terrible, merciless natural law at work. Thank God the summer was nearly over; now it was late in August, soon it would be autumn; weather would surely bring the battle to an end; the winter would provide a breathing space, a respite from the killing.

The next day the Oberstleutnant was relieved of his command. He received a telephone call at 0815 hours; his replacement would be arriving at 0900 hours. A major Schauff. There were apologies for the short notice. Order from High Command. If it was any consolation, commanders of several Geschwader were being replaced by younger men, operational pilots who would personally lead their units into battle. It was a new policy. Please accord the new Kommodore every courtesy and assistance. . . .

Schauff wore the badges of the brave: the Knight's Cross and the German Cross in gold. Lean, powerfully built, he exuded confidence. The possibility of failure did not interest him. The only thing that mattered was winning. A highly successful fighter pilot, he had served in the Luftwaffe since the early 'thirties; he had twenty-one victories to his credit, more than half of them scored against the British.

Ninety minutes after his arrival he was standing in the briefing room before his pilots, the Group commanders behind him. His grey eyes traversed the ranks. They were the standard mixture: veterans and fledglings, soft cheeks and distant gazes. It was eerie how one could sort them out; a few months of operational flying did something to the way a man regarded the world.

He gave them plenty of time to look him over. No hurry. The longer they waited the greater the impact.

At last he placed his hands on his hips.

'You've failed!' he declared.

A few of the young heads jerked spasmodically as if they had been hit. There were scowls; there were wide-eyed looks: predictable reaction. Interesting the way different gatherings of men reacted as one.

'You've failed,' he went on, 'to destroy the British Fighter Command. It's still operating, still powerful, still hurting us. Our bombers have been shot down by the dozen. You've seen them. You've seen the crews dying. You've seen the damaged Heinkels and Dorniers staggering back across the Channel. You've seen them ditching. We have let our comrades down, gentlemen! That is the simple, brutal truth!'

A murmur of dissent from the frowning faces. Again Schauff let his gaze roam along the lines of pilots. He took his time. In his experience silence was often far more effective than a barrage of words.

'I can assure you,' he told them, 'that this state of affairs is causing the utmost concern and anger at the highest levels. It will *not be tolerated*! Until the British fighters are wiped out, the invasion cannot take place! The eyes of the entire nation are upon us!' He indicated the map on the wall behind him. 'From now on, gentlemen,' he declared, 'we will be concentrating our attacks on fighter bases and on aircraft factories.' He jabbed at the map with a pointer. 'Here at Kenley! Here at Hawkinge! Here at Biggin Hill! All our resources will be directed at these targets. We will destroy the British fighter force – or we will be destroyed in the attempt!'

New tactics would be employed, he told them. Fighter groups would roam ahead of formations, clearing the sky, seeing the RAF defenders, engaging them before they could attack the bombers. Other fighter groups would fly above, below and alongside the bombers.

'The bombers must be protected so that they can do their job!'

A dark-haired pilot stood up. 'Herr Major, is the fighter force going to be expanded so that we can provide this protection?'

Schauff folded his arms. 'What's your name?'

'Dietrich, sir.'

'And how many fighters do you think we need to do the job, Herr Dietrich?'

'At least twice as many as we are presently using.'

'That is your expert opinion?'

'Yes, sir.'

'You're wrong! What is needed is twice as much determination, twice as much effort! The Englishman is a tough, dedicated foe. He is defending his homeland. There's only one way to beat him: to be even tougher and more dedicated than he is!' His jaw jutted; his mouth was close to a sneer. 'You think you've been doing one hell of a job, don't you? You think it's time to ease up; you've had a rough time! You're feeling sorry for yourselves! But not half as sorry as you're going to feel! I promise!'

'That bastard is going to kill us all,' said Dietrich slumping into a deckchair. 'He's got trouble with his vision. He only sees what he wants to see. I've met his sort before.'

'He's a good pilot,' Ernst said.

'Then he should stick to flying. He thinks he's Frederick the Great.'

Ernst glanced at his friend. The strain of combat flying was having its effect. Dietrich was becoming testy and nervous. He wasn't the only one.

These days the Messerschmitts were taking off on three, four, sometimes even five sorties in a single day, battling with the Spitfires and Hurricanes then scurrying back across the Channel, nursing their last few litres of fuel, often landing in the sea or on the beaches.

Men and machines were cracking under the strain. A sergeant was arrested and charged with drunkenness while on operations; he had consumed four glasses of brandy between sorties; he was unable to clamber back into the aircraft. A lieutenant was admitted to hospital with a wounded foot, apparently incurred in action over the south coast of England. But when the man had been in hospital two days he confessed that he had shot himself in the foot with his own pistol. Many pilots spent every available moment asleep. Others found it impossible to relax. Tempers became short. There were savage arguments, occasional fights. Some men rarely spoke; they became introspective, withdrawn, writing endless letters.

Ernst tried to sketch. He would take his pad to the tree-lined border of the field overlooking the gentle, rolling farmland. There were subjects galore. Farm workers. Pastures. Animals. But he accomplished nothing, only a few hesitant lines. The time was never right; the desire to create pictures seemed to have evaporated like a puff of smoke from an exhaust.

'Rudat says there's a mechanic who can look at a fellow and tell whether he's going to come back or not.' Dietrich puffed on his cigarette, blowing smoke from his nostrils in thoughtful streams. 'A lot of shit, of course.'

'Of course,' said Ernst.

'Swears the bastard looked at Strobel the morning he got it.

Apparently he told a chum. "That one's next." Nonsense, of course.'

'Of course.'

Mechanical response. One did, one said, what was expected.

Ernst rested the Feldpost letter form against a book. He wrote to Ilse. Recounting the incident of the forced landing. Creating an amusing little tale of it. A crash landing: ha ha. Very nearly got burned to death: chuckle, chuckle.

His letters to her were all part of the strange unreality of it all. The words seemed to have no connection with himself or what was really happening. He had devoted half a page to telling her how desperately he longed for her, how she was always in his thoughts, night and day, how he kept imagining the beautiful time when they would be reunited again. He invariably took half a page to tell her these things. It was expected.

But when he had written the familiar phrases he wondered. He tried to picture her in his mind. He couldn't; the image kept blurring. A pretty, laughing girl. But, in a curious way, a stranger. Why couldn't he recall the precise sound of her voice? Why did it seem to be a lifetime since he had last seen her? In fact it was only a matter of weeks. She belonged to another time, another existence. The cold, callous truth was, since he had started flying combat sorties she had hardly ever entered his thoughts. Perhaps in time his perspective would settle down and there would be room for her again. God, life was bewildering. Why couldn't he be like poor Strobel? The lean-jawed pilot from Wiesbaden had spoken joyously of his fiancée Anna, she of the majestic breasts and thighs like 'the portals of heaven'. There was a disarming candour about the way he remembered Anna: 'When she goes off it's like a volcano erupting. One day she'll kill me with delight – ah, but what a beautiful way to go!'

But Strobel hadn't died of delight in Anna's arms.

Dietrich glanced at his watch. He sighed.

'Time to move,' he muttered.

Ernst nodded, the fluttering in his innards starting up on cue like some wheezy old engine. He put the unfinished letter to Ilse inside the book; he had hoped to finish it; it vaguely troubled him to leave things undone when he flew. He wondered why. If he was killed what difference did it make whether he finished the letter? Why did he have to create problems?

But the pilots were pointing to the west, smiling.

Thunderclouds were piling up.

'Scrubbed!' chortled someone.

Beautiful word.

Six

The drizzle became a steady downpour as Vosser put the truck into gear. In the grey light the cobbled streets looked as though they were covered with ice.

Vosser switched on the windscreen wipers. They squeaked with every sweep, an odd-up-and-down sound vaguely resembling the wolf whistle that Americans were said to emit when they saw a pretty girl.

The canvas roof leaked; water dribbled in, splashing in great drops on the passenger seat. Ernst slid to the right and squeezed himself against the door.

'This truck,' declared Vosser, 'is a heap of shit. Lousy French job. It's going to fall to pieces one of these days. I keep telling them. But do they do anything about it? Like hell they do!'

Ernst nodded, hardly listening.

They trundled through the village, a dreary place in urgent need of paint and plaster. In the cobbled square stood half a dozen citizens, old folk who were apparently unwilling to terminate their conversation just because of a little rain. Strictly speaking, they were breaking the law. They were assembling. The Occupation Command had issued precise regulations on the subject; permission of the military commander had to be obtained with regard to any assembly of more than four persons.

One of the Frenchmen was a grizzled ancient who might have been a soldier in 1870. He stared at Ernst as the truck clattered by. There was defiance in the rheumy old eyes. A woman reached out and took his arm, as if to prevent him attacking the Germans with his bare bony fists.

How, Ernst wondered as the group vanished from his view, would he react if an old man assaulted him? Kick him away like an unruly dog? Keep walking and pretend it hadn't happened?

'A dismal lot, the French,' said Vosser. 'Their army outnumbered the Wehrmacht three to one. Did you know that?' Vosser raised one hand from the steering wheel to emphasize his statements. 'Hid behind the Maginot Line and waited for us. So what did we do? We went around it!'

Vosser's manner was familiar, as was so many NCO's when they addressed cadets whose commissions were not yet confirmed. A garrulous individual, Vosser had opinions on everything from international finance to the secret lives of film stars. It was, he said, common knowledge in America that Greta Garbo regularly went to bed with President Roosevelt – and that Mrs Roosevelt approved of the arrangement!

'Remarkable,' Ernst murmured.

'What's even more remarkable,' said Vosser with the self-satisfied tone of a man who possessed knowledge of vital importance to all mankind, 'is the fact that the king wants to get England out of the war, just like Leopold got Belgium out of it. But he can't! Churchill won't let him! You might think the king can do anything; I mean, what the hell's the good of being a king if you can't do what you want? But in England the king's got no power at all! Churchill can keep the war going as long as he wants. They should string the bastard up. He actually thinks he can *win* the war, silly old swine! Imagine! He's crazy, if you ask me. But it'll make no difference; we'll be over there in a little while. They say there are a hundred thousand landing barges ready and waiting at Calais. They're going to go at night. Catch the English at dawn! Our fellows will cut through them like a knife through butter. We'll be in London in no time. Then it'll be over. What're you going to do after the war?'

'I don't know,' said Ernst.

'You should think about it,' said Vosser like a father advising his son. 'It won't be long now. Me, I'm going to get into the taxi business.'

'I wish you luck.'

'This country has a shortage of taxis. Did you know that? It's a fact. There's a big future in taxis.'

'Really?'

'Yes, and yours truly is going to cash in on it. When the war's over there'll be money to spend. And when people have money to spend they want luxury. Makes sense, doesn't it?'

Ernst nodded. 'Are we nearly there?'

'Almost. Who're you visiting, a special little French sweetheart?'

'No,' said Ernst. 'It's official Luftwaffe business.'

'Oh.' Vosser sounded disappointed.

Ernst pointed.

'Drop me over there, will you?'

The same field, the same little house, a faded lime-washed grey. Yes, it was definitely the right spot. As the truck squealed to a halt he gazed over the field. The ugly scar was clearly visible in the grass. They had carted the aircraft's remains away; by now the faithful bird was probably resting on some junk heap waiting for the demolition men to come and cut her up and throw her, bit by bit, into the furnaces to be melted down and made into another aircraft – perhaps even one that he might fly.

'You want me to come with you?'

'No, it won't be necessary.'

'I'll wait here then.'

'All right.'

Ernst stepped out of the truck; the running board sagged under his weight. The door slammed shut with a tiny rattle. The rain had stopped; the air smelt fresh and clean. A soft wind stirred the trees bordering the road. It was a quiet spot; the house was the only building in sight. There was a village a couple of kilometres further along the road. He remembered glimpsing it as he had turned the Emil on to its approach to the field. His innards quivered gently as he recalled the moment; it might have ended there and then. A little less luck and a little more fuel. . . .

There was no one about – just Vosser, slumped over his wheel, watching with the indifference of all soldiers who have to wait for superior officers.

Ernst paused, turning over suitable French phrases in his mind. What was the French for 'Crash-landed'?

The house was small, even smaller than he remembered. Like so many French buildings he had seen, it had an oddly fragile look, as if the walls would crumble at a touch.

He opened the wooden gate; it squealed like an animal in pain. Half a dozen steps took him to the front door. A weathered brass plate bore the name 'Goutard'. He knocked.

The door was opened by a little girl in a bright blue dress. Her eyes opened wide as she absorbed his uniform and badges.

'Is your . . . father at home? May I speak to him please. . .?'

But the little girl had already turned and vanished into the house. He heard her voice, high-pitched with excitement. A moment later a woman appeared, wiping her hands on her apron.

Her dark eyes hardened as she saw him. She had firm, strong features; her black hair was cut in a casual, boyish fashion. She appeared to be about thirty.

She regarded him coldly.

'Does Georges Goutard live here?' he enquired.

'Why do you want to know?'

'I was the pilot of the aircraft that . . . er, fell in the field.'

'I see.'

Clipped, almost rude. She made no attempt to blunt the hostility in her tone.

Ernst said awkwardly, 'A boy – a very brave boy – helped me to get out of the plane. He said his name was Georges Goutard. He told me he lived in this house.'

She gripped the edge of the door tightly. Did she intend to slam it in his face? She seemed to be considering it. Then she said, 'Georges Goutard is my son.'

'I think I owe my life to him.'

'Is that what you came to say?'

He nodded. 'Yes, Madame.' He gulped. This was more difficult than he had anticipated. '. . . And I would like to give him something – a present perhaps.'

She shook her head 'We need nothing from you.'

'I see,' he mumbled, embarrassed. The woman's loathing was almost palpable. He cleared his throat. 'Madame, may I at least thank your son personally for what he did?'

She considered the request for a long moment. Then she shrugged. She turned and called to the girl who was secure inside the house, safe from this frightening stranger. Where was Georges? The piping voice replied that Georges was playing with Albert, outside, somewhere, she didn't know where.

'Go and find him,' said her mother. 'Tell him to come here at once.'

'I hope it's no trouble . . .' said Ernst.

She sighed, a curt little sigh. 'You wish to wait?'

'Yes . . . thank you.'

She closed the door. As if on cue, the rain started again.

Ernst sighed. A nightmare! Why the hell had he bothered to come? Clearly he was as welcome as the black plague. He should have sent a polite letter and left it at that. A fellow felt like a damned fool standing in a doorway, trying not to get soaked. Blast Vosser! The driver was leaning on one elbow, clearly enjoying the spectacle.

A footstep within. The door opened.

She glanced at the rain.

'I suppose you'd better wait inside.'

'Are you sure it's no trouble. . .?'

'Come on.'

'Thank you.'

He followed her into what appeared to be the parlour. The room was a surprise, the walls painted in dramatic tones and liberally hung with paintings, mostly landscapes in bright, striking tones. The furniture was unexceptional yet cleverly co-ordinated. Someone with adventurous taste had decorated the place.

'You may sit down.' She indicated a chair beside the empty fire-place.

'You're very kind, Madame.'

She stood at the door, arms folded, as if preparing herself to guard her home against this enemy.

Ernst thought frantically for something to say. Didn't women always like to talk about their children?

'Your daughter is very pretty, Madame. What is her name?'

'Giselle.'

'It suits her.'

'You think so.'

It was a statement not a question.

'How old is Giselle?'

'She will be nine in September.'

'And Georges?'

'He is eleven.'

'A remarkable boy.'

'You think so.' Again the statement.

'I don't know many boys who would have done what he did.'

'Don't you?'

'And so modest.'

'Indeed.'

'Unaffected . . . that seemed to be my impression. He took it all very much as a matter of course, as if he did that sort of thing every day.'

'He doesn't.'

'No, of course not.'

Her chin jutted defiantly at him. Somewhere in the house a clock struck seven.

Ernst said, 'Is your husband at home, Madame?'

'Why do you ask?'

'I just thought . . . I wanted to tell him about his son, that was all . . . nothing else.'

A letter would have done the job, met the obligation. Official thanks from the Luftwaffe. Did she have any idea what he had gone through to arrange transportation? The forms to sign, the explanations, the arrangements to make . . .

For this.

She said, 'You speak French well . . . for a German.'

A reluctant compliment. He thanked her. 'My mother taught me the language,' he explained. 'She lived for some time in Lyons. Her father had business dealings there, many years ago.'

'You have been to Lyons?'

'No, Madame, this is the first time I have visited France.'

'Perhaps "visited" is not quite the correct term.'

'I'm sorry.'

She shrugged. 'Why did you land in the field here?'

'I had engine trouble.'

'Trouble?'

'It stopped.'

She smiled. It transformed her. For an enchanting instant she looked like a schoolgirl. But the smile was shortlived. It vanished abruptly as if she had suddenly remembered that she shouldn't smile in the presence of this German.

She looked down at the palms of her hands. She had long, slender fingers. 'A man in the village accused Georges of aiding the enemy,' she said.

'I'm sorry.'

'He said Georges should have left you to rot in your aeroplane.'

'I see.'

'He said that because Georges saved you, you are able to fly again. And fight the English. Perhaps you will fight Frenchmen too, because they say many French airmen have gone to fly with the English.'

Was the Hurricane pilot a Frenchman?

Ernst said, 'I hope Georges doesn't regret what he did.'

'He may,' she replied candidly. 'But I don't know. He keeps his thoughts to himself.'

'He has great courage.'

'He's afraid of the dark,' she said, her expressive lips curving into the suspicion of another smile. He waited but it died before birth. She looked at him. 'How old are you?'

'Twenty, Madame.'

She nodded thoughtfully. Then she got to her feet. 'Where *are* those children?' With a sigh she made her way to the rear of the house.

There was a framed photograph on the mantel: the woman with her two children and a man. He looked old. Middle-aged. He had thinning hair and keen, intelligent features.

Presumably the man was her husband. He looked old enough to be her father.

He heard her calling. Giselle's voice answered. A door slammed.

She returned, shaking her head in the long-suffering way of all mothers. 'Georges has gone off somewhere with a friend. I keep asking him to tell me where he's going but he keeps forgetting. Children never think that their parents might worry about them.'

'I'm sure you're right.'

'I am,' she said.

He stood up. 'I'm sorry I missed your son, Madame. I would like to have thanked him personally for what he did.'

'He would have liked to have seen you,' she said. 'He's mad about flying.'

'Perhaps he'll grow up to be a pilot.'

'Perhaps.'

'I wish I could take him for a flight. He'd enjoy that, I suppose.'

'Enjoy it?' She smiled. 'There's nothing in the world he'd enjoy more.'

He wished he hadn't mentioned the notion. 'Unfortunately it's not permitted to take civilians up in Luftwaffe aircraft.'

The smile vanished; her mouth hardened. 'Particularly French civilians, I suppose.'

'No, no, any civilians,' he hastened to assure her. 'They're very strict about it. Military regulations, you know.'

'Of course.'

'They've got regulations for everything.'

'I'm sure they have.'

'Yes.' He swallowed noisily. Then he caressed his chin. 'But I wonder about Georges . . . it's rather a special case, isn't it, when you consider what he did.'

'I would say so.'

'Well, all one can do is ask . . . and wait and see. I've never heard of anything quite like this but that doesn't mean it's impossible.'

'Quite so.'

'I'd better talk it over with Schiegl. He's our adjutant. I can't promise anything, you understand.'

'I understand.'

'But I'll do what I can. I'll explain the circumstances and make it clear what Georges did. Perhaps they'll agree; perhaps they won't. It's hard to say – in fact, impossible.'

She nodded as if a bargain had been struck.

He said, 'Thank you for letting me talk to you, Madame.'

She shrugged. She gazed at him for a moment, then said, 'When you Germans came I was terrified that you would take my house and throw us out on the street. You're the first one to come here. And you're no more frightening than the boy who brings the milk to the back door.' Her eyes roamed his face. 'You strike me as a gentle person, not really the sort who should be a soldier.'

'Perhaps you're right,' he admitted. Did it show?

'You don't like being a soldier, do you?'

'Not very much,' he replied. 'But when I was eighteen I had to go into the military . . . and I wanted to fly. So here I am.'

'It is very frightening, flying in combat?'

The directness of the question took him aback. He thought for a moment. He nodded.

'There isn't much time to be frightened during combat,' he said. 'But there is a lot of time to be frightened before combat and after it.'

She said, 'You would be a fool if you weren't frightened.'

'A fool?'

'Anyone who is not frightened has no imagination. And anyone who has no imagination is a fool.' She glanced at the photograph on the mantel. 'My husband said that once. I think he was right.'

'He is your husband?'

'Yes,' she said. 'He died a year ago.'

'I'm very sorry.'

'He was a teacher. He used to ride his bicycle to the school every day. One morning he walked out to his bicycle, started to get on to it, and fell dead. A seizure of the heart, the doctors tell me. There was no warning. He had been in good health.'

'A tragedy,' Ernst said. Then he found himself telling her about his father, about the long battle with tuberculosis, the lingering death just before Christmas.

'We have both suffered terrible losses,' she murmured. Now her voice was gentle, sadly lilting, she seemed to have become another person. 'What was your father's profession?'

'He was an office manager for an insurance company.'

'An important job.'

'I suppose so, but I don't think he liked it much. He wanted to be a doctor . . . and then he wanted me to be a doctor.'

'My husband was a good teacher,' she said. 'But at heart he was a poet. His poetry was good, I think, very imaginative. He had some poems published in literary magazines, but it is difficult to make a living as a poet.'

'I suppose it must be.' Ernst picked up his cap and made his way to the front door. He glanced again at the paintings. They were exciting, possessing magnificent vitality.

'You like painting?' the woman asked.

'Very much, Madame.'

He looked closely. Many of the frames were clearly much older than the paintings themselves; some were home-made.

Then the name in the corner of one landscape caught his eye. Goutard!

'That's your name, Madame!'

'I dabble,' she said, pleased as all artists are when anyone takes an interest in their work.

'They're very good.'

'Thank you.'

'Your brushwork is . . . *splendid*; that's the only way I can describe it.'

Her cheeks flushed with pleasure. 'Do you paint?' she asked him.

'A little. But I feel more comfortable sketching. But when I try oils, or even watercolours, nothing seems to work!'

Now those eyes that had regarded him so frostily sparkled with delight at the sharing of a common interest. For fifteen minutes they talked about painting, about painters, about techniques, about problems and solutions. The moments flashed by; they chatted like two old friends, excitedly. Then as if by signal, they stopped.

She smiled. 'I just realized, I don't know your name.'

'Forgive me. It's Brehme. Ernst Brehme.'

She nodded thoughtfully seeming to weigh the sound of the name. 'My name is Jeanne,' she said. 'There's no need to call me Madame, not now!' Her smile began to fade. 'Will you fly to England tomorrow?'

'Possibly.'

'I can't wish you luck if you fight the English.'

'I understand.'
'But I hope you come back safely.'

Seven

It was a period of non-stop effort. The RAF fighter force had to
be destroyed; the battle had to be won. The way had to be cleared
for the invasion, the final, decisive operation of the war. Day after
glorious cloudless day the fighting went on. Pilots became dazed
by the continuous action, almost incapable of reacting when comrades died. Many became dangerously negligent. Clauser misjudged his landing approach by a ludicrous margin, ploughing
into a farmhouse in which a man and a woman were eating dinner;
miraculously everyone survived. Berger dived vertically into the
Channel; it was the opinion of many that he had fallen asleep at
the controls; haggard and apprehensive, he had been unable to
sleep. Now he slept permanently. A Heinkel, unable to reach its
base near Paris, attempted a landing at the fighter base. It trailed
smoke. As the bomber touched down one undercarriage leg collapsed. The wing slammed into the ground. With a sharp metallic
screech, the aircraft cartwheeled, erupting in fire. One man, a
gunner, managed to scramble free of the wreck. But he was alight,
a pitiful, writhing torch. He was alive when the rescue crews
reached him. He babbled about an appointment in Hamburg.
Very important. Vital that he wasn't late. He died as they gave
him morphine.

A third of the unit's pilots became casualties. Replacements
came in eager, smiling groups; one by one they disappeared,
sometimes within hours of their arrival.

Ernst lost track of the number of sorties he had flown. He
found that for several days he could carry out his duties in a
curiously disaffected way. Then emotion would catch up with
him. It would be an agony of nausea, of trembling in anticipation
of the inevitable. Soon it would be his turn. It had to be; the odds
couldn't be denied. It was part of the bargain.

Dietrich was of the opinion that the whole business was extremely bad for a fellow's nerves. He shot down a Hurricane near

Hastings; a telex arrived informing him that he had been awarded the Iron Cross, First Class.

Ernst continued to write dutifully to his mother and to his sister Maria, to Ilse, to an aunt in Wuppertal, an uncle in Bamberg, a cousin in Memmigen. He told all of them how eagerly he was looking forward to seeing all of them again, very soon. But he had no illusions. He would never see any of them. He had no future so it was better not to think about the future. Only the moment mattered: only the men around him were real; everyone else belonged to a never-never land that it was becoming increasingly difficult to remember clearly.

In the evenings when at last flying was done for the day, he and Dietrich would make their way to their room and hurl themselves on their bunks. They would grin wearily at one another and shake their heads as if denying that they were really a part of this lunacy.

'So they didn't kill you today.'

'Not today.'

'They will.'

'I know. They'll get you too.'

'But they'll get you first.'

The Heinkel reared up, like an animal in sudden, excruciating pain. It staggered, then rolled slowly over on to its back. Two members of its crew parachuted to safety, as the bomber fell out of the sky.

The victorious Hurricane banked, looking for more prey.

Oberleutnant Hans Baatz swung in pursuit. Ernst followed, automatically scanning the sky, covering his leader's tail.

'Jesus . . .!' someone bellowed over the R/T.

'Jump!' someone else yelled.

White tracer trails streaked the sky. A man drifted by, dangling beneath his open parachute.

Baatz hurled his Emil after the Tommy. He fired. Missed. Turned. Fired again. Missed again.

The horizon tumbled, disappeared, reappeared, then slid away to become glittering blue. The R/T crackled with voices; exhortations, warnings, appeals for help, cries of despair.

The Hurricane pilot knew his business, turning, skidding, never doing anything long enough to present a target. A wily fellow, this one.

He escaped. Baatz had to break off, frustrated. It was time to head for home. Far below, a single-engined aircraft trailed black

75

smoke, a thin stream that painted a line across the sky. The aircraft was descending gently, taking an inordinately long time to reach the earth.

The sun was already sinking low on the horizon. Another day of killing and being killed. Five sorties. God only knows how many aircraft went down, friends and foes. At times the sky was criss-crossed by the fiery trails of doomed machines.

End of sport for the day; the respective teams could return home.

I'm still alive, Ernst said to himself. It was a discovery of only mild interest. Still alive and kicking in spite of the efforts of countless Tommies. How many fighters did the bastards possess? HQ persisted in declaring the RAF Fighter Command was on its last legs. But HQ didn't have to meet RAF Fighter Command in battle day after day. The Englishmen kept coming up to fight, just as strong, just as eager as on the day before. So what was being accomplished? Who was winning? Was anyone winning? Rumour had it that there were secret peace talks going on at this very moment, in Stockholm, or in Lisbon, depending upon your source. But no one really believed such talk. The battle would go on for ever, until every aircraft in the world had been destroyed and every pilot killed.

Ernst's gaze flitted over the instruments. Revs, pressures, temperatures. As he did so he caught a glimpse of the shape in the mirror. A streamlined, flitting shape. A dangerous shape!

Rattle of guns! The Emil shuddered as the Englishman's bullets smacked home. Holes appeared in the wing, a neat line of them. Engines howling, the Spitfires streaked past. Ernst saw a Heinkel fly past, straight and level, but the bomber was engulfed in fierce, wind-battered flame. A tiny, pink face appeared at a perspex window.

The formation was scattered by the surprise attack. An Emil went down vertically, minus most of its tail unit.

'Bastards! Look out behind you!'

'Yellow Six! Cover me!'

'My God, my God, my God, my God, my God, my . . .'

Abruptly the transmission ceased.

The sea began to revolve, then it disappeared.

Where was Baatz?

He blinked. The sky was full of aircraft, milling about, confused, disorganized. A Heinkel whirled earthward, a huge torch from which five men fought to escape. And failed.

And then, in the sudden surprising way of aerial battles, it was over. The enemy had vanished. The battered formation began to close its ranks for the flight home.

Ernst eyed his wing, frowning, a sickening coldness in his guts. Old Friend Fear. The Emil was flying in an unusual altitude. The controls had a strange, spongy feel. The wing surface had been badly damaged. And that meant some disturbance to the airflow, to the lift. But what else was wrong? What was damaged beneath that sheet metal skin?

The thing could fracture at any moment. The tiniest turbulence might do it. The last aerial straw. He swallowed, his mouth dry and sour. How much time would he have to scramble out of the cockpit and jump? Would the broken wing fold at the root and wrap itself over the cockpit, trapping him? Such things happened. Deep breaths. He had to fight the near-panic flutterings of half a hundred nerves.

He pressed the transmit button on his control column.

He told Baatz about the wing damage. Baatz descended to examine Ernst's aircraft from below.

'One undercarriage leg is partially down. It looks loose. Seems to be moving slightly.'

Which explained the odd feel of the aircraft. Ernst glanced at the mechanical position indicator on the right of the instrument panel; it showed the gear locked in place within the wing. Hydraulic failure probably. That meant no brakes. Some of the newer Emils had emergency hand pumps to cope with just such a problem. But Ernst's aircraft was relatively elderly. There was only one option: release the undercarriage locks and let gravity do the rest. With luck the undercarriage legs would swing down and lock in position.

More deep breaths. Worry about the wing first. If the wing failed there was no need to worry about the undercarriage.

'Coast ahead,' said someone.

At that moment the British attacked again. Spitfires came up out of the setting sun, catching the formation completely by surprise. A Heinkel on Ernst's right staggered, vomiting flame. He glimpsed the Spitfire's delicate form as the fighter rolled on to one wing and dived away, back toward England.

He turned, following Baatz. A second Spitfire hit him. Bullets struck home like hammer blows, shaking the entire airframe, punishing it. The whole thing had to collapse; it couldn't possibly take such punishment and remain whole. A ridiculous sense of outrage hit him as the sea slid away on his right; it wasn't fair that the British should attack again, not when his machine was in such pitiful condition . . .

Baatz fired at a Spitfire, without result. It was a pointless gesture, a waste of ammunition; the Tommy was clearly out of range. By now all the RAF fighters had turned for home, their pilots no doubt chuckling, congratulating themselves on their success.

Headphones buzzed with messages to the Air-Sea Rescue. Bomber down, crew in dinghy . . . fighter down, pilot missing. . . . Hurry!

The sea was swirling greys and blacks, punctuated by tiny sparkles as the low sun caught a wave. Ernst flew alongside Baatz, nursing his badly wounded machine. The wings were in sad condition, the metal skin punctured by machine gun bullets; he imagined the structure within, flexing, bending, the components cracking, breaking, one after the other. . . .

No, he was still in the air, his aircraft still in one piece. He was still breathing. And now the coast was only four or five minutes away. Hold together a bit longer, he asked the Emil. You can do it. You've come all this way. You can manage the rest of the trip. . . .

'All right?' Baatz's voice. He had a curt, incisive manner, he rarely wasted words.

'So far.'

'Your undercarriage leg looks about the same.'

Which wasn't particularly good news. If the leg hadn't dropped during the last series of manoeuvres there was surely little chance that it ever would. Which meant that the leg had probably been hit and was jammed in that position. Which ruled out a normal landing. Wheels-up or wheels-down the end result would almost certainly be a pile-up and a bonfire. Baatz told him to jump. Ernst acknowledged. Jumping was a bowel-loosening prospect. In theory there wasn't much to it. Turn the machine to head back to the sea, then roll her and fall out. Count to five and pull the ripcord. Simple. But in practice things could go wrong. The tail could get in the way or the chute might have been hit by gunfire earlier and might fall to bits the moment it opened. . . .

But weigh the pros and cons. Consider the options. Balance the chances of survival.

There was really no choice. If the undercarriage didn't cooperate he had to jump.

The coastline slipped below. He asked Baatz to watch, then he reached forward and tugged on the undercarriage emergency release.

Please.

'Your port leg is down,' Baats reported. 'But the starboard leg is still in the same position.'

'Very well,' said Ernst, 'I'm jumping.'

'Good,' said Baatz matter-of-factly.

The earth tilted gently as Ernst pulled away from the formation. Now the sun was a mellow ball of fire settling down on the horizon; below, the fields and villages were already in shadow.

He struggled to recall the endless lectures on bailing out, the advice, the tips that were supposed to prevent everything from sore toes to total pulverization.

Tug the canopy jettison lever. Miracle! It worked! Wind burst into the cockpit, as the perspex and metal structure spun away; dust and dirt swirled about him. Ahead lay the Channel. No time to waste. Release the harness attachment, grip the pull firmly in right hand. Loosen helmet straps around the throat (remembering stories about airmen who had broken their necks because they had jumped with their helmets too tightly fastened).

Right. . . . Now! Stick back. Blue sky in view. Speed dropping off, off, off, airspeed dropping. Hard aileron and rudder. Starboard wing up and over. Suddenly there was nothing but the earth to see and . . .

Oh God! He was falling free! Tumbling! Earthandskyandearthandsky . . . glimpse of the aircraft wobbling away on its own.

Pull the bloody handle!

Nothing happened.

He continued to plummet.

Christ, he thought, quite calmly, it didn't work; it must have been damaged in the fight, riddled by bullets. For Christ's sake why didn't he stay with the aircraft? He saw his father, reaching out, trying to save him.

But suddenly there was a crack of thunder just above him. He bounced, the air banged out of his lungs. He saw one of his flying boots tumbling away, disappearing into the gathering shadows below.

Alive! Good God he was alive!

Above him the chute flapped like a sail, the ropes creaking as they took his weight.

Thank you, God, a million thanks for your mercy.

He felt as if he had just been born again. Life was fresh and new.

And as funny as hell. The whole thing struck him as hilarious. He couldn't stop himself giggling like a simpleton as he dangled in the soft evening air. It was indisputably the funniest damn thing ever, a joke of incredible proportions, something to laugh about for the rest of one's life . . .

Two Messerschmitts flew close by. Baatz and Dietrich. They waved, no doubt puzzled to observe him shaking with mirth. He waved back, still laughing. They turned for home.

Now it was strangely quiet; he listened to his own laughter, he tried to stop laughing, but couldn't. Laughter was a motor that wouldn't stop. He was still laughing when the cottage came looming up out of the shadows. He saw the chimney, felt the scraping of the rough bricks against his hands; then he was on the roof, slithering, tumbling, slates clattering. And spluttering weakly with mirth. He tried to stop himself sliding down the roof. He saw the edge, the gutter, the tiny garden, oddly colourless in the half-light; the narrow path, a large roller, incongruous on such a minuscule plot. He grabbed at the gutter. Missed. He fell. Again he was tumbling helpless in mid-air. And again he came to a sudden, breath-punching stop. Dazed, he look up. His parachute must have become entangled in the chimney. He was suspended, a couple of metres from the ground.

Hilarious. Even funnier than before.

'I envy you,' said Dietrich, making himself comfortable on the edge of the bed. 'Feeling better, are you?'

'Much better,' Ernst assured him. 'A bit stiff and sore, that's all.'

'What do you do all day? Feel the nurses? Have you had a feel with Nurse Horst? Not yet? Just tell her she has beautiful legs and thighs. That's all. She's randy as hell. She'll fix you up, believe me. She's awfully good at it. You may not think so by looking at her but under that starched bosom is a woman in a state of constant throb. She's frustration personified.'

Ernst smiled. You never knew when to believe Dietrich. It was best never to believe him.

'I know she reminds one a little of Winston Churchill,' said Dietrich. 'But if one closes one eyes it can be bliss, pure bliss. By the way, when are they letting you out?'

'I'm not sure. Kriker says I have to rest a bit longer.'

'One good session with Nurse Horst and you'll sleep like a baby.'

Dietrich had been paying visits several times a day, keeping him up to date on unit news. The pace of operations seemed to have slackened since that last, horrendous day in mid-September.

'We've got some new faces,' Dietrich reported. 'The usual crop. Every one wanting to be another Richthofen and have every girl in the country. Rudat had to pancake on the beach yesterday. Banged up his aircraft pretty badly but he's all right; didn't even get his feet wet.' He got to his feet, unwinding his long, lean body, stretching and yawning in his oddly feline manner. The Iron Cross was prominent against his left breast pocket, a badge proclaiming that here was a man who had met the enemy in combat and had conquered.

'I'll drop in tomorrow,' he said.

Kriker, the Medical Officer, arrived an hour later. A pudgy, perspiring man, he examined Ernst, sighing, managing to convey the impression of being hopelessly overworked because pilots persisted in doing foolhardy things.

'Back still sore? Pain here and here? Sleeping better? Opening your bowels regularly? Shock mostly. Nothing too serious. Soon have you back on duty.'

'How soon, sir?'

'A few days. Get you properly calmed down.'

'I am calm, sir.'

But Kriker was already on his way, scribbling on the chart, muttering to himself and shaking his head. 'You should count your blessings,' he said in his reproving tone. 'You were damned lucky that time.'

The hours dragged by at a maddening pace; the highlights of his days were meals and visits both professional and social. Ernst felt his strength returning, his nerves quieting. Operational strain, Kriker had mumbled; simple as that; too much flying, too much combat; something has to bend under that sort of strain. But why had he, Ernst Brehme bent before the other men who had flown and fought much longer? Different individuals, different characteristics, Kriker had declared; no mystery about it.

As his condition improved, Ernst became bored. He found himself envying anyone who was outside, no matter how onerous or hazardous his duties. The weather had broken; there were several days of steady rain that lashed against the hospital windows.

The sun returned for a few hours. Ernst was permitted a short walk in the grounds. It was the first time he had been outside for ten days. The walk had served only to sharpen his boredom; why the devil was he being kept here so long? God, a fellow could go mad in this place.

The evenings were short now. It was almost dark by the time he had finished his supper. The usual tasteless Medical Department fare. He wrote to Ilse, assuring her that he was well, almost fully recovered; she had nothing to worry about; then he wrote almost the same letter to his mother and the aunt in Wuppertal, the uncle in Bamberg and the cousin in Memmigen. It was good of them to write to him so faithfully; he enjoyed reading their letters. But as Dietrich had pointed out, every letter received meant a reply to be penned; relatives each had one letter to write; the unfortunate serviceman was expected to reply to all of them. The arrangement was totally unfair, in Dietrich's opinion. The one letter should be circulated, or duplicated. . .

The nurse came in to collect his plate.

Nurse Horst!

It was hardly fair to say she resembled Winston Churchill, although her chin had a somewhat masculine line to it.

A large, well upholstered woman, Nurse Horst.

'Did you enjoy the meal?'

'Yes, it was quite good, thank you.'

A curt nod. A clatter of plates and implements. Great heavens, how could anyone ever muster the courage to attempt a seduction of that formidable creature? That firm, professional mouth! Those stalwart shoulders. Those strong, capable hands! But there *was* something about the way she held herself . . . a certain poise; it certainly couldn't be called flaunting . . . and yet . . .

She took his temperature.

'How are you this evening?'

'Very well, Nurse, thank you.'

Another nod, like a military salute. She turned, her shoes squeaking on the polished floor.

He didn't think about saying it. He didn't ponder the pros and cons in any meaningful way. It simply happened. He heard himself saying,

'You have really beautiful legs, Nurse.'

She stopped.

He gulped, cleared his throat noisily.

God, what had made him say such a thing?

She turned, the supper plates still her hands.

A faint touch of pink now coloured her cheeks. She was smiling, a peculiarly shy little smile.

She looked down at her legs.

'Do you really think they're nice?'

'Yes . . .' he croaked. And they were.

'What do you like about them?'

'Er . . . their shape.'

'You think they are nicer than Nurse Buder's legs?'

'Much nicer. I've never noticed Nurse Buder's legs.'

'I think you have nice legs too,' she said with a tiny giggle. 'I've seen them, you know.'

'I suppose you have.'

'I've seen a lot more than that.'

'Yes, I can believe that.'

She paused, listening, then deftly pushed the door shut with one foot. She put the supper things down.

'Are you quite comfortable?' she enquired. 'Sometimes you can get a little sore from lying in bed too long. Perhaps you'd like me to massage the spot a little bit. Would you like that?'

Strong, capable hand indeed! She tackled her task with obvious relish. And with considerable skill.

When the discreet knock came on the door, Ernst was half out of bed, clutching one of Nurse Horst's bountiful breasts, attempting to kiss her and at the same time respond to her whispered expressions of adoration.

'Jesus Christ!' she hissed.

There was a flurry of frantic tugging at clothing and bedding, a scrambling for shoes, a brushing back of hair. She opened the door.

Schiegl stuck his balding head into the room.

'Hullo . . .' Disconcerted, he stepped back as Nurse Horst gusted past him. 'Good gracious,' he said to Ernst. 'She seemed to be in one hell of a hurry.'

'An emergency,' Ernst explained.

'Ah,' said Schiegl. 'Of course.' He beamed at Ernst. 'How's the patient?'

'Quite well, thank you, sir.'

'Good fellow. You'll be out of here in no time. Treating you well, are they?'

'Very.'

'Glad to hear it. Hours drag a bit, I suppose. Gets a little lonely.'

'Not so far,' Ernst assured him.

'Glad to hear, old fellow. I've got a bit of news for you.'

'News?'

'The Goutard thing.'

'Goutard?'

'You remember, the business with the boy.'

'Boy?' Ernst tried to get his tumbling thoughts in order. Then it came back to him. Of course! Georges Goutard, the boy who had helped him out of Yellow Three. 'You mean, the idea of getting him a flight? It's been approved?'

'That's right, old fellow. Just heard this afternoon. The PK people seem to think it will make a good human interest story. The press will love it, they said. It's all been authorized. We're to make the necessary arrangements without delay.'

Eight

The journey took more than an hour by bicycle. It was dark when he pulled up beside the house. He pulled the cycle off the road and wheeled it up the narrow path to the front door. He straightened his tunic and adjusted the set of his forage cap – his Fliegermütze. A chilly wind had sprung up; there was a feeling of autumn in the air.

The door opened before he had time to knock.

Giselle eyed him gravely.

'Hullo,' she said. 'You've come back.'

'I hope you don't mind.'

'No,' she said. 'I don't mind.'

Then Jeanne appeared. She wore a paint-daubed smock. She smiled when she saw him.

'Ernst. I thought I heard your voice.'

'I hope I haven't called at an inconvenient time.'

She shook her head as she opened the door wide for him.

The wireless was playing. A string quartet. The phrases seemed to form a soft web of sound, real enough to reach out and touch.

'I brought some pictures,' he told her.

'Pictures?'

'Of Georges at the field. I know a fellow in the Photographic

Section, I asked him to make an extra set of prints. I thought you might like to have them as a memento.'

She smiled that splendid smile.

'It was a kind thought, Ernst.' She beckoned to him, closing the door behind him before switching on the light. She took off her smock and tossed it on a chair. 'How are you? I haven't seen you for ages.'

'I had a short spell in hospital but I'm quite well now.'

'Were you wounded?'

'Not really. A little accident. Nothing serious.'

He sat down and gave her the pictures. It was delightful to watch her reaction to each one, to see the corner of her mouth twitch into a smile at the sight of her son. She had not accompanied Georges to the airfield, despite Ernst's request that she be included. The request was refused without comment. A decision was reached; it was not to be questioned. And so Georges had been picked up at his house in a Mercedes field car and whisked off to the field alone. Ernst had seen him only briefly during the visit; there had been time enough for a handshake and a few words, all recorded by the photographer and the chain-smoking correspondent, both members of the military propaganda unit whose task it was to provide the press with officially-approved war news.

'Georges had a marvellous day,' Jeanne said. 'He's been talking about it ever since.'

'He doesn't talk about anything else,' Giselle declared.

Georges came into the room, his small face serious as usual. He shook hands with Ernst and said he was pleased to see him and hoped he was enjoying good health.

'I'm very well thank you.'

'Good. Have you been flying much?'

'Not much. The weather isn't good now. Things are very slow.'

'I suppose it must be a welcome relief after all the operations in the summer.'

Ernst smiled at the boy's somewhat pedantic phrasing; he assured him that it was indeed a welcome relief.

Jeanne said, 'Ernst has brought some pictures.'

His eyes lit up. 'Of me? At the airfield?'

'Yes, of you.'

'Oh dear,' said Giselle with a sigh.

'They took *hundreds* of pictures,' Georges said. 'That photographer never stopped.'

'Of you?' said Giselle, sounding incredulous.

'Hush, dear,' said her mother.

'I didn't get a copy of every picture,' said Ernst. 'But I think this is a fairly good selection.'

Georges lost no time in arranging the prints on the floor before the fireplace. He dropped on to his knees; his eyes lit up with pleasure as he saw himself conversing with Major Schauff, Captain Schiegl, Captain Roder and some of the pilots, including Dietrich; clambering aboard the Weihe communications aircraft, being assisted into his parachute harness by a bored-looking crewman, waving soberly from a cabin window.

'You look as calm as if you've been flying all your life,' Ernst told him.

'I wasn't nervous,' Georges said. He recounted how he had seen the house from the air, how the river had looked like a ribbon of glass, how the pilot had let him take the controls for a few minutes. 'I flew it,' he beamed. 'I actually flew it!'

'I *know*,' said Giselle. 'You've *told* me that. *Lots* of times!'

'You don't have to look at the pictures if you don't want to,' Georges retorted, grabbing the prints and clutching them to his chest.'

'I want to see them.'

'Then behave yourself.'

Jeanne said to Ernst, 'It was very kind of you to arrange everything.'

He smiled. 'I didn't really do much. I just asked. I wasn't sure they'd agree to it. But apparently someone got on to the news people in Berlin and they thought it was interesting, a French boy helping a Luftwaffe pilot out of his crashed plane. So they sent a photographer and a journalist to the field. They interviewed Georges.'

Georges said, 'They asked me a lot of questions. But they were easy. I answered them all. The most difficult thing was to understand them. Their French was terrible.'

Ernst laughed. 'Sometimes their German is terrible too.'

Jeanne asked how the news people intended to use the pictures.

'I think they're going to do an article in *Der Adler*.'

'What's that?'

'It's the Luftwaffe magazine. It's published in several languages.'

'French too?'

'I think so. I'll find out. And I'll get a copy for you when the article is printed.

Yet another sigh from Giselle who was clearly dismayed at the prospect of Georges receiving even more attention and becoming even more swollen-headed.

'It was a very nice airplane,' said Georges looking at a photograph of the Weihe in which he had flown. He sounded like a man who has owned a number of machines and remembers that one with particular fondness.

'I would have liked to take you up in my 109,' Ernst said.

Georges nodded. 'But it's only got one seat,' he explained to the females.

Jeanne looked through the prints. 'It's strange seeing my little son with all those German uniforms.'

'Everyone liked Georges,' Ernst assured her.

Georges confirmed that. 'They were very nice to me,' he said. 'I told you that, didn't I?'

'Yes, you did. I remember.'

'Major Schauff said he hoped he would have a son just like me.'

She smiled wryly, as if saying that she knew he had been used for propaganda purposes, but if the wish was to play a game in which everyone believed the whole thing had been an example of Teutonic altruism, then she was prepared to go along with it.

She said, 'It was kind of the Major to say that.'

'He meant it,' Ernst assured her.

'I'm sure he did.'

Georges said to Ernst, 'Have you shot down any more planes?'

Ernst shook his head. 'I was shot down myself,' he said. 'I had to jump. Luckily I was able to reach the French coast before I got out.'

Georges was impressed; his dark eyes were unblinking as they fastened on Ernst. 'Were you in flames?'

'No. My plane was hit many times but I didn't catch fire. The trouble was, my undercarriage was damaged so I couldn't land.'

'It must be fantastic to jump by parachute.'

'Yes,' Ernst said, 'quite fantastic.'

'Your plane crashed?'

'Yes, the last time I saw it it was heading out to sea.'

'That's two you've crashed.'

Ernst smiled, nodding. 'Yes, and I've only got one in exchange, so I'm not a very good bargain, am I?'

'Don't worry about it,' Georges advised.

'I'll try not to,' Ernst promised.

His eye caught Jeanne's. He asked her what she had been painting.

'Would you like to see?'

'Very much.'

He followed her into the studio, a small sitting room with an easel, a stove, a table and a couch. The canvas was facing the one window, away from him. She grinned.

'Close your eyes.'

'Very well.'

He felt her fingers close on his arm. He allowed himself to be led a few paces. She positioned him carefully.

'All right,' she said, 'you may open your eyes now.'

He did so. And clapped his hand to his mouth in surprise. She had painted a watercolour of his Emil, upside down, its back broken, lying in the field. And Georges, like a tiny conqueror, standing beside it, one foot on its shattered wing. The stance was perfect. The human spirit triumphs over the machine.

'It's perfect,' he told her.

'You're very kind.'

He shook his head in admiration. 'You inject such vitality into your work . . . it's *alive*. You have a great deal of talent.'

She smiled, pleased.

'You promised me you would show me some of your work.'

'One day.'

'I hope so. I'd love to see some.'

'It's very dull,' he said, 'compared with yours.'

'You're being too modest.'

'Just honest.'

She grinned. God, she was beautiful when she let her smile have full rein.

He looked again at the watercolour. 'That's really my aircraft; my number on the side. It looks exactly right.'

'I sketched it before they came and took it away. I wanted to get the details correct.'

'Nice to think of it in a painting. It deserved the honour, getting me back over the Channel. It's immortalized.'

'I'm glad you're pleased,' she said.

He said, 'You should be painting professionally.'

'I was at one time,' she told him. 'I worked for an advertising agency. In Paris. I painted girls putting on lipstick and distinguished looking men smoking cigars.'

'You were wasted, doing that kind of rot.'

'I didn't think it was rot. I worked very hard at it. Remember, a lot of what we call great art was originally commissioned; it was commercial art, in a way. Perhaps when the history of art is written they'll say that some of the finest work was done in advertisements.'

They went back into the living room. The children had left.

'It was thoughtful of you to bring the pictures,' she said. 'May we keep them?'

'Of course.'

'Thank you.'

Suddenly there seemed to be nothing more to say. The wind had picked up strength; it pressed against the side of the house like a thousand hands.

Ernst said, 'I suppose I should be going.'

She looked up at him. 'You may stay for a cup of coffee. If you wish.'

'Thank you. I would enjoy that.'

She nodded. 'Very well.' She went into the kitchen, returning in a few moments. 'The coffee is on the stove. I will be back soon. It's time the children were in bed.'

Ernst listened to her footsteps. There was a squeaky giggle from Giselle. A few words, muffled and indistinct. Georges' voice. A splendid boy, Georges; remarkably courageous. Odd to think that you owed your life to an eleven-year-old.

It was a pleasant little house. So cosy after months of military living. This house smelt like a home, reminders of a recently cooked meal, the same sense of relaxation. Not a single uniform in sight, except his own. A fellow needed to get away from the military environment from time to time. . .

The coffee began to boil. He went into the kitchen. The lid was dancing on the pot. He reached to grasp the handle. His fingers closed on it – and immediately let go. Agony! He emitted a squeak of pain. The damned thing was piping hot! Wincing, he flapped his hand in the air, vainly attempting to cool his fingers.

'What's the matter?'

She came hurrying into the kitchen, purposefully, as she must have rushed to her children many times.

'It's nothing . . . the coffee pot. . .'

'Did you burn your hand?'

'Not really . . .'

'Let me see. Burns can be nasty.'

She took his hand in hers to examine the damage.

He gulped. Her touch was exciting, shockingly exciting. It set his blood pounding; it galvanized his very being.

Ridiculous! he told himself. Control yourself, you idiot!

He was obliged to take a deep breath because he found that he hadn't taken in air for several minutes.

She looked up at him. Deep, dark eyes. Mouth twitching into a smile. 'I think you will still be able to fly your aeroplane. The wound doesn't appear to be serious.' She gazed at him, as if waiting for a response. But he couldn't conjure an intelligent command. She nodded. 'Go into the other room. I will bring the coffee.'

He did as he was told. He stood by the dining table, waiting for her, feeling as awkward as hell, thrilled and not knowing quite why. He hadn't – was *sure* he hadn't – ever thought of her sexually. God, he couldn't *possibly* think of her in such a way. She was a *mother* – at least ten years older than he was, perhaps even *more*. . . . if he had any sense he would leave the place this instant and never come back. He had acted correctly as far as she and Georges were concerned; he owed them nothing. . . .

'Sit down,' she said as she came in from the kitchen, carrying a tray. 'I'm sorry I don't have anything stronger to offer you. I don't even have wine in the house. Isn't that a dismal confession for a Frenchwoman?'

'It doesn't matter,' he said, his voice a trifle strained. 'I don't drink. It doesn't agree with me for some reason.'

'My husband enjoyed a glass of cognac,' she said, pouring the coffee. 'He always offered cognac to our guests. But I'm afraid there's none left now. It's difficult to find these days. And terribly expensive. Not that it matters much. I get very few visitors. It's too far from the village. My husband liked it here; he valued his privacy. But I find it . . .' she shrugged. '. . . a little too private.'

He said, 'Have you considered selling the house?'

She laughed, wholeheartedly, as if he had said something funny. 'Obviously you don't know much about the housing market in this part of France.'

'No, I don't . . . I'm sorry . . .'

'There's nothing I'd like more than to sell this house. It's almost the only asset my husband left. But at the present time it's worth only a third of what he paid for it. And I don't think anyone would buy if I did put it up for sale. But I keep hoping; if I wait long enough the value of housing may go up again.'

'I hope it does.'

She nodded, smiling. 'So do I.'

'If you sell the house, where will you go?'

'Back to Paris. My mother lives there.'

'Were you born in Paris?'

She shook her head. 'Toulouse. When I was two we moved to Nice; ten years later we went to Paris. My father worked in the theatre; he designed sets for plays and operas. He's dead now.'

'I'm sorry.'

Georges and Giselle came downstairs wearing their night attire: voluminous shirts of warm flannel reaching almost to the floor. They said goodnight and how glad they were to see Ernst again. Then, giggling secretly, they ran upstairs.

'They are very polite,' Ernst said.

'I try to teach them manners. Life is pleasanter when people have manners, don't you think?'

'Yes.'

'What will you do when the war's over? Paint?'

'No, I have sense enough to realize that I don't possess the talent.'

'Will you continue to fly?'

'I've thought about it,' he said. 'I believe there'll be a lot more travel by air after the war. Perhaps I could learn to fly an airliner. That would be a pleasant way to make a living, I think.'

'Very pleasant,' she agreed. 'More coffee?'

'Thank you.'

'Do you find it difficult to think ahead, to when the war will be over?'

'Yes, yes, I do.' He glanced at her. 'How do you know?'

'Just a feeling.'

Remarkable. She seemed to know what one was thinking. A keenly perceptive person, this Frenchwoman.

And beautiful.

No. God, no! He mustn't start thinking in that ridiculous, infantile way! It was absurd. She was merely being friendly and hospitable; nothing more, absolutely nothing more, and the sooner he came to realize that fact the better. What possible interest could she possibly have in him? None, absolutely none. So, don't be a bloody fool, he instructed himself. Try to be grown up; act like an adult.

'Have you always loved flying?'

'Yes, ever since I can remember.'

'She smiled. 'Do you still love flying?'

'I suppose so; I'm not sure. It's all so different to what I expected. But I'm not sure what I expected. Not this, anyway. Sometimes I feel like an imposter – a civilian, pretending to be an airman.'

'You're growing up,' she said in a little more than a whisper. 'You're looking at yourself honestly and realistically. You must always look at life honestly and realistically.'

Those soft brown eyes could do nothing else.

'I try to,' he said.

'I'm sure you do . . . but sometimes it's difficult, no?'

He felt the colour rising in his cheeks. There was a feeling – an almost palpable vibration – between them. God, it was unthinkable; surely she didn't like him in that way . . . a mere *boy* . . . a *German* at that . . .

'I think,' he said, his voice husky, 'I should go.'

Her expression didn't change. 'As you wish.'

He said, 'But the truth is . . . I don't wish to go.'

There he had blurted it out. Would she laugh at him? Mock him?

She said simply, 'Then stay.'

A truck trundled past the house, changing gears with a clatter and a groan as it approached the corner. It sounded as if the road was damp. Inconsequentially, he thought of his bicycle left outside, getting wet, rusting perhaps. Stupid, pointless thoughts.

'It's . . . er, kind of you,' he stammered.

'Not really,' she said, her eyes never leaving him. 'It's agreeable having you here.'

He cleared his throat. 'It's agreeable being here.'

'Strange, isn't it, that you should have picked that very field to land in?'

'Very strange.'

'It must have been planned that way.'

'Perhaps.'

'Do you believe in predestination?'

'Sometimes.'

'And sometimes not?'

'That's right.'

'Interesting,' she murmured. 'Very interesting. Is your hand better?'

He nodded. She took his hand.

And then she was in his arms; it happened in a curiously automatic way, as if it was the most natural predictable thing in the world. They kissed, hungrily, fiercely. He felt as if she was dissolving into him. They separated; they gazed at one another. Her hand touched his face, her fingertips gently, deftly exploring his features.

'You are so sweet,' she whispered.

'You are beautiful,' he told her. 'And you feel . . . marvellous.'

She grinned. She looked eighteen. Ilse's age.

'Kiss me again,' she whispered. 'Please.'

He obeyed.

Their lips touched, lightly at first, but then more firmly, tongues probing. God, was there another woman in the entire world who could kiss like this? She gave everything to the task. She was magnificent. He felt the swell of her breasts against his chest; her fingers kneaded the back of his neck; his spine tingled; he had the odd feeling that his blood was about to boil.

Again they drew apart, but their hands were still interlocked.

She said. 'You look at me in a strange way.'

He said, 'I'm sorry. . . . I don't intend it to be strange. But I can't quite believe this is happening. I am . . . surprised.' It was a grossly inadequate description.

'Surprised? Not shocked? Disgusted?'

'No, no, of course not!'

In her matter of fact way she said, 'Don't you think I am a dreadfully forward creature? And don't you think I'm far too old to be doing this with such a young man?'

He shook his head and placed his hand lightly on her mouth. 'Don't say that. You're not old. You're perfect. But I still can't believe this. I shouldn't say that, I know. I wish I knew the right things to say to you.'

'You're doing very well. I think you've had a great deal of practice.'

'No. Honestly.'

She smiled; her hand caressed his cheek.

He kissed her neck; he heard her gasp softly with pleasure. He cupped her left breast in his hand; simultaneously her hand found his groin. Then, gently, she disengaged herself.

'What's wrong?'

'Nothing.' She stood still for a moment, listening, looking up at the ceiling. No sound from the children. She turned and beckoned to him. He followed her into the studio. There was a book open on the table, a pair of glasses reposing on the pages.

'We won't be disturbed in here,' she said.

She fastened the latch on the door.

He had to clench his teeth. His legs were wobbly with excitement. In some weird, topsy-turvey way he wanted to run and yet the last thing in the world he wanted to do was run.

He stood, looking at her.

She reached out a hand. He took it and drew her to him.

They kissed.

He had to draw back. His desire for her was too grotesquely obvious. She told him not to be embarrassed; she said it was flattering. Incredible creature! She guided his hands; he fumbled with her buttons, one by one until at last they were all undone. She slipped the dress off her shoulders and let it fall to the floor. Then, without a moment's hesitation she took off the rest of her things. She stood naked. Beautiful. Totally feminine.

He touched her breasts; the great dark nipple hardened beneath his fingers.

'That feels extremely pleasant,' she said.

'Does it?' Moronic response. But it was the best he could do under the incredible circumstances.

'I have to complain,' she said.

Alarmed, he croaked, 'What is it?'

'You.'

'Me?'

'You are shamefully overdressed.' She fingered the buttons of his tunic. 'Don't you know it's ungallant to let a lady take her clothes off without taking yours off?'

'Is it?' he said. 'I'm sorry.'

She smiled and kissed him gently.

This was nothing like the unsatisfactory fumblings with Ilse. Then, the whole idea seemed to be to pretend that they weren't doing what they were, in fact, doing. Now, there was no shame, no embarrassment. Jeanne was as aroused as he was – and she revelled in it. She wanted him. She desired his body. She took pleasure in helping him strip. And when he was naked she admired him, studied him from head to foot. She nodded approvingly.

'You are splendid,' she declared. 'I don't think I have ever seen such a beautiful creature as you.'

He held her face between his hands. God, there were so many things he wished to say that he couldn't say anything. All he could do was gaze at her, looking deep into those dark eyes, studying every contour of her face.

Their bodies melted into one another.

She had to restrain him.

'We are in no hurry,' she murmured, stroking his chest. 'Pleasure is to be savoured.'

They sat on the couch.

Neatly, precisely, in an oddly feline motion, she folded herself into the curve of his body; she grinned, immensely pleased. She drew his hand down; she kissed him, then her mouth roamed freely, without shame. Ecstacy was close to pain. God, it would surely throttle him; for a panicky instant he felt as if he was no longer capable of drawing a breath. Then he heaved air into his lungs in one huge inhalation and expelled it in a great sigh. She smiled.

'I do hope that was a sigh of contentment and not of boredom.'

'Boredom . . ? God, no, I assure you . . .'

She was only joking, she told him.

Damn! What a clod he was! Couldn't he ever respond as an adult and not as a stupid child? But she didn't mind, she said. He was charmingly honest; it was a rare quality.

'I feel as if I have known you for ever,' he said.

'Yes, I feel that too.'

God, what an incredible day! To think that it started out in such a totally ordinary way! There should have been bells and fireworks.

'I can't stop looking at your body,' he said. 'It's perfect.'

'Thank you for saying so. But my breasts were once firmer and my thighs slimmer.'

'I wouldn't want you different in any way.'

His fingers slid between her breasts. Her skin felt like silk; every curve, every valley was an exciting place to explore. Surely no two people in the entire history of the world had ever known such contentment.

She guided his hand. 'There, my dear . . . there.'

And then she drew him upon her. A steep dive, almost vertical. Full power. Speed mounting, mounting. Earth rotating slowly, steadily, then faster and faster until the details blurred, tumbling joyously into one another, revolving, running, merging into one glorious release, a total surrender to the senses. Rapture, perfect but temporal. He wanted to cling to it, revel in it, submit to it. . . . But it passed, leaving a gentle glow.

He opened his eyes. She was smiling at him. So tenderly. So sweetly. And yet there was a kind of comradeship in her smile; they were two veterans who had come through a campaign triumphant.

She kissed the tip of his nose, his eyes, his ears, his cheeks, finally his mouth. 'Sex with you,' she declared, 'was as good as I thought it would be. And that's very good. *Very* good.'

'I'm glad,' he murmured, wishing he could think of some better response.

'You fit so very nicely.' She grinned. 'Now I've shocked you.'

He shook his head. 'You surprise me,' he admitted. 'Again and again. But I don't think I could ever be shocked by you. I feel so close, as if we really belonged in the same body. I didn't think *this* could be so marvellous.'

She said, 'It can be marvellous or it can be a bore. It all depends on the participants and how they respond to one another.'

'I don't think anyone ever responded so . . .'

Damn! He remembered! Her husband!

'What were you saying?'

'Nothing.'

'You remembered my husband.'

Such perception! He nodded. 'I was jealous.'

'That's very sweet. But you don't have to be jealous of him. He was a dear man but he was nothing like you.'

They talked. Of their likes and dislikes. Of their homes and their childhoods, their parents, their families. In a gentle, almost platonic way it was as thrilling as their sexual congress. She loved Balzac and Dickens, Chevalier and Piaf. As a child, she told him, she had watched her father create the sets that transformed the stage; she longed to perform, to dance, to sing. 'But then I suddenly realized I didn't want to do either. I *knew* what I wanted above everything! To be the first really *great* woman painter! Someone to be ranked with Rembrandt and Matisse, Van Gogh and Gauguin!'

'And Picasso of course.'

'Of course!' she laughed, touching his chin, his lips. The smile faded. 'By the way, there is something else you should know about me.'

'Yes?'

'I'm Jewish,' she said.

Nine

The clouds were a grey mass, dirty and stringy like the hair of some old witch in a children's story. The stuff became thicker and closer to sea level as the cluster of Messerschmitts neared the mid-point of their journey across the English Channel. Ahead, the clouds seemed to merge with the surface; there was no discernible division; amorphous grey cloud dissolved into amorphous grey water. The Channel was almost motionless, eerily so, its surface like oily glass. It was hard on the nerves, flying at such an altitude; all too easy for one to misjudge one's height, for one's vision to play fatal tricks, for one to fly straight into the bloody Scheisskanal.

Ernst flew on the left, Baatz on the extreme right. They flanked the two bomb-carrying Messerschmitts, each with four 50 kg bombs fastened to the ETC-50 racks beneath their bellies. Poor bastards. If *they* touched the water it would be the bombs that hit first.

But it was essential to fly low. The English radar was tirelessly vigilant. The only way to evade the invisible probes was to fly beneath them. Suicidally low.

The object of the operation was to attack any suitable target that presented itself on the other shore – railway station, factory building, airfield; the choice was virtually unlimited and left entirely up to the Schwarmführer, in this case, Baatz.

Such Jabo (Jagdbomber: fighter-bomber) sorties constituted the Luftwaffe's current daylight operations against Britain. During the summer, the loss of heavy bombers had been crippling; now the Heinkels and Junkers flew only at night when the Spitfires and Hurricanes did not operate.

Ernst shifted in his seat seeking relief from the icy needle of air that danced about the cockpit. Damn the ground staff! They had examined the engine cowling again and again, without success. There were no cracks, they reported; there was simply no way for air to enter the cockpit. No doubt they thought he was imagining it, finding fault with their work to compensate for his own shortcomings.

First the frigid stream hit one knee, then the other.

Ernst peered ahead. No sign of the coast.

It was like flying into a great grey bag, except that one was not permitted to see the sides or the bottom of it. The cloud kept playing tricks; that bit there suddenly resembled a cliff, that bit a lighthouse. No! False alarm! Relax, reverberating nerves. As you were, eager hands and feet.

Anyone but Baatz would have called the conditions impossible and would have turned for home. A determined airman, Leutnant Baatz. Limitless reserves of guts.

A few degrees of navigational error could send an aircraft up the east coast of England to disappear in the North Sea. It was easily done in poor visibility like this. Disquieting thoughts, best squashed.

Met had promised clearing skies. Met was wrong again. For the umpteenth time . . .

There! The coast materialized out of the murk.

Baatz rocked his wings. The cliffs began to swell in the wind-screen panel. Details: grass, rock, a shack. Then the guns opened up. Tiny balls of red and burning white came wobbling across the water, slowly, then accelerating and hurtling by.

A glimpse of a sandbagged emplacement, the jutting barrel of an anti-aircraft gun, steel-helmeted figures looking up, one pointing; a bicycle resting against the sandbags.

No need for R/T silence now.

'Where the hell are we?'

No one knew.

'Near Folkstone, I think,' said Baatz, answering his own question.

His wing angled at the soft green grass, slicing across a narrow road on which a bus trundled, apparently unaware of the enemy above. The ground came skidding around as if it were on a giant roundabout. Images, like glimpses of snapshots: a village, squat little houses with thatched roofs clustered around a tiny square; a monument of some sort standing in the middle like a sentry; two women carrying umbrellas and shopping baskets, standing, open-mouthed.

Gone. Vanished behind. A solitary barrage balloon emerged from the gloom. No one fired. Odd. Wasn't the balloon guarding something? Something of significance? Was the formation being lured into a trap, an ambush waiting behind the next hill?

Stupid, funky thoughts.

Silently he implored Baatz not to venture too far. It was too easy to get lost in this weather. And the further inland they flew the further they had to fly back to the coast. And the more precious fuel they consumed.

Suddenly the barrage erupted.

Solid flak. Walls of it.

Behind it, the airfield. A line of concrete revetments, each occupied by a Hurricane fighter. A propeller turning, dissolving in motion. Men in overalls, some in blue uniforms, running, scattering, crouched.

The bombs fell away, the Emils lifting as they were relieved of their weight. The bombs had ten-second fuses so that the carriers would have a chance to get clear before the explosions.

One bomb bounced over a revetment, watched by a surprised mechanic who was scratching his head.

Tracer criss-crossed the field.

Ernst fired at a Hurricane that was in motion, taxying erratically, frantically trying to set up for a take-off run. His shells and bullets snapped into the ground immediately behind the Hurricane. Its pilot was straining forward in the cockpit as if urging his mount to greater effort.

Cracking explosions as the bombs went off.

The Hurricane somersaulted on to its back.

More flak, angry, determined flak.

Follow Baatz. The ground tilted. The stick trembled, fighting his urgent commands.

'Where are you, Yellow Five?'

'Behind you.'

'Good. Let's try again.'

The field skidded, straightened. Sparkling death danced by. The gunners couldn't possibly miss. Too many of them, too many guns. The air was solid with lead. No hope, not a chance of getting through this in one piece. Idiotic to hope.

He caught a glimpse: a fire burning away to the left. The result of one of the bombs? An ammunition dump perhaps. Lucky hit.

Cordite came stinking into the cockpit as he blazed away at the parked aircraft. Fire erupted. Was gone. Hits on sandbags. Hurtling, blurring images that vanished before one could line them up as targets. One fired; one fired again. Impossible to see if one hit anything. Everything sped by to disappear somewhere in the void behind. There wasn't an instant to spare for anything if it wasn't in direct line of flight.

Two Hurricanes clambered off the ground, tucking their wheels beneath their wings.

A two-second burst at one. It staggered. Vanished.

Baatz was turning at last.

Where were the Hurricanes? Where were the other two Emils?

'Time to go home.'

Casual, almost bored tone. Incredible person, Baatz.

Suddenly it was tranquil. Quiet fields slid beneath their wings. There was no flak. The field was already several kilometres to the rear. Now no one seemed to have any interest in the presence of the aircraft of the Luftwaffe. A farmer on a tractor looked up, then returned to his work.

'Reform,' came Baatz's command.

He acknowledged, but reforming was easier said than done.

Where was Baatz?

Where were the others?

They reported in. All safe and sound. But every man out of sight of his comrade, dodging in and out of the low-hanging cloud.

Baatz ordered his flock to proceed independently on course 190 degrees magnetic.

At some point they would probably see one another; one by one they would reform.

Quick glances in every direction.

No sign of anyone, in the air or on the ground.

Weird, how quiet it could be after the pandemonium of a few moments ago.

Did he hit that Hurricane? Perhaps someone saw it crash. It was possible. Quite possible. Unlikely, though, in the confusion. Unlikely as hell.

He had to fly low, to hug the ground; that was the way to surprise the anti-aircraft batteries. Speed past them before they could sort out from what direction one was approaching.

A railway line flashed by. A meandering river.

Gaze ahead, try to pierce the gloom, to see radio masts and church steeples before flying into them.

A string of houses; each one identical to its neighbour.

A woman hanging out washing. A child skipping.

Gone.

A line of trees, hurtling at him like soldiers.

Gone.

The sea! The ground vanished. Water sped beneath his wings.

He pressed the transmit button on the control column.

'Yellow Five. I'm over the coast.'

A crackle.

He repeated the message. Nothing.

He shrugged. Course: one ninety. Fuel: just over half. Pressures, revs, temperatures: all normal.

Reaction time. The shakes. The sour, sick taste. He sweated despite the icy air. God, how weak he felt; it was almost too much for him to maintain enough pressure on the right rudder pedal to keep the Emil flying straight.

The feeling would last until he landed. It always did. Then, slowly, laboriously, as if organ by organ, the upheaval would subside; things would settle back to normal.

He flew half in and half out of the clouds, the wispy grey blanket rushing by, grazing his head; for instants it would envelope him completely; then he would glance quickly at the turn and bank indicator and the airspeed indicator. A man's senses could play tricks with him when he no longer had a horizon to judge his attitudes.

A voice on the R/T. Baatz? No; someone with a Baden accent; someone from another unit, someone with his own problems. He too had become separated from his formation. He sounded scared.

Then the radio was silent. The greyness still sped by; below him the sea moved at more modest pace. He glanced at his watch. In a minute or two he would see the French coast.

What was she doing at this moment?

Laughing at the memory of him? Had his mouth dropped open and had he stared at her like an idiot when she had told him she was Jewish? She had smiled at him; yes, he remembered distinctly. No doubt he had amused her. A good joke to play on the hated Boche. Seduce them, then tell them the truth.

He shook his head. No, it was impossible to believe she had planned the whole thing simply to anger and embarrass him. Not her with those gentle eyes.

God, it was perplexing. Anger at her one moment, fondness the next. Life could be utterly impossible at times.

'The RAF are claiming three Messerschmitts,' Schiegl declared, removing his spectacles and fingering the bridge of his nose. 'We haven't got the names of the pilots yet, but I suppose we must assume that it's probably Baatz and the others.' He picked up his pen. 'You didn't see anything of them after you left the airfield?'

'No, sir,' Ernst told him. 'We were scattered, you see . . .'

'What airfield was it? Have you remembered?'

Ernst shook his head. 'I don't think Leutnant Baatz knew. We simply came across it. I suppose it could have been Detling. We were in that general area.'

'The aircraft on the field were Hurricanes, you say.'

'Yes, sir, definitely Hurricanes.'

'You consider the attack was successful?'

'I think so. We certainly surprised them. The bombs hit something. I saw a fire. We must have damaged several aircraft.'

'The flak was intense, you say.'

'Yes, sir.'

'Your aircraft wasn't hit.'

'I was lucky.'

'But the others weren't so lucky.'

'I suppose not,' said Ernst.

'Do you think the flak might have got them over the airfield?'

'No, definitely not. We were clear of the field when Baatz instructed us to head for home independently. Everyone was all right at that point. I heard them all on the R/T. Baatz told us to steer one ninety and reform if and when we saw each other.'

'Strange that four aircraft could leave an airfield after an attack and be incapable of seeing one another.'

'The ceiling was down to a hundred metres or less. We were in cloud the moment we got away from the field.'

'I see,' Schiegl sighed as he scribbled his report. He glanced up. 'You were very fortunate, Brehme,' he declared. 'Very fortunate.'

Dietrich was sprawled on his bunk reading a book. He beamed when he saw Ernst. 'Hello, old fellow. Someone told me you'd been killed.'

Ernst took off his jacket and hung it up. 'Schiegl seems to think I should have been killed.'

'He's an old soldier. Old soldiers regard survival as something to be slightly ashamed of. Did they get Baatz?'

'So it seems. The English are claiming three Messerschmitts. Baatz, Schüler and Reissner.'

'Lucky you.'

'I don't know what happened to them. They vanished. The visibility was terrible.'

'I watched you all take off,' said Dietrich. 'Anyone in his right mind would have turned back, there and then. But, of course, Baatz wasn't in his right mind. He was ambitious. Had to show everyone from the Reichsmarschall down what a splendid airman he was. The pity of it is he took Schüler and Reissner with him.' He grinned. 'Anyway you got back quite safely.'

'Quite safely.'

'Smart fellow,' said Dietrich. 'By the way, did you have a pleasant time last night? I went to bed before you got back and you got up at the crack of dawn.'

'It was quite enjoyable,' Ernst said as he tugged the black suede and leather flying boots off.

'I'm glad,' said Dietrich.

Was the tiniest emphasis on the second word? Did Dietrich, in fact, know precisely what went on? No! Impossible! How could he?

'We talked a long time. I find it enjoyable to talk French.'

'I'm sure you do.'

'But I won't be going back.'

'No?'

'There's no need.'

'Of course.'

'I've said thank you. I've given them the pictures of Georges when he was at the field.'

'Quite.'

'So there's no reason for me to go back.'

'But I think you should,' said Dietrich.

'Why?'

'To return this, old fellow.' Like a magician bringing a rabbit out of a top hat, he produced a pink garment, a slip of some sort, something flimsy and frivolous, something that looked uncomfortably familiar.

Ernst gulped.

'What's that?'

'Don't you know?'

'No, of course not.'

Dietrich shrugged elaborately. 'Well, all I can say is that I found it on the floor this morning beside your bed. Only too eager of course to jump to the worst possible conclusions, I presumed it had somehow become attached to your overcoat or your tunic. So, quite unknowingly you brought it back here. And it fell on the floor. You didn't notice it because you were understandably weary and anxious to retire. And our friend the orderly didn't see it because it was still dark when he came in to wake you. Don't you think the decent thing to do would be to take it back to its rightful owner?'

Ernst opened his mouth to say something. But he didn't know what. He shut his mouth again.

Dietrich carefully folded the garment and put it on the table.

'All right if I leave it there?'

'Yes . . . of course. . .'

Dietrich went to the window and studied the field with uncommon interest. 'I've always liked French women,' he said. 'In my experience most German women have a distressingly practical streak in their natures. Admirable in business but less so in bed. French women, on the other hand, seem to have mastered the art of being sensible and yet utterly feminine. Don't you agree?'

Ernst muttered something about never having given the matter any thought.

Dietrich burst out laughing. 'God, but you're a comical bastard at times! What the hell are you looking so embarrassed about? Do you really think it offends me to have such a deliciously female bit of attire in our austere quarters? Do you really think for one tiny instant that it shocks me – *me* – to think that you might have spent a free evening in bed with a French woman? My dear silly fellow, I'm only jealous of your success!'

Ernst nodded his thanks. It was just, he said, that the whole thing was a bit complicated.

'Such things usually are,' murmured Dietrich. 'What's the problem? Jealous husband? No, you told me she's a widow. Delightful. Some of my most beautiful friendships have involved widows.'

'I don't think you'd want to have a beautiful friendship with this one.'

'I wouldn't?'

'I found out something about her,' said Ernst.

'Yes?'

Ernst drew a breath as if the telling needed extra effort. 'I found out that she's Jewish.'

'Really.'

Dietrich took the revelation with a singular calm.

Ernst went on, 'And that, of course, is why I haven't the slightest intention of ever going back there.'

Dietrich nodded thoughtfully. 'How did you find out about her being Jewish?'

'She told me . . . er, afterwards.'

'Did you ask her?'

'No. The thought hadn't occurred to me.'

So she presumably thought it was something you should know.'

'Yes, I suppose so.'

'Did you like her until then?'
'Yes.'
'Very much?'
'Yes.'
'And did she like you?'
'Yes . . . I think so . . . yes.'

Dietrich folded his arms. 'Then, if you want my opinion, you're being a bloody fool.'

Ernst stared. 'But I told you . . . she's *Jewish*!'

Dietrich shrugged. 'Does that fact offend you?'

'Yes . . . well, it shocked me when she told me.'

'Why?'

'Because of everything I've heard about Jews and what they're doing to Europe and the world; what they did to our country in the 'twenties.'

'Did she do those things?'

'Of course not, she's the widow of a schoolteacher.'

'Attractive?'

'Yes, very.'

'Interesting?'

'Interesting?'

'I mean, you enjoy talking to her as well as fucking?'

'Well . . . yes, very much.'

Dietrich shrugged. 'Then, my dear fellow, you have found a gem. And gems should not be discarded lightly. Even if they have unfortunate religious affiliations!'

Ten

Afterwards, he often wondered at the fragile structure of happenings that make a man's life change its direction. Suppose he hadn't force-landed in that particular field; suppose Georges hadn't come to his rescue; suppose that absurd little slip of Jeanne's hadn't fastened itself to a metal fitting on his coat; suppose Dietrich hadn't seen it. . . . But those happenings had occurred; and they resulted in a period of intense happiness, an enchanted period when absolutely everything was right with the world. He had cycled back to her house, the slip folded ...d concealed in his greatcoat pocket. Unsure of his reception (he had, after all, left hurriedly and perhaps even rudely the evening before), he was relieved to be greeted with warmth. She had invited him in, offered him coffee. He took the slip from his pocket and handed it to her. He hadn't taken it intentionally, he assured her. Their eyes met. Simultaneously, they burst into laughter and fell into each other's arms. He was close to tears with the sheer joy of it all. Feeling her so deliciously close to him, it was beyond belief that a few short hours ago he had been determined never to see her again, pumped up by a lot of pointless prejudice. Thank God dear old friend Dietrich had been there to make him see what made sense and what didn't. A man needed such a friend. What possible connection was there between Jeanne and all the bleating from Berlin about the Jews wanting to strip the world of its soul, to destroy the tall, long-limbed Nordic races with their roseate-bright skin (average male cephalic index: 75)? There was, he knew vaguely, some difference between a Jew and a Zionist. He didn't understand it, or care. Holding her, feeling the softness of her hair against his cheek, it didn't matter that she was Jewish. Or even a Zionist. It was of no significance that she was eleven years older. He cared only for the person, the being who was more precious than anyone he had ever known. She was a marvellous creature, beautiful, adorable, sometimes infuriating, but always stimulating. She seemed to know him and understand him better than he knew and understood himself. When he was with her he felt alive as never before; she had a way of forcing him to see every aspect of every question, every angle of everything from art to rugby. She opened doors; she made him think and respond; it was as if he had been only half aware of the world before he knew her. The longing for her intensified (sometimes he felt a distinct ache deep inside) as the late autumn days began to shorten and the rain became chillier and more frequent. There was little operational flying now; at every opportunity he dashed off on his ancient Peugeot bicycle, pedalling his way through the village, along the bumpy paved road lined with tall elms. He would round the gentle bend; there would be the house, standing alone. She was always waiting (she could watch the road from her studio window); the door would open a moment before he reached it. For the children's benefit their greetings would be hypocritically casual; she usually managed to sound genuinely surprised, as if he was the last person she had expected to see. It was a secret little game. The children seemed to like him; they greeted him as if he belonged. Soon he was just another adult, someone to be virtually ignored. It was splendid; he felt as if he was married to Jeanne and this place was his; he could relax; he could be himself, he could be perfectly, splendidly content.

He found to his simultaneous relief and dismay that he had no qualms about continuing to correspond with Ilse, exchanging the usual fond greetings. Somehow it didn't seem wrong; she belonged to that life; Jeanne belonged to this life. He was still fond of Ilse; a fine girl, a good companion. What he felt for Jeanne was quite different. Was it love? He often wondered. Was what he felt the magic thing that all the songs chanted about? How did one know? Did she love him? Surely the answer was yes. How could any woman be more loving? But he was a German; she was Jewish. And eleven years his senior. Facts. But they seemed to possess no significance; men still talked scornfully about Jews; the German newspapers still carried cartoons of hook-nosed, money-grabbing 'Eternal Jews'; everyone agreed that Jews had been at the very foundation of Germany's economic troubles after the Great War; they had nearly succeeded in bringing the whole structure crashing down. Britain and America were run by the Jews; everyone knew it. It was all part of a sinister plot of International Jewry.

And yet what did it all have to do with Jeanne?

He didn't know. He didn't care.

On the tenth of December, Schiegl told him he was one of the lucky ones.

'Lucky?'

'Yes, old fellow, you're going home for Christmas!'

'What?'

'Leave!'

He protested; let someone else take his place; there were so many others who deserved Christmas leave far more than he; the married ones, particularly those with children . . .

'Good fellow,' said Schiegl with an approving pat on the shoulder, 'but you're going and that's the end of it.'

He bought presents for Jeanne and the children – a necklace of real gold (it cost him a week's pay) for Jeanne; a model airplane kit for Georges, a doll for Giselle. He spent the night with her. Before dawn he set off on his bicycle, returning to camp to collect his pass, his railway warrant and his leave pay. His heart ached. He dreaded going home. The people there were now the strangers, the foreigners. This was home; this little corner of Northern France. This was where he belonged. When his train set off for

Germany, he felt tears pricking his eyes. God, anyone would think he was returning from, rather than going on leave!

They were there, waiting for him on the platform. His mother, blinking, anxiously studying the length of the train as it squealed to a halt. Twelve-year-old Maria, looking years older than when he last saw her. Uncle Albert. Aunt Katerina. The Schüllers, neighbours. And Ilse. Beautiful. Eager. Hands clasped, fingers working excitedly. Eyes traversing the bobbing faces, apprehensive. Was she worried that he might have sprouted two heads during his absence? Or lost a leg or two, neglecting to inform her? They spotted him! Pointed! Hurried to him. He was in their arms; the world became clutching hands and tears and smiles and mumbled words. He looked healthy; he looked thin; he looked tired; he had grown; he was exactly as remembered so very fondly. He was swept along on a tide of affection; he kissed Ilse on the cheek; her grin said she understood, she knew he couldn't possibly kiss her the way he really wanted to, not here on the platform in front of everyone. It was, she told him, pure heaven to have him back safe and sound; her prayers had been answered; she was the luckiest girl in the entire world. He felt as if he was in a play – a jolly, amusing thing in which everyone hugged and grinned and cried a little, holding, clutching, reluctant to let go now that he had at last returned to them. Then to the house. Champagne bubbling into glasses. Jovial toasts to the returning hero. His mother's hands still reaching for him, touching him as if to reassure her that he was really home at last. Questions about the battles. Answers, some flippant, some serious. Gratifying in an almost sensuous way to be the centre of attention. The house, so familiar yet so surprising. He had never really looked at it before. It was infinitely more luxurious than he remembered. Fine panelling. Beautiful appointments. Worthy of the Reichsmarschall himself.

In the morning he awoke early, disturbed by the wind rocking a shutter. Where was he? Back in hospital? He relaxed, remembering. He lay in bed listening to light rain pattering at the window. Guiltily he admitted that he wanted to leave here, to hurry back to Jeanne. The dreadful, unforgivable thought kept haunting him: he had seen his mother, he had kissed her; he had answered her questions, assured her that he was well; he had done his duty as a son. So why was it necessary for him to stay longer? Bastard! Hell of a thing to think! Despicable swine! He nodded; he agreed. But it changed nothing. It was the truth. What was

Jeanne doing at this moment? Was she still asleep? Was her dark hair splashed over the pillow? Was she emitting that fascinating sleep sound of hers, that half-groan, half-hum?

He had escorted Ilse home the previous evening; she had slipped her arm under his, clasping his hand deep inside his greatcoat pocket. All the way to the Gebhardt house he had thought how curiously different her hand and Jeanne's hand felt. She had chattered gaily about friends, about the city, about clothes and parties. It was, she told him for the hundredth time, so absolutely perfect having him back for Christmas; she had hardly dared hope for it; she wasn't even going to think of the time when he had to go back. In the darkness he had smiled sadly; going back was *all* he could think about. Some fellows arrived home on leave to find their girl friends lost to others. But not him. Faithful Ilse.

She asked him to come in and see her parents; they were longing to see him, she said. And indeed they welcomed him with uncommon warmth. Herr Gebhardt shook his hand, even patted him congenially on the arm. Frau Gebhardt embarrassed him by planting a resounding kiss on each cheek while she clasped his face between her large warm hands. The warrior returned from the wars! So handsome, so heroic! Herr Gebhardt declared that the Luftwaffe had been doing an admirable job; Ernst thanked him, as if on behalf of his comrades. Herr Gebhardt said that it was a matter of the greatest regret to him that he was now considered too old to serve in the army as he had done, only too willingly, in the Great War. Besides, he hastened to add, he most certainly was not too old; he could still do everything that he could twenty-five years ago.

'That's true,' said his wife. And she giggled, meaningfully, embarrassing Ernst yet again.

The rain was heavier now. There was no point, he decided, in actually coming out and telling Ilse that he no longer cared for her. It would be cruel. Why spoil her Christmas? The kindest thing was simply to let things slide: be pleasant, be a good companion. But nothing more. Time would pass. Soon he would have to return to France. Inevitably her feelings would cool. A girl like Ilse, beautiful, charming, reasonably well-to-do, would certainly have no trouble at all finding a replacement for him.

He nodded. Yes, it was the best way. No reason at all to bring matters to an unpleasant boil. Let nature take its course.

The house smelled of goose and candles, sugar and red cabbage, all mixed up with gingerbread and cigar smoke. Time had been turned back. For a moment he was a small boy again and it was Christmas, the enchanted days; his father was downstairs sniffing at the oven.

He had one dinner at home, another at the Gebhardts. He drank a little too much; words became inextricably entangled with one another when he attempted to utter them; the faces before him became peculiarly heavy and ugly. But gallantly he informed Frau Gebhardt that she was the reason her daughter was so extraordinarily beautiful. More giggles from the matron. More kisses. The second day gone.

The war seemed to have had little effect upon life in the city. The shops were full; there was money to spend. Most people were of the opinion that the war was over. The English had clearly been beaten even if they had not as yet actually conceded defeat; they were being their usual irritating selves. Many soldiers had already been demobilized and had returned to civilian life. Military orders for uniforms, for supplies, for arms, had been drastically reduced. Some factories were said to be in the process of converting their equipment to the production of peacetime products.

His mother was handling widowhood as well as could be expected. But how was a fellow to know what she was really thinking? If she was suffering agonies of loneliness, she would never tell him. It simply wasn't her way.

His mother said she hoped he was finding his French useful. Wasn't he pleased that she had insisted on his learning the language? Yes, he assured her; he was most grateful. It was proving most beneficial.

Occasionally the British sent over their night bombers. But, his mother told him, they were few and far between and even if they managed to find the city they never hit it. One had crashed five kilometres from the house, transforming itself into a pitiful pile of twisted wreckage in a plumber's back garden. The crew killed. And for what? They had achieved absolutely nothing. Why couldn't the English come to their senses and admit defeat? Hadn't the Führer made offer after offer to them? No one could have been more reasonable. But the stubborn fools in London still refused to listen.

'Do you love Ilse madly? Do you intend to marry her?' Maria folded her arms across her narrow chest, frowning purposefully like an advocate posing a key question in court.

'None of your business,' Ernst told her; he reached out to ruffle her hair.

'It is my business,' she replied, neatly dodging his hand. 'I want to know. I have to be prepared.'

'Why do you have to be prepared?'

'Because I'm your sister. And if you marry her she'll be my sister-in-law.'

'Don't worry about it.'

'But I have to.'

'No, you don't.'

'Does that mean that you're not going to marry her?'

'It doesn't mean anything.'

'You are going to marry her, aren't you?'

'I don't know.'

Abruptly she sat back in her chair. She pointed at him. 'I know what's happened!'

'Really?'

'You've fallen in love with a beautiful French girl. At this moment you're pining for her, longing to get back to her.'

Jesus Christ.

He cleared his throat. 'You do talk an awful lot of rubbish.'

'I wonder,' she murmured, cocking her head to one side. 'I don't blame you. It's the sort of thing that happens in wartime.'

'How do you know?'

'I read books.'

'You shouldn't read such books. You're too young.'

'If this was ancient Rome I'd be considered grown up.'

'But this isn't ancient Rome and you are most certainly not grown up.'

'What's her name?'

'Whose name?'

'Your French girl friend. Do you have a photograph of her?'

'No . . .'

'Ah! I knew it! Let me see it! Please let me see it, Ernst. Please! I promise I won't tell Ilse! She'll be broken-hearted, of course. She may kill herself when she finds out. Girls do sometimes. I don't think boys do but I know girls do.'

He saw Ilse that evening. She was alone; her parents were visiting the von Schanzenbachs who lived in Kalk.

It was pleasant to kiss her, to fondle her handsome breasts and to smell the freshness of her young body. But now the activity was a sort of duty, a routine to be performed for her sake rather than his. 'We've never done it properly,' she whispered.

He said, 'I know how you feel about it. And I respect you for it. You want to save yourself for the right and proper moment. . .'

She said, 'This is the right and proper moment.'

God. 'Do you really think so?'

'Yes,' she said. 'You're home on leave . . . after fighting . . . I've thought about it so much and I know I'm right.'

He shook his head. 'But I'm going to go back to France soon. God knows what might happen.'

She said. 'I want to be yours . . . really yours.'

'You are,' he said.

'You know what I mean.'

'Yes, I know what you mean.'

'My parents won't be back for hours.' She kissed him, hard, almost fiercely. 'You used to ask me . . . you *pleaded* with me so many times.'

'They might come back early.'

'No, they're always late when they visit the Schanzenbachs.'

He gulped. 'But now . . . now, I realize you were right when you said it was wrong . . . *sinful* in fact, that's what you said.'

'I've changed my mind,' she said.

'You shouldn't have.'

In some inexplicable way of females she burst into tears and ran upstairs. He sat for ten minutes in the darkness listening to Christmas music on the radio. Then he walked back to his house. Yes, he told his mother, he was indeed home early. He went upstairs to his room and spent the rest of the evening looking through the books and toys and assorted mementoes of his youth. He found half a dozen sketchbooks. Most of the work was abysmal but some suggested a certain embryonic talent. He studied the sketches. He shook his head. Damn it, there wasn't one possessing the joy of life that Jeanne put into every work, so effortlessly. Her work was alive; his was dead.

He felt as if he was looking through the belongings of a stranger – just as he had sorted through Strobel's possessions on orders from Schiegl. The object of that exercise had been to remove any embarrassing items – dirty French postcards, letters from girl friends, contraceptives and the like – before the stuff was returned to the deceased's home.

The balsa wood model of Richthofen's Fokker triplane sat at

an awkward angle. It had lost a wheel. He searched for it, eventually finding it up the barrel of the toy howitzer.

Ilse telephoned him the following day. She had lain awake all night, thinking. She felt utterly ashamed. She was wrong; he was right. She didn't deserve such a noble man. Could he ever forgive her? All right, he said. Would he like to come to the house for a cup of coffee? He would. She looked gorgeous. When it was evident that her parents were at a safe distance he kissed her. She pulled him on to the couch where they contentedly manipulated each other's genitals.

His leave was a procession of meals, meals at home, meals at the Gebhardts', meals at neighbours', meals at Uncle Albert's and Aunt Katerina's. Uncle Albert, his father's brother, talked about business; about problems with machinery, problems with workers, problems with raw materials, price problems, bureaucratic problems. Uncle Albert was the managing director of a shoe factory. It was clear that in his view Ernst was the lucky one, able to run away to play with his airplanes and his war while his uncle had to grapple with the real enemies. What a self-important little bore Uncle Albert was! Incredible that he had never realized it before. Did combat help to clarify one's vision of people?

It was interesting to observe how each visitor would, for a few dutiful minutes, talk about Ernst and about the air war. Soon, however, the conversation inevitably switched to the things they knew and understood. Weddings, births and deaths. Themselves and their families. The bright future for the Germans: amazing new cities ('Plans are already being drawn up for an entirely new centre for Berlin') and a People's Car for every worker ('Deliveries will be starting this summer, you mark my word'). Many visitors were middle-aged people who had seen their savings vanish twice since 1918. They were intensely and unashamedly grateful to Hitler, the Leader who had taken them out of the nightmare of rampant inflation and unemployment, the one man who had seen the Jews for what they were: parasites who grew fat and prosperous sucking the life blood out of the German economy. Nodding to one another, they agreed unanimously: the cure may have been hard but it was correct. The patient *survived*! Only a brilliant man with vision and perception could have done it. Thank God Germany had had such a man when he was so desperately needed.

Eleven

It was a clear, crisp night. Moon-made shadows danced through the spokes of his bicycle wheels as they bounced noisily on the cobbles. His mudguard clattered against the bike's frame; almost rusted through, it would soon fall off if he did nothing about it. One of the mechanics would fix it for him.

A security patrol stopped him, taking him for a civilian. The error was understandable, since he wore a plain raincoat over his uniform and his head was uncovered. It was amusing to note the abrupt, almost frantic change of attitude when the two corporals discovered the cyclist's rank. They were full of apologies; they hadn't realized that the Herr Leutnant was an officer and with the greatest respect they would suggest that the Herr Leutnant wear his uniform cap at all times. Ernst told them that the damned thing refused to stay on while he pedalled; that was the reason he kept it in the carrier attached to the handle-bars. Yes, they understood fully, the Herr Leutnant certainly had a point but it couldn't be denied that regulations did insist on caps being worn at all times.

'Very well, fellows,' Ernst said, 'to please you I'll put it on.' The corporals nodded their approval, saluting as he pedalled away. Safely out of sight around the first corner, he removed the cap. He was less conspicuous without it; a young man in a raincoat was hardly worth a second glance; a Luftwaffe officer riding a bicycle most certainly was. The fewer people, military or civilian, who noticed him, the better.

Tonight the road was almost deserted; a couple of military trucks were the only vehicles he encountered. The houses were shuttered; the villagers were safely tucked in for the night.

A small dog ran across the road to relieve itself on the village monument to the dead of the Great War.

The journey to her seemed to take for ever! Had they lengthened the damned road while he was away? Was his bicycle working less efficiently? Another three kilometres to go. He knew the way by heart, every metre of it. The narrow bridge over the stream. The house with the blue roof. The cross-road. The small dark forest. The bend in the road. . .

There!

He braked and jumped off the bicycle while it was still in motion, whisking it off the road, its ancient frame clattering on the stone path.

Was she watching from one of those dark windows? She knew he would be coming tonight; he had explained his timetable in detail: the departure time of the train from Köln, the time of the change at Brussels and the train for Paris. In fact, he was only half an hour behind his most optimistic prediction: at the Military Transport Centre in Paris he had been obliged to wait ten minutes for transport to the airfield.

He propped his bicycle against the wall in its usual place.

Deep breath.

He knocked.

He heard footsteps. Hers. Beautiful balanced step.

The door opened.

Her smile had a fixed quality.

'Hullo,' she said as if he was a salesman or at best a casual neighbourhood friend.

He opened his mouth but the words were frozen somewhere in his throat.

Then he saw the other woman beside Jeanne, an older woman, her head set at an odd angle, as if she anticipated trouble.

Jeanne opened the door wide and asked him to enter. She turned to the older woman.

'This is Ernst Brehme. I told you about him.'

The older woman didn't respond.

'Ernst,' said Jeanne, 'I'd like you to meet my mother. Madame Levy.'

Mother?

He had to stir himself. 'It's a pleasure to meet you, Madame,' he lied, extending his hand.

But the older woman had already turned and was walking into the front room.

Jeanne closed the door and switched on the light.

'My mother is visiting us,' she said.

'How nice,' Ernst managed to say. Then he greeted the children; yes, he was back; yes, he had had a good holiday at home; yes, he would tell them all about it very soon.

Jeanne beckoned.

'Perhaps I shouldn't stay. . .'

'No, come in,' she said.

He followed her into the front room, feeling the old woman's frigid gaze on him as he sat down beside the fireplace.

'Ernst has been on leave,' Jeanne said.

A grunt.

'Did you find your mother well?' Jeanne asked him.

'Yes, thank you. Very well. Er, did you have an enjoyable Christmas?'

'How could we?' the old woman demanded to know.

'Madame?'

'Would you have had an enjoyable Christmas if your country was full of a lot of nasty foreigners?'

'I don't know . . .'

'Mother,' said Jeanne, 'behave yourself. Ernst is a guest in my house.'

But her mother was not to be silenced.

'I don't like Germans,' she declared, her eyes flashing defiance.

He gulped. 'I'm sorry,' he said.

'Why are you sorry?'

'Because . . . because our presence apparently spoiled your Christmas.'

'You speak French moderately well.'

'Thank you, Madame.'

Jeanne said, 'Ernst's mother taught him French.'

'She was French?'

'No, Madame. But she knows the language.'

'Would you like some coffee?' Jeanne asked.

God, she looked delicious; how he wanted to reach out and touch her. He ached for her. But all he could was nod. Yes, thank you, coffee would be nice.

Jeanne went into the kitchen.

The old woman's forefinger was levelled at him. 'I had a terrible journey here,' she snapped. 'All I wanted to do was come here and visit my daughter. Heavens, you might have thought I was M. Churchill himself. The questions! The papers!'

'I'm sorry . . .'

'I had to have passes signed by this little idiot and that one too. Self important nobodies. What was my crime? That I wanted to travel to visit my widowed daughter? Is that so strange? Don't widowed mothers want to visit widowed daughters in your country? God knows how you managed to win the war. You're as stupid about bits of paper as us.'

'I'm sorry you had a difficult journey . . .'

'You're always sorry.'

Jeanne came in with coffee. 'Mother, stop being a bully.'

'He keeps on saying he's sorry.'

'Perhaps he is.'

The old woman shook her head as if trying to control herself. 'I'm tired of you Germans. You caused all that trouble when I was young and now, damn you, if you don't do it all over again now that I'm old! I have lost patience with you all!'

'I'm sorry . . .' he began and stopped.

'Mother, be quiet,' said Jeanne. 'Ernst had nothing to do with any of that.'

The old woman peered at him through narrowed eyes. 'You're an officer, aren't you! You look very young to be an officer.'

'Ernst is a pilot,' Jeanne explained. 'All pilots are young.'

'And they die young, most of them,' observed her mother.

'You're incorrigible,' Jeanne said.

Her mother declared, 'René Fonck was the best pilot in the Great War,' in a voice that defied argument.

Ernst nodded. Why disagree? Why attempt to convince her that Richthofen scored the more victories?

'Ernst has a young sister,' Jeanne said. 'She's twelve, isn't she?'

'Yes.'

'What's her name?'

'Maria.'

'Pretty name.'

'I prefer Marie,' yapped the old woman. Her dark eyes flitted from Ernst to Jeanne and back again. No doubt she was cogitating upon the precise relationship between the two of them. Her mouth hardened momentarily, as if at that instant she considered the possibility of an actual *affair*, a physical involvement.

Suddenly he remembered the bag. He had left it in the bicycle carrier. He jumped to his feet, bumping into the table, setting the coffee things rattling perilously.

'Forgive me, I forgot something. I will be back in just a minute.'

Outside in the chilly cold he cursed silently. Damn her mother for being there! On *that* night! Was there no justice? No mercy?

Deep breath. Compose yourself, man! Be patient! Steeling himself, he retrieved his treasures and took them back into the house. Canned meats, chocolates, butter, candied fruits – delicacies that had long since disappeared from the shelves of French shops.

Jeanne and the children were delighted. But the old woman sniffed as if the stuff had a bad smell.

'Where did you buy all this?'

'We have a store . . .'

'We?'

'The servicemen . . .'

'So good to know you're all so well fed while French citizens go hungry!'

'Mother, I insist that you stop this!' Jeanne sounded as if she was scolding one of her children. 'Ernst has nothing to do with whether goods are in shops or not. He's a friend of mine and a guest in this house.'

'He's also a Boche,' snapped her mother.

Ernst rose. It was hopeless. 'I'd better go. Thank you for the coffee.'

'No.' Jeanne's hand pressed him back into the chair. Her eyes told him how she longed for him, how she wanted him in spite of everything.

'Tell me,' said the old woman, now elaborately polite, mocking him with good manners, 'what part of Germany do you come from?'

'Köln, Madame.'

'How interesting. It was once a French city, I believe.'

'Yes. There are many people of French descent.'

'But not your family?'

'No, Madame, I don't think so. My father's family is originally from the south, from Bavaria; my mother's family has lived in the Rhineland for many generations.'

It went on for another thirty minutes and two more cups of coffee. With the old woman civility was somehow worse than acrimony. At last Ernst stood. He said it had been a pleasure to meet Madame Levy.

'I doubt it,' she responded with a tight smirk.

'I hope you enjoy your visit.'

'I doubt that too,' she said.

Outside, he clasped Jeanne's hand. She whispered her apologies; she had known nothing about her mother's visit. The Post Office was partly to blame, delaying the letter from Paris, not delivering it until the morning after her mother's arrival.

'How long will she be here?'

'Not long . . . I don't know; she hasn't said.'

An appalling thought struck him. 'She doesn't intend to . . . to *stay*, does she?'

'Permanently? No, no, of course not.'

'But how long?'

'I don't know exactly . . . a week, perhaps two.'

God, a lifetime! He shook his head in despair.

'I can't come back while she's still here.'

'I'm sorry,' said Jeanne.

'She hates me.'

'She doesn't hate you personally. If she got to know you she'd feel differently. I know she would. She's not an unkind person, Ernst. But she's had a nasty time in Paris with the occupation people; they requisitioned her flat for soldiers or clerks or somebody. She had to move in with a friend.' She squeezed his hand. 'I'm very sorry; I know how disappointed you must be. I'm disappointed too.'

Disappointed! It was like calling the war a disagreement.

'Will you telephone me when she's gone?'

'Yes, of course. Shall I ask for you?'

'No, they are very strict about personal telephone calls. Just leave a message with the operator. Tell him . . .' He thought for a moment. '. . . Tell him that my watch has been mended and is ready to be picked up.'

She smiled in the darkness. He touched her lips lightly with his.

'I missed you so terribly.'

'I missed you too, my dear.'

Hasty glance at the house. She had to go. Of course, damn and blast everything.

'Can't you get out one evening? We could go somewhere together.'

'But how can I? How can I explain it?'

'Can't you say you're visiting a friend?'

'Yes, but she'll want to come. You don't know my mother.'

'I think I do,' he murmured.

There were two stoves in the Readiness Room, named – for no apparent reason – Tristan and Isolde. Both stoves radiated a good deal of heat; indeed if one sat too close to either it was possible to be painfully scorched. And yet there was no way to achieve a state of all-round warmth in the Readiness Room. Inevitably one side was roasted while the other side – that facing away from Tristan or Isolde – was beset by chills from the draughts that somehow managed to find a way in.

Dietrich shivered. He tugged his flying jacket tighter about his shoulders and cursed the place and the evil Frenchmen who had designed and built it, obviously intending to conquer the conquerors by sending them all home with pneumonia. He was bored. It was nothing new. Boredom was a familiar condition to airmen of every nation. They described their lives as interminable periods of utter tedium punctuated by brief moments of stark terror. Boredom was, in the normal course of events, manageable. One could read, one could exchange lies with one's fellows, one could doze; whole days passed not unpleasantly. But when boredom was combined with discomfort it became quite insufferable.

What was he to do about it?

He decided to write a book.

The notion tumbled into his head, formed, final, as if it had been germinating in there for weeks, months, even years, without his knowledge. A splendid idea! Here he was, involved in perhaps the most significant struggle of modern times, in the thick of the action, living it, experiencing it. So why not write about it? Tell everyone at home what it was really like, convey the savagery and the humour, the courage and the cowardice, the fear and, yes, the boredom.

He nodded, agreeing wholeheartedly with himself. It was the perfect answer to his problem. Why on earth hadn't he thought of it before? It was lying there, simply pleading to be thought of; and he had completely ignored it. (But, he reasoned, no doubt Tolstoy had experienced much the same sort of incredulity when it had suddenly occurred to him to write *War and Peace*.) He must make notes, record conversations and incidents, detail the facts and figures. A fellow needed a veritable storehouse of material from which to fashion a masterpiece. He would write about real people, real events. He would start off by describing the unit itself: the pilots, the groundcrews, the commanders, the cooks, individuals all, some admirable, some odd, some downright obnoxious: real human beings with all the frailties of the species. Already he could see the critics' comments in the review columns of the press: ' . . . A work of art.' ' . . . Dietrich writes with extraordinary power and conviction.' '. . . The author will unquestionably be compared with Tolstoy – and rightly so.'

He smiled. A fellow pilot asked him what he was smiling about.

'I see something magnificent,' Dietrich told him.

'I don't,' said the pilot.

'I pity you,' said Dietrich, still smiling.

Siemer stood like a ramrod, head back, eyes fixed on a point somewhere above Ernst's head.

'Corporal Siemer reporting for duty, sir.'

'Stand at ease, Corporal.'

'Thank you, sir.'

The floor shook slightly as Siemer stamped. Ernst sighed, unaccountably irritated by the young corporal's parade-ground manner. He told him to sit down.

Somehow Siemer managed to maintain his erect stance even as he lowered himself into the chair.

Ernst wanted to prod him, to make him unbend. Had Wolfram experienced the same desire when a cadet named Brehme had reported to him?

Siemer's file contained glowing remarks: 'above average' and 'good material'. Why hadn't he been recommended for officer training?

'How many hours?'

'Two hundred and sixty-eight, sir.'

'What types?'

'One hundred and thirty hours on the Klemm 35, sir; sixty on the He 51 and the Arado 65; and nearly eighty hours on the 109, sir.'

'Where did you fly the 109?'

'At Schleisheim, sir.'

'Which models?'

'The "C" and "D", sir.'

'Tired old things, I imagine.'

Siemer nodded, his firm mouth cracking into the suspicion of a smile. 'Yes sir, some of them had been in Spain, they say.'

'You'll be flying the "E" model here – the Emil.'

Siemer nodded, eyes bright. 'I'm looking forward to it, sir.'

'It's got a Daimler-Benz engine instead of the old Jumo. There's a lot more power to play with but it makes her want to swing on take off; and it makes it a little more tiring up in the air because you have to keep a lot of right rudder on to keep her flying straight. Perhaps one day they'll put a rudder trim on the 109. And they've moved the radiators back to the rear of the wing. It does its job there but it's vulnerable to damage from stones and dirt thrown up when you taxi.'

Siemer kept nodding; obviously eager as hell. But how eager would he be when the Tommies started shooting at him? Sad that the only way to find out was to send him up to be shot at.

'Where's your home?'

'Hannover, sir.'

A.–E

'Well, you're on an operational station now,' Ernst told him – just as Wolfram had told him so many months before. 'We're not such sticklers for discipline and saluting as they are at the training schools. The important thing is to make you a useful member of the unit. You'll be flying as my wing-man. First of all you've got to learn to be my shadow. Your job is to cover me, protect my extremely valuable arse. All right?'

Siemer's smile broadened, the ramrod was beginning to bend.

'Yes, sir.'

'Any questions so far?'

'No, sir.'

'Remember that there's no room for individual heroes. We fly as a group; we depend on one another.'

Was Wolfram listening somewhere, laughing as he heard all his words again?

'Yes, sir.'

'Are you married?'

'No, sir, but . . .'

'Engaged?'

'In a way, sir. But nothing formal, if you understand.'

'I understand. What does your father do?'

'He's a carpenter, sir.'

They flew that afternoon, streaking into the winter sky, turning, diving, zooming at the leaden clouds, threading their way between the towering mountains of mist, glimpsing the sun then rolling and plummeting, slicing through smoky floors to find more caverns and valleys below. It should have been a delight but Ernst was impatient; the aerial panorama bored him; he had seen it all before. He returned to base, Siemer trailing at precisely 200 metres.

The telephone operator's pudgy face bore a knowing smirk. He shook his head. No, he had received no message about a watch having been repaired; as soon as such a message was received it would certainly be passed on to the correct party without delay.

Sanctimonious bastard.

'It's a valuable watch,' Ernst said. 'That's why I'm concerned.'

Again that smirk. Had too many people used the watch repair story already?

'You should have given it to Oster.'

'What?'

122

'Oster in Instruments. A watch-maker in civil life. Very good, they say.'

Dietrich was in the Readiness Room, folded into an easy chair, his knees jutting up to provide a rest for the notebook in which he was industriously scribbling. He looked up and smiled in the vague way of someone whose mind is a thousand kilometres away.

'Any news?'

Ernst shook his head. He sat down and took a battered magazine from the table before him and gazed at it without interest.

'Shame,' said Dietrich. He studied Ernst for a moment. 'It isn't the end of the world.'

'Did I say it was?' Ernst snapped.

Dietrich observed. 'You're not at your best when frustrated.'

Ernst shrugged. He apologized.

'You mustn't let it get you down,' said Dietrich. 'When one lady becomes unavailable, as so many do, in my experience, the only solution is to look elsewhere. Without delay.'

'I don't want anyone else,' said Ernst.

'Oh dear,' said Dietrich as if hearing bad news. 'She must be a remarkable lady.'

'I've never known anyone like her.'

'I see.'

'She has a marvellous way of looking at life; she loves to argue, to discuss anything under the sun, to turn subjects upside down. She's quite incredible.'

'I'm sure she is,' Dietrich murmured. 'But she's unavailable.'

'Only because of her damned mother.' Ernst rolled the magazine into a tube and hit the table. 'I've got a horrible feeling she's going to stay for ever.'

'Let us pray she doesn't do that,' said Dietrich. 'For my sake as much as yours!'

'She hates Germans, that old woman.'

'It's not unknown among the French,' said Dietrich. 'But do try to look on the bright side. There's a good chance you'll be killed tomorrow. If that happens you won't have to worry about all this.'

The English coast appeared through the overcast. The leader, Stelzer, rocked his wings, the three Emils drew closer together, as if instinctively seeking mutual protection against the guns ahead.

A quick glance over the shoulder. Siemer? Yes, he was still holding station well. Two hundred metres away, watching his leader's tail, as he had been taught. Be reliable Siemer. Please. Familiar tingles up the legs and back. Funky nerves readying themselves for the ordeal. Jesus. At last one could understand poor old Wolfram's concern about his rear end; it was sobering knowing that it was the responsibility of a total neophyte, an unknown quantity who might turn and run at the first burst of gunfire. One had to pay as much attention to a new wingman as to the enemy.

The past weeks had seen a number of changes. Several senior pilots had been posted to other units. Roder had taken over as CO. An intense, pedantic individual, he spent endless hours in his office, frowning anxiously at his paperwork, checking and rechecking figures and facts, driving the clerks to distraction. He had been responsible for elevating Ernst from wingman to leader, but he had done it with little enthusiasm. It was, he had declared, time for Ernst to assume greater responsibility. Ernst had thanked him. But Roder had shrugged as if to say that it was beyond his control; all the good men had gone; he had to do the best he could with what was left.

Ernst had flown several trips with an experienced sergeant acting as his wingman. But the sergeant had been posted. Siemer arrived, his replacement. A sturdy, dependable-looking fellow, Siemer, obviously determined to do his duty to the best of his ability. No doubt his carpenter father was bubbling with pride that his son had become a fighter pilot, one of the élite! The notion persisted that all fighter pilots were aristocratic young men with too much money, far too fond of girls, champagne and high speed for their own good.

The cliffs were unpleasantly close now.

But still silent. Had they managed to slip unnoticed between the flak emplacements and the radar transmitters?

Bang! Tiny lights flashed. Sparklers came curving, swaying low over the choppy water. Light stuff. But lots of it. The whole English coast bristled with flak; pity the Wehrmacht troops who would eventually have to storm these beaches.

The cliffs grew at an incredible pace. Suddenly they were there, close enough to reach out and touch. The edge of the land, looking as if it had been sliced off by some huge knife. Scraggly bushes thrust themselves out of the chalky wall, clinging desperately for survival; rocks wobbled, about to tumble into the breaking waves below. Now, abruptly, it was rolling meadow that flashed beneath the yellow-painted noses. Over it went, rolling on to its side as Stelzer led the formation into a turn to the right. A sizeable town ahead. Eastbourne or Hastings probably. Nasty area. Too much flak. As if to prove the point, a battery opened up, lacerating the air with its burning, twinkling projectiles.

Another hasty glance. Siemer was still there, faithful follower. What was going through his mind? Did he fill his trousers when the guns opened up? Plenty of pilots had. Thank God for the 8 mm armour plate now fitted behind the seat and the thickened perspex panel in front. Since their seats were attached to 300 litre fuel tanks, many pilots added their own protective devices: flat plates of thick steel on which they sat. Uncomfortable but comforting.

Houses, row after row of them, seeming to tumble towards him at lunatic speed. Tiny chimneys trailing smoke at right angles. Washing flapping on lines. People turning, looking, pointing, some running.

'There's an army camp somewhere around here,' said Stelzer in the unhurried manner of a man out for a Sunday afternoon drive.

'Yellow Leader, off to port!'

'That's it!'

Bombs away!

Ernst saw one hit the ground and bounce, somersaulting, wobbling, as if it was trying to straighten up. It hit a small camouflaged building, smashing cleanly through the wall, vanishing. A khaki-clad figure ran headlong, bent almost double.

Flak sprayed at them, lethal fountains of the stuff. The squat buildings sped below. A parade ground, flagpost, Union Jack fluttering. A platoon of troops, scattering, some firing their rifles. A military truck, skidding as the driver frantically changed direction. A smacking thud as something walloped into the fuselage behind him. Wrench the bird into a vertical turn. Earth whizzing by in a circle as if on a roundabout. The stink of cordite in the cockpit. Limbs working automatically, an extension of the machinery, more components in the complex little vehicle.

Ernst winced as a window panel cracked. He wanted to shrivel, to crouch lower in the seat. Not much protection in an Emil. Paper-thin metal skin. High-octane fuel beneath one's seat.

Christ!

A twin-engined aircraft! Flying straight and level, apparently unaware of the presence of the German fighters!

A Blenheim.

'Yellow Six, I'm attacking.

Siemer acknowledged, coolly, correctly.

'Victor.'

There he was, maintaining his position as ordered.

No evasive action by the Blenheim.

What was the matter with it? Was everyone asleep?

It grew in his gunsight.

No movement from the turret amidships, nestling on the bomber's spine like an observatory.

Bore in. Close! Closer! God, no one in the turret!

Fire!

At once, as if stung, the Blenheim reared up on one wing. Shells exploded around the wing roots, slicing through its fragile structure.

A glimpse of its underside – pale grey with oily streaks from the engine nacelle that contained the half wheel of the retracted undercarriage. Dull finish. Tiny lines where the countless small metal panels joined to form the whole.

Stick and rudder hard to the right. Earth rotating.

The crippled bomber lurched as Ernst dived away. Flames streamed from the wings, gobbling greedily at the fuselage. The Blenheim tumbled then seemed to correct itself. Something fell away. A man? No time to find out. Suddenly, the stricken bomber collapsed in mid-air, a writhing mass of flame, wings folded. It plunged straight into the side of a hill; burning fragments went bounding down the slope like pretty toys.

'Hullo, Yellow Five; I saw it crash. Congratulations.'

Ernst thanked Siemer. All very formal and polite, he thought as he sucked in air, his innards reacting to the release of tension. He glanced back. The column of black smoke was being blown almost at right angle, to hug the ground. No sign of parachutes. Poor bastards. No hope for anyone in a crash like that. The only thing to say for it was that it must have been quick. Damned quick.

The Channel lay dead ahead.

He landed back at base twenty minutes later. He clambered out of the aircraft, still feeling wobbly but managing a suitably modest smile as everyone crowded around to congratulate him on his victory. There was the combat report to complete: type of aircraft claimed; air witness (if any), ground witness (if any), type of ammunition used, number of rounds of machine gun ammunition, number of rounds of cannon ammunition, map references, time, date . . .

Dietrich was sitting in the Crew Room reading a limp copy of the *Illustrierter Beobachter*.

'Congratulations.'

'Thanks.' He sat down and looked for something to read.

'I've been thinking,' said Dietrich.

'What about?'

' "Eagles of War". Well?'

'What the hell are you talking about?'

' "Eagles of War". A title! Damned good, eh?'

Jesus. 'Splendid,' he said. Dietrich and his bloody book.

'By the way.'

'Yes?'

'Any news? Developments?'

'No.'

'I have a notion.'

'A notion?'

'An idea. It may appeal. It may not. . .'

Twelve

He approached the house cautiously. It looked quiet enough. Peaceful, one might even say. So it might reasonably be presumed that Dietrich had been there, done his stuff and had gone, all according to plan. Or had something gone wrong? Was it possible that he hadn't even arrived? Yes. No. Yes. Damn! They should have organized something to ensure that the one would know what the other had done. Stupid omission.

Dietrich *must* have been. There was no reason for him not to have been. Correct? Definitely.

But suppose he hadn't been; suppose he arrived at the *same* time . . .

No. No point in thinking like that.

Deep breath. Shoulders braced. It was utterly still. His shoes sounded like drums on the cobblestones; the bicycle squeaked and groaned as he wheeled it over to the house.

He swallowed, preparing himself for the moment of confrontation. God knows what might have happened . . .

The door suddenly burst open, startling him.

Jeanne stood there, silhouetted against the light from within.

All he could think of was the blackout regulations.

'You'd better close the door,' he said.

She stepped forward leaving the door open, peering into the darkness.

'Ernst? Is that you?'

'Yes.'

'Thank God! I didn't know who it was!'

'Yes . . . it's me.'

She ran along the path to him.

'Please help!'

'What's . . . what's the matter?'

He had to clear his throat.

She clutched his arm. 'They've taken Mother!'

'Taken her?'

'Yes! Why would they do that, Ernst? Why?'

'Surely not . . .'

'They *did*, I tell you . . .'

'Er . . . precisely who did this?'

'The army . . . I think it was the army. An officer came here about half an hour ago. He talked about her papers and her travel warrants. Something wasn't in order.'

'It's nothing to worry about,' Ernst said. It sounded strangely unconvincing.

'The officer said he was from the office of the administrator for the region. He said Mother hadn't had her pass counter-signed by the Security Area Commander. She said she didn't know she had to have the damned thing signed . . .'

'You don't have to worry,' he insisted.

'He *took her*.'

'He'll bring her back. Honestly.'

She looked up at him. 'How do you know?'

Quick intake of breath. 'It was Dietrich.'

'Dietrich?'

'You see, he was the fellow who talked to your mother.'

She shook her head, quickly, frantically, as if trying not to lose control. 'What are you talking about, Ernst. Please tell me. Who is Dietrich?'

'A friend of mine. Really quite a nice fellow.'

She opened her mouth then closed it. She stared at him. 'You mean to tell me you did this?'

'In a way . . . yes.'

'That officer. He was a friend of yours?'

'Yes, so you see there's nothing to worry about. He's just taken your mother for a little drive. He'll bring her back very soon . . .'

There was a moment of awful silence. In the distance a train chugged its noisy way to somewhere.

'*You* did this?' Jeanne's tone was incredulous; she kept shaking her head as if she was unwilling to believe it of him.

'It was the only way we could think of . . . to get your mother er, out of the house . . . so to speak.' He tried a friendly chuckle; it emerged as a sad splutter.

Jeanne had grown in stature; she loomed above him, her soft sweet eyes now hard, vengeful.

'You bastard! You arrogant bastard!'

Her voice was terrifyingly soft, little more than a whisper.

He reached out to her – but she shrank away from him as if he was diseased.

'It was just a joke,' he explained. 'Nothing to get upset about . . .'

'She was terrified.'

'But there was no *need* for her to be terrified.'

'She didn't know that, you stupid thoughtless swine!'

'Please, Jeanne, I only did it so we could be together . .'

'You're horrible!'

'No . . . you don't understand . . !'

'She thought she was going to be thrown in jail! Tortured! Killed perhaps!'

'No, that's absurd! Please listen to me. . !

'Get out of my house!'

'She was quite composed,' Dietrich said. 'Quite brave, I suppose, considering everything.'

'You took her back to the house?' Ernst asked.

'Of course. It was eleven thirty on the dot, just as we'd planned.'

'And she was all right when you let her out at the house?'

'Perfectly all right. She told me it was a poor way to spend an evening. Then she marched off into the house.'

'Jeanne was angry as hell.'

Dietrich frowned. 'Didn't you tell her it was a joke?'

'Yes, but she didn't think it was very funny.'

Dietrich shook his head. 'Odd creatures, women.'

They came from the north: tiny, slender things flying low.

Another unit, no doubt. Showing off. A beat-up of the rival unit's field. Typical fighter pilots' high jinks – just the sort of thing that HQ frowned upon so severely.

Something wasn't right.

'Christ,' said a pilot, sounding only mildly surprised. 'They're Spitfires!'

At which moment the intruders opened fire, their gun ports twinkling prettily. Tracers slashed across the open field. On the ground, men dived for their lives, hugging the cold earth; bullets smacked through the air above their heads, chewed into the ground beside them.

A parked Emil burst into flames, shuddering convulsively as it absorbed a hail of bullets. One undercarriage leg collapsed; the aircraft sank to one side like a dying beast. Another Emil, caught during a take-off run, spewed fire from its engine cowling and careered across the field in a series of wild, uncontrolled skidding turns until it tipped on to its nose and exploded. A Spitfire screamed in at zero feet, blazing away with all eight guns into the huge open door of Hangar No 4. The mechanics working in there hurled themselves to the concrete floor as the place became a nightmare of ricocheting bullets.

A trio of Blenheims now roared in low over the field, bomb doors gaping. Small black shapes tumbled free, wobbled, then straightened, describing graceful arcs as they hurtled toward their targets. The Administrative Building received two direct hits; its wooden walls burst outward; the roof suddenly rose as if it had found wings. An instant later it disintegrated into a shower of tiny fragments. A 250-pound bomb hit the old Citröen bus that brought the French civilian workers to the field each morning. It vanished, leaving a hole and two wheels. On fire, a truck from the Radio Section collided with two parked Messerschmitts, smashing easily through their fragile wings and sending the whole mess into a ball of flame.

Then, abruptly as it began, the attack ended. The British fired their last shots, dropped their last bombs. They turned for home.

But one was in trouble. A Spitfire trailed smoke. Its engine emitted hoarse coughs. The pilot jumped.

*

They brought the Spitfire pilot back in the field car. He sat in the rear seat, clutching his unfurled parachute. A hefty sergeant sat beside him with a rifle. The Englishman was a Flying Officer, a slim fair-haired young man dressed in a baggy uniform with a red and white spotted scarf in place of his collar and tie. He seemed slightly shaken but otherwise unharmed by his parachute descent. He glanced uneasily at the group of Luftwaffe men who quickly gathered around the car as he got out.

Roder was a surprise. He spoke English well. In his earnest way he explained to the Spitfire pilot that he had absolutely no need to be nervous; the Luftwaffe fought under a strict code of honour. 'Besides,' he added, 'we have a great deal of respect for the Royal Air Force; and airmen are brothers no matter what uniform they wear.'

The Englishman seemed to suspect some sort of trap. 'That's nice to know,' he murmured flatly.

'You will be our guest for a short while. We will be having lunch shortly. We hope you will join us.'

The Englishman nodded. 'All right.'

Roder thrust out a hand. 'Hauptmann Roder, how do you do?'

'Ackroyd,' said the Englishman. 'Flying Officer.'

Ackroyd began to relax after his second glass of Mumm champagne. He said he came from a place called Hemel Hempstead; he was twenty-three years old and he had recently became engaged to a girl named Daphne, personal and private secretary to Lord Somebody-or-other who apparently owned half the merchant ships in the world. Ackroyd seemed surprised to learn that the German pilots considered the Messerschmitt equal if not superior to the Spitfire. Puffing a Remschma, glass of champagne in hand, he shook his head in the definite way of a man who knows his subject inside out. He claimed that Göring himself had asked the Luftwaffe fighter leaders what they needed to win the battle last summer; according to Ackroyd, Galland had responded with a request for squadrons of Spitfires! The Germans shrugged, mystified; the story was new to them. And singularly unlikely. English propaganda, no doubt; as everyone knew the English were past masters at creating the wildest fiction to further their political ends.

The pilots compared notes; it was intriguing to look one's adversary in the face, to see the look in his eyes, to study the cut of his uniform, his badges, the quality of his equipment.

Early in the afternoon the armed guard came to take Ackroyd away. He shook hands with everyone and said he had enjoyed his lunch and the conversation. He wished everyone well. Someone told him he would be a prisoner only a short time; the war would soon be over. Ackroyd disagreed; no, the war would continue for many years and England would win.

'Quite a pleasant fellow,' said Dietrich as they watched the truck take Ackroyd away to captivity.

Ernst found the Englishman irritatingly quick to compare everything from food to aircraft with what was produced in England.

'It's an English trait,' said Dietrich. 'They are convinced that they are the cleverest, fairest, most brilliant people on earth.'

The unit had to be put back on fully operational status. The damage had to be assessed, repairs made, reports written, requisitions made out, priorities established.

The work went on at a brisk pace. Within twenty-four hours most of the worst damage had been patched up; replacement aircraft had arrived; the Pioneer Corps were busily erecting temporary buildings for the clerks and the mechanics. Roder telephoned Major Schauff and reported that the unit was fully operational once more.

Whereupon the RAF arrived to bomb and strafe the place all over again.

The mist enveloped him like a clammy sheet as he cycled through the village. The hooded street lights cast half-hearted glimmers on the damp pavement. A gendarme, shoulders caped, managed a casual movement in his direction, part-salute, part-wave. Ernst nodded in reply. He felt as wobbly and edgy as if he was going into combat. The same tightness around the throat and sourness in the mouth. He had written Jeanne half a dozen letters. He had apologized profusely; it was a stupid prank, he admitted; but no harm had been intended. Couldn't she understand why he did it? Couldn't she forgive him? He asked her to telephone. The watch story. Did she remember? But he received no message. He had to explain in person; there was no other way.

Jeanne, don't you realize how much I need you?

And don't you need me?

As he pedalled, he wondered. Did women need men in the same way as men needed women? Did they think the same thoughts? Did they ache in the same places?

The appalling truth was that the old woman could have died from the shock of it all. It was possible. And it would explain only too clearly why Jeanne hadn't responded to his letters.

He shook his head. It didn't bear thinking about.

Dietrich had been of little help. He said it was clear the affair had gone on too long; it had become complicated. When affairs became complicated, he claimed, they became tedious and then it was time to end them as rapidly and cleanly as possible and go on to something fresh and new.

God, if it hadn't been for Dietrich he would never have gone back to Jeanne; if it hadn't been for Dietrich that mad episode with her mother would never have taken place.

Damn Dietrich!

The house materialized through the mist. It looked cold and forbidding; windows shuttered, door firmly shut. But it was occupied; a slim column of smoke curled from the chimney.

He paused, one leg supporting the cycle, one foot on the pedal as if readying himself for a rapid departure. He took his cap from the carrier and put it on.

Was she watching from a window? Was she at this very instant hurrying downstairs to open the front door?

The front door stayed solidly in place.

Deep breath. Straighten cap. And coat. Now.

He propped his bicycle against the dripping fence. Under the circumstances it would have seemed presumptuous to wheel it right up to the house as he had done so many times in the dear, distant past. The worse-for-wear brass plate still bore the name Goutard. No sound from within.

Another deep breath.

He rapped. Once. Twice.

His heart thudded against his ribs.

Someone moving inside. Approaching.

The door opened.

Georges. He smiled readily enough.

Ernst nodded and extended his hand. 'Hullo, Georges.'

'Good evening, Ernst.' Georges held the door open and seemed vaguely surprised when Ernst didn't walk straight in.

'Is your mother at home?'

'Yes. I think she's in her studio. Do you want to see her?'

'Yes, please.'

If you only knew how much, Georges. There's a good fellow; go and get her, please, please.

Ernst stood on the threshold, neither inside the house nor outside. It seemed to be the appropriate place for him.

He heard someone moving upstairs. Giselle? The old woman?

He didn't care about the old woman being there, as long as Jeanne wasn't angry with him.

A movement within. Steps. She emerged, wiping her hands on a rag.

'Please close the door.'

She said it in a matter-of-fact way. A distant, disinterested way.

'Yes, of course.' He closed the door.

'It makes the house cold when you keep the door open.'

'I'm sorry.'

God, she looked adorable, even though she held herself stiffly, defensively.

He said, 'I came to apologize to you and to your mother.'

She said, 'My mother has gone back to Paris.'

Thank God!

'I . . . I hope she's well.'

'I think so.'

'I'm very glad.'

'Are you?' she asked, as if demanding to know his political affiliations.

'Yes. Really. I thought she was a nice lady . . . and it's quite understandable, why she feels as she does about *us* . . . the Germans, that is, not *us*, meaning you and me, of course.'

'Of course,' she said.

'Are the children well?' he enquired, anxious the change the subject.

'Yes, except that Giselle has a slight cold.'

'I hope it's better soon.'

'So do I,' she said.

Silence.

Then, for the first time it seemed, she looked at him. She sighed. A tiny, impatient sigh.

'Your coat is soaking,' she said. 'And your hair is all wet. Why didn't you wear your cap?'

'It falls off when I pedal,' he told her.

She gazed at him then her lips trembled as she fought the mirth bubbling inside. The battle seemed to last for endless minutes. At last she capitulated. Chuckling, she rose and went into the kitchen, re-emerging a moment later with a towel. Those marvellous eyes were warm and welcoming now. She pointed at him. He was to take off his coat at once and hang it up near the fire and without delay; he was to dry his hair if he was not to suffer the most dreadful consequences.

134

He was only too happy to obey. She arranged his coat, hanging it from the mantel so that the fire could warm and dry it. He towelled his hair. She watched, the ghost of the smile still on her lips. She reached out and fluffed his hair; she nodded; it was dry. He caught her arm; for a moment they gazed at each other, then he drew her to him.

'Will you forgive me?'

'Perhaps . . . some day.'

'Please, very soon.'

'How soon?'

'Tonight?'

She smiled. He kissed her. God, it was so overpoweringly good; he felt as if he would explode with the delight of her.

'I've missed you so . . .'

She touched his cheek; her fingertips lightly traced the outline of his mouth.

'I was very angry . . . but still I missed you.'

'I didn't mean any harm.'

'I know.' She gazed deep into his eyes. 'You were like a silly little boy who couldn't have the sweets he wanted, so you were ready to do anything to get them. But I'm not a bag of sweets, my dear. I am a person. I have a life outside you and this house.'

'I know.' He nodded humbly. 'Was your mother really frightened?'

'Terrified. She thought she was going to be shipped off some-where. Sent to a camp. You think such things when you are Jewish.'

He shook his head. 'I had no idea it would be taken like that. And I thought you would be *pleased* . . . isn't that absurd? I can't think what I was thinking about. No, that's not true. I do know what I was thinking about. I was thinking about you and how I missed you and how I had to do something, anything, to get your mother out of the way. I'd like to apologize to her. Do you think I should write her a letter?'

'I don't think so. It's probably better if she never knows the truth.'

'Perhaps you're right. Is she coming to visit you again?'

'She might. But I don't know when. She's frightened, but she's a very determined person.'

'I believe you,' he said.

She smiled. He leant forward to kiss her again. But there was a footstep in the hall; the door handle turned.

135

Georges came in glancing at the two of them as any child might glance at his parents sitting beside the fire. He said he was looking for his chemistry book; he had to do his homework. Jeanne pointed to the small black table beside the window on which she had arranged several small china figurines.

'You left it there.'

He found the book and regarded it with distaste.

'I hate chemistry,' he told Ernst in the manner of someone revealing an awful secret. 'Did you like it when you were at school?'

'Not much,' Ernst admitted.

Georges nodded, apparently relieved; it was good to know that older, more important people felt the same way as he did about chemistry.

'Did you have to do homework?'

'Yes, of course.'

Georges sat down. He wanted to know how much Ernst had been flying, whether he had been in battle, whether he had had any more exciting escapes.

Ernst said no; things had been quiet, except for the English attack on the field.

'Did they do a lot of damage?'

'Enough. To make matters worse, when we had it all patched up, they came and did the same thing again.'

'Did you see them?'

'Yes, the first time they came, we were in the Operations Room. We saw them coming but we thought they were our own aircraft.'

'What sort of aircraft were the English flying?'

'Spitfires and some Blenheims.'

'The Blenheims with the short noses or the Mark IV with the long noses?'

'The long-nose types, I think.'

'We could hear them but we didn't see them. What do you do when the weather's bad and you can't fly?'

'We check the aeroplanes and we practice gunnery on the range; often there are lectures and sports.'

'It must get boring.'

'Yes, sometimes.'

'Is that why you come here?'

'Yes . . . you could say that.'

Jeanne turned to her son. 'It's almost time for bed, young man. Where's Giselle?'

'I don't know.'

'Then find her, if you please, and tell her to start getting ready for bed.'

Georges sighed long-sufferingly. 'If you insist.'

'I do.'

When Georges had gone, she said, 'Shall we sit here until they've gone to bed?'

'If you insist,' he replied attempting to emulate Georges' high pitched voice.

She grinned – and she was eighteen again. They clasped hands, fingers stroking, caressing, their eyes locked in delicious intimacy.

'I prayed you'd come,' she said.

'But you didn't reply to any of my letters.'

'I know.'

'But why didn't you . . . if you wanted me to come back?'

'I'm not sure; I just couldn't.'

God, women were irrational creatures. But glorious. He said, 'I feel so happy that I wouldn't mind dying, here and now.'

'I know exactly what you mean.'

'You always know what I mean.'

She gazed at him, studying every contour of his features. Her eyes seemed enormous, great wells of affection, almost hypnotic.

She said, 'So now your friend Dietrich knows about us.'

'Don't worry about him.'

'I don't worry for myself,' she said. 'It's you.'

'No. Dietrich is a good fellow.'

'I'm sure he is but suppose he just happens to tell someone else about us.'

He shrugged it off as something totally inconsequential. 'The only thing that matters is what we feel for each other.'

She smiled gently as her fingers touched his face. 'You are so beautifully young and, in a way, so innocent. I know you feel strongly about me – and I am intensely, marvellously happy about it; you can never know what it means to me – but I wonder what it would do to your career if they found out about us. And what would your family – your mother – say?'

'I don't care,' he said.

'You are a German officer and I am a Jewess – and much older than you. Hardly the ideal companion, I think.'

'But I think you're ideal,' he told her. 'And that's all that matters.'

She placed her hands together beneath her chin as if she was about to pray. She continued to gaze at him, smiling; but now there was a trace of sadness in her smile.

'Suppose you weren't a fighter pilot, my dear; suppose there was no war on. Would it still seem so simple to you?'

'Of course.' Stoutly.

'Do you ever think of the future?'

'Naturally.'

'How far do you think into the future?'

'How *far*?'

'Yes, a day? A week? A year?'

'I'm not sure. . .'

'I am,' she said. 'You think of today, and perhaps tomorrow. Beyond that it's impossible, isn't it?'

Sometimes her perspicacity was frightening. He had to admit that what she said was true. He had never considered it properly, but of course she was right. She thanked him for being honest.

'Does it matter?' he asked her.

She took his hands. She shrugged. 'Perhaps it will matter one day,' she said. 'But tonight, no, tonight it doesn't matter at all.'

Dietrich opened a weary eye.

'You're a noisy bastard,' he muttered.

'Sorry,' said Ernst, struggling to remove his clothes in the darkness. 'I'm being as quiet as I can.'

Dietrich glanced at his watch. 'Nearly four,' he groaned. He propped himself up on his elbow. 'I take it the lady has forgiven you.'

'Yes, isn't it marvellous.'

Dietrich ran a hand through his hair. 'I hate to mar this moment of ecstacy,' he said, 'but I have news.'

'News?'

'Yes. We've been posted to Poland.'

Thirteen

It seemed like the end of the world, an ugly little clearing hacked out of the black pine forest, possessing no amenities, no services, constantly battered by fierce gales and blowing snow. Someone declared that it had been an aerodrome in the Great War, a base for aircraft of the German Imperial Army Air Service. If so, it seemed unlikely that anyone had been near the place since. The landing strip itself was a nightmare of holes and bumps. Two of the Messerschmitts had suffered damage putting down there. One had already been written off, its carcass soon to be picked clean for spare parts.

Crews worked night and day erecting huts and tents, setting up mobile generators, field telephone lines, canvas hangars, washing facilities, stoves, fuel dumps, creating a technical establishment in this harsh wilderness.

It was bitterly cold, still the middle of winter – while in France it was already spring. Why had the unit been sent here? What was the point, when the action was in the west and in the south? Was it some sort of punishment for failing to destroy the RAF's Fighter Command last year? Was it an experiment to determine the worst conditions under which the 109 could operate?

Dietrich noted in his journal: 'It's interesting to observe the reactions to this dismal place. To the regulars it's just another inconvenience in the lifetime of inconveniences, something to be borne with a disgusted shrug, the unpleasantness of the moment somewhat ameliorated by the knowledge that no matter where one is posted one can be certain that one will be eventually posted somewhere else. To most of the pilots and the younger enlisted men the whole thing is monstrous, a subject for endless grumbling, reason for vitriolic arguments, even on occasion, physical combat. Finally there are the ambitious professionals. The career men. The whole object of their existence is to be noticed, their performance approved by the right people further up the military ladder. To the ambitious professional the war is an opportunity rather than an ordeal. This period in Poland is a test; they are being watched; on their handling of the myriad problems of every day may depend the progress (or lack of it) of their careers. So the worse the conditions, the more uncomfortable the facilities, the more onerous the difficulties, the happier are our heroes. Fortune is presenting them with the most precious of all gifts: a chance to show their mettle. No matter that they have to work eighteen hours a day to achieve the absolutely impossible; no matter that they drive themselves to the brink of nervous exhaustion and their men to the brink of mutiny. Quite unimportant. The result is what matters: how *They* at HQ will react.

'Our Kommodore, Major Schauff, is tireless. He supervises

every stage of every job. Nothing is too insignificant for his closest attention. Nothing escapes him. His energy, initiative and patience are incredible – but we must remind ourselves that here is a man who is taking an examination, the result of which may well elevate him to the Staff. He addressed all the Geschwader's pilots on the first day we arrived here; indeed most of us were still in our flying clothes when we were summoned into a sagging, draughty hut. Schauff declared that we had enjoyed a soft, indolent winter in France. We were here, he said, to train, to learn how to rough it. I had the temerity to ask why; he told me that I would find out when it was decreed that I should find out. He fixed me with that steely look of his; I have a feeling that I am not the most popular of his pilots. Schauff then proceeded to inform us that the first project was to prepare a second landing strip; all non-commissioned ranks were to assist in the clearing of snow; officers were to organize the work crews and supervise their labours. Twenty-four hours later the field (if it can be so described) was declared fully operational – and presumably someone at HQ made an approving note in Schauff's record – and no doubt Schauff did the same for the officers under his command, including, of course, Roder who is in command of our unit. Thus everyone was made happy – everyone, that is, who mattered. For the rest of us the whole thing was an exercise in futility.

'For less than a day after we had made the God-forsaken place operational, the weather closed in. There was a blizzard that lasted most of the following week. The winds sounded like wolves howling in the damned forest. We spent the time shivering and looking at one another and disliking each other a little more each day.

'This is a place without diversions. The nearest village is twenty kilometres away; it is a bleak collection of peasants' huts; it looks as if nothing has changed there since the Middle Ages. One visit is sufficient; there is absolutely nothing to do there except stroll about and look at the Polish women who bear a strong physical resemblance to barrels. Even strolling isn't recommended; the area is said to abound with trigger-happy partisans who possess a singular lack of affection for us all.'

A letter from Jeanne. She talked about Manet and Cezanne, about the rococo style of Watteau, the neo-classicism of J. L. David, the romantic work of Delacroix and Gericault. A strange letter to pass from lover to lover. But it was a letter that would, it was hoped, excite no suspicion in the mind of the Official Censor.

Ernst and Jeanne had worked it all out on that last night, clinging to one another, shedding tears without shame: a code involving painters and their works, an awkward elaborate means of communicating but infinitely better than no means at all. To the censor it would appear to be nothing more sinister than a series of letters between a French art expert and a Luftwaffe officer who was a student of the subject. What could be more innocent? Ernst had already written to Jeanne asking a series of questions about Rouault; from it she would know that he had been sent to Poland. Her letter told him that she and the children were well and that he was always in her thoughts and that her feelings were unchanged. He read and reread the letter; he ran his fingers over the surface of the paper as if trying to sense where she had touched it. It was all sickeningly unsatisfactory. When would he see her again? Would he ever see her? It was easy to see why men deserted. To hell with the consequences. To hell with tomorrow. Only today mattered . . .

'Schauff says we're here to train,' said Clauser of the long jaw and sad eyes. 'But what for? What can we learn here?'

'We're all learning how to live without sex,' muttered Dietrich. 'The idea is to learn how long it takes for permanent erections to affect flying ability.'

'You've got a dirty mind,' said Ziegler who hadn't.

'True,' said Dietrich.

'The Middle East,' said Schleipmann. 'That's where we're going. They've sent us here to prepare us for fighting in the desert. The military mind works that way.'

But Hecht, a stocky, red-faced Munich man, was of the opinion that there was to be trouble with Russia.

No one agreed. Germany had a pact with the Soviets, a mutual non-aggression agreement, a triumph of negotiation, a masterpiece of diplomacy, another of the Führer's triumphs that had astounded the world.

The door opened, admitting a torrent of frigid air. A pilot named Haschert hurried shivering into the comparative warmth of the Crew Room.

'Foul bloody place!' he bellowed in his lisping Swabian accent, 'I was starting to freeze to the toilet seat! A man could do himself a serious injury in there! It's not right, I tell you! Something should be done about it!'

They laughed, telling him how suspicious his wife was going to be when he went home on leave with parts of his privates missing.

141

'It's no joke,' declared Haschert in his dour way. 'We've got to have a stove in there!'

'You'll just have to learn to crap faster,' said someone.

'I can't,' Haschert said. 'I've tried and I can't.'

Dietrich said, 'The British evacuated Dunkirk faster than Haschert can evacuate himself.'

'Don't be disgusting,' snorted Ziegler.

'Simply a natural function performed by everyone every day . . . except for Haschert, of course.'

'What's for lunch?'

'How can you think about lunch when we're discussing Haschert's bowel movements?'

'Who wants to play Skat?'

At that moment the shots rang out, a ragged burst, then several individual shots. They sounded oddly hollow against the wind.

'What the . . .'

'Wait for me!'

Ernst tugged on his flying jacket and followed the others outside. The wind-driven snow was blinding, each flake stinging, needle-like, as it struck his face. Dietrich pointed. Wehrmacht guards, rifles drawn, were clustered by the trees.

'What's going on?'

'They were nosing around, sir.'

'Who?'

'There, sir,' said the soldier, pointing.

Ernst stared in horror. Two bodies lay sprawled in the snow, limbs twisted, grotesquely, unnaturally.

'Christ,' breathed Dietrich.

The dead were boys, youngsters, sixteen or seventeen. They wore the graceless garb of Polish peasants. Both had been hit half a dozen times. Their eyes were half open, staring vacantly into the snow.

One of the soldiers was examining a light, single-shot rifle.

'It was his, sir. That one's. Got a round up the spout.'

Dietrich snapped, 'Did you have to shoot them, for God's sake?'

'Orders, sir. Anyone seen nosing around. No questions asked.'

'They're just village kids,' said Clauser.

'Partisans, sir. Lots of them around these parts. Turn your back on them and they'll stick a knife in you.'

'Couldn't you have arrested them or something?'

'No, sir.' Firm shake of the steel-helmeted head. 'We've had some experience with these bastards. This is the only thing they understand, if you get my meaning.'

'Perhaps they were just going for a walk . . . and sort of stumbled on the field.'

'Doubt it, sir. This sort doesn't just go for a walk anywhere. Now perhaps you gentlemen should go back to your quarters. There may be more of this sort about.'

Ernst took one last look at the forlorn, ragged figures in the snow. White faces, dulled eyes; their blood spattered on the snow, already disappearing under new snow. Children, not much older than Georges and Giselle . . . and Maria. Was it really necessary to kill children?

The weather cleared at last; the snow tapered off, the winds abated. Crews once again dug out the landing strips, mechanics tugged brittle, metal-hard tarpaulins from engine cowlings. They heated the engine oil before pouring it back into frigid crankcases. Still it was hard work to stir the big twelve-cylinder DBs back to life. Fitters grew purple-faced as they heaved on obstinate starter cranks to spin the engines' flywheels. Eventually they fired. Propellers spun, blasting back gales cold enough to freeze a man's nose off his face.

Swaddled against the chill, the pilots clambered into their narrow cockpits and set off along the bumpy strips. They reconnoitred the harsh, frozen land, learning to find their way from one unpronounceable place to another and back again. Rudat got lost, ran out of fuel and ended his flight upside down in a forest. He was lucky to escape alive from the crash, even luckier to be found by a passing Wehrmacht patrol. One pilot inadvertantly dropped a bomb in one of the huge black marshes. The explosion dragged an eerie figure from the boggy depths: a German soldier dressed in the field uniform of the Great War, apparently perfectly preserved. For a weird moment he had lain spreadeagled on the surface staring at the sky. Then he had slipped back into his lonely grave.

The unit moved to another field, just as bleak as the first; a week later they moved again.

Day by day the temperature rose. Reluctantly, it seemed. At last it was possible to touch a metal propeller without gloves – and without leaving large portions of skin on the blade. The forests were suddenly punctuated by clusters of flowers that seemed incredibly bright against the sombre background. The days became hotter, although the temperature still dropped to below freezing at night. The pilots took to sitting outside and soaking up the sunshine. They played Skat and Siebzehn-und-vier; they complained about the food and the accommodation; they wondered when there would be leave. They talked about the impending arrival of the new 'F' model of the Messerschmitt 109 – the 'Friedrich' which had already replaced the Emil in some units. Disquieting stories had circulated about the new type. Several test pilots were said to have reported mysterious vibrations; moments later their aircraft had broken up in the air. Something wrong with the tail design, the experts declared; problems with high frequency oscillations. Rumour had it that the people at Messerschmitt were frantically modifying the new models as they came off the production line, strengthening their tail sections before the aircraft were despatched to the front line units. But what distressed the pilots most was the news that the Friedrich actually carried *fewer* guns than the Emil. Had everyone gone mad at Luftwaffe HQ? They had approved the removal of the two wing cannons, replacing them with a single cannon firing through the propeller hub. They claimed that the new cannon would have a higher muzzle velocity than the older weapons mounted on the Emil; moreover, according to them, the clustering of weapons in the nose was more effective than the combination of engine-mounted and wing-mounted machine guns and cannon on the Emil. It was all very well for the armchair flyers to make such declarations; as far as the pilots were concerned, reducing a fighter's punch was a lunatic step backward.

Now it was sweltering day and night. The ground became rock-hard; the landing strip shimmered, appearing to vaporize in the dazzling glare. Mechanics dripped sweat into engines as they worked, wearing only shorts, their shoulders and backs the colour of mahogany. In the aircraft the heat gave new life to a score of smells that had been neutralized by the merciless winter; the odours combined to create a single, unique scent, yet its components could still be identified: fuel, oil, rubber, leather, sharp little hints of cordite, old sweat, old fear.

Letters arrived from both Ilse and Jeanne, the one discomfortingly passionate, the other ludicrously formal. He placed the two letters on the table before him. They seemed to offer conclusive evidence that the world was completely, utterly mad.

The next day, at dawn, they attacked Russia.

December 31, 1944 19:45 hours

You are attentive and polite to Reichsmarschall Göring; you smile
at every joke and nod at every compliment. You are well trained;
rank still commands respect, even if the individual doesn't. For
this special occasion, Göring has dressed his rotund self in all his
finery: a pigeon-grey uniform, piped in gold cord, breast eagle
hand-embroidered in gold, collar patches of gold, field-marshal's
batons surrounded by gold laurel leaves. He even wears his special
Reichsmarschall's dagger made by the students at the Berlin Technical Academy; its fittings and scabbard are gold; diamonds and
rubies adorn its pommel; its grip is made of solid ivory. He wears
his Grand Cross of the Iron Cross and his Pour le Mérite. He
looks like something from a comic opera, a clown dressed up as
a commander for the delight and amusement of the audience. But
there's no denying that the man possesses charm. The young
pilots hang on his every word; their eyes follow him as he waddles
among them. For here, close enough to touch, is the legendary
Hermann Göring, the comrade and confidant of the Führer
himself; side by side the two of them had fought in the streets of
Munich and Berlin to carve a place for the struggling Party. And
you must admit he can talk, this monstrous marshal. He knows
how to dazzle and galvanize his audience. He flatters them, feeds
their hungry egos. They will wipe out the Allied air forces, he
tells them; their actions will open a brand new chapter in the war,
one that will see a complete reversal of Germany's fortunes, soon
to be followed by the downfall and despair of her enemies. The
Allies believe the war is almost over, he chuckles (and the pilots
chuckle too because he wants them to), but in fact the war has
hardly *begun*! German ability, skill, inventiveness, German courage, German *will* are about to change the entire course of the
conflict! The young pilots swallow it all, eager to believe, wanting
to be told that they will perform glorious feats of arms, that they
will avenge their fellow citizens who have suffered so cruelly at
the hands of the Allied bombers. The Reichsmarschall tells them
they are his eagles, every one worth ten Yanks or Tommies; they
lap it all up, the poor bastards (few of whom have more than a

145

hundred hours in their log books). Their soft, unlined faces glow, nourished by the sort of stuff he dishes out so effectively.

You nod modestly as Göring refers to you. One of the greatest fighter pilots in the history of warfare, he calls you, a brilliant example for every one of them. (God, it's bloody bilge, but you keep nodding, keep smiling. Training tells.)

At last it's time for him to go. Thank God. You listen dutifully as he wishes everyone good hunting! It is his sorrow, he declares, that he is not permitted to fly at the van of the formation. 'Get a good night's sleep, my children, so you'll be fresh and eager in the morning!'

They cheer him. It's quite incredible. These silly naive little boys treat him as a hero! Lunacy triumphs once more.

He takes your arm in a huge, beefy hand and you make your way out of the Mess to a thunder of cheers and applause.

'It's inspirational, talking to such men,' he declares. He means it; there's a tear in each puffy eye.

You find yourself admiring his uniform. It is made of some splendid silk-like material; the thing is a masterpiece of the tailor's art. They say he has two hundred such uniforms, in various hues and weights for summer and winter wear; they hang in his personal dressing room at Karinhall like rows of gorgeous tents.

'I only wish I could spend every day with my pilots,' he rambles on. 'This is where I belong, on operational airfields, with front-line flyers. I spend too much time in offices.'

'A great pity,' you hear yourself say.

'A tragedy,' he tells you, warming to his subject. 'I feel at home here.'

You tell him you understand perfectly.

An aide hurries forward with the Reichsmarschall's flowing cape, another pigeon-grey creation, with gold piping around the collar and glittering gold clasp and chain.

'A sincere pleasure seeing you again, my dear Brehme,' he says, beaming. 'I can assure you your promotion won't be long in coming; soon you'll be Herr Oberst to all your staff!'

You thank him. At one time promotion to colonel would have seemed almost beyond belief; now you accept it without emotion. Of what significance is rank when the air force is disintegrating day by day? Soon there will be nothing left to command. You tell him that it was a thrill for your pilots to see him in person. He nods, agreeing.

'Our friends across the line are going to get the very devil of a shock tomorrow morning,' he declares, chins a-wobble. 'You have a splendid unit, my dear Brehme. Every man has just the sort of fighting spirit that is going to make all the difference in the days to come.' Around us, officers smirk, as if Göring's opinion still mattered. You wonder if he knows what has happened to the Luftwaffe. Does his staff report the truth? Or do they simply tell him what will please him?

You hear youself saying what an honour and pleasure it was to have him at the Mess, how his presence inspired every man present.

'I feel inspired too, my dear Brehme.'

He clasps your hand. His sincerity envelops you. You have to shake it off. Then everyone is saluting everyone else. The engines of shimmering staff cars burst into life. The visitation is over. Göring and his entourage vanish into their Horsts and Mercedes. They wave gloved hands in farewell.

The procession drones away into the night; no doubt they will soon be enjoying themselves at more New Year's Eve festivities. But you and your pilots have to retire early. You will be shaken into wakefulness while it's still pitch-dark; indeed it will still be dark at take-off. God knows how many pile-ups there will be before the formations get into the air.

How big will the force be? If it's big enough perhaps the inexperience of most of the pilots won't be so critical. Perhaps sheer numbers will do the job.

Three *thousand*?

Is it really possible? Does Germany possess that number of aircraft? And pilots?

The met reports are disappointing. Clearing skies. Higher barometric pressures. Damn! You hoped for snow and sleet and fog, anything to make them call this madness off.

You thrust your hands in your breeches pockets and step outside, down the wooden steps to the gravel path. There's a soft wind, pleasantly fresh and cool after the smoky hall. Out on the field the mechanics are working like Trojans to ready the fighters for the morning, feeding in the belts of 13 mm machine gun ammunition, fastening the drums of 20 mm and 30 mm cannon shells in position, securing the bombs to the ETC 501 bomb racks.

You stroll among them; they come to attention and salute. You tell them to carry on with their work; you wish them a happy and prosperous new year. They wish you the same. It's sad to see their respect in their eyes. They regard you as a knight, the superhuman warrior who will turn the tide of battle. Doesn't the Führer keep saying it will happen? Then unquestionably, it must happen.

Good fellows. But as naive as their pilots.

One of the mechanics, a curly-haired lad, remarks that tomorrow, the first of January, 1945, will be a glorious day in the history books.

'Unquestionably,' you agree.

As you walk away you wonder, whose history books, ours or theirs?

You feel old and tired. Your entire life seems to have been spent in one cramped, draughty cockpit after another; your eyes are weary from piercing impossible distances, straining to interpret the shape of fleeting, skidding aircraft, trying to identify them as friend or foe; your brain is numbed; there can be no emotion left in you. You are a relic of the conflict, like some ancient weapon left to rust on the battlefield. Your nerves are bad; your hands tremble like an octogenarian's when you hold them outstretched. You sleep fitfully, haunted by nightmares of fire and falling, always falling.

The damned war has been raging for ever. You remember peace but the memories are fragmented, somehow lacking substance, as if they are figments of someone's imagination – someone else's, not yours.

You turn and walk in the direction of your quarters. The attack takes place at dawn. As you walk you remember another attack that took place at dawn.

Part two

"Ace"
June 1941

One

It was a fantastic sight. The stubby little Soviet fighters squatted in trim rows, dozens of them with their big radial engines, every shining propeller set in the vertical position. They might have been awaiting inspection by a visiting general.

The red stars stood out like targets on wings and tails.

A shooting gallery! Set the nose in the right direction. Squeeze the triggers. Watch the bullets and shells curving through the air, bouncing, striking home, exploding. A nudge on the rudder pedal; a tiny shifting of the nose while maintaining pressure on the triggers. Another target! More hits!

On the ground the confusion seemed to be complete. The Russians offered no defence; the few men to be seen were frantically running for their lives, looking for cover, not for guns with which to fight the 109s. One after another the parked aircraft erupted, collapsing in flame, like dying creatures. Now the field had become a massive collection of bonfires, burning individually but merging fifty metres over the field in a giant cloud of oily black smoke.

The voices in the earphones were high-pitched, excited. Too many targets! If only there was more ammunition! The Russians were crazy!

'Look out, Yellow Five, I'm right behind you! Pull up, pull up – or I'll shoot your arse off!'

'Look at the bastards burn!'

'One's trying to take off!'

A madman!

A tiny Rata was in motion on the ravaged field, picking up speed, passing out of sight into one column of smoke, reappearing, disappearing again.

A brave man! But foolish. Two 109s attacked him, one immediately after the other. The Ivan actually got off the ground. Then he staggered, wobbled. One wing fell. Hit the ground. Crumpled. The big blunt nose snapped down. In an instant the machine was a pyre, scattering flaming fragments of itself that skidded and tumbled about the field.

Ernst jammed his stick and rudder to the left. The horizon rolled on edge. The column of smoke from the blazing Rata was horizontal as it flashed past. A tiny figure of a man ran frantically for cover – apparently running up an almost perpendicular hill.

The ammunition counter indicated a mere handful of rounds left. Enough for one more run. But when the field was before him once more he looked in vain for anything to shoot at. The whole place was on fire; every aircraft, every building. He hurtled through a pillar of smoke, beyond it, he could find only more smoke.

He followed the others back to base, the few remaining rounds still in place.

Forty-five minutes later, refueled and re-armed, still tasting the coffee he had gulped down while in the cockpit, he was back in the air, streaking low over the dusty Russian plains, waggling his wings at the endless lines of Wehrmacht infantry, packed in trucks, speeding eastwards.

The target was another airfield.

Incredibly, unbelievably, these Ivans were as unprepared as were their comrades at the first field. Did they possess no telephones? No means for commanders to transmit warnings? Or didn't they care? Again, long lines of aircraft, propellers just so, bright metal glinting in the morning sunlight.

Low level attacks, guns blazing, scattering the newly-issued SD–2 fragmentation bombs along the orderly ranks, watching as the targets dissolved in flame, one after the other.

The place swept past once, twice, three times, four times, as he attacked. Great black columns of smoke rose vertically into the still air, like nightmare skyscrapers.

A Rata upside down on a hangar roof. A man running for cover wearing a shirt but no trousers. A 109 making its firing run too low, hitting the ground with its propeller, momentarily recovering from the impact then, abruptly, shockingly, becoming a ball of fiery wreckage bounding across the grass and colliding with parked aircraft, already blazing. A water tank falling, bursting, sending its contents splashing into one side of a hangar, emerging from the other. Men diving into ditches, flattening themselves on the scrubby turf, covering their heads with their arms.

Christ! An Ivan in flight!

He was at the northern end of the field. Perhaps he had just arrived; perhaps he had gone for an early-morning flight and had returned to find the place transformed, a shambles. He seemed stunned. He was flying in a gentle bank, turning; the idiot might have been on a sight-seeing trip.

Easy meat.

Ernst was in the ideal position, five hundred metres above him and behind him.

A quick glance behind. Faithful Siemer was there.

'I'm attacking!'

'Victor. I'm covering you.'

Didn't it occur to that lunatic Ivan that he was in danger? He *had* to realize it!

No one could be that slow!

Ernst held his breath, fingers on the triggers. He bore in until he was close enough to see the oil smears on the fuselage, the dents in the metal cowling, mud clinging to the foothold: a dazzlingly, crystal-clear image; every detail of the Russian machine sharply crisply defined.

A three-second burst.

It tore the Rata to bits. Pieces of tail and fuselage broke away; one undercarriage leg dropped out of its well beneath the wing. Flame snaked back from the engine. Violently the little fighter twisted, snapped on to its back then plunged, whirling, to vanish into a forest and become a mushroom of fire.

Siemer confirmed the victory in his matter-of-fact way. Then he said, 'There's another one.'

Ernst glanced to his left. A Rata had taken off, somehow evading the darting Messerschmitts. Now the Ivan was desperately clawing for altitude. He came directly into Ernst's field of fire.

Another three-second burst. Down went the Ivan, wrapped in fire, spinning furiously all the way into the ground. The pilot jumped. But too late. He hit the earth a moment after his aircraft, bouncing once then lying still.

A pair of 109s sped across the field, hugging the ground, guns blazing. Tracers winked as they sliced through the thick plumes of smoke. Beside a hangar, an old training biplane absorbed a stream of lead; it jumped as if scalded; vomiting flames, it tipped itself on its nose against the wall of the hangar.

A machine gun at last began firing from a sandbagged emplacement.

It was still firing when the attack force turned for home.

The German pilots glanced at their watches. It was not yet eight o'clock in the morning, Sunday, June 22.

*

The first days in Russia were incredible. The hours passed in a blur of action; when men tried to remember it all, they found it became impossible to separate one sortie from another; they flew from daybreak to sunset, invariably at tree-top level, attacking airfields and stations, military convoys, infantry, horse-drawn transport. As soon as their ammunition was exhausted they would hurry back to base for a quick drink and a bite to eat while the mechanics filled their tanks and re-armed their guns. Then back into the air. Another target.

In the evenings, as the glowing red ball of the sun slid below the dead-flat horizon, the exhausted pilots sprawled in deckchairs and on the grass. Some slept, dead to the world, still garbed in flying gear, R/T connections dangling from their fingers like umbilical cords; others were wide awake, on edge, as if the sorties were being flown all over again, blurring images flashing before their eyes by the score, senses trying to keep pace with the lunatic speed of it all.

'It was like shooting clay pigeons.'

'Nice of them, the way they lined up their crates for us.'

'I think they were waiting for a general to come and inspect them . . . and we came instead!'

'How many do you think we destroyed?'

'Hundreds.'

'How many have the Ivans got left?'

'God knows. I didn't know they had as many as we saw today!'

'If they're no better than those poor bastards we ran into today, it won't matter how many. They were useless. I felt sorry for them, I really did.'

'They're a primitive people, the Russians. Non-technical. Machinery confuses them. My father knows them. He fought them in the Great War.'

'Those Ratas look like American racing planes.'

'They're slow; no match for a 109.'

'But they're manoeuvrable as hell. I saw one do a one-eighty that was incredible. One moment he was heading this way, the next he was going in the opposite direction. Don't stay on their tails, that's my advice.'

'They burn like hell.'

'What plane doesn't?'

The German pilots also discovered that the Russian Rata fighters packed a powerful punch in the form of two 7.62 mm ShKAS machines guns firing at an impressive 1800 rounds per minute and two 20 mm ShVAK cannon that could deliver 800 rounds per minute. In fact, the Soviet pilots had considerably more firepower at their disposal than did their Luftwaffe counterparts; what's more, their agile little fighters were well supplied with protective armour. Thus the Ivans should have been far tougher opposition than they were. The difference was in the individuals flying the aircraft, their skill, their training, their self-confidence. All the things that had been said about the Soviet Union seemed to be coming true. It was vast but backward, a gigantic morass of ignorance and intrigue, every citizen suspicious and afraid of his neighbour, the deadly weight of bureaucracy crushing any individual initiative.

Fearing dissension, Stalin had ruthlessly eliminated most of the competent officers in the Red Army. Now he was the supreme commander. But was he issuing orders? There appeared to be a total lack of organization. Everywhere along the line the Russians were in headlong retreat. Whole divisions disintegrated, individual soldiers hurling away their arms and running to surrender. They were terrified, demoralized, backward peasants with only the vaguest idea of who they were supposed to be fighting.

Some claimed that the Russian people would now rise in revolt, grasping this heaven-sent opportunity to throw off the yoke of their Communist oppression once and for all.

No German soldier or airman doubted the necessity for the attack on the Soviet Union; it had all been meticulously explained before the invasion began. Yes, it was true that a treaty existed between the two nations. But the Führer now realized that the Soviets had signed it simply to pacify the Germans, to lull them into a false sense of security. The truth was, the Russians couldn't be trusted. They had occupied Lithuania; more recently they had talked of moving into Rumania. It was all a prelude to their real aim: the invasion of Germany.

So, the German servicemen had been informed, it was vital that they strike fast, to compensate for the disparity in numbers by surprise, by initiative, by technical and moral superiority. It wouldn't take long. In a matter of weeks they would be in Moscow, the nerve-centre. Then, inevitably, the whole rotten Communist structure would come crashing down.

Europe would be saved for all time.

The new SD–2 fragmentation bombs were effective weapons – but treacherous. Everyone detested the small missiles, the 'Devil's

Eggs', as they were called. Rudat landed after a sortie, believing he had dropped all ninety-six of his SD–2s on the enemy. In fact, however, the first row had remained on the rack, held in place by air pressure. As he approached to land he slowed; the air pressure eased. One by one the bombs tumbled free. The last two fell out at the instant of touch-down. Rudat's 109 was blown almost in half; the forward section burst into flames and rolled across the grass to smash itself to blazing smithereens against the huge pines that bordered the field. Another pilot landed safely, taxied to dispersal and was clambering out of his cockpit when his last SD–2 fell out and exploded on the ground. The pilot escaped but a mechanic was hideously injured and the aircraft reduced to a blazing wreck.

But these were minor setbacks in a period of stunning successes. The German advance seemed irresistible; the Soviet forces kept falling back, confused, disorganized, abandoning weapons and supplies, even alcohol on occasion. The victorious Wehrmacht troops despatched tens of thousands of prisoners to the rear, often with no more than a couple of armed soldiers as guards. What a sad, demoralized lot the Ivans were! Pathetic peasants, they seemed only too glad to be out of the battle; they obediently shuffled into line and awaited their captors' pleasure.

Ernst sketched an endless column of them, slouching as they plodded past the airfield on their way to captivity. A cocky little Feldwebel strutted along beside them, wagging an imperious forefinger. Close up the ranks! Move faster! No talking! The prisoners regarded him with vacuous eyes, obeying his commands without a murmur. They outnumbered him five thousand to one yet between them they seemed to possess less strength of will than he did. One of the prisoners fell. The others simply trudged on, ignoring the unfortunate who rolled at their feet, coughing in the stinking dust. The Feldwebel stopped the column and, with gestures and bellows, commanded two of the Russians to break ranks and assist their fallen comrade.

It was another world, this harsh, dour land of Russia; the people who populated it seemed to be of a different species, resembling European man only superficially. Ernst longed for the day when he would leave this place for ever. Some of the airmen talked of staying here after the victory and farming the rich lands; rumour had it that the Führer planned to present enormous tracts of land to servicemen who had helped in the defeat of Soviet Russia; they would move their families here, build homes, then settle down to live like feudal lords with some two hundred million Russians at their beck and call.

'I'd made a damned fine lord and master,' said Dietrich as he unbuttoned his shirt to absorb the blazing summer sun. 'I'd personally deflower all the village girls when they reached sixteen.'

'You'd die young,' said Ernst, still sketching.

'But very, very happy,' said Dietrich. 'Anyway, on second thoughts I'm not at all sure that I'd like to be lord and master of a place where everyone was waiting for the right moment to stick a knife in your ribs. How could a fellow relax at his deflowering in that sort of environment?'

'I'm sure you'd find a way,' said Ernst.

Dietrich nodded, agreeing. He pulled his cap forward so that the peak shielded his eyes from the sun. 'Everyone's saying it will be all over in a few weeks. I tell you, old fellow, we're going to have to think seriously of making a living!'

'There's still England to be taken care of.'

'The English will come to their senses when Russia falls, you mark my words.'

'Perhaps you're right.'

'Of course I am. Aren't I always?'

Ernst grinned. He had sketched the stocky Feldwebel; it wasn't too bad; the figure had an amusingly bumptious stance although the head should perhaps be set at a perkier angle.

'Peace will present a lot of problems to a lot of fellows,' Dietrich declared.

'You'll write your book,' Ernst said, 'and make a fortune.'

'True,' said Dietrich. 'And you?'

'I don't know. Perhaps I'll stay in the Luftwaffe. I like flying.'

'Ah, but in a few years you'll be too old to fly and they'll stick you behind a desk, officer in charge of lavatory paper supplies or something. You should become an artist. You have talent.'

'But not enough.'

'You think your French girl friend is better?'

'Infinitely. She's brilliant. Really.'

'Then I suggest you marry her and live off the fruits of her labour.'

Ernst smiled secretly. The thought of marrying Jeanne had already occurred to him.

Ernst shot down a twin-engined bomber that appeared from the north flying in the careless, aimless fashion so common to Soviet aircraft at that time. The rear gunner fired wildly as Ernst approached; clearly the man was hopelessly inexperienced or terrified out of his wits. Or both. Ernst turned to attack. At last the bomber made some attempt to evade. But it was half-hearted, as if the pilot harboured no real hope of escaping. A short burst set the port engine on fire. The bomber began to turn, losing height. The rear gun was static, jutting impotently at the heavens from its transparent bubble.

Another quick burst. The bomber shuddered and rolled quickly over on its back, it fell, streaming flame and smoke, diving straight at first then whirling into a hopeless spin.

A man jumped; his parachute flared and snapped open. The wind carried him back toward the German lines as his bomber smashed vertically into the open ground.

When Ernst landed he was met by Schiegl. The adjutant informed him that the Russian was dead. German troops had found him, still wearing his parachute, a bullet wound in head, a Tokarev pistol in his right hand.

'He shot himself?'

'Presumably. They took his body to the MO.' Schiegl shrugged.

'Did you see him?'

'Yes. They asked me to look after his documents. He was a captain. Twenty-seven years old.'

'What was his name?'

'Bretovich.'

'Married?'

'Yes. Two children. Both girls. Came from Kiev.'

'He must have been mad to kill himself.'

Schiegl shrugged. 'I suppose he didn't fancy being captured. Odd lot, the Russians.'

Late that afternoon, Dietrich went missing.

Two

'He was losing oil,' said Beyer, Dietrich's wingman, a young sergeant. 'The stuff was spewing out all over his cowling. I saw it,' he added as if wondering whether he was believed.

Roder shook his head. A bad business.

'Was there any fire?' Ernst asked.

Beyer said he didn't see any fire. Oil had covered Dietrich's windscreen. 'He knew he couldn't make it back to our lines; he called me and told me he was going to try a forced landing. Then the Ratas jumped us. A dozen of them, at least. That was when we got separated.' He rubbed his soft brow, still branded by the edge of his helmet.

'A dozen, you're sure?' Schiegl, the records keeper, jotted the data in his notebook.

'Yes, sir, at least a dozen.'

Ernst said, 'Did you actually see him crash?'

'No, sir. But I saw him go down, steeply, with three or four of those bastards right behind him.'

Ernst sighed, sick at heart. Stinking luck. Poor Dietrich. He deserved a better fate.

'Where did this happen?'

Pale-faced, gnawing nervously on his lower lip, Beyer crossed to the Operations Room wall chart. Like the vast majority of maps in use by the Germans, it was inadequate, in places grossly inaccurate. 'Somewhere here,' he said, indicating an area with his forefinger.

Anger flared within Ernst, its very impotence making it keener. 'Christ, man, that's more than a hundred kilometres square, probably more!'

'I know. I'm sorry.'

Schiegl puffed on his pipe. He patted Beyer's shoulder in his avuncular way. 'It's damned difficult to pinpoint anywhere in this bloody country,' he said. 'But was there anything – a river, a village, a forest – anything to help us find him?'

Beyer shook his head. 'I'm sorry . . . I didn't see anything; those Ivans were on my tail . . . and it was cloudy . . . I lost sight of him,' he admitted. 'I'm sorry,' he said again.

'Couldn't be helped,' said Roder, frowning. He turned and strode out, as he opened the door a gusty wind blew dust and bracken into the Operations shack, sending the Daily Orders flapping on the bulletin board.

Schiegl told Beyer that there was nothing he could have done for Dietrich. He nodded, smiling. 'Go and have something to eat, old fellow. Take your mind off things.'

'Thank you, sir.' Beyer turned as if to say something to Ernst; then he walked out of the room without another word.

'A good lad,' said Schiegl approvingly.

'You think so?' Ernst muttered. The bastard had left Dietrich to the tender mercies of those Russian pigs.

'It wasn't his fault,' said Schiegl.

'He's alive and Dietrich is dead.'

'We don't know that definitely.'

But there couldn't be much doubt. Even if Dietrich succeeded in getting his crippled aircraft down in one piece, what chance did he have? The Ivans were said to have special tortures reserved for Luftwaffe pilots, whom they apparently categorized as aristocrats, haughty enemies of the proletariat.

Ernst went outside. The stars looked like hard little diamonds against the clear blue sky. The air smelt good, clean and fresh. He watched a trio of mechanics remove a 109's tyre, cut and torn by the sharp stones that carpeted the field.

One of the mechanics laughed at a companion's joke. Ernst's temper flared.

'Keep quiet!'

The mechanics turned, startled.

'Sir?'

Ernst mumbled an apology and turned away.

The Rata slid into Ernst's sights as if by pre-arrangement. The stubby little fighter grew by the instant. Ernst might have been in communication with the Russian pilot. A kind of icy joy gripped him. Wing up. Glimpse of pale, dirt-streaked undersides. A turn to the left, the natural direction for every pilot. Ernst was already making his corrections. It was beautiful. A copy-book attack. Get in closer! Closer!

The helmeted head twisted in alarm.

Fire! A brief burst, but superbly sufficient.

The agile little aircraft had become a blazing torch, writhing as if in agony.

Two Ratas hove into view. Spotting the 109s, they turned and dived for their lives. Ernst followed them. Idiots! Didn't they know how much faster the 109 was than their crates? It was so incredibly simple. Line up one of them. Press the triggers. Nudge the rudder. Line up the second victim. Fire! Down he came. The first Rata burst into flames but the second simply fell to pieces in mid-air as if the German bullets had smashed every connection in its structure.

Another Ivan skidded across his path.

Ernst knew – *knew* – what would happen.

Sure enough, the Ivan snapped into a turning dive to the left.

Ernst was already in position to cut him off. The Russian's head jerked in surprise as if the last thing he had expected to see was a German 109. Ernst had a curious feeling that he could read his victim's mind. The two of them were one, partners in a lethal aerial ballet that ended abruptly, violently.

The Rata's wing tore free at the root; the Ivan managed to jump free. His chute opened; he vanished into a dense forest.

Roder was all smiles, patting his desk as if in commendation.

'My dear Brehme, you were quite incredible!'

'I was lucky,' Ernst said. He was exhausted. He had been sick after landing; hanging his head out of the cockpit he had watched the horrible mess splashing down the metal flanks of his aircraft.

Roder shook his head, still smiling.

'No, it was far more than mere luck. You were methodical, my dear fellow, absolutely splendidly methodical, chopping them down one after the other – and not wasting a round of ammunition in the process! Most impressive. This calls for something a little special,' he added, producing a bottle of Henkeltrocken from his desk. He poured two glasses. 'To your continued success!'

'Thank you, sir,' Ernst muttered. The champagne seemed strangely fiery, threatening to burn a hole in his empty stomach.

'Tell me,' said Roder, with the air of a man unearthing the key to an enigma, 'was it the loss of your friend Dietrich that made you forge into those Ivans the way you did?'

Ernst hesitated. He had asked himself the same question. 'I'm not sure,' he said, 'but I think so. When I saw them I was eager to get at them . . . and when I did it suddenly seemed so easy. I knew just what to do and how to do it.'

Roder nodded, knowingly. 'Sometimes it takes a jolt like this to get a fellow going at full throttle, so to speak. Most pilots have a tendency to hold back, to be a trifle too cautious. Which ironically is often a damn sight more dangerous than pressing into point-blank range, hitting the enemy then skidding out of the way as if someone else was already on your arse-end, blazing away. You did it. I watched you, you know. I like what I saw.'

'Thank you, sir.'

'You have great natural ability.'

'I don't think so, sir . . .'

'But I do. And I know. Keep up the good work, my dear fellow!'

The victories came quickly now. But quaking nerves had to be steeled, shuddering muscles commanded to do what every instinct screamed at them not to do. Ernst found that in a strange, almost frightening way he could become one with the victim, anticipating the instant when the Ivan became aware of the danger hurtling upon him, firing only when there was not the slightest possibility of missing, when there was no chance for the enemy to survive. Ernst soon became the top-scoring pilot in the Gruppe, then in the entire Geschwader, the envy of the younger, less experienced pilots, an oracle from whom one could learn the secrets of this deadly craft.

Ernst received his Iron Cross First Class from a burly general whose ruddy nose was marked with tiny purple lines. The man's skin was mottled and pock-marked. He looked ravaged. But his handshake was firm and his smile warm.

'I understand you're doing quite brilliantly, young man.'

'Thank you, Herr General.'

'Your family must be very proud.'

'I think so . . .'

'Think!' The general guffawed. 'I'm quite sure of it!' He slapped Ernst's arm. 'Confucius would consider you a superior man, Brehme. Modest in your speech but not in your actions! Well done! Keep up the good work and we'll all be home for Christmas!'

While the PK cameramen clicked away, the general told the assembled airmen that they were crusaders, warriors privileged to take part in the most important military operation of modern times. Nothing that had happened in the last hundred years even approached the present struggle in significance. They were, he declared, deciding the fate of Europe for generations to come; their sacred duty was to cut a malignancy from the very soul of civilization – and that foul thing was communism!

The general pointed a righteous finger westward. 'Churchill himself used those words,' he cried. 'Yet now he talks of sending aid to the Soviets! Is he mad? Doesn't he ever sober up enough to comprehend the true nature of communism? The trouble with the English is that they're terrified of losing their pre-eminent position in the world – a position, I might add, attained solely by war! Ah, they're good, the English, at proclaiming themselves peace-lovers, yet there's hardly a country on earth that hasn't bled because of wars with England. Yes, this earth is full of people who preach peace but practice war. Take the Jews. World Jewry is dedicated to war. The Talmud teaches murder and destruction. And Bolshevism is the political result of world Jewry!'

The general positively shook with indignation as he uttered these words, his face becoming progressively more purple. But his colour moderated as he waved farewell to the airmen from the doorway of his Ju52 transport. He took off in a cloud of choking dust.

The photographers wanted more pictures of life at the field – and what the Propaganda people wanted they invariably got. Local commanders were only too eager to oblige. Publicity was good for a man's career. So the pilots clambered in and out of their aircraft, wearing suitably confident grins. They were still grinning obligingly when they were photographed at the supper table in their improvised quarters and writing letters under flickering oil lamps. The idea seemed to be to depict life at the airfield as a sort of holiday; it was a jolly all-boys-together place where a good time was being had by one and all.

Several of the pictures appeared in the papers a few days later, including one of Ernst (described as one of the leading Luftwaffe aces on the Eastern Front) accepting the general's congratulations. It was a flatteringly effective shot. Ernst shrugged it off. A lot of nonsense, he told his comrades. But secretly it pleased him. To think that a large proportion of the population would see that picture! Millions of Germans! Old school friends, relatives, former comrades; they would recognize him and tell everyone about him! At this very moment hundreds of people might be talking about him. He contemplated sending a clipping to Jeanne but he decided against it; better never to remind her of his involvement in the war.

The news from the other sectors continued to be incredible. Now the Wehrmacht had taken close to half a million Russian prisoners. Vast numbers of Soviet tanks had been lost – indeed it was said that the Germans had knocked out or captured far more tanks than they themselves had possessed when they entered Russia. Day after day the airmen saw the infantry, endless columns of them, dusty, dirty, often verminous, waving enthusiastically as the 109s streaked past. They were marching thirty or forty kilometres a day, pursuing an apparently-shattered enemy. The German troops bubbled with confidence and enthusiasm. And the Ivans continued to surrender in droves – despite Stalin's much-publicized order threatening to hold as hostages all the families of soldiers who permitted themselves to be taken prisoner.

There was a week of thunderstorms and torrential summer rain that turned the airfield into a quagmire. Mud became the enemy – viciously sticky, slippery mud that oozed and spread as if it possessed life of its own. It immobilized vehicles, aircraft and men. Only the little Russian ponies could negotiate the viscous stuff, stepping with a quaint delicacy, quickly, deftly removing their hoofs before they could become embedded. Sturdy, dependable creatures, the ponies were apparently capable of surviving indefinitely on a diet of birch twigs and the occasional mouthful of thatched roof from a peasant's cottage.

With the increased humidity came the mosquitoes, countless millions of them, insatiable, tireless. Life became a contest between the eaters and the eaten. Men felt themselves tumbling over the brink of insanity as they slapped at some part of the anatomy for the hundredth time in the last five minutes. One pilot burst into tears during breakfast. Mosquito nerves. Kriker had to feed him pills to settle him down.

Then the skies cleared. The sun shone. The mosquitoes moved on.

The field dried. The war could continue.

'I pray for you every moment of every day,' Ilse wrote, as passionate as ever. 'When I saw your picture in the newspaper I was ecstatic; I showed it to everyone; I nearly burst with pride! And then I felt terribly sad because it was only a picture; I was holding a piece of paper, not you.'

It went on and on. She provided news of countless friends. Theo was now a sailor; his girl friend Helga ('You remember, the one with the big breasts that you said must weigh her down') was training to be a nurse. Martin came home on leave and took Eva ('Bruno's fiancee') out to a restaurant; rumour had it that they slept together repeatedly during his leave. Gerda Keller was said to be pregnant ('but no one is saying by whom'). Ilse wrote diligently, providing all the latest gossip. But he wasn't interested. Theo and Helga and Martin and Eva were like characters in a half-forgotten book. A long letter arrived from his mother replete with the latest on relatives and neighbours. Wearily (he had been flying nearly ten hours that day) he took the Feldpost letter form. But what to tell her! That he had that very afternoon seen a

Russian pilot fall into a propeller, seen him reduced to mincemeat in an instant? That he had watched a nineteen-year-old pilot from Bremen burn to death, trapped in his aircraft after a landing accident? That he had killed half a dozen men in the last forty-eight hours? That sometimes he was violently sick after combat? That sometimes he couldn't sleep and sometimes he could sleep for twelve hours at a stretch? That when he did sleep his dreams invariably involved cavorting on silk cushions with half a dozen nubile naked maidens (and, for some reason, Dietrich) or falling five kilometres, trapped in a cockpit because the canopy jettisoning mechanism didn't work, watching the fire creep toward him?

He wrote his mother: 'This is an immense land, flat and hard. The villages are crude, ugly places without any buildings of distinction, except on occasional big house still surviving from the Czarist days. The Russian peasants live in mud huts with thatched roofs. There is usually one window – but it is fixed in the wall and can't be opened. Inside you find one or perhaps two rooms. Most huts possess a huge stove in the centre of the floor. It heats the whole place. In the winter the animals live inside with their owners. We have taken over some of these huts. No matter how often we fumigate the places there is still the smell of the animals!'

It was a pleasantly undisturbing letter, just like so many letters sent by servicemen from every nation to anxious parents. Why make things worse for the people at home by telling them the nasty truth? Far better to pretend the whole thing is a sort of grand tour paid for by the government, far better to describe the weather and the peculiarities of foreign places and peoples and to recount amusing stories about all those comical characters with whom one is fortunate enough to be serving.

Even further removed from reality was the correspondence with Jeanne. Ludicrously formal ('Dear Leutnant Brehme', 'Dear Madame Goutard'), the letters included not a single mention of the war. They were dissertations on artists, on style, on techniques. Ernst would read her letters, then he would hold them, running his fingers across the lines she had written. It was contact of a sort, maddeningly unsatisfactory and yet somehow meaningful, because she had touched the paper; her fingers had pressed here along the folds, there where the stamp had been applied.

A pilot named Straub occupied Dietrich's bunk. A thin, humourless individual. Straub possessed only one book, the Bible. He devoured it every evening with the intensity of a student studying his textbook for an important examination. Straub belonged to a large family, every member of which was, according to him, a paragon of virtue and industry. There seemed to be no profession, no skill, no sport in which Straub had not excelled. There were doctors, musicians, professors, burgomeisters, bankers, journalists, bridge players, tennis players, soccer players; predictably there had been a Straub who had been of inestimable help to the Führer in the earliest days of the Party. Straub had a collection of framed photographs of parents, brothers and sisters, uncles and aunts and cousins. He arranged them on the table beside his bunk, like sentries surrounding his Bible.

Flak got him: a SkVK heavy machine gun mounted on a truck, part of a convoy of retreating Russian soldiery. Straub's 109 streamed flame, rolled on to one wing, hit the ground and cartwheeled to fiery oblivion.

They sent the Bible and the framed pictures back to Straub's parents with the customary condolences '. . . a fine comrade . . . he will be sorely missed . . . an inspiration to every member of the unit.'

Peltz came next. A blunt, talkative fellow of twenty-one. He was candid about his ambition; he intended to be an ace. He had heard that Ernst was a success, so wasn't it good fortune that they occupied adjoining bunks? What was the secret? What were the tricks of the trade? How should a fellow set about getting a big score? How many Ivans had Ernst shot down before he received his Iron Cross? How many more before he got the Knight's Cross?

Peltz was shot down on his second operational sortie, having fired not a single round at the enemy. His 109 caught fire. He jumped; his chute opened. He waved at Ernst as he dangled beneath the canopy. But he landed well inside the Soviet lines. He wasn't heard of again.

Then there was Lang. He was quiet and introspective. He read poetry by Eichendorff and Uhland. He vanished one fresh August morning.

Ernst's score continued to rise at a remarkable rate. Roder wanted him to record his victories on his rudder – tiny red, white and blue roundels signifying the RAF machines he had shot down, red stars for the Russian victims. All the major aces followed this practice, Roder declared. Mölders, the first man in the history of warfare to shoot down more than one hundred enemy aircraft, had every one of them marked on his rudder, complete with the date of the victory. But Ernst decided against it; somehow it smacked of tempting providence.

'You're a strange fellow,' grumbled Roder. 'Good heavens, most pilots are falling over themselves to daub their aircraft with victory symbols, but not you! Never mind! If that's the way you prefer things, by all means continue!'

The star was permitted his idiosyncracies.

The days became fresher. Rainstorms battered the field again. At night the temperature dropped close to freezing. The summer of 1941 was coming to a close.

Ernst shot down one of the new YAK fighters: thirty minutes later the unit stormed through a formation of PE-2 bombers. Ernst got one on his first pass, setting both engines on fire. His second victim blew up and fell in a shower of burning fragments into a marsh.

When Ernst reached base, the place was in semi-darkness. Another five minutes would have meant a night landing – an unpleasant prospect on the narrow, tree-lined strip with only a few oil lamps to guide one in.

He taxied to his dispersal.

A mechanic appeared out of the gloom, beckoning. This way! Faster! Faster!

Ernst glared. Impatient bastard!

The mechanic wore a fur cap against the evening chill. He had an irritatingly imperious quality to his gestures, as if he was doing the flyer a favour!

Ernst cut the motor. The propeller slowed and stopped. Ernst unbuckled his harness; the fur-capped mechanic jumped on to the wing root and gripped the edge of the cockpit.

'It's about time you got back,' he said in a gruff voice.

Ernst gaped. 'Who the devil . . ?'

'I've got better things to do than sit around until you decide to come home,' the mechanic declared, unperturbed. 'My supper's getting cold.'

'You impertinent devil . . .'

The mechanic laughed.

And Ernst knew.

Dietrich! 'Good God, it *is*!'

Dietrich whipped off the fur cap; his dark hair fell across his forehead. He leant into the cockpit and clutched Ernst's head in both hands as if it was a prize item of fruit at the vegetable market.

'Thought I was dead, didn't you? Got nicely accustomed to life without me, didn't you?' He laughed, loudly, defiantly. 'But I'm alive. They told me you were flying so I thought I'd greet you when you got back.'

Ernst clambered out of the cockpit, still hardly able to believe that Dietrich had really returned. It was incredible. He kept shaking his head as he looked Dietrich up and down. There was so much to say that he said nothing, until: 'You look like hell.'

Dietrich's face was haggard, the cheekbones sharply defined; he had lost at least ten kilos, perhaps more. He grinned.

'I knew you'd say something sweet to welcome me back.'

'But what happened? It's been almost a month.'

'More than a month, old fellow. I know. I've been keeping a meticulous record. Thirty-two days, seven hours and forty-eight minutes, to be precise. The longest thirty-two days, seven hours and forty-eight minutes in my life. I spent most of it hiding in a stinking little barn with half a dozen pigs for company! And Russian pigs are dismal conversationalists, I can assure you!'

'So you weren't hurt when you came down?'

'Not a scratch. Sweetest wheels-up landing I've ever done. Got out. Looked around. No one to be seen. So I set the machine on fire – after one hell of a lot of trouble, I can assure you. The things absolutely refuse to burn when you want them to. Then I ran like hell! And ran! Didn't see a soul. Peaceful as could be. Spent the first night in a forest. You remember all those children's stories about boys and girls settling down and sleeping soundly in cosy beds of twigs and leaves? Bloody nonsense! I damned nearly broke my back trying to get comfortable! Didn't sleep a wink! Almost froze to death! To make matters worse I was scared stiff I'd run into some of those partisans. Then, after about twelve hours I suddenly realized something. You stupid bastard, I said to myself, how the hell can you possibly run into partisans? This is *un*occupied territory! No need for partisans here, you moron! So I started walking west. I was as hungry as hell. I was thinking of trying to steal some food. Then I started seeing lots of Russian troops. Nasty looking characters. I steered clear of them and came across this broken-down apology for a farm. I hid there. Ate bits of dried-up vegetable and God only knows what else. Filthy muck! But it kept me alive till our troops came – which was when I damned nearly got shot by a grenadier; the fathead thought I was a Russian. His mouth dropped wide open when I started talking German. He looked as surprised as you did!'

'I thought you were dead.'

Dietrich smiled wryly. 'I thought so myself a few times.'

'You can have your old bunk back. Three different fellows have had it while you were away. They've all gone.'

'All three of them?'

'All three.'

'Things must have been pretty hot around here.'

'Hot enough, I can assure you.'

Dietrich grinned and patted Ernst's arm. 'I hear that congratulations are in order. You've been doing great things.'

'I've been lucky.'

'It's much more than luck from what I'm told.'

Ernst recounted how anger, the desire for revenge, had sent him barrelling into the enemy formations, knocking down one Ivan after another. 'It suddenly seemed quite easy. It was as if for a year I'd just been practising. Now I knew what to do and when to do it. I think I was always too hesitant before; I worried too much about what action the other fellow was going to take. Now I seem to know. It's difficult to explain.'

'Genius always is,' said Dietrich in his cryptic way.

That evening they celebrated Dietrich's return, consuming most of the unit's remaining stocks of wine, beer and schnapps. A fitter who was skilled at cartooning drew a large sketch of Dietrich hiding in his farm, disguised as a cow – and looking apprehensively at Russian troops approaching from the left and a pair of virile bulls approaching from the right. A discarded portrait of Stalin provided the frame; the drawing hung on the wall behind Dietrich's chair.

When called upon to speak, he wobbled to his feet. 'Never,' he said, 'did I ever believe that I could actually be glad to see your ugly faces again.'

Dietrich wrote: 'I made something of a fool of myself last night. Couldn't be helped. It happened. Why do I cringe in shame when I remember? Why do I persist in believing that my fellow-airmen are laughing at me? They're not, of course, any more than I would laugh at any of them if the situation were reversed. The trouble is, all of us pretend. We make light of everything. War is a big sports event and we are the players. The curious thing is how successfully we can delude ourselves. Most of the time. It takes something unpleasant to kick us back to reality. When I stood up and started to be my casual, witty, amusing self (or the self that I take pains to project) I experienced an extraordinary emotion. I looked at those faces, the faces of my comrades – some of whom

I didn't even know – and they were overpoweringly dear to me. I wanted to rush to each of them and hug him. I *loved* every man there. I had never before felt such affection for any fellow man – or woman. That was when I burst into tears.

'I still cringe when I remember.

'My friend Ernst has become a phenomenon during my absence. He is the talk of our unit. He is held in awe by the other pilots. And quite rightly so, because he is an exceptional pilot, or rather, an exceptional destroyer of enemy aircraft. He is the one of ten thousand or so, the one who seems to combine just the right qualities, abilities, senses. And stunning good looks.

'Strange that I still like him!'

While Dietrich was away on medical furlough the unit moved to a new field. The pilots' quarters were a motley collection of huts, some abandoned by the Soviets, some still being erected by the Pioneers. Ernst was assigned to a mud-walled cottage, once the home of peasants and their stock. The animal smells had become impregnated in the baked mud walls and rough wood floors, impervious to soap or disinfectant. Water had to be pumped from wells, heated and brought in steaming cauldrons for the morning wash and shave. Oil lamps provided flickering illumination at night. Gigantic wood-burning stoves heated the shacks; they were tricky to light and when at last they were in action they turned the tiny rooms into ovens. It was a time of shortages. The supply people kept failing to provide the simplest necessities: soap, toothpaste, razor blades, toilet paper. Quantities of everything were always said to be in transit but somehow they never arrived. The shortages affected serviceability too; some damaged aircraft had to be cannibalized to provide spares; almost daily, Ju52s flew in boxes of ammunition and cans of fuel to enable the unit to take part in the day's operations.

The Soviets' resistance was definitely stiffening now; the Wehrmacht continued to advance but every village became a battleground. Miserable little clusters of huts and sagging buildings cost the lives of thousands of troops, German and Russian; they slaughtered each other in savage hand-to-hand combat, their bodies sometimes lying for days until the burial parties could catch up to the front line.

They abandoned the field and occupied another twenty kilometres to the east. Ironically it was a field that they themselves had systematically demolished one sunny day in August. Since then the Russians had repaired much of the damage, only to blow the buildings and facilities to pieces when they retreated. Fires still burned as the first 109s landed. A wrecked Rata lay upside down in one corner of the field, the stiff, staring pilot at the controls, clutching the joystick with both hands. There was no sign of battle damage. Presumably the unfortunate pilot had crashed on take-off when his unit was departing; his comrades had simply left him when he fell.

By nightfall the tents and portable huts had been erected; the 109s dispersed, the airmen accommodated.

A mechanic named Knobloch felt the need to relieve himself while changing the oil filter on a DB 601. He walked 200 metres to where thick forest marked the edge of the field.

He unbuttoned his overalls and contentedly watered the bark of the tree, observing how it now glittered in the moonlight. Three shots rang out in rapid succession. Knobloch slumped to the ground. One bullet had caught him directly above the right eye, a second in the chest, a third in his exposed genitals. Troops scoured the area but found no sniper. The second night an instrument man was hit in the knee as he made his way from his quarters to the flight line. But a guard had spotted the flash of a rifle in the trees. He pointed the way to a squad of infantrymen. They stormed into the trees. There was a shot. A soldier fell. The Germans returned the fire. A body tumbled from a tree. They dragged the prisoner into a clearing, bleeding profusely, close to death. They stared, amazed. They had captured an old woman, at least eighty, dressed in the rough, shapeless cloth of the Russian peasant. Her weapon was an ancient Moissin Nagant rifle of Czarist vintage. The old woman laughed at the Germans, baring blackened teeth in a mouth bright with blood. She spluttered an incomprehensible curse, then died, a smile on her lips.

They patrolled the area between Smolensk and Roslavl where vast fields of flax were flattened and used as staging sectors for tanks and other vehicles newly arrived from Germany. Crews readied them for active service; diligent supply clerks spent their days walking up and down with their clipboards, checking serial numbers and requisitions, supply statements and modification memoranda.

From the air the place looked like an enormous toyshop, the merchandise lined up in rows, as if waiting for customers.

Dietrich said there was something pathetically virginal about all those tanks and trucks fresh from the factory, paintwork so pristine, metal-work so crisp and trim. A couple of days at the front would reduce them to the battered, scratched, dented condition common to every other conveyance in Russia.

HQ demanded ceaseless patrols, all too aware of what a tempting target the tanks and trucks created. But for weeks the Soviets ignored the place. Patrols were a joyride, a diversion.

Then one day when the ceiling was low and threatening and gusty winds battered the circling fighters, the Ivans struck. A formation of the new Il–2 Stormovik ground assault aircraft came streaking in from the east. Sleek, efficient looking aircraft. There had been reports about them, rumours that they were incredibly tough, formidable machines. This was the first time they had been seen in this sector.

They bore in low, hugging the flat ground.

The 109s pounced.

Revi gun sights on. Guns armed. Speed building, targets growing, the earth skidding away from them. Fingers caressing the trigger buttons. Voices chattering in the earphones, high-pitched, tight with the excitement of the moment. Air screaming past the canopy. A sliver of chilly air entered by the sliding panel.

Ernst selected his target.

Him.

Second from the right.

Ease back on the stick. Heave now. Hard work; the 109 wanted to keep going straight into Mother Russia. But at last the controls obeyed his command. The elevators deflected the semi-solid stream of air. The horizon shifted.

Now the Russians were dead ahead. Clinging together in tight formation. And every rear-gunner blazing away for all he was worth. Tracers curving through the air. Ignore them! Press in closer! Closer!

Helmeted head of the rear gunner, bent over his weapon. Firing in short, accurate bursts.

Damn him!

Ernst felt the impact of the Ivan's bullets. The bastard knew his business – and he possessed stout nerves. A thoroughly dangerous combination!

The Stormovik loomed in his sights. Red star bright on its metal flanks. Rear gunner still firing. Still hitting.

Now!

Bulls-eye! Hit after hit on the long canopy, the wing root, the engine cowling.

Ernst broke away, turning, sweeping low over the flat ground, preparing to attack again.

The Stormovik was still flying.

On the ground every gunner was pumping away for all he was worth, just as likely to hit friend or foe.

Another burst at the Stormovik. Still more hits! Sparkling explosions as the shells struck home.

The rear gunner wasn't firing now.

An instant later Ernst saw why. Gloved hands still clutched the machine gun but the helmeted head had vanished, blown off cleanly. Presumably it was somewhere on the cockpit floor, rolling around as the Russian pilot attempted to evade his assailant.

More hits! But still the Stormovik flew. Incredible machine! Heavily armour plated, according to the reports, specially designed for the ground attack role. A sort of flying tank. Did it take an anti-tank gun to shoot the thing down? How much lead could an airplane absorb and still keep flying?

The Stormovik's rudder was torn, bits of fabric and metal flapping furiously in the wind. But tail damage tended to be the aerial equivalent of a flesh wound; ugly but not fatal. One had to blast an adversary's tail right off to bring him down – and it might take every last round to do that. No, the only sensible course was to aim for the cockpit, the engine and the wings if they contained fuel. Did they? Ernst didn't know; he would find out. It was important to learn this crate's weak spots – if it possessed any.

Hasty glance at the ammunition counter. Only a few rounds left. God, was this bastard going to get away?

They sped over the flat, marshy countryside, by now far from the staging area. The rest of the Ivans had long since scattered. Perhaps they had all been destroyed; perhaps they had all escaped – the latter seemed the more probable if they were all as tough as this one.

Then the Ivan rose to clear a building.

For a moment his belly was exposed. Was it more vulnerable to gunfire than the upper half? Ernst fired.

A brief, final burst. But it was enough.

The Stormovik streamed fire.

Horrido!

The fight was over. The Ivan wobbled, skidded, on to one

wing. A tip hit the ground. The aircraft cartwheeled like something at a spectacular fireworks exhibition; then it dissolved in searing flame.

Ernst circled the funeral pyre, the busy fire gobbling at the twisted, shattered remains of aircraft and crew, the black smoke beaten low by the wind, pointing the way the Russians had come. Poor bastards, to die in defence of this wretched grey land. No one came running to the wreck; apparently no one had even seen the aircraft crash. The Ivan might have come down in the middle of a desert, for all anyone cared.

He turned for home.

Three

The cold rain thundered down on the leaky thatched roof of their hut as the pilots clustered around the radio listening to the voice of their Führer. Adolf Hitler declared unequivocally that the Red Army had been destroyed and would never rise again. The war against the Soviet Union was as good as over, he assured them; all that now remained was herding the prisoners into camps and mopping up the remaining pockets of resistance.

There were grins of satisfaction from the pilots. They nodded, heartened to hear such things from the Führer himself. Even distorted by radio interference, his voice possessed extraordinary power; it captivated every listener in the hut.

'They're talking peace terms already,' said one man when the broadcast had concluded.

'How do you know?'

'Obvious. The Führer wouldn't say such things unless it was all settled. You wait and see.'

'We'll have some leave in Moscow.'

'God, I'm looking forward to a hot bath.'

'I'm looking forward to a hot woman.'

'Incredible to think it's all over.'

'Not quite.'

'But as good as. The Führer said so.'

'The Ivans are beaten and they know it.'

'We took three quarters of a million prisoners at Vyazma.'

'I know. I saw them. The lines stretched over the horizon. Unbelievable sight.'

As the weather turned colder the vermin moved indoors. There was no stopping them: rats, mice, cockroaches, lice, fleas, maggots, ants, weevils; all were determined to find warmth and nourishment no matter how vigorously the humans resisted.

The pilots would place scraps of food, sausage or bread, in the centre of the floor. Within moments the industrious pests would scurry out of the floor heading for the treasure. Vengeful, the pilots would leap into action, stamping like flamenco dancers gone mad. It provided satisfaction but little else; the crushed remains of the insects served only to attract more of their kind, eager to consume their comrades' remains.

The weather deteriorated. For a week it rained continuously; the field became an ocean of mud that found its unpleasant way into everything – engines, shoes, clothes, food. In the morning the stuff was topped by a layer of lice – not thick enough to support vehicle or man but just thick enough to make life a little more uncomfortable and hazardous.

Dietrich returned from leave. He looked chubbier and fitter. He reported that Germany seemed prosperous and peaceful; the news from the East was so incredibly good that everyone expected the troops home before Christmas. It was said that Auto-Union planned to revert to peacetime production of automobiles in 1942.

Thrilling news; it all seemed to bear out what the Führer had said only a few weeks before. The campaign was as good as over.

But pilots continued to die. Ents and Oertgen, Guntzer and Knose. And God only knows how many Russians.

Ernst rarely flew without scoring a victory; indeed he was becoming well-known for his rapid-fire multiple kills, hitting one Ivan, skidding immediately to the next and another and perhaps yet another – all before the Russians seemed to know what was happening.

Fan-mail poured in. A female from Düsseldorf, by name Clarita Bothemberg, wrote: 'Ever since I saw your picture in the *Völkischer Beobachter* I have been dreaming of you. You are so handsome and so brave. You deserve everything a real German girl can give you. When you come on leave please telephone me. Düsseldorf is not far from Köln. The journey will be worth while, I assure you. I will be waiting.'

Some letter were more bloodthirsty than ardent ('slaughter the Asiatics . . . my heart jumps for joy when I think of all the

Bolshevik swine you have killed.'). Others explained in clinical detail precisely what the writer wanted to do with Ernst. ('. . . then I will massage you with a special oil I possess, working it carefully, diligently into every muscle, every pore in your beautiful and desirable body.').

One grey November morning he shot down a PE–2 and a YaK fighter. Upon his return to base he was ordered to report to Hauptmann Roder's office without delay.

There was another officer with Roder, a tall, elegant colonel in his late thirties. He stood up as Ernst entered; the motion had a deliberate quality, as if it had been practiced and perfected. He had pronounced cheekbones which gave his face a curiously emaciated cast, although in every other way he seemed remarkably well nourished.

Roder was all smiles. And smiles didn't suit him.

'Two more, eh, Brehme? Well done!'

'Thank you, sir.'

'Well done indeed,' said the visitor. He spoke quietly but with authority.

Roder said, 'Sir, may I introduce Leutnant Brehme.'

'Delighted,' said the colonel. 'I've heard a great deal about you. You're becoming quite a celebrity, young man.'

'Thank you, Herr Oberst,' said Ernst.

The colonel smiled, a slow, thoughtful smile. His finely tailored uniform identified him as an officer in the Luftwaffe, but he wore no aircrew badges.

'My name's Wilde.' He produced a silver cigarette case. 'Care for one?'

'Thank you, sir, but I don't smoke.'

'Sensible fellow. Do you object if I smoke? No?'

The urbane colonel seemed in no hurry to reveal the nature of his visit. He puffed his cigarette and looked about the room before returning to Ernst.

'You've been accumulating an impressive score of victories.'

'Thank you, sir.'

'How long since you've been on leave?'

'Almost a year, sir.'

'A long time.'

'Yes, sir.'

Wilde had an odd way of glancing as he spoke; it was as if he was saying one thing but thinking something else.

'You deserve some leave.'

Ernst nodded; the fact was not to be denied.

Wilde said, 'I'm involved with the press. My job is to make sure the papers know what the Luftwaffe's up to. Make equally sure they don't know anything they shouldn't know. That sort of thing.'

'Yes, sir.'

'Married?'

'No, sir.'

'Girl friend?'

'Well . . . yes, sir.'

'I imagine so, with your looks. You have to fight off adoring females, I shouldn't wonder.'

'I wouldn't say that, sir.'

'But I would,' said Wilde with a tight little smile. 'I understand you've been getting a good deal of mail.'

'A few letters, sir . . .'

Roder reported: 'Eighteen in the last mail delivery, twenty-seven in the previous delivery; fifty-three in the one before that . . .'

Wilde hadn't taken his eyes off Ernst. 'All those letters must put you to a great deal of trouble.'

'Not really, sir. A clerk in the Orderly Room types out replies.'

'The clerk types out a standard thank-you letter,' declared Roder, brisk and businesslike. 'All that's necessary from Brehme here is his signature – or just his initials if there is a particularly large batch.'

'Excellent,' said Wilde. He studied Ernst in leisurely fashion. 'You photograph remarkably well, young man.'

'Thank you, sir.'

'It's pure luck,' said Wilde as if to say that there was nothing to thank anyone for. 'Some faces are made for the camera, some aren't. Simple as that.'

'Yes, sir.'

'The rare thing is when the face that photographs well belongs to someone who is worth photographing.'

'I see, sir.'

Wilde said, 'You'll be getting leave very shortly. I'd like you to come to Berlin. We'll arrange an extra seven days for you.'

'Sir, what do you want me to come to Berlin for?'

'We'll take some more pictures.'

'Of me?'

'Of course.'

'I see.'

'At this point there's no telling how we'll use the pictures – or indeed whether we'll use them at all. The whole thing may be a waste of everyone's time.' He smiled. 'We'll try to make your time in Berlin as entertaining as possible. Well?'

Roder said, 'A most generous offer, if you ask me.'

But Ernst wondered about the reactions of Dietrich and the others.

'I appreciate your interest, Herr Oberst, but I really don't think I want to be a photographer's model. . .'

'I understand perfectly.' Wilde stubbed out his cigarette. 'I'm sure I'd feel the same way. But you must understand something. Don't think for a moment that it's anyone as lowly as me who had this notion. I'm merely the messenger, old fellow. I happened to be coming to the Eastern Front, so I was asked if I would discuss the matter with you. Some very important people are interested in you, Brehme. I suppose that hadn't occurred to you.'

'No, sir, I . . .'

'I can assure you that it would be in your own best interest to accede to this request. When the Doctor sets his mind on something he usually manages to get it.'

The Doctor? Goebbels? Head of the Ministry of Propaganda and Public Enlightenment?

'You mean . . ?'

Wilde beamed. 'Precisely, old fellow. Shall we let him know that you agree? I know he'll be delighted . . .'

A Ju52 transport to Warsaw, another to Hanover, a third to Brussels, a fourth to Paris. The Special Pass (signed by Wilde) made it all so easy. Scheduling clerks were only too pleased to find a last-minute seat for the Herr Leutnant. Clearly his journey was of national importance; here was a man to be treated with the utmost respect despite his junior rank.

At Paris a Weihe was found to fly him to the fighter base at Denain; there, the Motor Transport Officer happened to have a supply truck going in the very direction the Leutnant desired.

The driver was as garrulous as Vosser.

'I saw your picture in the paper, Herr Leutnant.'

'Really?'

'It's a privilege to make your acquaintance, sir, a genuine privilege. It's not every day that someone like me gets to meet someone like you, someone who has *done* something, if you get my meaning.'

'It's kind of you to say so.'

'Not kind, sir, no not kind at all. Just plain honest. I always try to be honest.'

'Sensible of you.'

'I think so and I'm most pleased that you agree, sir. It's good to be able to have the opinion of someone of importance, someone who's had his picture in all the papers. Wait till I tell my wife that I've spoken to you, had you sitting beside me here, not more than an arm's length away . . .'

He heard himself responding, even managing to impart a tone of interest in what the fellow was saying. In truth he heard the words but they had no significance. He could think only of Jeanne. The incredible, almost unbelievable truth was that in a few minutes he would be seeing her.

Please, he prayed, please let everything be the same.

His innards quaked.

It was terrifying to contemplate the awful things that might have happened in the months since he had last seen her. Those lunatic letters had conveyed nothing but the fact that she was still alive. Was it really asking too much of any woman to expect passion to survive such a separation? Dietrich claimed it was. Damn Dietrich. Damn his shrug and his sly grin and his observation that one had to be realistic; one had to face facts. Damn facing facts. He felt just the same as he had all those months before, therefore she had to feel the same. Please.

She didn't know he was coming.

If only she had a telephone he could have given her at least a few hours' notice. But what the hell was the point of thinking about it? She didn't have a telephone and she couldn't get a telephone even if she wanted one. No new telephones were available for civilian use.

'I wanted to fly,' the driver was saying. 'But it was my education that let me down. I told the officer that I was quick to learn things but he just kept shaking his head. Not a hope. Forget it . . .'

'A shame,' Ernst heard himself say.

'I thought so,' declared the driver. 'I have a good way with machines, always have. Bicycles, cars, trucks. Took to them all like a duck to water, if you get my meaning.'

'I do.'

Dietrich had declared that one of the few advantages to service

179

life was the magnificent opportunities it provided to slip quickly and fairly gracefully out of affairs that had run their course. The idiot seemed incapable of getting it into his head that this affair had most definitely not run its course. It was just, Dietrich had said, that he felt a certain sense of obligation since he had been to some extent instrumental in getting it started in the first place.

'You don't have to feel responsibility,' Ernst had told him.

'Can't help it, my dear fellow.'

'There's no need for it.'

Dietrich had disagreed. 'You're such an intense individual. You sail into life in the single-minded way you sail into formations of Ivans. The trouble is, you're a damn sight more vulnerable on the ground than you are in the air.'

'Vulnerable? What do you mean?'

'I mean,' Dietrich had said in his patient-teacher-to-dense-pupil manner, 'that I don't want to see you get hurt.'

'I don't intend to get hurt.'

'Then think for a moment about all the reasons why the two of you are really not very well suited to one another.'

'Thank you for your advice.'

'Think about those reasons. That's all I ask.'

'I do.'

Dietrich had shaken his head; his hair had tumbled across his forehead. 'Look, damn it all, old fellow, have a good time. Enjoy yourself. You deserve it. But don't get so bloody serious about it!'

'Personally I think the Führer will celebrate Christmas in the Kremlin,' declared the driver.

Ernst pointed. 'Drop me there, please.'

'There, sir?'

'Yes, I'll walk the rest of the way. I feel like a little exercise.'

'I wouldn't walk around much by yourself, sir. Not here. You're in France now, sir.'

'I know. But I'll be all right.'

A half salute, a half-wave in reply. The truck pulled away with a groaning of gears.

Ernst stood there. His heart pounded, his throat was dry; his stomach revolved like a DB's flywheel. He could see the house peeping through the elms at the curve in the road. Dear house. Dear elms. Dear curve.

Please be there, Jeanne. Please, please.

180

His footsteps clattered on the pavement

His mouth tasted sour – damn, his breath would undoubtedly smell stale and rotten. Why didn't he think to suck something sweet?

Like her nipple.

Damn you, you bastard. You nasty-minded, randy bastard. Stop thinking of her naked. Stop thinking of yourself rolling around clutching her, possessing her. Perhaps she's sick of waiting for you. Perhaps she's already married to someone else. It's possible, isn't it? Almost a year since you were here. What can you expect?

Don't think such things. That's an order!

God, but he was frightened.

Frightened of disappointment.

Frightened of change.

A bird squawked, startling him. The damned creature was chuckling, he was sure, enjoying a good laugh at the stupid German.

A wispy curl of smoke at the chimney.

Was she there at that familiar fireplace with the picture of her late husband on the mantel . . .?

Why, he asked himself deliberately as his footsteps quickened, do you think of her husband at this precise moment?

Suddenly he was scared of knocking on the door.

Scared of finding out.

Finding out what?

'Ernst!'

There she was, at the door, smiling, beckoning, adorable face alive with joy.

A moment later she was in his arms; melting into him, clutching him, saying things he couldn't hear but loved to hear all the same. He told her he was sorry he couldn't tell her that he was coming; it didn't matter, she told him; there wasn't time, he told her; she was so happy, the told him; he prayed that she would be there waiting, he told her.

She pulled back and studied him, biting her lower lip as if trying to stop it quivering.

'You look thinner.'

'You look beautiful.'

'And tired. Are you very tired?'

He told her he didn't know; he hadn't thought about it.

'How long have you been travelling?'

'Twenty-four hours.'

'You must be exhausted.'

'I suppose I must be. Are the children well?'

'Very. They're both at school.'

'And you?'

'I am well too, Ernst,' she said, her eyes roaming his face, her fingers touching his cheek.

He said, 'I've got a feeling that I'm going to start crying, I feel so incredibly happy. Isn't that silly? Absurd . . .'

'No, my darling, it isn't silly . . . not silly at all . . .'

They lay together, satiated, languorous, drifting in the sad delight of slowly fading passions.

'I've dreamed about this a thousand times.'

'Only a thousand?' She gently chided him.

'A million!'

'That's better.'

'You too?'

'Of course. Do you think I forgot about you when you went flying off to Russia?' She clung to him, her cheek rubbing softly against his chest. 'My dear, I worried so about you, wondering what you were doing, whether you were safe . . .' She lifted her head and gazed at him, directly. 'How long can you stay?'

'I have three weeks' leave.'

'Beautiful!'

'But I must go home. I have to spend a few days there. I wish I didn't have to . . .'

'I understand.'

'Then I have to go to Berlin for some days.'

'And after that you go back to Russia?'

'I suppose so.'

'I prayed for you every day.'

'Jewish prayers?'

'Just prayers. Asking God to please protect someone who is very dear to me.'

'I love you,' he said. 'I love everything about you.'

As if in wonderment, she slowly shook her head. 'Sometimes I can't believe this is happening.'

'I feel the same way.'

She touched his face, kissed him on the eyes, the nose, the mouth.

He asked her if she loved him.

Her lips touched his, lightly. 'Of course I love you, my darling. I adore you. How could I not love you? But . . .'

'But what?'

A tiny sigh. 'Do you really want me to list all the problems?' She snuggled close to him.

'We must be married,' he said. There, it was said, once and for all.

Her fingers tightened on his shoulder. 'That's such a serious thing to talk about on your first day of furlough . . .'

'Don't you want to talk about it?'

She said, 'It is a lovely thought, of course.'

'Is that all it is to you?'

She sat up, turned and propped herself on her elbow, looking down at him. 'Have you thought about the problems?'

'Problems can be solved.'

'Some can't.'

He said, 'I want to marry you and I'm going to.'

For some reason the statement sounded almost petulant, like that of a schoolboy demanding another portion of pie.

'Now? While the war is on?'

'I don't know . . . perhaps later.'

'And what will your mother think of you marrying a French Jewess more than ten years older than you?'

'I don't know. And I don't care. I only care about you. The others, everyone else, can go to blazes.'

Brave words. But they seemed to stick in his throat. He could see his mother's horrified eyes, hear her outraged voice. Why had he done this to her? Why had he disgraced her?

Jeanne stroked his hair, gazing at him. 'I can't imagine why this beautiful young man loves me. I feel so old . . .'

'No . . .'

'But I do. And yet at other times I think it doesn't matter; I think a miracle has taken place and everything will be all right simply because we feel so much for each other.' She pulled his head close to hers as if protecting him from the outside world. 'It's strange, you know, when my husband Georges died something seemed to die within me too. I never imagined I would be able to love anyone else.'

Jealousy pricked him like a particularly nasty sharp-clawed insect. It was disquieting to realize that she had once loved another man, totally. That the man was now dead seemed strangely unimportant.

She said, 'I loved him of course, but it was something very different from what I feel for you.'

Better? Worse? He said, 'Wasn't he much older than you?'

'Fourteen years.'

'It seems a lot.'

She shrugged. 'I never thought of him as older. He was a good, gentle man. You would have liked him.'

But would the late Georges have liked Ernst? Hardly. He rolled his head so that his cheek was resting against her right breast. He tried to reach the nipple with his tongue, and failed.

'We will be married,' he told her. 'I insist on it.'

'You haven't asked me yet.'

'Asked you?'

'You haven't proposed marriage to me. A gentleman is supposed to do that.'

'You're right, I'm sorry.' He sat upright and placed his hand formally across his chest. 'Will you do me the honour of . . .'

She interrupted him, those liquid eyes fixed on him.

'Have you told your mother about me? Who I am? My nationality, my age, my religion? The fact that I have two children?'

'Not yet, but I will.'

'Perhaps you'd better not, my darling,' she said, clutching him, drawing him down on her. 'Perhaps she would find some way to prevent you coming here again to see me and I don't know how I could carry on if that happened.' She kissed him. 'Yes, I would love to be your wife, I would love to have your children. Perhaps it will be possible . . .'

'It will. It must be.'

'I hope you're right. But let's not worry about the future, not now. The next few days are ours. And they're precious. Like jewels!'

The extraordinary thing was how readily his story was accepted at home: only three days' leave granted; urgent official business in Berlin; love to stay longer but impossible on this occasion. So all-consuming was his mother's pleasure and pride in his accomplishments that he could have spent a mere afternoon at home without arousing any suspicion. She would have believed anything he cared to tell her. His picture had appeared in the papers. He was one of the Luftwaffe's top-scoring fighter pilots. A hero. A celebrity! A name to be reckoned with!

Herr Gebhardt strutted around like the ring-master at a circus, talking about Ernst's successes as if he had personally arranged for every one.

Ilse said it was terribly unfair that he wasn't given more leave, he who had done so much for the nation. Boys like Ferdi Happner who did nothing more dangerous than push a pen in some army office in Brussels were at this very moment at home enjoying no less than *fourteen* days' leave! Where was the justice in that?

He found it easy to lie to Ilse – as easy as it was to hold her and fondle her. He had entertained vague ideas of telling her the truth, saying there was someone else. But somehow the right moment never presented itself; the moments slipped by; the smiling faces passed before him as if on parade.

He would have to tell Ilse about Jeanne; he would have to tell his mother too.

But not now; later.

The photographer, Max Bosch, was a fair-haired man with a mobile, irritable mouth. He might have been of any age between thirty and fifty. His cold blue eyes examined Ernst's features from every angle. Had Leutnant Brehme ever considered a career in acting? He was particularly well suited to film: a matter of bone structure and the set of the features.

'Your face looks better on film than in real life,' he declared. 'It's a priceless gift for anyone with ambitions in the cinema.'

'But I have no such ambitions,' Ernst said.

'You'll probably change your mind,' Bosch stated. He managed a tight little smile. 'You are a handsome man, Herr Leutnant. Very fortunate. Nature has been generous to you.' He nodded to Colonel Wilde who was sitting in a corner of the studio, leafing through sheaves of glossy photographic prints. The nod was one of approbation: acknowledgement from one professional to another of a job exceedingly well done.

For the next few hours, Max Bosch and his young (and terrified) assistant took innumerable photographs of Ernst, looking happy, angry, determined, confident, merciful, merciless. Move the head just so. No, too much. Now back a little. Tilt it slightly. Just so. Hold that. Now smile. Now frown. Now look this way. Now that way . . .

At the end of it, Ernst felt limp although he hadn't moved from the spot on which Bosch had firmly placed him.

'You did very well, my friend,' said Bosch. 'You really are a splendid specimen. Excellent features, voice, deportment. Almost perfect, I'd say.'

'Careful, Max,' Wilde purred.

'But I suppose you like females,' Bosch said to Ernst.

'Females? Yes. Why do you ask?'

Bosch sighed. 'As I said, "*Almost* perfect". Have you ever posed in the nude?'

'No, of course not . . .'

'Perhaps you should consider it.'

Bosch took a large envelope from a filing cabinet and handed it to Ernst. Inside were a couple of dozen prints: young men, slim and naked, all demonstrably stimulated as they wrestled with one another, clutching genitals, engaging in an incredible variety of sexual acts.

Wilde chuckled. 'You mustn't mind Max. He has a one-track mind.'

'I am simply a lover of beauty,' purred Bosch.

'As long as the beauty is young and male. And willing.'

Ernst placed the envelope on the table, carefully, as if he was afraid it might explode.

'How long will you be in Berlin?' Bosch asked.

'Not long,' Ernst told him.

Wilde chuckled. 'Very sensible reply, old fellow. Max, we have to be on our way. Sorry to drag him away, but duty calls.'

'Delicious to have met you.'

'You mustn't mind Max,' said Wilde as they stepped into the chauffered Opel waiting outside in the Alexanderplatz. 'He's a little odd but he's a fine photographer.'

'I've never met anyone quite like him before.'

'I can believe it. Homosexual and proud of it, that's Max. He's quite incredibly blatant about it. Which is dangerous these days. Lots of zealous Party people are all too anxious to point the finger at anyone who has that sort of inclination. But Max survives. He's good. Therefore he's useful. As long as you're useful you survive. It's the law of our strange little jungle.'

Ernst nodded automatically; a bewildering place, the capital.

They met Herr Straub in the radio station. He was fleshy and amiable. And orotund. It was, he assured Ernst, a signal honour to meet such a distinguished member of the fighting forces. And so young. Twenty-one? How splendid to be twenty-one! The gallant Leutnant had accomplished so much so rapidly. Straub suggested a brief conversation before the actual interview, a creation, if you will, of the foundation of knowledge upon which the truly successful interview was invariably based. Nothing whatever to be nervous about. A chat between friends; an exchange of ideas.

And then Ernst found himself at a microphone. He heard Straub introducing him to the entire nation! Heroic son. Brilliant pilot. Victor of countless aerial combats. Yet simple and modest. A marvellous example to the youth of our beloved nation. An inspiration.

The sense of unreality persisted as Ernst heard himself answering. Yes, the struggle was fierce on the Eastern Front but yes, the German forces were proving themselves far superior, man for man, plane for plane, tank for tank. Yes, the Russians had suffered staggering losses, vast amounts of equipment, awesome numbers of men. Yes, there could be little doubt that Moscow would soon fall and with it, inevitably, the entire Soviet state.

In the next few days there were more interviews, congratulations, smiles, handshakes, platitudes. Goebbels declared Ernst to be quite perfect, as if he had been selected for a part in a play.

'Curious, isn't it,' he said in his clipped, incisive way, 'how the combinations of lines and angles in a man's face can communicate to many millions of people.'

'Most curious, Herr Reichsminister,' gulped Ernst who had only the vaguest idea what the diminutive but vibrant Goebbels was talking about.

'The trouble with most heroes,' said Goebbels, 'is that they don't look and act the part. You do.'

'Thank you . . .'

'When one of my aides saw the first picture of you receiving your Iron Cross, he said, "That man personifies total victory." He was right. Letters from ordinary citizens confirmed it by the thousands.'

'You are very kind, Herr Reichsminister . . .'

Goebbels said, 'Your home is in Köln, I believe.'

'Yes, Herr Reichsminister.'

'I lived there for a short time. I was working for the Dresdener Bank. An unhappy period. Are you returning to the front soon?'

'In three days, Herr Reichsminister.'

'I wish you continued success.'

He walked about the city, along the Unter den Linden, gaped at the Brandenburg Gate and the statue of Frederick the Great, strode the hallowed halls of the German National Gallery, window-shopped along the Friedrichstrasse, even ventured into the lobby of the Adlon Hotel where the rich, powerful and famous always stayed in Berlin. He was admired frankly by countless women, from mere girls to matrons who looked even older than his mother. Some recognized him from the newspaper pictures. In the Kaiser Gallery a perfumed, splendidly attired woman noticed him looking into a radio shop. Did the handsome Leutnant admire a particular set? Perhaps some arrangement might be made. For a moment Ernst thought she was involved with the shop; soon it became obvious her interest was purely sexual. Was the Leutnant on leave? Was he merely passing through Berlin? Perhaps he might care to while away a few hours in an extremely luxurious apartment on Tauentzienstrasse.

He met a jovial, prosperous-looking Göring at the Air Ministry offices. The Luftwaffe chief thumped Ernst on the shoulder and congratulated him on his performance while PK photographers recorded the scene for posterity. The usual questions; the usual answers; smiles, handshakes, salutes, followed by a rapid termination of interest when the filming had been completed to everyone's satisfaction.

While Ernst was in the capital important news was received from the far east. The Japanese had attacked and destroyed the American fleet in Hawaii. Another triumph of air power! Now at last the greedy, opportunistic Yankees were in the war. Now they would have to make war rather than money by selling arms to the combatants. Everyone in Berlin seemed to regard the developments at Pearl Harbor as excellent news. But not Wilde.

'The Japanese are fools,' he declared. 'The Americans will stagger and retreat for a little while. They have no choice; they are unprepared for war. But when they recover from the shock of this attack they will organize themselves and their factories and they will wipe out Japan. I just hope they occupy themselves with that task and leave us alone!'

Four

Dietrich wrote: 'Our star performer returned from leave last night. Looking as if he had just stepped down from a recruiting poster.

Immaculate. Ridiculously handsome. It was an occasion of importance; royalty might have been returning to court. Our CO was out there to greet the hero. Had he enjoyed his leave? Did he have a good time in Berlin? Did he meet anyone important? When E. told him of chatting with none other than Hermann Göring, Reichsminister and Luftwaffe Commander-in-Chief, and Josef Goebbels, Chief of the Ministry of Information, both confidants of the Führer, our esteemed leader seemed to be in imminent danger of death by awe. The man's colour changed visibly as E. (in his characteristically modest manner) recounted the gist of his conversation with these titans. How long, one wonders, until our hero is chatting with the Führer himself?

'It is pleasant to have E. back. I like him in spite of the fact that he has long since proved himself to be infinitely better at his job than I am. He is a fascinating individual. Obviously his amazing ability as a fighter pilot makes him highly unusual. But there's more. He possesses a curious innocence, a purity. (I can't help but use the term much as I dislike it.) He is being thoroughly and somewhat shamelessly exploited by the Propaganda people. Yet it has no effect upon him. He doesn't change. He shrugs off the fervent adoration of God only knows how many citizens. It never occurs to him to take advantage of his position, of his rapidly mounting reputation. He apparently possesses no conceit. I suppose I am forced to admit that he is *good*. Certainly it's the quality all his photographs project; no doubt this is what excites the Propaganda vermin.

'E. took off this morning. First sortie since his return. He shot down three Ivans in as many minutes – and used a quarter of his ammunition to do it. He really is quite incredible. Beside him, I feel like an ugly aging incompetent. And yet, amazingly, we remain the best of friends.'

The weather was vile. Every day brought lower temperatures. Roads were blocked by snow drifts, battered by freezing gales. A mechanic wandered away during a snowstorm; he was found two days later, frozen stiff less than half a kilometre from the flight line. His arms snapped off when they tried to pry the body free of the ground's icy grip. The savage weather reduced air and ground activity drastically. But there were constant probings of defences, vicious little battles which rated only a line or two in communiques from HQ but which left thousands of Russian and German troops dead and dying in the snow. A regiment of Cossacks had bivouacked on the edge of the field. Ukrainians all, they had joined the Germans soon after the invasion, eager to assist in the downfall of the Soviet state. The Cossacks delighted in capturing Communist Party bosses. They called the senior officials 'Goldfish', the junior officials 'silverfish'. Good sport was to hang the captives upside down and peel of their skin, sliver by sliver, while making bets on how long the poor bastards would take to die.

'Did you see your French friend?'
'Yes.'
'She was well?'
'Very.'
'Her children too?'
'Yes.'
'I take it her mother wasn't visiting at the time?'
'Correct.'
'So you and Jeanne are still friendly.'
'Yes.'
'Would you prefer that I drop this subject?'
'Yes.'

The weeks passed, an endless endurance test, a ceaseless battle against the cold, the vermin and, from time to time, the Russians. On nine days out of ten, flying conditions were appalling; in Germany and France they would have been considered impossible. But the fighters kept taking off, groping through flurries of snow, the pilots fighting to keep their nimble aircraft upright in the ferocious gusts that swept across the Russian plains. Cold, biting and merciless, made every flight an ordeal. It was impossible to stay warm; eventually one accepted the fact; one learned to live and fly and fight with numbed, aching hands and feet. One learned to grope one's way through blinding snow. But even clear, sunny days were not without their dangers; one brilliant afternoon early in March, a pilot named Götz flew straight into the ground while landing. The conclusion was that he had been confused by the dazzling whiteness of the snow-covered field and had misjudged his height. It was easily done.

The ground staff found that they could start frozen engines by mixing fuel in the crankcase oil. The fuel evaporated as the engine turned. Astonishingly the system worked without causing fires. They used sledges instead of the usual vehicles to transport supplies about the field. They wiped the guns clean of almost all their oil. Now the guns wore more rapidly but they no longer froze solid when they were needed. But there was little the crews could do to keep the R/T sets working; components simply shattered in the savage cold. Rubber tyres became hard and brittle, splitting with monotonous regularity on the rough airfield surface.

Ernst's score mounted almost daily. Seven Ivans one day; eight another. He had become utterly professional; firing at precisely the right moment, wasting hardly a round of ammunition. Letters kept arriving from admirers, keeping the clerk, Fromm, busy tapping out acknowledgements on his typewriter. PK photographs duly appeared in magazines and newspapers all over Germany, invariably resulting in even more fan mail. A recruiting poster for the Waffen SS appeared; the stern young face beneath the steel helmet resembled Ernst; it must have been painted from one of the photographs taken by the peculiar Max Bosch. Then there was another poster: soldier, sailor, airman, linking arms with a burly factory worker, all four of them marching confidently toward victory, all four of them bearing more than a passing resemblance to Ernst.

The fighting got harder. In some areas the Soviets counter-attacked, achieving local successes. Again and again the fighters went out in horrific conditions to assist. Reuter (who claimed that his father was an intimate friend of Field Marshal Keitel) went down in flames during a mission to escort JU52 transports taking supplies to troops encircled at Demjansk. Lederer collided with a parked PE–2 during a low-level strafing run on a Soviet airfield. Büch spun vertically into a forest at full throttle, apparently shot dead at the controls. A nineteen-year-old named Bulitz arrived one Wednesday morning, took a 109 out for an acclimatization flight at 13:35 hours and crashed upside down in an icy marsh at 13:41 hours. The reason remained a mystery but Schiegl wrote Bulitz's parents that their son had died a glorious death in action fighting for the Fatherland and that he would be sorely missed by his many friends in the unit.

At last, miraculously, the cruel grip of winter was loosened by the spring sun. The field was flooded; the water couldn't drain beneath the ground because it was still frozen. Ironically the Ivans came to the Germans' aid, flying low over the field and dropping bombs. The flood water rapidly disappeared into the new craters. The field was soon operational again.

*

Major Roder had managed to put on a surprisingly good meal. His servant, a slow-talking Saxon named Schwartz, attended in white jacket. The tablecloth was heavily starched, the silver glittering. But Major Roder's hut stank. Of excrement. Of sweat. Of dirt. Of animals. Of vermin. Of head and cold and age and death.

'Schwartz's tried everything,' said Roder as he sipped his Frascati. 'But still the stink persists. The only solution is to burn the damned place down and start all over again. Which, in my opinion, is true of the whole of Russia.' He smiled in his stiff, slightly affected way.

Ernst smiled in return, nodding as Roder declared that it had been on his mind for some time to have Ernst to dinner.

'It's one of the problems of command, keeping in really close touch with one's men.'

'I'm sure it must be, sir.'

'You're doing extraordinarily well.'

'Thank you, sir.'

'I think I can safely say that it won't be long before you're wearing the Knight's Cross.'

Ernst felt his cheeks burn. 'Thank you, sir.'

To wear the coveted Knight's Cross was every serviceman's dream. The black cross, 48 mm square, cast in light metal, was a proclamation that the wearer was a hero *extraordinaire*, a man deserving of the deepest respect – and the best seats in restaurants and cabarets. Only the superlative fighter pilots – men of the calibre of Mölders and Galland – wore the Knight's Cross at their throats.

'I hardly need tell you, my dear Brehme, how delighted I am to have you under my command.'

'I'm pleased to be here, sir.'

'Glad to hear it,' said Roder. 'Very glad. HQ is greatly influenced by success in the field – after all, how else can they measure efficiency? A pilot of your calibre not only does an excellent job of increasing the unit's total score, he also acts as a catalyst, an inspiration, if you will, to the others. I can assure you that there are no pilots in this Gruppe who don't dream of exceeding your score. And so I think they try harder, they get in a little closer – in other words they are better at their jobs!' He jabbed the air with a bony forefinger. 'The task we must now address ourselves to is to make the best use of your priceless experience! What we need is a really scientific method of teaching aerial combat. And, my dear Brehme, what better teacher than yourself?'

'I'm no teacher, sir.'

192

'Of course not, I understand perfectly. But I feel sure you are aware of the problem. We're leaving far too much to the individual. We send new pilots up and hope for the best. What I want to do is to *prepare* them for battle just as doctors are prepared for patients' complaints. A worthwhile venture, wouldn't you say?'

'Yes, sir, of course, but . . .'

'Think of it this way, my dear fellow. You possess the knowledge and skill that every pilot needs to succeed – and to survive. Now what can we do to make that knowledge and skill available to those who need it? I look upon you, Brehme, as a vast reservoir, if you get my meaning, a storehouse, a veritable cornucopia of information. What I have in mind is the preparation of a series of bulletins, hints, ideas, that sort of thing. We might think of issuing one a day. Nobody will have any trouble in absorbing one good fact a day! Cumulatively we will have prepared a superb handbook on aerial combat! A bible! Fromm takes shorthand. You can dictate your ideas, then brush up the grammar, that sort of thing, when he types it up.'

'Sir, I really don't want to be considered an expert . . .'

'But you are, my dear Brehme, you most certainly are!'

'Yes but the things that work for me won't necessarily work for everyone else.'

'Well, we just have to make them work!' declared Roder.

'I simply feel that every pilot should fly in the way that best suits him,' Ernst told Dietrich. 'It's wrong to force people. This bulletin idea could really be quite dangerous.'

Dietrich chuckled. 'My dear fellow, Roder isn't thinking about the effect – if any – your wise words will have on the other pilots. That's of practically no importance at all. What really matters is how HQ will react. Roder will bundle up all the pages of the Gospel According to St. Ernst and ship the lot off to HQ. There the big-wigs all see what a brilliant administrator he is. They'll say, "That fellow Roder has a bright future because he exploits the talents he has at his disposal." He'll probably be a general by the end of the year!'

Ernst said, 'And then he'll find himself in your book.'

'Of course. Unwittingly he will make me rich. And I shall live on Majorca and drink far too much wine and chase girls who get younger and younger as I get older and older. I fancy myself as a dissolute old man.' He grinned and rubbed his eyes. He looked weary having flown five sorties since dawn. 'But, come to think of it, in this mad business one likes to think of oneself becoming any sort of an old man. One gets the impression that the Ivans are determined to prevent it.'

He had a point.

The fighting had become vicious as the weather improved. Now the ground was firm enough for tanks and heavy vehicles. The machinery of war could again be deployed. A massive, final assault was said to be in the offing, one that would smash the Reds once and for all.

But there could be no doubt that in the air at least the Soviets were better organized, better equipped and considerably more aggressive than they had been before the onset of that ferocious winter. The new LaGG and Yak fighters appeared in increasing numbers. They were better machines than the Ratas and Chatos that had been shot down in droves the previous year. But still the Luftwaffe far outflew all but the best Russian pilots, the Red Guards. Was it training? Was it temperament? Was it leadership? The questions were discussed endlessly. No one knew the answer but everyone thanked God the questions were still valid.

The weather grew milder; the sun dried the last soggy patches in the field. Ernst shot down a LaGG before breakfast. The Soviet fighter lost both wings as it plunged earthward, hitting a cluster of houses and sending the lot up in flames. When he returned to base his undercarriage refused to work. He jettisoned his canopy and his fuel and glided in to a bumpy but successful dead-stick landing. A PK photographer was on hand; after Ernst had clambered out of the battered 109, the photographer asked if he would be kind enough to get back in the aircraft and then clamber out once more, this time with a cheerier smile on his lips.

He flew to East Prussia to receive his Knight's Cross from the pudgy hands of Hermann Göring. It was, said the Reichsmarschall, a great personal pleasure to present this coveted award for courage to Leutnant Brehme, no one in all the illustrious history of the award had ever deserved it more. The Reichsmarschall's personal aircraft flew Ernst to Wahn field, near Köln. A sizable crowd waited to greet him. There were handshakes, speeches, photographs by the score. He embraced his mother and Maria, then Ilse, looking remarkably appealing in a light blue outfit. The entire world seemed to want to touch him, as if he was a good luck charm.

He didn't see Jeanne. He couldn't telephone her so he wrote a letter explaining his dilemma and hoping that she understood how difficult it was for him. He hoped for more leave shortly. He would definitely come to her at that time.

She wrote to his military address. It was, she said, such a pity he didn't have time to visit during his recent furlough. Then she wrote half a dozen paragraphs about The Sleeping Gypsy by Henri Rousseau.

Enormous armies clashed as the Germans thrust south-east towards the Volga and the oilfields of the Caucasus. The great days of June 1941 seemed to be repeating themselves: the irresistible Blitzkreig, the devastating combination of infantry, tanks and aircraft delivering lightning blows where the enemy least expected them.

The Soviets fell back, leaving a burning wasteland in their wake. Villages, farms, depots – all were put to the torch. The Wehrmacht advanced under a sun that was often obscured by the black ceiling of smoke.

Major Gollob of JG77 became the first pilot in history to achieve a score of one hundred and fifty enemy aircraft destroyed.

For flyers, one week was indistinguishable from the next. They flew countless sorties, settling on new airfields almost daily as they followed the triumphant troops. Ernst's skill was awesome; he became the fourth highest scoring fighter pilot in the Luftwaffe, then the third.

The unit was ordered to return to Germany for rest and refitting.

Five

He was so absurdly happy that he couldn't stem the tears, damn them; they streamed from him as if he had sprung a leak. Thank God the children were at school and so missed this laughable display.

'I'm sorry,' he spluttered. 'I can't think what got into me.'

She was smiling, her head slightly inclined as she absorbed the sight of him. She asked if he would feel better if she cried too; she could if he wished.

He sniffed and shook his head.

'You must think I'm mad . . . I'm where I want to be, the only place in the world where I want to be . . . and you're close and I can reach out and touch you . . . and I can see you and hear you . . . and I'm ruining everything with these ridiculous tears.'

'Does it matter so much to you?'

'I feel foolish.'

'You shouldn't. Even strong, brave soldiers have their limits. You are not made of steel. You are flesh and blood and you have been under terrible stress. Now it is suddenly released.'

He dried his eyes. 'You look marvellous. Are you well? The children too? God, its been so incredibly long since I saw you . . .'

'You look older,' she said.

'You don't. You are as lovely as I remember. Lovelier.'

'But you are just as handsome,' she said.

'But older.'

'A little.'

'I told you I would come to you.'

She nodded, acknowledging the fact. 'Was it difficult for you, to leave your mother?'

'I spent two days there. I told her that I had to attend an important meeting in Paris for a few days. I will see her again for a couple of days more before I go back to my unit. We're getting new airplanes.'

'Are they finer airplanes than you had before?'

'I doubt it. But at least they'll be new. Our present birds are worn out.'

'Like their pilots.'

'Do you think I'm worn out?'

'You look tired.'

'In a very little while, my dear, I'm going to demonstrate that I'm not the least bit tired!'

She smiled and touched his face. They kissed, holding tightly, revelling in the nearness of each other.

It was perfect. She had greeted him joyously. She had been warm and tender every moment. So why did he have that nagging suspicion, that everything was not quite as it should be?

'The English attacked Abbeville,' said Georges. 'I saw them. Spitfires. They were very low. I suppose you don't see Spitfires in Russia.'

'I've seen P–40s and Airacobras,' Ernst told him. 'But not Spitfires, although the Ivans are supposed to have some.'

'Do the Russians have any fighters as good as the Messerschmitt?'

'I don't think so. And I'm glad of it.'

Georges grinned. He had his mother's expressive mouth, so serious one moment, so alive with joy the next.

There was a knock on the front door.

Jeanne called from the kitchen that she would answer it.

Ernst heard her in the hall, unfastening the lock. He heard a man's voice, flat-toned but with a note of familiarity. A neighbour? Ernst could catch no more than the occasional word; Georges was still chattering away about the Spitfires that had flown over the house, so low that the pilots could be seen; one had waved to Georges and had waggled his wings as he streaked overhead . . .

Jeanne closed the front door.

Giselle called from the stairs.

'Who was it?'

'Pardon?'

'Who was at the door?'

'M. Amiel.'

'What did he want?'

'Nothing.'

At supper Giselle said, 'M. Amiel likes my mother.'

He heard himself say, 'Is that so?' Casual. Polite. Almost disinterested. But he felt as if someone had hit him in the stomach.

Jeanne said, 'He likes you too, Giselle. He said so.'

Georges asked, 'Do you think you'll come back to France for good?'

'I hope so,' Ernst told him.

Later, when the children were in bed, he asked her about Amiel. 'Who is he? Why was he calling?'

She shrugged. 'Don't concern yourself about him.'

'Why not?'

'Because I ask you.'

'Who is he?'

Another shrug. 'A man.'

'Does he live nearby?'

'In the village.'

'Why did he come to the house?'

'He's a butcher.'

'A butcher?'

'Yes, is that so strange? I buy meat from him – when he has any to sell.'

'He chooses odd hours for deliveries. He is married?'

'A widower.'

'How convenient.'

She sighed, her eyes closed for a long moment as if she was seeking patience. But when she spoke her voice had lost its edge.

'Please, my dear, let's not talk about this any longer.'

'Why not?'

'There's nothing to talk about.'

'Does he like you?'

'I don't know.'

'Women always know when men like them. You told me that yourself.'

Lips tight again. Voice sharper. 'You remember what you want to remember.'

'What were you talking to him about?'

Her eyes flashed. 'The price of meat! The weather! The god-damned Germans! Now be quiet about it!'

They sat in silence. Then she touched his hand. A breath of fresh air? A walk? He agreed. They went out into the darkness and trudged the quiet fields. It was peaceful, calming.

On the way back, with the pale outline of the house already in view, she said:

'He wants to marry me.'

His blood chilled. 'Why didn't you say so?'

'I didn't want to upset you.'

'Do you love him?'

'No. I feel nothing for him. I hardly know him.'

'Then why does he come to your house?'

'He's lonely. His wife died a year ago. He's a harmless person. I told him I wasn't feeling well. He went away.'

Ernst took her in his arms, pulled her body hard against his.

'You're going to marry me,' he told her. 'I love you and you're mine and I'll kill anyone else who even dares look at you!'

But she didn't laugh as he expected.

She said in an oddly flat voice. 'It's all so simple for you, isn't it?'

'Simple?'

She shrugged in her expressive way. 'You're a hero. You go off to battle and you fly your airplane and you collect your medals.

And when you come down to earth you expect to find me waiting . . .'

'I thought you wanted . . .'

'Please let me finish. This is not easy for me. I feel so much for you – much more, I think, than you can imagine. The last thing in the world I want to do is hurt you. But I have to be realistic. Can you understand that? I have to face facts. I'm not young. I have children, responsibilities. . .'

'I know; I understand.'

'How can you?'

Anger caught him around the neck again; he could feel the fingers tightening, squeezing. 'I suppose your friend Amiel can understand what I can't understand!' He had to cough to clear his throat. 'Damn that swine! Now the two of you are talking about marriage . . . behind my back!'

She said, 'It's true he asked me to marry him. But we hardly know each other. He's a shy person. I think he asked me because he wanted to tell me that his intentions were honourable. Silly . . . someone his age.'

'How old is he?'

'I don't know. About forty-five, I think.'

'God.' Methuselah.

She held his arms, clutching them tightly with both hands. 'Listen to me. Do you really know what sort of relationship we have?'

'Yes . . .'

'Do you? Do you realize that if you're killed I won't know. One day I'll notice that it's been a long time since your last letter. Then I'll wait and wait . . .'

'I'll tell Schiegl to make some arrangement. I never thought . . .'

'Of course you didn't. Why would you ever stop to think of such things? You're not part of my world, my darling. If you survive the war – and I pray to God you will – if you survive you'll probably be a general or something. And do you really think you'll be able to marry a French Jewess, more than ten years your senior, with two children? No, my darling, this is a lovely game we're playing. It's beautiful. I adore every moment of it. But I know it for what it is: a game. I'm your little secret tucked away in France, always waiting for you when you come down from the clouds.'

Numbed, he said, 'I thought if two people felt as we do there is always a way to work their problems out.'

She said. 'You have a girl friend at home in Köln.'

'How do you know?'

'You're famous. Your pictures appear even in the French papers. They write articles about you. And about your pretty girl friend.'

'She means nothing to me.'

'But you see her when you go home?'

'For appearances' sake, nothing else.'

'Have you told her about me? Have you told your mother?'

'No, you see I. . .'

'I don't blame you. It would only cause a lot of awkwardness, wouldn't it – and you see your mother so infrequently. . .'

Christ, she could read his mind.

'I know I'm hurting you, my darling.' Her eyes brimmed as she released his arms and turned away. 'And I don't want to hurt you. But I have to say these things. I have to be honest with you. I have to be frank.' She touched his face. 'You're so beautiful, so strong, but so young. You think this is life. It isn't. Life is working at a dull job. It's saving to buy clothes for children. It's washing and ironing. And buying insurance. Do you understand what I'm saying?'

'I think so,' he said humbly.

'You're the most precious, most wonderful thing that ever happened to me. But you're not *reality*.'

'And Amiel *is* reality?'

'Perhaps. And, my darling, I think you will find reality one day. You'll meet a girl of twenty. You'll wonder, "Why did I waste so much time with that old witch in France?" '

'Don't say such things!'

'I have to.'

'You want to marry this Amiel creature.'

'I don't,' she said.

'But you might marry him,' he persisted.

She shrugged. 'I suppose it's possible.'

He winced as if she had struck him. But the irony was, now that he had reason for tears, he was dry-eyed.

'You must hate me,' she said.

'No,' he told her, 'I feel dead inside. I feel as if you had just killed me.'

Six

Dietrich was concerned. He had never seen Ernst in such a black mood. 'The fellow is virtually unapproachable,' he noted in his journal. 'Grim-faced, silent, he goes about his duties with all the enthusiasm of a prisoner on his way to the scaffold. The problem is undoubtedly his French girl friend. The affair had to disintegrate sooner or later. I knew it. I even told him so. But of course he informed me that it was none of my business. No doubt he'll get over it as everyone always does get over this sort of thing; but knowing him, I suspect he'll take an inordinate time about it.

'We are currently refitting with new F-3 models of the 109, powered by DB 601E engines that use 87 octane B4 fuel instead of the 96 octane C3 fuel on the earlier model. A little more power but a little more weight. It's the same old story; the designers can't resist adding a kilo here, a kilo there. And more weight means less manoeuvrability. Perhaps we'll get the FW 190 one day.

'In addition to obtaining new aircraft we are also replenishing our sadly depleted complement of pilots. We look them over. We study their log books. Poor bastards. The sad truth is, the Eastern Front has been gobbling up pilots more rapidly than the training schools can turn them out. This obviously is a state of affairs that no self-respecting bureaucrat can put up with. What's the answer? Well, clearly the whole training process must be streamlined and brought thoroughly up to date. Concentrate the courses! Condense the instruction time! Teach the absolute essentials! Ignore all the frills! The result is that nowadays the instructors are being forced to send pilots to the front-line units with fewer and fewer hours' experience. While this presumably satisfies some bureaucratic balance book at the Air Ministry, it only succeeds in exacerbating the problem in Russia, because the ill-trained men invariably fall before they have learned to survive, leaving gaps to be filled by new men with even less time in their log books . . .

'We regard the fresh young faces with some suspicion, for these men are unknown quantities, a different species until they prove themselves in combat. One's life might well depend upon one of these eager young flyers in their crisp new uniforms, their pilots badges still bright. Statistically it is certain that one of them will lose his nerve the first time an Ivan fires a gun at him. In all probability three out of four of them will be dead within six months.

'There is a cocky one, supremely confident of his ability to knock down Ivans by the score and become the toast of the nation. A nervous one, with torn fingernails, stomach doing loops as he considers the frightening uncertainties that lie ahead. There is a studious one, intent on every word uttered by his CO, a humorous one, whispering witticisms to his comrades, a dedicated one, thinking only of his Führer and the opportunity he has to serve the Fatherland.

'The usual mixture.'

How could she be so damned cruel? What had he done to deserve such treatment? Damn her, she had *turned* on him! She virtually *blamed* him for being an airman! Was it his fault that he had to go to the front? Did he choose to go? Did he have a choice?

His head pounded. It felt as if it would explode. He wished it would. No more hideous nightmares: Jeanne and Amiel, pink and naked, bodies in passionate contact, limbs intertwined, her hand on his erect organ, her mouth gaping and smiling with joy; Amiel, ancient, grey-haired, vile body lined and baggy . . .

God, a man could go completely mad hounded by such thoughts. It had all seemed so perfect; she kept telling him she loved him. Now this. Was it because she was French and Jewish? Did she hate Germans so much? Had she led him on simply to plunge him into despair?

No, it was impossible to believe it of her.

Not Jeanne.

But why in God's name did she do this?

The first new-boy, the jokester, spun into a field, engine screaming at full bore. He was instantly reduced to unidentifiable fragments, a finger here, a toe there. He had been attacking a Stormovik. It was his third sortie. Presumably he had been shot dead at the controls by the Russian gunner. A week later to the day, the nervous one went down in flames. He jumped. But his parachute didn't open. He plunged into trees behind the Soviet lines. A letter went to his parents in Kassel regretting that he had been posted missing in action and that further information would be forwarded as soon as it became available. None did.

The patriot, Fleuth by name, became Ernst's shadow, eager to learn every trick of the trade from an acknowledged master. Tirelessly he sought Ernst's advice on every aspect of aerial combat. What could he do to improve his shooting eye? Were head-on

202

attacks recommended? Would Ernst always abandon a sortie if his R/T became unserviceable? Was it wise to continue to glance behind even during an attack? Was it better to dive away after an attack or skid away? How could one learn to spot the enemy more rapidly?

He vanished in a smear of flame and smoke that trailed across the bright blue sky, held its form for a few moments then quickly disappeared as if it had never been.

'You'll get over it,' said Dietrich.

Ernst looked up from the book he had been reading but not absorbing. 'Get over what?'

'It,' said Dietrich. 'I know it hurts like hell. Aches. Stings. It's worse than a toothache. Feels as if it's going to drive you around the bend. That's wounded pride, dented self-esteem. It'll mend. You'll recover. Everyone does.'

'I don't know what you're talking about,' said Ernst.

Dietrich shrugged elaborately. 'Very well, I won't say another word on the subject.'

'Good.'

Ernst stared at the page; the words formed sentences which became paragraphs and pages. But none of it made sense. He kept reading the same words over and over again.

Silence for five minutes, broken only by the sighing of the wind outside.

'What a curious fellow you are,' chuckled Dietrich at last. 'Millions of women all over Europe are wetting themselves just thinking about you. They'd jump into bed with you at a moment's notice. You could have a different one each night for the next ten years. But no, you're only interested in your Frenchwoman! She must be a marvel.'

Ernst said nothing for a moment. He considered ignoring Dietrich's remark completely. But Dietrich meant well.

'She's unusual,' he admitted, placing a book-mark at the page he had been reading.

'She must be.'

'She says she has no future with me.'

'Smart girl. She's quite right, of course. The trouble is, you don't want to admit it. Women are remarkable creatures. They're simultaneously romantic and pragmatic. It's a terrifying combination for a mere male to contend with.'

'I know you mean well . . .'

'I make a point of never meaning well,' said Dietrich with that smirk of self-satisfaction that signified the creation of yet another *bon mot*.

This one irritated Ernst rather than amused him.

'This is none of your damned business!'

'True,' said Dietrich, 'that's why it's so intensely interesting. Besides, I'd like to help if I can, bring to bear some of my own ghastly errors. . .'

Anger seemed to explode in Ernst's chest. Dietrich was a target, someone on whom to vent his frustrated anger.

'Keep your mouth shut! That's all I ask of you! I don't need your damned smart remarks or your advice. . !'

The PE–2 dissolved in a great fountain of flame. The blast from the explosion thudded into the flanks of Ernst's aircraft, sending is skidding, shuddering.

As Ernst fought to regain control he saw the man.

A spinning figure, arms flopping loosely, grotesquely.

Damned nearly tumbled into the 109's propeller.

Missed by less than a metre.

For a scintilla of an instant Ernst found himself gazing into the Russian's eyes. A big man. Broad, strong face, apparently un-harmed by the ghastly fire-ball out of which he had fallen. Indeed there seemed to be no damage to the upper half of his body.

But nothing remained of the lower half. He had been sliced cleanly as if by some giant knife.

Was the Russian still alive when he spun past Ernst's aircraft? Did he see? Did he comprehend? Did he *feel*?

That night he saw the poor bastard of a Russian. Again and again. But in the lunatic way of dreams the Russian had become a Frenchman, Amiel. And the Frenchman was grovelling about on Jeanne spreading an unspeakable smear of bloody entrails all over her white body. . .

In the morning they rendezvous'd with a formation of Ju 87s. Escort duty. A dirty job: protecting the vulnerable dive bombers against Soviet fighters. The bombers' task was the destruction of a wooden bridge in map sector 4J, 12A6, a tactical necessity if the advance was to be maintained. Heads would unquestionably roll if the bridge was not destroyed as ordered.

The entire Staffel took to the air, Roder leading.

A grey, overcast day. The landscape looked as if it had been photographed in black and white. No; there was a touch of colour;

a small barn on the bank of the river possessing a roof of bright orange. An uncommon sight in this bleak land.

The flak opened up as soon as they were over the target. Heavy stuff. And accurate. A Ju was hit. It lurched, spouting flame. Then it fell to pieces and plunged, bits of wing and tail in fluttering pursuit. The remains crashed into the bank of the river, missing the bridge by only a few metres.

The German fighters attacked the flak emplacements, sweeping low over troops and tanks, lining up the targets, firing short bursts, conserving precious ammunition in case Soviet fighters put in an appearance. The Ivans knew the value of that bridge, damn them. They sent up solid walls of flak. Christ only knows how anyone flew through it in one piece.

Bombs exploded in great spouts of water to the left of the bridge and to the right. But not on it. One bloody miss after another.

Ernst circled low over the river. The bridge still stood. Flimsy looking thing. One bomb would do the trick. Reduce the damned thing to matchwood.

Another near miss.

Ernst glanced up as the last angular-winged Stuka began its plunge. The pilot, having closed his radiator flaps and switched off his supercharger, was now intent on lining up his target with the red lines painted on the side panels of his cockpit canopy, like Plimsoll lines on a ship. If he missed, if the bridge survived (no matter how many airmen didn't), the sortie would have to be flown again. HQ would insist on it, indifferent to reports on the volume and accuracy of flak. Destruction of the bridge was vital; it justified the loss of any number of airmen.

Down, down, down.

The bomb fell free. Retract air brakes! Throttle back! Open radiator shutters! The plunging Stuka began to pull out, then staggered, burst into flames and spun earthward.

But its bomb hit the target!

Or did it? Disappointment quickly followed elation. When the smoke cleared it was clear that the bomb had indeed struck the bridge, but its point of impact was at the extreme end of the structure, just where it met the road. The bridge itself still stood.

Another 87 became a casualty. It wobbled; black, oily smoke streamed from its engine. Inexplicably, it turned back, staggered across the river, straight towards the Ivans. God knows why the flak didn't blow it out of the air. Every gun in the area opened up on the poor labouring cripple. It was hit! It staggered, leaving a trail of smoke. One man jumped; his chute opened. The aircraft flew on, then turned. Neatly, it rolled on to one wing, then hurtled earthward. Flak peppered the sky around it, but still it plunged. It hit the bridge in the centre of the span, bringing the entire structure down in an eruption of splintered timber.

When the fighters landed, the ground crews were busy organizing yet another move. To a field named Morosovsk. Near Stalingrad.

Seven

A gigantic pall of smoke hung motionless over the city. It was as if the very air had died, yet another casualty of the conflict. The savage blooding had continued, intensifying day by day, as the blazing summer days gave way to the chilly winds of autumn. Every house, every room, was a battlefield. Ivans died, burnt to a crisp by flame throwers, defending a doorway as if behind them was the Kremlin itself. Germans by the hundreds fell as they advanced across a street, a few miserable metres. Rumour had it that Stalin had ordered that the city bearing his name was to be held no matter what the cost. So reinforcements poured in from the east – troops, tanks, vehicles, supplies – to strengthen the defences of Stalingrad. At the same time, the Germans sent more men and armour to hasten the fall of the place. Hitler was as determined to take it as Stalin was to defend it. And so the horror of a city kept consuming human beings like some ghastly mincing machine.

Daily the fighters took off from Morosovsk. Sometimes they escorted the Heinkels and Junkers that bombed the city incessantly. Sometimes they flew tactical sorties, attacking specific targets on the ground, screaming at rooftop height over acres of desolation, blazing away at a shell of a building that housed a mortar battery, pinning down Soviet soldiers as they attempted to move about among the mountains of smoking rubble.

The Ivans were putting new aircraft into the battle: the La–5 and Yak–9 fighters and some of the Hurricanes, Kittyhawks and Airacobras that their British and American allies had been shipping to them by the boat-load.

Street by street the Germans advanced, pushing the Russians back or killing them where they stood. The fighting was vicious, merciless. Bitter hatred for the enemy seemed to motivate men as much as love of country. In Germany the papers kept announcing that the city was virtually won; it was merely a matter of accounting for a few isolated pockets of resistance, here and there.

'Our star performer continues to astound everyone,' Dietrich wrote. 'He is the complete professional, superbly economical with ammunition, timing every move, every turn like a ballet dancer who has performed this same routine many thousands of times and knows precisely what to do and when to do it. I admire him enormously, but I am worried about him. He has become uncommonly introspective; he still broods over that damned Frenchwoman. Meanwhile accolades continue to pour in. Visiting generals – German, Italian, Hungarian, Finnish – come to shake his hand and be photographed with him. The PK men are forever haunting him with their cameras. Any day now he'll be promoted to Captain; undoubtedly he will replace Roder as CO.

'It's sad how little it all seems to mean to him. He does what is asked of him; he smiles when he is asked to smile; he salutes at the appropriate time and says the appropriate thing. Then he goes off by himself to sketch or read. He wades through Goethe and Schiller. He seems to be searching for a meaning to it all. Aren't we all? God, we have become a sober lot since we came here to Stalingrad. There is something about this city, something about the sheer brutality of the battle that infects everyone. Why, we fly continuously, usually at low level; it's a rare day when we don't encounter Ivans. In the evenings we simply sit exhausted, semi-comatose, listening to our few records, drinking whatever is available. Our accommodation is a collection of stinking little Russian huts – yet they are luxurious compared with the holes the infantry have to live in.

'It is turning colder. In the morning we find our aircraft glinting with frost. Puddles are frozen solid. The winds are already stinging like whips. What seemed unthinkable has happened: another winter in Russia. God, how we detest it. We begin to feel that we will never leave it; men and machines will continue to grind each other to pieces in this awful place until nothing is left alive anywhere in Europe.

'They are equipping us with new aircraft. Our weary old Friedrichs are to be relegated to the training schools and the scrapheap. In their place, the 109 'G' – the 'Gustav'.

'A Technical Officer came to introduce us to our new mounts. He was like a bespectacled Father Christmas, pudgy and rosy-cheeked. "You've got a great deal more power at your disposal," he told us, eyes a-twinkle. "They've redesigned the cylinder block to obtain the maximum bore and yet at the same time maintain the original cylinder centres. And a most efficient job they've done, too. The compression ratio has increased: 7.3 for the port cylinder block and 7.5 for the starboard block. Your maximum permissible revs are now up to 2800." He informed us of these facts in the manner of a headmaster granting an extra half-day holiday. "You'll note that the cockpit canopy has been redesigned for pressurization – a sign of the things to come, let me add. And a final item that will interest you: the GM–1 nitrous oxide injection system for extra power when you need it."

'A pair of the factory-fresh fighters had been delivered; we had examined and flown them. And we were somewhat less than enthusiastic; the Messerschmitt engineers have unquestionably provided their aging fighter with more power and heavier armament but in so doing they have added a disturbing amount to the weight. Every extra kilo has the machine a little less manoeuvrable and therefore a little more vulnerable. The fuselage sports a great bump, a fairing for the breechblocks of our new 13 mm MG 131 machine guns. No one likes the changes in the cockpit. In order to strengthen the canopy for pressurization, the designers have thickened the structural members. Thus they have reduced visibility from the cockpit. Doesn't anyone realize how important visibility is? Why weren't the pilots consulted before all these changes were made? Why can't we keep the Friedrich? Or better still, the Emil?

'The Technical Officer nodded as he listened to our comments. He'd heard them before. You could see the fat chump thinking: Pilots are all the same: reactionaries, suspicious of change, clinging to the tried and true. An odd breed.'

Three trucks trundled on to the field one bitter afternoon. They disgorged a quartet of dancers, a magician, a comedian, a juggler, a girl singer, a piano accordionist, a violinist and a plump gentleman who played the drums.

The show took place in a hangar that evening, the performers using a stage that had been hastily assembled earlier in the day.

The orchestra was strident, the dancers enthusiastic; the comedian told joke after joke, each dirtier than the last; the magician seemed bored; the juggler seemed frightened. The girl singer – her name was Ursula Schreiter – was petite and pretty; she sang of tender farewells and joyous reunions, of faithful sweethearts and the perfect happiness that was waiting for everyone just around the next corner. She had an appealing catch in her voice that could bring a tear to any eye. The audience adored her.

At the end of the show Fräulein Schreiter told the airmen that it had been a privilege for the company to perform before the men of the Eastern Front. Valiant heroes, all. Constantly in the thoughts of everyone at home. Their heroic deeds the subject of every conversation, stirring every German heart. Familiar words but she made them fresh and vital.

'And no one,' she declared, shoulders braced, arms outstretched, 'has stirred more German hearts than a man who is here tonight. You all know who I mean. The ace of aces, the terror of the Red Air Force, Leutnant Ernst Brehme!'

Thunderous applause.

She appealed to the front row where the officers sat. Would the Leutnant be good enough to stand? 'We would count it a great privilege if he would come forward, up on stage, so that we performers might meet him.'

'He's here!' someone yelled, pointing.

'Don't be shy!' someone else yelled.

Reluctantly Ernst got to his feet and went forward, to the accompaniment of good-natured cheers and applause.

The performers were lined up on stage, the men paunchy and middle-aged, wearing seedy dinner jackets, thinning hair carefully dyed; the female dancers were panting and sweaty, their make-up blotchy. Only Ursula Schreiter looked as delightful at close quarters as she had from a distance. She grinned charmingly and took Ernst's hand as he clambered up on to the stage. She thanked him for coming forward – and promptly gave him a resounding kiss on the lips, to the delight of the assembled airmen and soldiers.

Ernst thanked her.

'That kiss,' she declared, 'was on behalf of every German woman I have ever met. I can assure you, handsome, charming Leutnant Brehme, that there are several million women in Germany who are ready and eager to deliver more of the same, in person!' The audience howled; Ursula Schreiter knew her audience; she had them at her command. She told them how girls had tried to stow away with the company on hearing that there was a chance of meeting the redoubtable Ernst Brehme. It was nonsense, of course, and everyone knew it. But it was what was needed in that place, at that time.

Afterwards there was a party in the Operations Room. The orderlies had found a few bottles of Henkeltrocken and some Dortmunder beer. Müller, the cook, managed to create a plateful of unidentifiable but reasonably tasty canapes for the occasion. The entire unit was singularly proud to demonstrate its appreciation of the entertainers' efforts, Roder proclaimed, already a trifle wobbly on his feet. The evening, he said, had been a delight; never had such welcome visitors crossed the threshold of their humble quarters. . . . He rambled on through scattered applause and boos. At last he stopped, looked about as if to remind himself where he was, and sat down.

Someone started the gramophone. A young pilot named Meister asked Ursula Schreiter to dance. Smilingly she accepted. In a moment the other girls were dancing too. The male members of the troupe sat in a corner with glasses of beer and watched the proceedings in the disinterested, almost unseeing way of men who watch the same thing happen night after night.

'Nice of them to come,' Roder kept saying. 'Damned nice.'

He talked as if the entertainment troupe had journeyed to the field on a general whim, at their own expense.

Ernst refused another drink. He had to fly in the morning.

'Let's pray for stinking weather,' muttered Roder conspiratorially then dissolved in guilty laughter at his own daring.

'Aren't you going to ask me to dance, Leutnant?'

Ursula Schreiter stood with one hand on her hip. She was prettily flushed after her exertions with Meister.

'I don't dance,' Ernst confessed.

She thought that remarkable. But she said she would be only too happy to teach him.

'I shouldn't bother if I were you. He has an incredibly poor sense of rhythm.'

Dietrich. Hand in pocket. Hair tumbling over his forehead.

'I, on the other hand,' he said, 'am a superb dancer. And I will be only too happy to demonstrate the fact. But before doing so, may I tell you how much I enjoyed the show. To be frank, Fräulein Schreiter, I didn't expect much. In my experience military concert party shows are about as thrilling as visits to the dentist. And to be frank again, most of this evening's performance did little to change my opinion. And then you came on. You have a unique way with a song. I know. I have good taste in matters musical. For example I was impressed by the way you changed key twice in the last sixteen bars of one song. Very neat. Very professional. I suppose it must be an instinct, that ability to project emotion. You do it very well.'

Ernst moved away, leaving Dietrich to his conquest. The party was gathering momentum; there would be some thick heads in the morning.

Outside it was cold, the stars bright and hard in the frigid sky. He flipped his coat collar up. A sentry saluted; Ernst wished him good night. In the distance the thud of guns could be heard. At Stalingrad the killing went on twenty-four hours a day.

He walked along the wooden duckboard path.

'Leutnant Brehme.'

He turned. A girl's voice. Ursula Schreiter came hurrying along the path. She wore a pilot's fur jacket; it was far too large for her but it suited her delightfully.

'Where are you going?' she asked.

'To bed.'

'So early?'

'I have to fly first thing in the morning.'

'Where do you have to fly to?'

Ernst smiled. 'There,' he said, pointing in the direction of the gunfire.

'We have to leave tomorrow,' she told him. 'We're going to a place called Lugansk.'

'I hope you come back soon.'

'Do you?'

'Of course. Dietrich too.'

'He was a nice fellow,' she said. Past tense. 'It's cold out here,' she said. 'Would you like to have a glass of cognac? I have some good stuff, French.'

'But the party . . . it's in your honour.'

'Too many people,' she said. 'Well?'

He started to shake his head, to refuse and leave her. But her eyes were roaming his face just as Jeanne's eyes had once done. He followed her to one of the huts that had been provided for the entertainers; it was sparsely furnished but comfortable by the standards of Russia. She asked him to excuse the mess; her suitcase was open on the bunk; there were several costumes hanging

211

from the ceiling, a jumble of make-up on the washstand. She closed the case; and put it on the floor.

'Please sit down. There,' she added, indicating the bunk.

'Do you come from a theatrical family?'

'No. My father is a machinist. And yours?'

'My father died nearly three years ago.'

'I'm sorry.' She poured the cognac.

'To your very good health.'

'And yours.'

She said. 'You're not married.'

'No.'

'I thought not. The last newspaper article I read about you said you weren't. But you must have a special girl friend.'

'I did once,' he said. 'Not now.'

She shook her head in wonderment. 'I bet women are throwing themselves at you all the time.' Her voice had become slightly husky. 'God, you're a lovely man, Leutnant Brehme.' She studied his features. 'You're quite perfect. You look as if they took you off a Grecian urn. I think you're the handsomest man I've ever seen.'

There was an intriguingly matter-of-fact way in which she spoke, simultaneously tough and tender.

'You're beautiful,' he said, the brandy warming him.

She shook her head. 'I'm pretty,' she said. 'And I'm sexy. But not beautiful.'

Her face was close to his. He kissed her lips. She closed her eyes and murmured appreciatively. God, the closeness of her was exciting as hell! She smelt delicious; he'd forgotten how intoxicatingly a woman could smell . . .

She didn't resist when he kissed her again, when his hand wandered to her breasts and slipped down the front of her dress to touch her hardening nipples.

'You touch well,' she said. 'Shall I leave the light on?'

'Yes.'

'You want to see what you're doing?'

'Yes, I suppose so.'

She nodded approvingly, smiling. 'Would you like to help me unbutton my dress?'

'I would like that very much,' Ernst told her.

'You have beautiful hands,' she said, touching them.

'You have beautiful breasts,' he said.

'Yes,' she said, looking down at them as they were recent acquisitions. 'They are nice, aren't they?'

*

'I owe my life to the bastard,' Dietrich noted in his journal. 'It's quite impossible to deny the fact yet it's equally impossible to thank him for what he did. We were busy with a formation of Stormoviks and Kittyhawks. They caught us flatfooted. Meister went down in flames, nose-dived straight into the ground and blew himself to smithereens. The next moment I found my aircraft being ripped apart. A cannon shell hit the armour plating panel behind my head, almost tearing it off, twisting it as if it was made of putty. Without it I would certainly have been decapitated. Half my instruments had vanished from the panel; the cockpit started to fill with smoke. I remember thinking: Damn, not today! I wasn't expecting it today! A strange sense of outrage gripped me. This wasn't fair! Temporary madness, of course. The brain responds in odd ways when it decides that death is imminent. There were two Ivans behind me, blazing away for all they were worth. I was a sitting duck, as good as dead.

'Then in a matter of perhaps three seconds, it was all over. Both my assailants were heading earthwards, burning. Our hero had struck again in his inimitable quick-fire style.

' "All right?" he called me. I could see him in the cockpit, looking in my direction.

'I told him I was unharmed and that the smoke in my cockpit was clearing. I didn't thank him for what he did. I couldn't. I was still too furious with him for stealing Ursula away. That's what he did, *stole* her. He escorted me back to base. When we landed we walked away from our aircraft without exchanging a word. Childish behaviour; no other way to describe it. We had been friends a long time. But it's over. I hate him, literally *hate* him, when I remember Ursula running after him. But I think I hate that Jewish bitch in France most of all; she's a continent away and yet she's managing to destroy him, bit by bit . . .'

Eight

The snow bestowed a short-lived beauty on the battlefield, blanketing the corpses and the mountains of rubble. The snow sparkled as the sun emerged, countless billions of jewels packed in

213

layers, hills and valleys, smoothing and softening the angular profile of battle. But pity the poor bastards fighting down there, crouching in their holes, ducking behind doorways, clutching their ears as high explosive sent the snow dancing in to the sunlight and tossed up old bodies and bricks that had been turned over a hundred times. The temperature plummeted, to zero, then far below. Troops lit fires in braziers as they waited for the next assault. Wounded men died where they lay, frozen solid, limbs stiff as boards.

Catastrophe had overtaken the German Army. After capturing more than three-quarters of the city of Stalingrad the Wehrmacht had been unable to advance another metre. The Soviets held them, fought them to a standstill. Then they attacked. Their losses were appalling but still they came, swarming out of foxholes, leaping over debris blazing away with their PPSh submachine guns. The Germans fell back. Street by street, building by building, losing all the territory they had won at such horrific cost in earlier months. On the outskirts of the city Soviet armour began a giant pincer movement. A quarter of a million troops, the entire Sixth Army under General Friedrich Paulus, was encircled.

Now the impossible was to be attempted: supplying the Sixth Army by air, flying in six hundred tons of fuel and ammunition and weapons and food. Daily. The Luftwaffe field commanders said it was impossible. But Berlin said it must be done; the Führer wished it. So the transports were summoned from every front. Three-engined Junkers arrived from the Middle East, still bearing their desert camouflage; ambulance machines wore Red Crosses on their wings and fuselages; there were training aircraft flown by boys with fewer than a hundred hours in their log books, ancient Junkers ready for the scrap heap and aircraft so new that they lacked radio equipment; there were bombers, reconnaissance machines, communications aircraft, anything that was remotely capable of serving as transports.

The JU 52s materialized through a curtain of snow flurries, wobbling, swaying, buffeted by angry, capricious winds.

Ernst banked and turned across their path, displaying his wing markings to reassure the transport pilots – and the gunners. The 'Aunties' flew in loose formation, an aerial convoy laden with sufficient supplies to enable the beleaguered Sixth Army to fight and live for about twelve hours.

Soviet flak peppered the sky. The Ivans had stationed scores of guns along the route into Stalingrad: a gauntlet of fire of nearly two hundred kilometres. The transports flew from Tazinskaya to the landing field at Pitomnik within the city of Stalingrad. At any point during the journey, Red Air Force fighters were likely to put in an appearance, the pilots only too eager to add to their scores by knocking down a couple of doddering tri-motors.

The Messerschmitts kept circling, unable to reduce their speed to that of their charges without simply tumbling out of the air. No sign of Soviet fighters, thank God. The weather was problem enough without having predatory Ivans to contend with. The transports ploughed on through the muck, homing in on the beacon at Pitomnik. When the airlift began, transports had flown in one at a time. But too many had been shot down en route; thus the convoy system was instituted, just as the Allies had organized convoys for their shipping because of the threat of U-boats. But the system compounded the ground handling problems. Pitomnik, an advance fighter base, possessed no facilities for handling a couple of dozen transports at a time. The result was that the transports had to wait in line to be unloaded – wasting precious time and even more precious fuel. Pitomnik was a pilot's nightmare, its treacherous landing strip nothing but packed, frozen snow. The whole area was dotted with wrecked aircraft, twisted, burnt-out carcasses, every item of salvageable equipment long since torn out for use by the trapped starving soldiers of the Sixth Army.

A Ju was hit!

It lurched, staggered, tipping on to one wing. Smoke streamed from the port engine. Flames licked about the cowling, battered into fierce intensity by the howling slipstream.

Ernst winced as he watched. But there was nothing he could do for the poor bastard of a pilot except wish him luck. The orders were unequivocal: fighters were forbidden to escort damaged transports that failed to maintain their positions. The fighters' responsibility was to the survivors, those who still had a chance of getting through. Stragglers had to be left to their fate.

The Ju was turning, still streaming smoke. Cartons tumbled from the aircraft's rear door, the crew frantically dumping the cargo in an effort to lighten the wounded bird. But it was hopeless. The Ju kept descending, its angle increasing as it rolled slowly, until its broad wing was almost vertical to the ground. Now the flames had taken their greedy grip on the wings and fuselage. The doomed aircraft disappeared into the flurries to become a glow slipping steadily earthward until it vanished.

A sudden glint of sun as Pitomnik came near, peeping between giant mountains of cloud. The air was viciously bumpy. The aircraft pitched and tossed, pilots labouring to keep their overloaded craft upright.

Damned flak. Carpets of it, black pimples in the air. Fly too close to one of those pimples and one could smell the explosion as one heard the patter of razor-toothed steel fragments hitting wing and tail.

'Indians dead ahead!'

Christ! Yes, there they were. Bastards! Coming in for the kill! Some would latch themselves on the tails of the ponderous transports. Others would prefer to wait until their victims were on the final approach to the tiny, slippery strip, even more pathetically vulnerable than they had been during the trip in from Tazi.

'Follow me! We'll head them off.'

'Victor!'

The glittering white ground tilted. Glimpses of burned-out trucks and tanks. Huddled soldiery. White faces turned up toward the hurtling aircraft. Ahead, Pitomnik field, the single icy strip splashed by sudden sunshine. Beyond, the city, the vast charnel-house.

The Soviet fighters scattered as the 109s tore into them. Ernst hit one on his first run. A red-starred wing folded and ripped away. The fighter whirled into a frantic spin. The pilot jumped. His parachute unfolded, only to flare, an impotent flutter of white that followed the man to the ground.

Ernst dived away then climbed, turning.

There! One of the Ivans had slipped through the 109s and was harrying a Ju 52, like a savage wolf at a plodding carthorse. Murdering swine! Ernst skidded the 109 mercilessly to line up the target. Already the Ju was shuddering as the Russian's bullets sliced through its fragile flanks. But Ernst had the LaGG in his reflector sight. Now! A quick burst. Perfect! The Ivan became a ball of fire. He reared. Stalled. Tumbled. Disintegrated in a shower of sparkling fragments.

A Ju 52 went down in flames rolling helplessly from side to side, great almost-vertical banks. Some poor gallant, agonized soul was still at the controls, trying to get the wounded tri-motor down in some semblance of a landing. But he failed. The transport rolled over on to its back, the fixed undercarriage thrusting skyward as flames consumed the wings. Then it was all over. Fire and snow mingled in an instant of horrific beauty as the Ju smashed headlong into the ground a mere kilometre short of the strip.

More Ivans came pouring in! God almighty, why did the weather have to choose this precise moment to clear? The damned sun was beaming down, almost blindingly bright. Blue skies! Clouds vanishing! A single-engined fighter plummeted, wreathed in flame. Aircraft came skidding in every direction, flashing before startled eyes. It was like a lunatic air display for the benefit of the gaunt remnants of the Sixth Army huddled in their icy foxholes. Desperately the transports descended, making for the minuscule landing strip. But as each one lined up for the landing, a Russian fighter – a Rata or one of the new LaGGs – would fasten itself on to its unprotected tail. Then in turn the Ivan would be attacked by a 109. Then sometimes another Ivan would pounce upon the 109. Tracers danced through the dazzling sunlight.

One Ju landed with flames eating at the wings. Bumping, bouncing, it slewed off the strip and careered into the centre of the field. Ground crewmen dashed for the burning transport. But before they reached it there was a massive explosion; the big aircraft dissolved in fire.

Ernst shot down a Rata as it fired at a Ju. The Soviet fighter snapped into a dive and crashed headlong into a 109. Locked in a blazing embrace the two fighters tumbled, parts fluttering in the sunshine like leaves on a bright autumn day.

Incredible that there weren't more collisions. Incredible that every aircraft didn't hit every other aircraft. There simply wasn't enough air to contain them all.

A Ju touched down safely. But a Soviet LaGG came screaming in pursuit, trying to kill the transport even after it had landed. A 109 opened fire. Hit the Ivan in the cockpit area. The LaGG flew straight into the ground, bouncing, streaming flame, smashing headlong into a pair of Heinkels parked to the side of the landing strip. And now the stupid flak gunners were firing at the 109! Firing at their own aircraft! Madness! Ernst found himself bellowing at the German gunners. Stupid waste of breath! He was becoming as crazy as everyone else! Another Ju managed to put down on the snow-packed strip, somehow evading the Soviets who swarmed about the field like mosquitoes in summer.

Someone else went down in flames to vanish in an eruption of fire. No way of telling if it was friend or foe. No time to worry about it one way or the other. Time only for attacking or evading. Killing or being killed.

A Ju ground-looped as it touched down. No doubt the aircraft was flown by one of the inexperienced youngsters dragged out of training school for the airlift. The poor devil simply didn't know how to handle a Ju in a violent crosswind, on a short, impossibly slippery strip. The transport lost its undercarriage and squatted gracelessly on the snow, revolving three, four, five times before finally coming to rest. No fire, thank you, Jesus, for your mercy. Now the ground crewmen would drain every last litre of fuel from the Ju's tanks, rip out its radio equipment and then cannibalize its remains to keep other aircraft serviceable.

A Soviet fighter tried to machine-gun the ground crews as they clustered around the wrecked Ju. Ernst saw him in time. Banked. Fired. The La-5 dropped a wing and dived vertically into the frozen ground.

Ernst glanced at his ammunition counter. Zero. Every last round gone. And the fuel situation would soon become critical.

Time to turn for home.

He pressed the transmit button on his control column.

His engine stopped.

Nine

Colonel Wilde adjusted his trousers as he sat down. He wondered how long he would have to wait. One could never tell. A secretary at the opposite end of the room spared him only a fleeting glance before returning to her typing. She was dumpy and remarkably unattractive. Odd. There was a time when the Reichsmarschall had only the prettiest women on his staff; he insisted on it, personally selecting each individual.

But times had changed. Possibly the formidable Frau Göring had had something to do with it.

A door opened. Footsteps. A bespectacled officer, clutching sheaves of paper, hurried importantly through the waiting room without looking to the left or right.

Colonel Wilde cleared his throat. Not long now. The question was: what was the Reichsmarschall's mood this morning? Damned unpredictable, the fat one. The soul of affability one day, a tyrant the next, a self-pitying nincompoop the following day.

'The Reichsmarschall will see you shortly, Herr Oberst.'

To Wilde's surprise the girl had a charming voice, low-pitched and moderately sexy.

He thanked her; she started to respond, then there was a movement next door; at once she became intent on her typewriter, scowling at it, her porky fingers jabbing at the keys as if punishing them.

Even the secretaries were edgy at Luftwaffe HQ these days. It was a difficult period. Stalingrad had fallen. A quarter of a million men – the entire Sixth Army – had surrendered and trudged away to God only knows what fate. They had surrendered because they no longer had ammunition or food. The Luftwaffe had failed to supply them. No matter that the task was completely beyond the air force's capability. The Reichsmarschall had promised. And the promise had not been fulfilled. Worse, the debacle had virtually wiped out the Luftwaffe's transport force. The Russian countryside was littered with their remains. Göring had immediately blamed his advisors, his general, his staff officers – everyone who had so strenuously advised him against accepting the task in the first place. The difficulties were insuperable, they had told him. Even if the Luftwaffe had possessed a sufficiently large force of transport aircraft (which it didn't), the vile winter weather and the primitive airfield conditions would have combined to guarantee failure, even without the efforts of the Red Air Force and the flak gunners. Everyone had told Göring these things. He hadn't listened. The Führer insisted on the Sixth Army being supplied by air; the Luftwaffe was the only means of doing the job, ergo, in some magical way it would be done.

According to the gossips, a positively awesome torrent of wrath had exploded on the Reichsmarschall when Stalingrad fell. The Führer, it was said, had verbally whiplashed the Reichsmarschall, reducing him to a sobbing, quivering hulk of abject apology. For days afterwards he had skulked in his office refusing to see anyone, waiting only for a telephone call from the Führer, saying that he was forgiven. But the call didn't come.

It was only in the last ten days that Göring had become approachable to underlings once again.

But one had to be wary.

Oddly enough, Göring was in an uncommonly good humour this morning. He smiled as Wilde entered like a small boy who is expecting a present but doesn't know what it will be.

'Good morning, Wilde, you rascal.'

'Good morning, Herr Reichsmarschall.'

'Sit down. Been to any more of your famous orgies?'

'I can assure you, Herr Reichsmarschall . . .'

Göring beamed. 'You can't pull the wool over my eyes, Wilde. You and all your actress and writer friends, a decadent lot, in my opinion. Bloody Bohemians. Immoral as hell.'

Wilde sighed. 'Berlin is remarkably quiet these days, Herr Reichsmarschall. However,' he added as he noted the fat man frowning, disappointed, 'I did hear that there was a little soirée given by Martin Neiss, the film producer, upon completion of his latest epic. They say that the leading lady – Ulla Stolle by name – imbibed a little too enthusiastically and declared herself ready to take on every male in the room.'

Göring's small eyes lit up. This was the sort of story he liked.

'And did she?'

'No.'

'Oh.'

That same disappointed furrow in the fat brow.

'Only eight of the twelve,' said Wilde.

The Reichsmarschall emitted a giggle. 'And were you one of the eight, Wilde?'

'Me, Herr Reichsmarschall?'

'Yes, you, you devil. I'll wager you joined in the fun. Well, I can't say I blame you. She's a handsome woman. Magnificent figure. Breasts like a couple of those,' he said, pointing to the propeller boss on a silver model of a Focke-Wulfe 190 fighter. He chuckled, obviously pleased with his simile. For a moment he seemed lost in thought, perhaps imagining what it would be like to fondle Fräulein Stolle's bosom. At last, with a sigh, he returned to reality.

'Well?'

'Herr Reichsmarschall, perhaps you recall meeting a young fighter pilot last year; Ernst Brehme.'

'Brehme? Of course I remember him. Brilliant pilot. I gave him the Cross myself. Good looking boy. Keep seeing his picture in the papers.'

'Perhaps you heard that he had been shot down.'

'Dead?'

'No, he survived a crash landing when his engine failed over Pitomnik airfield. He got aboard a Heinkel that was taking off. They were no sooner off the ground than they were shot down. Everyone was killed except Brehme.'

'Lucky fellow.'

'Extremely lucky, Herr Reichsmarschall. He suffered a broken leg and some minor burns but nothing serious. He's at present in hospital in Poland.'

'I see.'

'He has become quite a noted celebrity in the last year or so. He possesses a singular quality: he seems to project his personality from the printed page. He's a fine looking fellow and he photographs extraordinarily well, from any angle. Pictures of him in the press have attracted an incredible amount of mail: offers of marriage, sex, money, thank-yous from classes in schools for the splendid job he's doing for the Fatherland, the usual sort of thing. You are of course personally aware how much adulation a successful fighter pilot can generate.'

Göring nodded, no doubt recalling his days as a flyer on the Western Front battling the Spads and Camels. For a few heady months in 1918 he had led the famous 'Flying Circus', JG.1, following the death of Manfred von Richthofen. In those days Göring himself had been a national hero, a darling of society, holder of the Blue Max, the Pour Le Mérite.

'I'm impressed by Brehme,' Wilde went on. 'He is rather charmingly modest and, oddly enough, quite shy in spite of being one of the most successful pilots of all time. It seems to me, Herr Reichsmarschall, that this might be an appropriate time to let the German public see and hear more of Leutnant Brehme.'

'Possibly,' Göring murmured.

'I'm sure you'll agree that the nation should be reminded of the incredible accomplishments of your Luftwaffe,' Wilde said, with the tiniest emphasis on 'your'. More nods from the Reichsmarschall in the gilt-encrusted chair.

'I would like to bring him back to Germany for a time, as soon as I arrange a schedule of broadcasts, interviews, suitable occasions for photography and so on.'

'I have no objection.'

'Thank you, Herr Reichsmarschall. But first I wonder if you might consider another aspect of the matter. It's my understanding that the Führer intends to visit the Eastern Front in the near future. As it happens, Brehme is in line to receive the Oak Leaves to his Knight's Cross. Do you think the Führer would consent to visit Brehme in hospital and bestow the award on him there and then?'

Göring's brow had furrowed. The thought of asking a favour of the Führer was daunting indeed.

'Why can't he come back to Germany when he's out of hospital and receive the award in the usual way?'

'He could, Herr Reichsmarschall, but I believe that public reaction would be infinitely greater if the event took place in a hospital close to the front line. It would, I believe, convey to every German the confidence and faith the Führer has in the Luftwaffe. The public emphasis has far too long been on the army and the navy, particularly the U-boats; and while I'd be the last to denigrate their achievements, I think we in the Luftwaffe must take steps to ensure that we are not relegated to second or even third place.'

'I agree,' Göring grunted.

'I am convinced the effort to arrange the investiture would be repaid many times over. Consider the impact of the scene: the hero, bandaged, but handsome still, not disfigured, thank God, receiving the Oak Leaves from his Führer, almost within sound of the gunfire.'

'It has a certain appeal.'

'I wondered whether you might be prepared to recommend such a visit.'

A stroking of the flabby chin. 'It's not easy to arrange anything with the Führer these days,' Göring complained. 'He's always changing his plans at the very last minute. Quite unpredictable.'

What you mean, Wilde thought, is that Hitler's still angry as hell and you are frightened to ask anything of him.

'I understand,' he said.

Göring's fleshy fingers were intertwined, momentarily resembling a group of Sumo wrestlers locked in combat.

'But I will certainly give the matter some thought.'

'Thank you, Herr Reichsmarschall. May I ask if you intend to visit the Eastern Front in the near future?'

'I'm not at all sure,' Göring said. 'Of course, there can be no question of my accompanying the Führer. He is quite adamant about it, refuses to consider the two of us travelling together to any of the fronts. He's right of course. God knows what would happen to the country if anything happened and we were both lost!'

'It doesn't bear thinking about,' said Wilde.

*

They were beneath his skin just below his left cheekbone: tiny, industrious worms, chewing, wriggling, drilling their horrible way through him. Four of them. Two going forward, toward his mouth, one going in the opposite direction and one working vertically. If only he would reach it and tear them out. He tried to rip his flesh off in layers. Nails in, biting, cutting. But no matter how deep he dug the worms were always just below. Then, when his face was in bloody shreds and he was moving along the fuselage to talk to the pilot, there was the attack. Bullets sliced through the metal walls just as he had sliced his own flesh. A world of shattering din. Wind whistling in. And fire. It leaped at him, reaching for him like some extraordinary monster. He recoiled at its hot breath. Turned. But there was nowhere to run. He could only stumble back, trying to protect his face with his arm while the aircraft wobbled, trembling on the brink of a stall. At last it fell. A glimpse of the ground through the conical transparent nose cone. A flat snowy area, revolving. Engines screaming. Air screaming. Men screaming. Snow rushing up to meet the plunging aircraft . . .

'Steady on, old fellow. You're quite safe now.'

'What?'

Fear still raced through every nerve although his eyes already absorbed the fact of the hospital and the doctor's face, his gentle eyes.

'You had a bad dream.'

'Damned worms in my face.'

'You mustn't scratch it. You'll damage the new layer of skin.'

'Can't you make it stop itching?'

'It's healing.'

'It itches like hell.'

'That's a good sign,' said the doctor, beaming.

'For you perhaps.'

'For you, too. It means you'll soon be out of here.'

The doctor's name was Drobnig. He was a pleasant man of about thirty-five, but he looked older because of his bald pate and the fussy little moustache under his thin, well formed nose.

Drobnig examined the left side of Ernst's face where the new flesh was reluctantly being accepted by the raw, burnt skin underneath.

'It's coming along very nicely.'

'I'm glad you're pleased,' said Ernst. Yes, he supposed he was relieved to be out of it for a while. No, it really didn't concern him that other pilots, such as Gollob and Graf, might lengthen their leads while he was out of action. Yes, he still enjoyed flying. . .

'Did you sleep well before all this?'

'Reasonably.'

'How many times did you wake up during a typical night?'

'Sometimes a dozen times. Sometimes not at all.'

'Digestion good?'

'Not very.'

Drobnig scratched his shiny pate. 'You need a long rest, my friend. Your nerves are in poor condition.'

'How long?'

'Six months. A year.'

'I'd go mad.'

'You're like drug addicts, some of you flyers.' said Drobnig, shaking his head in mock despair. 'You can't get enough of it to satisfy you!'

The morning mail. A letter from Ilse. Faithful Ilse. How many times had she written those same, dutiful things? He was always in her thoughts. She longed for him. She kissed his photograph every night and every morning. Would he please tell her the date of his release from hospital: she was looking forward to his leave more than anything in her entire life.

Sweet Ilse.

Beautiful Ilse.

He was, he admitted privately, damned glad that she was there at home, waiting. Thank God he had never told her about Jeanne. The disquieting thing was how readily he had been able to transfer his affection from Jeanne to her. He wrote words of longing to Ilse as if attempting to quash his thoughts of Jeanne.

He told himself that he should be ashamed. He supposed he was, but the feeling was of no significance.

A letter from his mother. She hoped and prayed that he would soon be completely recovered. She was well but tired because of air raids several times a week. A letter from Uncle Albert: he damned the Russians, the Americans and the British, as if he had suddenly woken up to the fact that they were far from contemptible opponents. Did Ernst remember Herr Hüttlich? He was killed in a raid. He had been at a Party meeting in the centre of the city. There was an air raid warning while he was on his way home. A bomb hit him. The funeral was on the fifteenth. What, Ernst wondered, did they bury? There was a note from Roder:

Greatly looking forward to his return to the unit. He would be sorry to hear that Stappen was shot down in flames. Presumed dead. Who was Stappen? Ernst didn't remember anyone by that name. A brief missive from Dietrich. A trifle formal but sincere nonetheless. He hoped Ernst was progressing satisfactorily – and feeling thoroughly ashamed that he was lazing in bed while his comrades were working. He complained about the Gustav; it was now so heavy as to be positively vicious, particularly on take-off. Ah, for the halcyon days of the Emil! The book was progressing magnificently and would unquestionably make a rich man of him. The enormously satisfying thought, he noted, was that today he, Ernst, might be famous throughout the land, but in years to come he might be remembered only because that noted author Walter Dietrich had written about him!

Good old Dietrich. All had apparently been forgiven.

What of Jeanne? Was she already married to that bastard Amiel? Was she living with him at this very moment? Lying with him in that great brass bed?

No, he refused to think about it.

He turned painfully to look out of the window that overlooked the shaggy, unkempt lawn. There were still patches of snow, but they would soon be gone. Another spring. But very different from the spring of twelve months earlier. Then everyone had talked confidently of the final thrust that would shatter the Soviets; the war would almost certainly be over by mid-summer. Now the Red Army was on the offensive, having taken a quarter of a million Germans at Stalingrad. It was the worst disaster in the history of the German Army. In Africa the British were pursuing Rommel along the Mediterranean coast. In Germany itself every major city was shuddering under the increasingly brutal bombing raids at night, with the Americans beginning to make their aerial presence felt by day. And God only knows how many bombers were being manufactured in those gigantic factories across the Atlantic. The man in the next bed, an infantry officer named Lucke, kept saying that the war was already lost. It was, he mumbled, a simple matter of arithmetic. Populations and productive capacity. No matter how you calculated it, the answer was the same. But for him it was all academic, he declared. He had a lung wound. He was dying. He could feel the life slowly dissolving inside him, disappearing bit by bit. He gave himself seven days, ten at the outside. He claimed that the hospital had once been the sumptuous mansion of a Polish count who regularly held orgies in the very room in which the officers now lay. 'A dozen or so girls at a time, all tumbling over each other. God, they knew how to live in those days. Every Sunday they gathered, in the afternoon, at about four.' Lucke devoted much time gazing at the floor. He claimed that on certain days, when he applied himself seriously to concentrating, he could succeed in making the naked men and girls return and go through their antics all over again.

Ernst found himself spending hours wondering why he wasn't killed at Pitomnik along with the other men on board the Heinkel. Why did they die? Why did he survive? A priest who regularly visited the patients cautioned him against questioning it. Accept it, he advised. Be thankful for God's mercy.

Mercy? Living had become a miserable, tedious business of pain and boredom, frustration and anxiety, all charged with a virulent hatred for a middle-aged Frenchman he didn't even know. 'Recuperative melancholy' was a common phenomenon in the hospital, according to Lucke. 'People are glad to find themselves alive,' he said, 'then they have too much time. They contemplate. They soon come to the conclusion that perhaps they aren't all that glad to be alive after all . . .'

Ernst had more than his share of visitors, mostly fellow airmen, pilots who had heard of his accomplishments and who came to tell him how greatly they admired him. They asked his advice on how they too might become Experten wearing the cherished Ritterkreuz, the ultimate badge of heroism. He answered their questions but he found himself taking remarkably little pleasure in it. Why had it all become so meaningless?

One afternoon two orderlies came to move him to a private room. He asked why; they shrugged; they didn't know; they were, as always, simply obeying orders. But The Dragon, the head nurse, told him that he was to receive an important visitor, for which reason the room was at that moment being cleaned, fresh flowers were being placed in vases on the bedside tables, two nurses were preparing to wash him and a barber was hurrying to the hospital at this very moment to shave him and trim his hair.

There was a strange air of unreality about the whole thing. Cameramen came in and set up their equipment. Security men followed them, examining every corner of the room – for God knows what. Then SS guardsmen entered and arranged themselves around the doorway in preparation for the great moment.

At last the Führer appeared. To Ernst it was as if he was

watching it all on a newsreel. None of the proceedings seemed to have any connection with him. He was a spectator, only mildly interested. He found Hitler to be shorter than he had expected; and older; the leader's face was tense and heavily lined; there were streaks of grey in the famous dark hair and moustache. He wore a simple military tunic adorned only by the Iron Cross First Class that he had won in 1917 as a despatch runner with the 1st Company of the 16th Bavarian Reserve Infantry regiment.

'You are an inspiration to every German,' Hitler declared, after bestowing the Oak Leaves. He kept nodding as if agreeing with his own words. 'I have followed your career with the keenest interest.'

'Thank you, my Führer,' Ernst responded as he had been instructed prior to Hitler's arrival.

'I hope your injuries are not causing you too much pain.'

'No, my Führer.'

'Good. I know how anxious you must be to return to the front. But it's important that you regain your strenth completely. You have some leave coming, I'm told. I want you to take it all and recover completely. You will do that?'

'Of course, my Führer.'

'Your mother must be extraordinarily proud of you. My office sent her a short note to say that I would be calling on you today.'

'That was very good of you, my Führer.' God, imagine the excitement the missive must have caused! No doubt half the population of Köln had already seen it!

Hitler seemed slightly ill at ease, almost diffident. He kept fingering his chin, thrusting his left hand in his tunic pocket and taking it out again. He asked Ernst's opinion of the Soviets.

'They are becoming tougher foes, my Führer.'

Hitler nodded. 'Their aircraft?'

'They're getting better. When we first fought them they were flying Chatos and Ratas, poor machines in comparison with our Messerschmitts, although very heavily armed. But in recent months they have introduced many new types – LaGGs, YaKs, MIGs. Some of them are almost as good as our equipment at low altitudes – and that's where most of the fighting takes place on the Eastern Front.'

'Their pilots?'

'They're getting better too, my Führer, but I think they still have a long way to go to equal the Luftwaffe pilots – at least those who were trained in the early days.'

'Early days?'

'I mean, my Führer, that the pilots who trained before the war or during the first year or two had many more hours of training before they went into action than today's pilots.'

'I see.' Hitler nodded, stroking his chin thoughtfully. But he took the point no further. Evidently the length of pilot training was not a matter which rated high in his order of priorities.

There were a few more minutes of conversation. Then a be-medalled SS officer stepped forward and whispered something to the Führer. A curd nod. A final handshake.

'I shall look forward to hearing more of your accomplishments.'

'Thank you, my Führer.'

Then it was over. The door opened. The guards came to attention; Hitler departed; the black-uniformed officers followed. The cameramen relaxed and yawned and began to pack up their equipment. They nodded farewells to Ernst and shook his hand with mumbled words of congratulations. In a few minutes they too had departed to be replaced by nurses and doctors, all eager to know everything about the visitation. What did the Führer say? What was he *like*? How was his handshake?

'You must be wonderfully proud,' said Dr. Drobnig, his pleasant face aglow with the glory of it all.

Ernst nodded. Yes, he supposed he must be wonderfully proud – somewhere, somehow. An event had occurred that was the stuff of every young pilot's dreams: a personal visit by the Führer, receiving the Oak Leaves to the Knight's Cross from his hands, exchanging niceties just like two *equals*! It had happened; he accepted the fact but it failed to stir him.

'I saw him,' said one of the nurses, giggling as if she had witnessed something naughty. 'I was standing only two metres from him. Imagine! My mother won't believe me when I tell her! She'll say I'm exaggerating. She always says that. Once I saw Willy Fritsch; I talked to him; I said I loved his films; he said I should have thought about being an actress – he did; he really said that! But she didn't believe me then, either . . .'

There were handshakes and pats on the shoulder. Ernst smiled obligingly; they were good-natured people excited as hell to have had their Führer walking and talking in this very room. The irony of it was that they were far more excited about it than he was.

'Some mail for you, sir.'

More mail. There were letters every day.

An orderly thrust the bundle into Ernst's hand. Most were

addressed in unfamiliar writing; admirers' letters, no doubt. But one had come from the front. The handwriting seemed vaguely familiar. He slit it open and looked at the signature before the letter itself.

From Schiegl, the old balding adjutant.

What was this about? A bar bill? A form to be signed?

No. Schiegl wrote how sorry he was to have to be the bearer of bad news. Dietrich. Shot down in flames. Killed instantly. Awful to tell you, knowing you were such good friends. The rest of the salutations became a collection of meaningless lines on the paper.

He glanced up. The Dragon was shooing everyone out of Ernst's room. No point in tiring him. He had to have his rest.

Drobnig shook his hand once again.

'Congratulations again. A great day.'

Ernst nodded. A great day.

Ten

'Dietrich deserved to live. He was writing a book about Russia and about the war. He kept on telling me how famous and rich it was going to make him. I think it would have been a good book too. But flak got him and blew him to bits in mid-air. . . . Then Lucke died the next morning.'

'Who was Lucke?'

'A fellow in the next bed. Chest wound. He told me he was dying. He could feel it happening.'

Ilse snuggled closer. 'I'm sorry about your friends.' She tightened her grasp on his shoulder. 'But I'm thankful it was Dietrich and Lucke and not you. I suppose it's selfish to say that but it's true. I wish you could stay at home for ever. When you're here with me I'm the happiest girl in Germany.'

'And the prettiest,' he said, almost automatically. She gobbled compliments like her family's powerful Weimaraner hound gobbled up treats of horse meat; both responded with instant outbursts of warmth and affection.

He fondled her left breast, working the nipple until it hardened, enjoying the closeness of her well-formed body, the softness of her hair as it brushed his cheek. They had made love that afternoon as they had made love every day since he came home on leave, lying naked on her perfumed bed while the gramophone churned out Greta Weiser songs. Her parents, who had once hovered suspiciously over them whenever they were in each other's company, now seemed content to leave them alone by the hour. Ernst was received in the Gebhardt home as if he was already one of the clan.

His opinions and comments were now accorded respectful silences, Herr Gebhardt nodding appreciatively at every other word, his small grey eyes constantly dropping to regard once again the medal at Ernst's throat, placed there by the hands of the Führer himself, as chronicled by countless photographs in newspapers and magazines, as well as on the newsreel at all the cinemas. Passers-by stopped Ernst in the street; others pointed him out ('That's *him*!'). The local press sent reporters and photographers to interview him at home. ('Air hero enjoys well-deserved rest at home.') He spoke at factories ('the craftsmanship of German workers gives us flyers a vital advantage over the enemy') and schools ('there can be no more satisfying career for a young man than to serve his Fatherland'). The speeches were provided by Oberst Wilde's department, all neatly typed in large characters to facilitate reading. At first he had been intensely nervous about appearing in public. He had stumbled over his words; he had missed lines and had been forced to go back and correct himself. But soon he discovered that the immense sea of faces, the buzzing organism before him was his slave. It adored him. It obeyed him. It hung on every phrase; it laughed when it was supposed to laugh, drew in its collective breath when he told it shocking or alarming facts, cheered itself hoarse when he said his thank-yous for its kind attention to his few modest words. And then it would become individual faces: workers in overalls, plump women and middle-aged men with balding heads and tired, lined faces, managers in black suits and wing collars congratulating him as they might have congratulated a star salesman upon his performance, schoolboys and schoolgirls, eyes wide with admiration. Hands reached for him, hungry for a touch, some soft and young, others hard and calloused. Was he lonely? Would he like a beautiful widow with a magnificent body who had learned about lovemaking from an Egyptian husband of royal blood? Did he feel the need for spiritual solace? A quiet evening of prayer with a truly patriotic German family? Would he like to see a collection of model airplanes, every type currently in use including a Messerschmitt 109 bearing his personal markings? Five scrap books packed with clipping about his exploits? A vacation in Bavaria, all expenses paid? Anything, it seemed, was possible for such a hero. But Wilde had counselled him, warning him against accepting favours. 'The trouble with admiration,' he had declared in his pedantic way, 'is that it is such an appallingly short-lived emotion. It has an unfortunate habit of turning to all sorts of nasty things like jealousy. A man may therefore ask you with the very best of intentions to come to his house and join his family for dinner. You will meet everyone and they will all talk about your splendid accomplishments. But only for so long. Soon, inevitably, people want to talk about themselves. When they do they find themselves beginning to resent the person they were admiring such a short while ago. Sad to say it probably has something to do with familiarity. Much better to be the glowing hero on the distant stage. Now, of course with women, the situation is rather different. They have by far the best way of expressing their admiration. Enjoy them for all they're worth, is my advice; but do try to avoid wives of generals and burgomeisters. It will make my job so much easier!'

'We must always be this happy,' Ilse murmured.

'Yes,' he said. What else was there to say? It made her content, that was reason enough, for when she was content she exuded affection and he could lose himself in it as if it was a huge, warm blanket.

She moved, brushing against his cheek. She apologized at once, reaching out and delicately touching the angry scars.

'I'm sorry. Does it hurt?'

'No,' he lied. 'It's quite all right.'

'I was afraid when you told me you'd been burned,' she confessed. 'I didn't feel any different about you of course, but I wasn't sure how I would react when I saw you. I'm not a brave person. It would have been awful if I'd fainted or something. But when you arrived, it didn't matter at all. And the strange thing is, the scars don't spoil your looks; they give you a sort of *devilish* look, like a man of the world who has been everywhere and seen everything. And I suppose in a way you are such a man.' She smiled, shaking her head. 'It's strange to think of you like that, because you're someone I've known so long, all my life, really. Will you have to go back to Russia?'

'I don't know. They're talking about sending me to a new unit.'

'Are you glad?'

'In a way, now that Dietrich is dead. It would have been hard to go back there without him.'

'I think they should give you a job at Luftwaffe headquarters in Berlin – or even in Köln here. Wouldn't that be marvellous, if you were working here? I could see you every day. It would be just as if you had a proper job in an office . . .'

'I'm a pilot not a clerk.'

'I know but don't you think you've done enough?'

'What's enough?'

'But it's so *dangerous* . . .' She gripped his arm as if to prevent him running from her, back to active service.

Everyone seemed convinced that an engagement would soon be announced. Both families apparently regarded it as a natural inevitability, like spring following winter. His mother kept referring to the 'increased responsibilities' that were on the horizon. She told him again and again what a fine young woman Ilse was, absolutely ideal in every way. What a thrill it was to see the two of them together. But Maria wanted to know about Ernst's French girl friend.

'I have no French girl friend,' he told her.

'Did she throw you over for someone else? Is your heart broken? Did she do it because you're a German?'

'You should become a Gestapo interrogator.'

'Perhaps I will. But tell me about your French girl friend.'

'I told you. I don't have any French girl friend.'

'But you did.'

'How do you know?'

'You're my brother. I understand the way you think. I can read your mind.'

'You're a witch.'

'No,' said Maria shaking her head. 'I'm just highly intelligent, observant and perspicacious.'

Ilse arranged for a photographer, Herr Dahlmann, to come to the Gebhardt home with his camera and lights. He took photographs of the pair of them seated together on the North Italian Renaissance sofa that was Frau Gebhardt's pride and joy. Afterwards, to Ernst's indignation and embarrassment, the photograph – handsome Leutnant Brehme, the Knight's Cross prominent about his throat sitting in delicious proximity to the stunningly attractive young Ilse – became the centrepeice of the Dahlmann studio window, beneath it the legend: 'Leutnant Ernst Brehme, hero of the Luftwaffe and his fiancée, photographed by Johann Dahlmann.'

Ilse shook her head apologetically.

'I didn't tell him we were engaged. He's simply jumped to conclusions. Do you mind terribly?'

'No,' he told her. 'It doesn't matter.' And it didn't.

'I'm very sorry.'

'I don't mind.'

'People will think . . .'

'I really don't care what people think.'

'No, I suppose you don't,' she said.

The days rolled by, pleasant enough in some ways but full of the tiresome trivialities of civilian life. There was an aimlessness that he found curiously disquieting after years at the front where the purpose of each day was sharply defined. If one had survived that day there was a feeling of intense satisfaction; one had defeated the odds yet again. Only the air raids provided a hint of that same satisfaction. They came two or three times a week, the crump-crump of their bombs clearly audible in the cellar where the family slept during raids. One night he and Ilse were at a cinema in the city when the alarms were sounded. A bomb landed close by, shaking the building, shutting off the electricity. By candlelight the patrons made their way to a street shelter, already crowded with citizens, some in night attire. A workman in overalls recognized Ernst. In a moment there were dozens of well-wishers, pumping his hand and patting him on the back. Ilse found room for the two of them on a bench between two families.

'Don't you wish you were up there shooting those bastards down?' enquired a fierce old lady with plump cheeks and a light brown moustache.

'Not very much, madam. You see, I'm a day fighter; I'm not trained to fly and fight at night. I'd be more dangerous to myself than to the British.'

They thought that hilarious; the famous Leutnant was a good fellow and no mistake.

'Is this your wife, sir?' enquired the workman.

'No, we're not married.'

'But you soon will be,' declared the old woman with a definite nod.

'Mother!' exclaimed a younger woman with a sleeping child in her arms. 'What a thing to say!'

'I say what has to be said,' was the reply. She turned to Ilse, almost angrily. 'You'd be a fool if you let this one get away, he's beautiful, good enough to eat!' she added with a throaty, meaningful chuckle. 'I can tell you, if I were fifty years younger you'd have a bit of competition from me . . . in fact not a bit but a hell of a lot!'

More howls of glee. An elderly man clutched Ernst's arm and told him that he had talked to Manfred, Freiherr von Richthofen, one rainy day in 1917 when the redoubtable Red Baron was recovering from a head wound. 'He was just out of the hospital, you see. Got dizzy from time to time. He was walking along a street and had to sit down. I helped him – not knowing, of course, who he was. When he recovered his balance he thanked me and gave me one of his cards. Engraved; beautiful. I've got it at home. Would you like to come and see it?'

'It's kind of you,' Ernst said, 'but we mustn't stay any longer than we have to.'

'Come tomorrow, then,' said the old man.

'I'm afraid I won't be able to . . .'

'He doesn't want to see some silly card,' said a female voice.

'Of course he doesn't,' snapped the woman with the moustache. 'He's on leave. He's got better things to do than look at cards – hasn't he, dear?' she said with a wink at Ilse.

A pair of bombs cracked down a few blocks away. The shelter seemed to wince; dust broke free from the ceiling and floated down like fine snow.

'Those bastards,' said the old woman. 'I'd like to get my hands on them . . .'

'You'd like to get your hands on any man!'

'I'll bring the card, sir,' said the old man, reaching for Ernst's arm and missing. 'I'll bring it the next time there's an air raid. I'll bring it to this shelter. Will you come?'

'I will if I can,' Ernst promised. 'But I don't live near here, you see; we were at the cinema when the warning went off . . .'

'Where do you live?'

'Near Höhenberg.'

'I can bring the card there.'

'But . . .'

'It's no trouble. I get the tram, you see. I can be there in half an hour. Just give me the address and I'll bring the card.'

'Well . . .'

'You want to see it, don't you?'

'Yes, of course . . .'

'I can bring it tomorrow. Ten o'clock in the morning. Would that be all right? Ten o'clock?'

Ernst nodded, defeated. Yes, ten o'clock would be satisfactory. He would look forward to seeing von Richthofen's calling card and hearing more of the man's encounter with the great flyer.

'That was very sweet of you,' said Ilse when they were on their way home. 'You made that old man very happy. Now he will be able to tell everyone that he went to the home of the famous Ernst Brehme.'

'And made Ernst Brehme very unhappy,' said Ernst.

'It's the price of fame,' she told him.

'The price is too high.'

Hauptmann Schiegl was weary. It had been a frantic day. Yet another move: hour after frustrating hour of trying to make a military establishment out of a miserable collection of shattered buildings; organizing, improvising, inventing, creating order out of chaos. God, did HQ have any idea what it was like moving a fighter unit? Did anyone really comprehend what was involved?

He loosened his collar and glanced at his watch. Nearly midnight. Trude would be in bed now, fast asleep, eyes tightly closed in that quaint, little-girl way of hers. Thank heaven she had at last acceded to his wishes and had moved from the apartment in Düsseldorf. Of course it was hard, leaving so many of her possessions. But there was too much danger from bombing there. So she had gone to live with her parents in Dresden, where bombing was almost unknown.

He rubbed his eyes and sighed. Before him was a veritable Everest of cardboard boxes, packed with paperwork by his clerk Salzborn. An idiot, Salzborn. Why hadn't the Selection Board put him in the infantry? Excellent cannon fodder material, Salzborn. Mind you, if things got much worse everyone in the Luftwaffe might well be handling a rifle before too long. . . . He shook his head. No use thinking defeatist thoughts.

He would have a quick look through the paperwork, then tackle it seriously in the morning – provided he was given an hour or two free of conferences and emergencies.

He pulled the first box toward him and tugged the string from one corner. It was already loose; Salzborn was incapable even of fastening a cardboard box securely.

Schiegl frowned as he removed the lid. Unfamiliar looking

papers inside. What the devil where they? Page after page, hand-written notes. . . .

Of course! Now he remembered. They were found in poor old Dietrich's quarters among his effects: they'd very nearly gone in with the rest of his stuff to be sent back to his next of kin with the usual note. But one always had to be careful with writings and photographs. God knows what embarrassments they might cause if the wrong sort of stuff went to Mutti. Anything suspicious was destroyed. So when he found the papers he had decided to read some of them and then decide what was best.

But there was so much of it. What was it? A diary? No, there seemed to be no dates. Just a lot of notes. One hell of a lot. Dozens of pages of the stuff, on the back of official Luftwaffe stationery. Saucy devil, Dietrich. Schiegl yawned and leafed through the pages, reading a paragraph here and there. His interest quickened when he found that Dietrich had been writing about the unit, about the flying, the fear, the superstitions, the equipment, the places, the men – names from the past: Wolfram and Strobel, Rudat and Berger, Baatz and Reissner. Scores of them. Damn it, one could no longer connect faces to those names or remember whether the man was short or tall, dark or fair. Incredible to realize how many had gone through the unit as if it was some sort of processing organization: take them, use them, kill them, forget them. He shook his head. What was happening to his thoughts? He was too tired to continue. He would retire, have a good night's sleep. He'd be better in the morning and he would decide what to do with Dietrich's scribblings.

He took a handful of the pages to put them back in the box. But something caught his eye. Something about Brehme. He and Dietrich were good friends, weren't they? Too good? Was there something . . .? No, nothing like that, indeed not. Dietrich was amused, it seems, by Brehme's devotion to some French woman. Apparently the lady was some years older than Brehme. But this didn't deter him; according to Dietrich he was absolutely captivated by her. Typical case of a young man's violent infatuation for an older woman. Nothing unusual about it. Many a boy has learnt about life from a mature female, he mused as he read on.

Then he stopped, his eyes popping wide.

But a *Jewish* woman?

No, surely not. It was unthinkable. *Quite* unthinkable.

Ilse kept holding her left hand up to display the gold band denoting her betrothed status. For the hundredth time Ernst assured her that it looked utterly adorable, precisely the right thickness and form, not too thick, not too thin, quite perfect in every way.

He had consumed a great deal of champagne. The restaurant was wobbling as if it was about to roll over on its back and tumble into a spin. Why did violinists persist in strolling by as they scraped, grinning down at the happy couple, showing discoloured teeth? Most disconcerting. The manager and the head waiter hovered about the table, obsequious little smiles rigidly affixed to their thin lips. It was, they said again and again, such a signal honour to serve Herr Brehme and his party.

'Ah, but it's not Herr Brehme and party,' snapped Ilse's father, loudly, clearly. 'It's Herr Gebhardt and party! Is that quite clear?'

'Quite clear, Herr Gebhardt.'

'Let there be no mistake about it! We can't have a hero with the Knight's Cross and Oak Leaves receiving the bill, now can we?'

'Certainly not, Herr Gebhardt, most certainly not.'

'I wish you didn't have to go tomorrow,' whispered Ilse, her strong fingers on his leg beneath the table cloth. 'God, I want you so badly.'

'I want you too,' murmured Ernst. But he didn't. He could scarcely keep his eyes open.

A guest ventured to their table. Would Herr Brehme object to having his photograph taken? Everyone would be so appreciative; it was simply marvellous – quite unbelievable – to meet such a hero in person, something to be remembered and cherished for a lifetime.

Ernst obliged and smiled at a camera as half a dozen hefty, middle-aged citizens crushed around him.

'I think that was rather rude,' said his mother when the party had gone.

Herr Gebhardt chuckled pompously. 'You must remember that your son is famous now, Frau Brehme. In a way he now belongs to the people!'

'Like a public toilet,' Ernst muttered.

'Pardon?' said Herr Gebhardt.

'Nothing,' said Ernst.

Maria said, 'Long engagements are unhealthy.'

'How do you know?'

'I read a book about it.'

'You shouldn't read such books,' said her mother.

'Why not? It's my duty to find out about life.'

The two mothers agreed that such books should not be available to young girls. Or boys, for that matter.

Ilse said, 'Thank God you're not going back to Russia. Belgium isn't far. You can come home lots of times, can't you?'

'I expect so,' said Ernst, stifling a yawn.

The talk turned to the future. Had Ernst decided upon a post-war career? Ernst stared at them. *After* the war? What were they talking about? Did they really think there was going to be anything *left*? Didn't they *know*?

Herr Gebhardt raised a judicial finger. 'He's looking into the law, aren't you? We had a good chat about it. He's keenly interested.'

Ernst's mother said she had no idea her son was thinking of a legal career.

'He's been meeting important people,' Herr Gebhardt pointed out. 'The *most* important people in the nation. There's absolutely no limit for a man with a record like Ernst's. Take politics. Why not? It's certainly not beyond the realm of possibility. A law degree will stand you in good stead my boy.'

Ernst tried to recall the 'good chat' about law that he was supposed to have had with Ilse's father. He had vague recollections of agreeing that the subject was indeed worth thinking about. Did that constitute a 'good chat'? They had subtle ways of manoeuvring people, these Gebhardts. If he wasn't careful, he advised himself laboriously, he would find himself studying law just as he had found himself engaged – not unwilling but not quite sure how it all came about.

'I foresee a brilliant future for this young man,' declared Herr Gebhardt, beaming as if he had just bestowed his blessing on the fortunate youth. 'The nation will be eternally grateful for what he has done.'

Ernst wanted to shake some sense into the idiot. The know-it-all didn't *know*. Didn't understand. Didn't see what was happening all around him. He still *believed*.

Eleven

'Frankly they're a rabble,' said Gablenz. 'We had two good men until last week. Schönberg and Fröhlich. Schönberg was in charge. Fine fellow. Played the violin. Went in on Thursday. A P–47 got him. A flamer. Fröhlich went the next day. Vanished. God only knows what happened to him. Schäfer's been trying to hold things together in the interim but I need him for Staffel Two. I'm damned glad to see you. Heard all about you, of course. Everyone has. How's your leg? Still need the cane, do you? Never mind, as long as you can fly, that's the important thing. I'll be honest with you, these lads need someone to respect. They also need someone to give them a little hope.'

'I'll do my best,' Ernst told him. 'But I don't consider myself Staffelkapitän material . . .'

'Never mind,' grinned Gablenz, glancing nervously from side to side, 'it's what HQ considers that counts. Ever flown the 190?'

'No, sir.'

'You'll like it. Good machine. I grew up on the 109 like you. Very suspicious of the 190 at first. Understandable, eh? A man gets used to a plane and when it keeps on bringing him home he starts to feel downright affection for the thing, don't you agree?'

'Yes, of course.'

'Of course. But the 190's all right; you'll see. Mind you, you'll find things different here in the west. One hell of a lot harder to shoot down the Yanks and Tommies than the Reds. Those bloody B–17s are the worst. Bastard things. Each one's got a platoon of machine gunners aboard. As for the damned airplanes, they're built like tanks. You've got to blow them to pieces before they'll go down. Head-on attacks are the best. Forts are lightly armed in the front end. And that's where all the important people are. With a bit of luck you can kill the two pilots and the flight engineer with one burst. But you've not got much time to do it in. You can imagine what the combined speeds are. Get too interested in what you're doing and you're liable to find yourself in the bloody navigator's compartment. I saw a 109 do that. The 109 disappeared inside the big bastard, I swear it did. Went right down the fuselage. It was like seeing a damned great whale swallow a little fish. Then the whole lot blew up, of course. He got his Yank but it was a messy way of doing it.'

Major Gablenz drank his coffee and grimaced, muttering about the bitter taste of it. He was in his late twenties, haggard and pale, with curly black hair combed straight back from his high forehead. His nerves were taut; he kept inhaling sharply as if he noticed a bad smell; his mouth twitched; his hands were never still. Like Ernst, he wore the coveted Knight's Cross at his throat; it looked well against the white leather flight jacket. He drew on pale kid gloves as he stood up. It was time to meet the pilots.

'You have a good leave?'

'Pleasant, sir.'

'Where's your home?'

'Köln.'

'I know it well. Had an uncle there. And an aunt of course. Both as deaf as posts. But vain. Refused to use hearing aids. Yelled at each other all the time. Can't think of Köln without thinking of those two bellowing away like drill sergeants.'

The Operations Room was a solid concrete hut, camouflaged with branches and leaves, its shape disguised by netting stretched from the roof to the ground.

The pilots stood to attention as the two officers entered. Incredibly young, those pilots. Mere children, dressed up in flyers' garb. Their uncertain eyes devoured Ernst as he walked to the front of the room behind Gablenz. So this was the legendary Brehme, the handsome pilot whose face had become almost as familiar as some of the Party leaders in recent months. A brilliant pilot. Knocked down Russian planes like nine-pins. Would he find that easy here in the west?

'You're damned lucky,' Gablenz told the assembled pilots. 'Fate has sent one of the world's great fighter pilots to be your commander. I'm not at all sure you deserve him but nevertheless here he is . . .'

Gablenz had an unusual way with him; he might have been introducing a performer on the stage rather than a commander in the field. Ernst stood up. His stomach still stung; his mouth had a metallic taste. He told the pilots that it was an honour to be sent to command them, that he would need their assistance in the early stages because he was unfamiliar with the western theatre of war, that he would look forward to getting to know each of them individually, that together they had a vital job to do . . .

'Damned good,' said Gablenz as they made their way back to the flight line.

'The usual sort of stuff,' said Ernst.

'Of course. That's what they need. Makes them feel secure. That's what it's all about these days. Poor bastards are sent out here to do battle when they're still learning how to fly their bloody airplanes. They're brave enough, most of them, but bravery's no damned good if they haven't got the flying skill to go with it. And most of 'em haven't. Now fuel's getting tighter and tighter. HQ keeps telling us not to waste any. Waste! What the bloody hell do they think we're doing? Running aerial tours of the Greater Reich? Jesus Christ, I use fuel so that some of these poor bastards can learn to fly their airplanes so that they might stand half a bloody chance to do some good when they get in combat. And what's the result? Complaints from HQ. Got to cut back on fuel consumption. Cut out any consumption not absolutely necessary. Good God almighty, wouldn't you call training the bloody pilots fairly necessary? I would, I can tell you. And I told HQ that too. In no uncertain terms! Didn't do any good. Never does. Those bastards fight a paper war. Reports versus memos. And to hell with the reality of the god-damned front!'

The 190 was an attractive aircraft, powerful, sleek, superbly balanced, squatting on its broad undercarriage. It looked positively eager to take to the air.

Half a dozen pilots and ground crewmen clustered around the cockpit, eager to be of assistance to the redoubtable Brehme as he set off on his maiden trip in the new type.

The cockpit felt right; the seat was sharply angled so that the pilot sat in a semi-reclining position – said to help in withstanding G forces in combat. The visibility was excellent; in contrast to the small canopy of the 109, the Focke-Wulf fighter featured a long transparent sliding hood that enabled the pilot to see in virtually any direction when in flight.

'Don't forget to keep the canopy closed when you've got the engine running, sir. The fumes get sucked into the cockpit if you don't.'

'Harness comfortable? Seat the right height?'

Helpful fingers indicated the instruments: the panel in front and consoles on either side of the seat. Comforting amount of armour: in front the steeply inclined windscreen made from 50 mm armour-glass; on the sides the 30 mm armour-glass quarter-lights; around the seat was more protection in the form of 5 mm, 8 mm and 12 mm armour plate steel – all neatly designed into the aircraft rather than added on later as was the case in the 109.

'Fuel tanks and pumps on.'

'Cooling grills set to one-third.'

'R/T connection there on your left, sir.'

'Stick right back to lock the tailwheel.'

Familiar quaking of the guts. He felt like a cadet again. Why the hell couldn't he have arranged a nice quiet test flight at dawn with no one else around to witness the proceedings? Perhaps he should have spent more time on conversion trainers before tackling this formidable machine. He'd been off flying for a long time; one could get rusty . . .

'You'll find she'll want to pull to the left on take-off but you'll hold her easily with the rudder.'

The fourteen-cylinder BMW started at first flick of the starter switch; the big propeller dissolved in motion; the airframe became alive with anticipatory vibration. He switched on the radio.

Someone bellowed something helpful, something lost in the din.

Ernst nodded his thanks and slid the canopy over the cockpit, swallowing the momentary feeling of claustrophobia.

Pressures, temperatures normal: instruments functioning.

The controller's raspy voice accorded him permission to taxi.

A final nod at the blobs of faces, the spectators, the helpers and the hopers – those who wished, consciously or unconsciously, for the great man to fall flat on his face.

Left leg hurting like hell. Aching in an unpleasantly rhythmical way: one jolt of pain every seventeen seconds.

Grey, overcast sky. Little activity in the air war today. The Yanks had taken a mauling yesterday. Now, presumably, they were licking their wounds.

Because the 190 was a tailwheel aircraft its big BMW radial effectively blocked the view forward; one had to swerve gently from left to right to check on the path ahead.

At the threshold of the runway he ran up the engine, testing the magnetoes. Time to roll. The controller gave him the green light.

Ten degrees of flap. Lock tailwheel. Elevator trim to neutral. Pitch to auto. Power on. Needle climbing to 2700 rpm. . .

God, she leapt forward, fairly gobbling up the slick black surface of the runway. At 180 kilometres she lifted off. Hasty glance down at the left to find the correct buttons for retracting the undercarriage and the flaps. At 2500 rpm she climbed steadily. He relaxed. He felt at home in this aircraft. Reasonably good take-off. Didn't disgrace himself, not yet. . .

Ah, the speed of her rolls! Fantastic ailerons turn! The sky revolved about him as if he had suddenly, wondrously become the centroid of the entire universe. A magnificent airplane! But possessing a temper. Power down. Stick back. Airspeed indicator sliding away to the left like a clock running down. Wham! She ceased to fly. At a fraction over 200 kilometres the left wing suddenly fell out of the sky. Over went the fighter, snapping on to her back, demonstrating firmly and dramatically that she was not to be trifled with. She demanded respect at all times; take her for granted and she could retaliate.

How delightful it was to fly simply for the joy of flying. To make the horizon do one's bidding: fall to the left, to the right; to experience gravity's tug-of-war, to skim the clouds, slicing them with shapely wings, to taste the sun, revel in its warmth while far below earthlings huddled in overcoats and complained about the ceaseless rain. Full power dive! Down into the murky caverns of cloud; then a breathless climb up, up, up into the dazzling brightness. A marvellous airplane, the 190, the controls firm, the entire airframe splendidly sensitive, throbbing with power. A thoroughbred. Gleefully he slammed the fighter into a vertical bank, applying gentle back pressure on the stick to keep her nose level. Hard reversal of the controls; now a merry whirl in the opposite direction, the earth spinning, obedient to his commands. He smiled at the instruments arranged before him; he felt the airman's instinctive desire to convey to his aircraft just how pleased he was with the assembly of spars and longerons, formers and ribs. It all felt like an extension of his own body, enabling him to soar and dive, turn and wheel like an eagle.

He wriggled his shoulders against his harness, easing the stiffness that came from bracing them too long. He had been nervous, fearful of problems with this spirited fighter. But he had worried needlessly. More turns and dives, more hurtling from cloud to cloud, performing aerial pirouettes, scaling the loftiest heights of misty mountains.

Damn! The clock on the control console at his right informed him that he had been aloft nearly ninety minutes! An hour and a half! Quite incredible how rapidly the minutes passed up here in this world of sunshine and space, a clean world – and in an odd way an uncomplicated world. Wouldn't it be superb to stay up here for ever? Never go back; keep climbing higher and higher. . .

Up here, wrapped in sunlight, far above the carpet of grey cloud, he found he could think of Jeanne, picture her, relive moments with her – without that familiar stinging ache thrusting itself through his guts. In some strange way all earthly emotions seemed to be in abeyance; altitude provided a kind of objectivity, a loftier view of life. Floating, balanced on an invisible ocean of air, he could understand why she did it. Damn it, what hell he must have put her through: those months of never knowing if he was alive or dead; waiting, always waiting. Being a secret. She deserved better. It was his fault. He was stupid, insensitive. Of course she loved him; of course he loved her. But what could ever become of such a relationship? Could he blame her for accepting Amiel. . . . Mr. Reality?

For Oberst Wilde the day began disastrously. Shortly after midnight the air raid sirens whined.

'There's a cellar below,' he told his guest.

His guest pouted prettily. 'But we can't continue doing what we're doing down there, can we?'

'Not unless we are willing to provide entertainment for a couple of hundred people.'

'It might be fun.'

'But people would talk.'

'Undoubtedly.'

'Pity. Then I suggest we stay here and entertain one another.'

'Delicious idea. I like what you're doing.'

'I'm glad.'

'You do it well.'

'Thank you.'

'I wish my husband would learn to do that. . .'

At that moment a British MC 500 pound general purpose bomb struck the corner of the apartment building. Its amatol exploded upon contact, blowing in much of the building's west wall, killing two elderly women hurrying downstairs on their way to the shelters. Oberst Wilde's bed collapsed; the radiogram that had been pumping out appropriately sensuous dance music was silenced as the electricity failed; pictures tumbled from the walls; a crystal chandelier in the dining room fell and shattered. Shaken, scared, Oberst Wilde and his guest threw on some clothes and dashed downstairs. In the stairwell leading to the shelter they encountered a certain Albrecht Schwalm. He recognized Oberst Wilde's guest immediately, for Albrecht Schwalm was her husband's cousin. Her husband was a Gruppenführer in the Waffen-SS.

Later that same morning, when Wilde had arrived at his office there was a message for him. Borchardt of Internal Security had dropped in. A matter of some delicacy. Perhaps the Oberst would be good enough to call when he had a moment to spare. One could almost hear the oily bastard talking, smiling all the time, cold little eyes like gimlets. . .

He was about to telephone Borchardt when she rang. Scared as hell. Fearful of the consequences of their meeting with Albrecht Schwalm. Wanting to know what to do.

'I'll think about it,' he promised, his head aching; he had not slept.

'This is *serious*, for God's sake!'

'Perhaps not,' he said, kneading his throbbing forehead. 'Your husband's cousin simply saw two people hurrying downstairs to the shelter. They didn't necessarily come from the same apartment . . .'

'I can't just *hope* that's what he thought.'

'I don't know what else you can damn well do!'

'You bastard!' she snapped.

When at last she rang off his headache had become a rumbling roar that threatened to split his skull. Had the whole dreadful business set off a dormant brain tumour? One heard of such ghastly things. . . . He told his secretary to ring Borchardt. A matter of delicacy, hadn't he said? Christ almighty, how many matters of delicacy could a fellow handle in one morning?

'And bring some coffee.'

The bigger Borchardt's smile the nastier his mission. He wished the Herr Oberst a very good morning as he settled himself in the visitor's chair.

'Coffee? Thank you so much, Herr Oberst. Delicious. Excellent quality. Swedish? I thought so. A distinctive flavour.'

'What can I do for you?' Wilde enquired. He had to grip the leather arms of his chair to steady himself, for his headache seemed to be in exquisitely delicate balance, sensitive to the smallest inclination to left or right.

'Actually,' smiled Borchardt, 'I think I may be able to do something for you. It concerns a young airman. A fighter pilot whose name is more than a little familiar to you, my dear Oberst. A certain Ernst Brehme.'

'I know of him,' Wilde admitted carefully.

'I wonder if you know that he had a French girl friend.'

You bastard, Wilde thought, don't you wish you could tell me he had a French *boy* friend?

'I believe I did hear something of the sort,' he lied.

'He had known her several years.'

'Yes.'

'I can see that the intelligence doesn't startle you, my dear Oberst. I reacted in much the same way when I received the news, which came to us in rather an odd way, via another pilot's diary. Great heavens, was my first reaction, what could be more natural than a charming liaison between a young fighter pilot and a local girl?'

'Quite so.'

'However, Ernst Brehme is not an average pilot. You have made him famous, Herr Oberst.'

'True.'

'For that reason we took it upon ourselves to make a few discreet enquiries.'

'Go on.'

'Certainly. We discovered that the lady in question is a widow, some years older than young Brehme. Eleven years and two months to be precise.'

'And you do like to be precise, don't you?'

For a moment Borchardt's smile became a beam, then, as if mechanically, it reverted. He said, 'It was also ascertained that the lady in question has two children; indeed her son, Georges, now thirteen, helped Brehme out of his aircraft when he crash landed in September of 1940. Subsequently the boy was entertained at Brehme's airfield, even taken for a flight in a Luftwaffe aircraft.'

'I remember, I remember.' At times Borchardt's voice sounded as agonizingly monotonous as a dentist's drill.

'The lady's husband was a teacher.'

'Really.'

'He died shortly before the outbreak of war.'

'Yes?'

'Name of Goutard.'

'How interesting.'

'What's even more interesting, Herr Oberst, is the lady's maiden name. It was Levy.'

'*Levy*?'

'Yes, Herr Oberst, your young hero's paramour is a full-blooded Jewess!'

Wilde's fingers tightened on the arm rests; one cracked audibly, sending a sharp pain lancing up his arm.

'You're sure? Some people have Jewish names but. . .'

'It was thoroughly checked, Herr Oberst. The lady's father was a man of some reputation in the French theatre, a designer of stage sets, I understand. Married one Marie Rosen in November of 1907 in Paris at the . . .'

'I don't give a damn where or when her bloody parents were married!'

'Quite so, Herr Oberst. It's not important. I thought you would prefer that I bring you this information personally. This seemed to be a case where letters and memoranda should be avoided, at least at this stage.'

'Most thoughtful of you,' Wilde heard himself say.

'My pleasure, Herr Oberst. I take it I may leave the matter in your hands.'

'Of course.' Go to hell, you smirking bastard! 'And thank you so very much for the coffee. I enjoyed it.'

Wilde closed his eyes as the door shut behind Borchardt. He clutched his head in both hands as if trying to contain it.

Damn Brehme, he swore silently. Damn his soul for doing this to me.

The stupid, ungrateful bastard. It was bad enough getting himself involved with some bloody French tart . . . but a *Jewish* one . . .

It was unspeakable.

Suppose the news leaked out. It could. Such things had a hideous way of reaching the public. Röhm's homosexuality . . . Göring's drugs . . . common knowledge. There was a chillingly good chance that Himmler already knew; Borchardt was altogether too friendly with his colleagues in the SS. . .

Wilde grimaced with the pain and the anguish. This thing could make a laughing stock of him.

Something had to be done.

The P–47s had reached the limits of their range. Now they had to turn back, waggling their wings in farewell to their comrades in the B17s, the Fortresses. The fighters would return to their bases in England, land, refuel, take off again and meet the bombers on their way back from the target.

This was the moment to prepare the attack, the moment to move closer, to fly alongside the formation, just far enough away to frustrate all those hundreds of machine gunners with their heavy Brownings, but near enough to study the bombers, report to the ground on their type, numbers, markings, course, height . . .

The bombers flew in a series of formations – 'boxes' – individual aircraft rising and sinking as if they were suspended on elastics, gun turrets rotating, searching the hostile sky like great glittering eyes.

A moment for deep breaths of oxygen, for trying to calm wobbling nerves. Gun sights on. Safety switches off. Gloved hands on throttle levers. The fighters picked up speed; they forged ahead, leaving the bombers far behind.

Now! The fighters swung into a tight bank to the left. Round in a semi-circle, the earth revolving far below, sun glinting on cockpit canopies. In a matter of seconds they faced the bombers. The great machines were packed in tiers, so tightly that it looked as if the formation had become a single, monstrous flying machine.

Suddenly, shockingly, the tempo doubled, tripled, quadrupled. Bombers and fighters hurtled headlong for one another. Instants became compressed – and yet somehow simultaneously became eternities.

Open fire at 500 metres; break off at 100 metres. Time for a burst of fire of perhaps two, more probably one and a half seconds. For most pilots it was an impossibly brief period of fire. They might score one or two hits with their machine guns or cannons. Most would miss completely in the frenzied excitement of the moment.

To destroy one of those huge armour-plated monsters it was necessary to deliver a solid burst of fire right into the vulnerable cockpit and wing. The statistics said it took an average of more than a hundred hits by 13 mm machine gun bullets, thirty hits by 20 mm shells, but only three hits by 30 mm shells. . .

Fire!

Ernst saw his shells exploding. Fragments of shattered perspex went spinning into the sunlight. A glimpse of helmeted faces. Of blood. Of fire. Of tracers lacerating the sky. Of great swaying fuselages, gun turrets turning, machine guns winking.

He banked as he roared over the bombers.

Christ. Still alive. Still breathing. Christ.

The horizon rolled to the vertical. A glance behind. His wingman was there, straggling a bit but still hanging on. A good youngster. Name of Grultig. The Fortress formation in the background. Two, three, four of the big bastards in trouble. One diving away on fire. The others falling back, slipping behind the formation but still flying. Stragglers. They didn't stand much of a chance. Lone bombers were doomed. A fighter went spinning away in the nasty loose manner of an aircraft without anyone in control.

No hits to be observed on the wings or what could be seen of the fuselage. He wondered numbly how they could miss, all those

Yankee machine guns, all blazing away, in unison. Well, in a minute they would have another chance to get him. Power on. Overtake the formation – already becoming loose in places – even though the leader was undoubtedly yelling at everyone over the R/T. Close up! Tighten formation! Now turn once again. Check guns and sights. Brace every nerve and muscle. Head for the bastards. Shrink down behind the cockpit coaming. Pick a target. That one. Mine!

For a fleeting instant he wondered why he picked that particular aircraft. Why not that one? Or that? No shortage of targets.

Great lumbering metal monster filling the sights.

Fire!

Perfect hit!

The Fort lurched, its shattered nose jerking heavenward. As Ernst pulled up the bomber stalled and tumbled – but still the top turret kept firing.

Around again for another attack, the cockpit reeking of cordite. No time to wonder and worry about the chances of surviving another assault on the Forts. No time to think of anything but selecting a target, lining up, instantly calculating the range. Squeezing the triggers. The aircraft shuddering with the recoil of the cannon and machine guns. Hits! Spewing oil.

Jesus Christ . . . too damned close!

He damned nearly hit the Fort. He glimpsed the startled faces of the pilots, one with gauntlet'd hand raised as if to protect his face. A name painted on the side of the aircraft – an English language name he couldn't understand. A glimpse of a naked girl painted there; she possessed red hair and enormous breasts. She was smiling but there was a bullet hole in the centre of her forehead.

A Fortress tumbled out of the sky minus its tail unit; the aircraft's four engines still functioned, their propellers churning the air in aimless motion. Away to the south a straggler, streaming smoke plodded hopelessly in the direction of England. But the damaged Fort would never reach its base; a pair of 190s screamed in to riddle it until it died.

The Americans were taking a beating. Their formation was uneven now – tight in spots but a shambles elsewhere. The fighters had torn great gaps in the bombers' ranks; as soon as the Forts attempted to reorganize their formations fresh attacks would create more chaos.

Another head-on assault at lunatic speed, the enormous targets swelling in the windscreen panel. A burst of fire. A glimpse of hits. Then pulling up, hurling the aircraft away as a hundred machine guns peppered the air, every gunner doing his best to kill.

'I've been hit!'

Who? Identify yourself. . .

Christ oh Jesus, it was Grultig. Wrapped in flames his 190 twisted its way earthward.

'Bail out! Jump!'

A wing tore free of Grultig's aircraft; the remains vanished into cloud.

They drove to the wreck of a Fortress. The bomber had made a passable forced landing in a ploughed field; although the aircraft was peppered with bullet and cannon shell holes there had been no fire. The crew had survived the crash and had been taken away for interrogation.

The big machine looked strangely forlorn as it squatted on its belly in the dirt, its tall tail dominating the view.

'I remember this one,' Ernst said, pointing at the nose art: the redhead with the gigantic bosom.

' "Miss Adventure",' read Gablenz.

'What does it mean?'

'It's a pun,' said Gablenz. 'It could be her name, like Fräulein Adventure, you see. Or you can read it as referring to an accident.'

'An accident?'

'It loses something in the translation,' said Gablenz.

They clambered aboard the bomber, examining its fittings, its instruments, trying out the pilots' seats, handling the controls, imagining what it was like to sit in one of these monsters and watch the fighters bearing in at you head-on.

'The distressing thing about this airplane,' said Gablenz, 'is the quality of everything. Look at the covering of these seats. Good stuff. The sound-proofing here on the roof. The instruments. Everything. All top-quality. And they can make thousands of these things . . . thousands! As many as they need! And they can fill them with properly-trained crews. This is just the beginning, my friend. God knows what it'll be like in a year's time. Still, you and I will certainly be dead by then so it won't matter to us, will it?'

Ernst smiled. 'They say the Yanks are going to fit their P–47s with long range tanks so they can escort the bombers right into Germany.'

'I don't doubt it,' said Gablenz. 'An inventive people, the Americans. When we in Europe see a problem we learn to adapt to it. But the Americans find a solution. I lived there once,' he said. 'In a place called Newark, New Jersey. I was very young; I don't remember much except that it was dirty and much too hot in the summertime. My mother was homesick, so we came back to Germany. If we hadn't come back I'd have become a Yankee and I might have been in one of those Forts today. And you might have shot me down! Funny to think of that, no?'

'Very funny,' Ernst agreed.

Gablenz was undoubtedly correct in his estimation of their life expectancy. Every sortie against those enormous formations was suicidal. What difference did skill and experience make when hundreds of sharp-eyed gunners were spraying the air? All it needed was one bullet – one of God only know how many hundreds of thousands. The only course was to consider oneself already dead. It was the only way to drive oneself to engage in this madness. He was utterly drained after every day's operations, nerves on fire, limbs aching with fatigue. On that day, incredibly, his aircraft had taken only a single hit, a little hole punched through the fin, neatly separating the top bar of the swastika from the rest of the emblem.

The unit had lost two pilots – two out of twelve – yet spirits were high. The youngsters thought only of their successes, the great four-engined Yankee bombers they had destroyed, the German homes and lives they had saved. Other units had mauled the Fortresses on their return from the target. In all, the Americans were said to have lost more than fifty Forts and five hundred aircrew. But what were such losses to a nation with such productive capacity as America? Lucke was right. It was all a matter of arithmetic . . .

Twelve

It was bundled in with a score of missives from schoolboys and housewives, adoring and admiring letters. Such letters arrived in batches, tied together by some dutiful individual in the Field Post Office who affixed labels and wrote Ernst's current service address in large, childish letters. It was necessary to sort the letters into two piles: those requiring only the standard reply and those that called for some sort of individual response. He would jot something down and the Orderly Room would do the rest. People wanted to know the oddest things: Ernst's astrological signs; what he liked to eat for breakfast. A man from Essen once requested information on Ernst's bowel movements, claiming that they had direct relationship to fighting ability; a woman in Dusseldorf asked whether Ernst had been breast-fed as a baby; she was conducting research to determine whether breast-fed babies made the best soldiers. Occasionally the letters were more personal. A girl in Aaachen requested a clipping of his pubic hair; a man in Stuttgart demanded a full length photograph of Ernst in the nude, with organ erect; it was required, he explained, for scientific reasons.

He opened the letter addressed to: 'Leutnant Ernst Brehme, Luftwaffe'. The letter was brief, written in French. Leutnant Brehme should be advised that because of him, Jeanne Goutard was dead, taken and killed by the Resistance. Leutnant Brehme should rot in hell.

It was signed Georges Goutard.

The message didn't sink in for a moment. The words conveyed nothing. He listened for a moment as someone tried to start a truck's motor, the starter mechanism howling as if in pain. Then, numbed, he read the letter again.

Georges was saying that his mother was *dead*? No, obviously there was some gross error, some stupid mistake. It simply couldn't possibly be. The *Resistance*? What would they want with her. . ? He had heard of such things . . . but not *there* surely . . . who knew? Who cared? What purpose could it possibly serve to kill her because of *him*. . ?

A joke? Was the whole thing a joke?

He found himself staring at the postmark as if the answer might be found there. But the markings were blurred. Had Georges actually written this letter? Was this his handwriting? Christ, why did he ask himself such questions? He didn't know Georges' handwriting, so why did he waste time wondering about it?

It didn't make sense. Nothing made sense.

The Readiness bell jangled. In a strange way it was welcome. It was understandable; one knew how to react. Throw on flying gear, hurry out to the aircraft, clamber aboard, fasten harness.

Then sit back and wait for the next signal. And think. And feel the jab of fear that it might all be true. And argue with oneself, grapple with the thing . . .

Signal to start engines! Green flare! Immediate take-off!

The Americans came in force that day. The German fighters attacked them again and again, landing, refuelling, replenishing their ammunition, taking off again, attacking again.

Afterwards Ernst could remember little of the action.

The next day the weather closed in. The Americans stayed at home.

As he neared the house he saw that it was unoccupied; the front door was locked but the curtainless windows revealed empty rooms. The place was deserted. She had gone. An instant of panic. No, it might mean nothing more sinister than that she had moved without having sold the house. She and the children might now live in the village.

He parked the field car and switched off. It was utterly still; not a breath of wind stirred the damp air.

He walked around to the back of the house. Nothing to be seen. A small shabby place, undistinguished in every way; but when he stood and gazed at it his eyes filled with tears and a thousand memories came to haunt him.

He returned to the field car. An elderly man came along on a bicycle. Ernst hailed him.

'Excuse me, sir. I wonder if I might ask you about the lady who lived here . . '

The old man was already shaking his head vigorously. 'I know nothing of her,' he snapped as he cycled by, picking up speed.

Ernst drove into the village, pulling up beside the plump gendarme who stood in the village square, rocking backwards and forwards on worn heels.

'Do you know a M. Amiel?'

The gendarme came to attention and saluted, eager to please.

'Most certainly, sir. I am well acquainted with the Amiel family. Perhaps you would be good enough to tell me to which member you are referring. There is the elderly M. Amiel, once the major of the community but now retired and, I'm sorry to say, in rather poor health. Then there are his sons. M. Paul Amiel is a dentist; he lives a matter of some fifteen kilometres from here. . .'

'Not the dentist. The butcher.'

'Ah, then, sir, you are referring to Mr. Maurice Amiel.'

Maurice. For some reason it stung, learning the man's Christian name.

'His shop is on the corner, sir.' The gendarme pointed across the square.

'Is here there now?'

'I couldn't say, sir, but I would expect him to be.'

'Thank you.'

Another salute accompanied by an unctuous beam. 'Thank you, sir, and may I compliment you on your knowledge of the French language. . .'

Ernst nodded and walked across the street; Amiel's shop was cramped and drab. A thin, greying man stood behind the counter talking to a customer. Both turned abruptly as Ernst entered. The woman seemed to shrink back at the sight of the German officer. But the man folded his arms and waited without apparent concern or even interest.

Ernst hesitated, suddenly conscious of the delicacy of the situation. He felt like a child who has stumbled in where he isn't wanted.

'M. Amiel?'

The man nodded slowly, almost reluctantly.

'I am Maurice Amiel.'

'May I speak with you?'

The Frenchman said, 'You are Brehme, I suppose.'

'Yes.'

'Will you wait? I must serve this lady.'

'Of course.'

Amiel indicated a door at the side of the counter. Ernst went through it into a tiny sitting room cluttered with undistinguished furniture that looked as if it had been positioned without care or interest.

A painting near the door caught his eye. Bright, vigorous, full of life: unquestionably Jeanne's work. His heart ached; God, this couldn't be happening; it had to be a nightmare. . .

Amiel opened the door.

'I'm sorry to keep you waiting.'

'It doesn't matter. I came to you . . .'

'I think I know why,' said Amiel. He indicated a chair. 'Sit down. I wondered if you would come.'

'I had a letter from Georges, her son.'

'He told me he intended to write to you.'

254

The man spoke softly, his eyes downcast. He wore baggy trousers and a rumpled shirt. He looked tired and ill.

'It said . . . that the Resistance had come and taken her . . .'

Amiel nodded.

Christ.

Ernst said, 'You mean it's true?'

'Yes.'

'She's dead?'

'I believe so.'

He spoke in a strangely flat way, almost emotionless, as if he had told the story so many times that it now failed to move him.

'I don't believe it.' Ernst stood up. 'I can't believe it.'

'I couldn't believe it, either,' said Amiel with a hopeless sigh. 'She spoke of you many times. She had a high regard for you even though you are a German.'

'What can we do . . ?'

Amiel shrugged. 'We can do nothing,' he said. 'It is not possible to discuss the matter with the Resistance. I think our only hope is that someday one of their number will be captured and will reveal what happened.'

'For God's sake, we can't just wait.'

'No? If you have any suggestions I will be pleased to discuss them with you.'

Ernst stared at the man. He seemed so weary, so apathetic.

'Where are the children?'

'In Lille. The authorities took them.'

'Can I see them?'

Amiel shrugged. 'I suppose you can demand to see them; I'm sure it will be arranged, for someone like you. But I wouldn't advise it. They blame you for what has happened . . . Georges particularly.

'But I . . .'

'They're very young, you must remember that. Children tend to see things in black and white; to them there's nothing in between; you are guilty or innocent.

'And I'm guilty?'

'I'm afraid so, as far as they are concerned.'

'But . . .'

'You don't have to explain anything to me. I don't blame you. In a way I suppose I hate you, yet I don't blame you. Curious, isn't it? Jeanne and I were to be married. Perhaps you knew that.'

'She told me.'

'Yes, I thought she probably did. She was like that; she wanted everyone to know the truth; she hated deceit and hypocrisy above all things. She said exactly what she felt; I admired that in her. I am a far more timid person. We were, I suppose, ill-matched but I do believe I could have made her moderately happy . . .'

He rambled on. Ernst hardly heard him. He kept glancing at the painting; he could almost see Jeanne, working away with her brushes, creating those deft little touches that were so daring, so individual.

'Do you mind if I ask your age?' Amiel asked.

'Twenty-three,' Ernst said.

'We're odd rivals, aren't we? You so young and dashing and successful; me, a middle-aged nobody.'

'I'd better go.'

'As you wish.'

Ernst stood. 'I'm deeply sorry about everything.'

'I know you are. The war is the villain. You're the enemy yet I have to respect you because you're a brave man. She told me a great deal about you. You always treated her with kindness.'

Ernst blinked away the tears that suddenly blurred his vision. He had to get away from this place, from this lamblike specimen who seemed able to accept Jeanne's death with such equanimity. Ernst wanted to fight back, to wreak revenge on the inhuman bastards who had done this monstrous thing. . .

January 1, 1945: 02:35 hours

You wake suddenly, automatically glancing at your watch. You have slept a couple of hours, no more. The dreams jarred you back to wakefulness. You were falling and the sky was full of crackling flames.

You feel wide awake, experiencing that disquieting feeling of having too much blood in your arteries, of having it pumped around your body at twice its proper pace. Pointless, trying to go back to sleep. Besides, a couple of hours is sufficient. It will all be over by breakfast time. You can catch up on your sleep afterwards. If there is an afterwards.

You clamber out of bed and pad across the cold lino floor to the window. You part the blackout curtains. Disappointment awaits you. No dense, swirling fog or blinding blizzard to force a cancellation of the whole thing; not even a good steady rain. You peer into the gloom. The mechanics are busy out there on the field, frantically working to have every aircraft serviceable for the operation.

Three thousand?

How near to that magic figure will they come? Only HQ knows; at this moment some tireless clerk is probably collecting readiness reports from all the units, adding up the figures, passing the totals on to Generalmajor Freisler at his gilt and white desk.

A thousand? Even that figure now seems optimistic. Besides what does it really matter how many aircraft they have found? It's the quality and experience of the pilots that will make Operation Bodenplatte a brilliant success or shattering defeat. If all the pilots taking part are as young and amateurish as the lads who had downed their suppers with Göring last night, then the outcome is inevitable.

It is the first morning of the new year, the sixth of the war. On January 1, 1940 you were in the middle of flight training, wondering whether you would receive your pilot's badge before the war ended. Are any of your class still living? Koniger, of the curly blond hair? Wolfe, the law student-turned-airman? Hochtl, with the talent for the piano and the eye for the girls? Kraft, who wrote poetry? Klopfer, the Party stalwart who could quote *Mein Kampf* by the page? And the others, whose names and faces have long since dissolved in your memory: have any survived the impossible odds as you have done? You remember encountering Hochtl on a sodden field in Russia. You also remember hearing a couple of weeks later that he had been killed in a mid-air collision with a PE–2 bomber. Didn't someone tell you that Kraft was killed over England, less than a month after graduation from Advanced Training Flying School? Klopfer wrote to you when you were awarded your Knight's Cross. Possibly he's still alive, on the Staff perhaps . . .

Why are you wondering about them now? It's years since you thought of any of them. You shrug, unable to answer your own question.

As the Kommodore of entire Fighter Geschwader, leader of more than a hundred fighters, you enjoy relatively luxurious accommodation: a private room with your own personal bathroom, a field telephone at your bedside, a servant, Fisch by name, to keep the place tidy, do your laundry, shine your shoes. A tiresome little man, Fisch, but good at his job.

You switch on the light in the bathroom. You regard your reflection without enthusiasm; your face is pale, your eyes dull and heavy; against your pallid skin the scar on your cheek seems angrily red. You touch it, running your finger lightly over the area, feeling the welt where the new skin is joined to the old. For the umpteenth time you wonder at the strangeness of a fate which will kill everyone aboard an aircraft and let one man escape with a broken leg and an insignificant burn on his cheek. Why? What does it all mean? The burn gives you a devilish look, according to Ilse, your wife of eight weeks. She considers it far more dashing and *modern* than a mere duelling scar. Her picture stands on your dressing table, a portrait taken by Scherer, the leading portrait photographer of Berlin. He worked diligently to do justice to the wife of such a notable personality. It is a striking photograph of a remarkably lovely woman. One day you entered your room to find Fisch clutching the portrait in both hands, gazing at it in wide-eyed, slack-jawed adoration. Startled, the idiot dropped the portrait and smashed the glass. He had it replaced the next day but a tiny corner of Ilse's forehead was scratched.

You wash your face and brush your hair before returning to the bedroom. You long to telephone Operations. Possibly everything has been cancelled; bad weather could be approaching. But you won't call, not yet. Pride forbids it. A telephone call at this ungodly hour is proof positive of the jitters, of a shameful inability to sleep. No, you will call in an hour and you will sound casual and calm and pretend that you have just woken up from a satisfying, entirely restful slumber.

Outside, only slightly muffled by the hangar walls, the din of an aero-engine shatters the stillness of the night. The pitch rises to a crescendo, then abruptly drops almost to silence, only to scream out again as if in torment. A heavy-handed mechanic is working that throttle lever, a mechanic who undoubtedly hates that recalcitrant engine with every fibre of his being. When did the poor devil sleep last? Or eat?

In their own way the black-clad mechanics fight as valiantly as any pilot.

You turn off the light and return to the window, opening it, breathing deeply of the chilly air, gazing out into the blackness as if looking into the new year and examining what it will bring.

Defeat? Without question, no matter what Freisler and Göring and all the others say. Defeat can't be avoided. And it can only be a matter of weeks, perhaps days away. The enemy is too strong, too well equipped, too confident. The enemy has everything that Germany lacks. Ever the Führer must admit it, if only to himself.

You met Hitler twice in the last twelve months. The first occasion was in February. He awarded you with the Swords to your Knight's Cross and Oak Leaves. He seemed weary then, worn down by the awesome responsibilities he bore; his conversation was curt; he was impatient to return to more important matters. The second time you saw him was in the autumn. He presented you with the Diamonds, the ultimate accolade, worn by only a handful of fighting men. A proud moment – but you were appalled by Hitler's appearance. He had become an old, shaky man, his skin blotchy, his eyes dull; he was a pathetic figure, who kept mumbling about greater, more powerful U-boats until an aide quietly reminded him that he was talking to an airman, not a sailor.

You have survived. God only knows how many hundreds of thousands of bullets have lacerated the air around you. You have felt them thud into your aircraft; you have heard them glance off your cockpit canopy; one entered through the port side of your aircraft, grazed your gloved hand and departed through the starboard cockpit wall. But you have survived. You have limped back to base with damaged controls, with coughing, wheezing engines, with undercarriage legs dangling uselessly beneath your wing, with flames licking about your fuel tank on top of which your pilot's seat is fastened. But you are still breathing, still functioning. Your nerves are bad; your digestion is worse; you can seldom sleep more than two or three hours at a time; sometimes you suffer from airsickness; often you vomit after combat. But these are the occupational hazards of your calling.

You are a national hero; you are famous. You can't go into a restaurant without fellow citizens clustering about your table eager to shake your hand and slap your shoulder. Other servicemen stare in awe at the decorations at your throat.

The sad thing is how little it means to you. Is it because of what happened to Jeanne? For months you courted death. You flew like a madman, pressing your attacks in suicidal ranges. But it was the fledglings who died, wrapped in fire, many of the poor bastards on their first operational sorties. Never a scratch on you. You kept returning to collect more medals and adoration – and to sign the typed letters saying how deeply you feel the loss of your brave son, sir and madam.

Will you keep on surviving? Is it your punishment? You shake your head at the notion. Stupid, thinking such things. Punishment for what? Didn't you mean what you said to her? Of course. You loved her. Adored her.

And married Ilse.

She smiles at you from the portrait. A beautiful girl. No wonder poor old Fisch was smitten. How many times has he imagined possessing her? Does he wonder about the shape of her breasts and thighs? They're perfect, Fisch, old fellow; she is flawless.

But she's not Jeanne.

Your wedding in Berlin was an event of national importance; the photographs appeared in every paper: you, Ilse and your smiling guard of honour consisting of some of Germany's leading fighter pilots, bemedalled heroes all.

You realize with a sad little twist of the guts that two of them have since died in action, another lingers in hospital horribly burned.

You gaze at her picture and you tell her silently that you married her because a French Jewess was taken by the Resistance . . . a French Jewess she had never met, never even heard of . . .

Ilse was there when you needed her. You clung to her because you were sad and shaken. And, as if by some natural process, you found yourself engaged. All the world smiled at you. Warmth enveloped you. You had the power to make people happy. Simply set dates and select guests. . .

It seems a lifetime since you last saw Jeanne. But the wound still stings as keenly; she haunts your dreams; you see her on this street or in that restaurant: you keep hearing her voice and re-membering things she said . . .

No, Jeanne, this is not the moment to think of you. Duty calls.

You lift the telephone receiver. You are immediately connected with Operations. Assuming a casual tone, you enquire about the morning's operation.

'No change in the plans, Herr Major.'

You hang up and stare at the telephone as if expecting it to say more. Then you hear footsteps. Fisch. You sit on the edge of the bed and hope you look as if you have just woken up. At the last instant you remember that you have brushed your hair; as the door opens you ruffle it, silently calling yourself a mental case . . .

'Ah, good morning, Herr Major. You are already awake.'

Fisch has a penchant for stating the obvious.

'I am indeed awake.'

'I trust you slept well, sir.'

'Very.'

'The motors didn't disturb you?'

'Motors?'

'All night long they've been working on the aircraft. Making the very devil of a racket.'

He puts a cup of coffee on your bedside table. It is vile. You tell him so. He apologizes, saying it is the best he can obtain. The two of you exchange the same niceties every morning.

'Will the Herr Major eat breakfast in his room?'

You nod and tell him to bring some bread rolls and more of his disgusting coffee. The nincompoop beams as if you've compli-mented him.

You shave with care, paying particular attention to the tricky areas around the lips. God knows why. Then you dress, in winter flying suit. You strap your Luger PO8 9 mm pistol (which you have never fired) to your right side. You pull on your well-worn flying boots with their suede legs and leather uppers; you attach a rubber bandolier of flare pistol cartridges to the left boot. In twenty minutes you will meet the Gruppe and Staffel commanders; then the pilots themselves.

You will be matter-of-fact. You will discuss the operation as if

261

it is no more significant than a cross-country training exercise. It is your style. Calm begets confidence, someone once told you. Good advice – besides you are physically incapable of delivering stirring, morning-of-battle speeches. You wouldn't have the faintest idea of what to say – or how to say it.

The telephone rings.

'Brehme? Good morning.'

It's Freisler. Oily as ever.

'Good morning, Herr General.'

'How are you this morning?'

'Well, thank you. And yourself?'

'Never better, my dear fellow. Delighted to see the weather is co-operating with us. Everything well with you?'

'Yes sir. One hundred and six aircraft will be operational; a couple more if we're lucky.'

'Splendid.'

You ask the question that's been haunting you. 'How many aircraft will we be sending on this sortie?'

Freisler chuckles confidentially, the born salesman reassuring a cautious customer. 'Enough, my dear fellow, have no fear.'

You are bold this morning. You ask, 'Can you tell me the number, sir?'

'Not specifically, not at this moment. But don't concern yourself about detail.'

You shrug. You were right; three thousand was their make-believe number, the magic figure to make men's eyes wide with wonder, to reinforce their courage; to manufacture confidence to order. Lie convincingly enough and men will do anything.

Freisler says he will do his best to see you before take-off. You thank him – and immediately wonder why. The bastard should be thanking you.

'Good hunting,' he says.

The first rocket is fired!

Start engines! A hundred propellers spin, cold engines wheeze into motion, catch, roar. The field trembles beneath their din.

You nod to Dorsch – and he pats your helmeted head as he always does. You tug the cockpit canopy forward and lock it in place. Dorsch leans over and gives the windscreen and quarter panels a final polish.

You glance at the instruments. Pressures good. The dials blur as the massive 14-cylinder BMW sends shivers through every spar and rib. You feel the vibrations through the rudder pedals and through the armour-plated back of your seat.

The end of the field is invisible, cloaked in semi-darkness behind a wispy wreath of mist. Not long now. Thank God the waiting and preparation is almost over. Is anything worse than searching for the right words to say to men going into battle? It's worse, you think inconsequentially, than making conversation while waiting for a train to pull out. You remember Ilse clinging to you, fiercely, her fingers intertwined about your neck, as the train began to roll. She looked into your eyes with an intensity that was almost frightening. You had to smile and unencumber yourself of her arms, telling her to look after herself and to write often, just as you had told her a hundred times already . . .

You waved until she vanished from your view.

The extraordinary thing was how confident the young pilots looked this morning, eager to fly against the enemy, to inflict a crushing blow on the Yanks and the British. They believed they could do it. But not the older, more experienced hands, the few who had survived more than a few weeks: they accepted their orders without comment; they kept their thoughts to themselves as they made their way out to their aircraft . . .

Are there a *thousand* aircraft warming up at this moment? *One* thousand instead of *three* thousand? You doubt it. And who will fly them? Are there a thousand Luftwaffe fighter pilots left in the west? And even if, by some miracle, they did manage to dredge up a thousand, how many are truly capable of flying this sortie? Two hundred? Three hundred? You shake your head, feeling the dull weight of impending failure deep in your innards. Has anyone really planned this thing? Or is it a final, futile gesture?

Why ask the question now? Why didn't you demand to know when you were first told of the plan? Why didn't you refuse to fly it? Why didn't you do something to save some of these young lives? Can you do nothing but obey?

Like a programmed doll you received your orders and you nodded, obedient.

Good soldier, Brehme.

Fool, Brehme!

The second flare!

The take-off signal! A flick of gloved hand at Dorsch, then brakes off and you begin to roll over the bumpy frozen turf, your wings rocking as your undercarriage absorbs the shocks. The din becomes almost a physical thing, a massive, unyielding pressure on your very being. Your aircraft gathers speed. A hasty glance at either side. The others are following, great swarms of them; it's like some great mechanical cavalry charge.

Lift-off. Ground dropping away, slipping down into the blackness that smears the earth. You are climbing into a clearing sky, into a new day.

In the semi-darkness ahead you glimpse the flashing navigational lights. They belong to a Ju 88 bomber. On board is a navigator whose job is to plot the course and lead the formation to its target. Each Geschwader has its own target; each will rendezvous with a Ju to lead the way.

There is strict radio silence; at briefing, pilots were forbidden on pain of court-martial even to switch on the aircraft sets to test them. There will be no snippets of aircraft-to-aircraft conversation for the enemy to pick up, nothing to alert them to what is coming. The aim is maximum surprise. Catch the Yanks and Tommies while they're still half asleep, still nursing their hangovers from their New Year's Eve celebrations, still trying to remember what day it is.

The Ju waggles its broad wings, a waggle of welcome, a waggle of relief too, no doubt, that the rendezvous has succeeded.

You glance behind. Did everyong get off safely? You shrug. There's no way to find out so why worry about it? You glimpse other fighters, rocking, dipping, as they settle into formation. It will, you tell yourself, be a bloody miracle if there are no collisions.

The formation flies low, hurtling over darkened houses and tranquil woods. The ground has a misty, vaguely ethereal look about it, beautiful in a curious way; the shadows seem to have more substance than the bricks and wood. There's a chilling desire to want to sweep lower, to look more closely . . .

You trim the aircraft slightly nose up so that you have to maintain pressure on the stick to keep her flying straight. Pressures, temperatures, fuel OK . . .

ETA at the target: precisely two and a half minutes. Light steals across the landscape just ahead of the leading edge of your wings.

It's incredible, you haven't seen a living soul since take-off. You and your formation are making enough noise to rouse the devil himself, but no one emerges from the toy houses. Only an occasional cow accords you a disinterested glance. The rest of humanity has more sense than you, staying in bed, making love or simply going back to sleep, grumbling perhaps, at the noisy bastards outside, so damned early in the morning . . .

Tiny patches of snow are huddled in the corners of fields; sad little remnants of the storms before Christmas. Why couldn't the storm have waited until last night? It would have been greatly appreciated, Lord . . .

Wasn't Dietrich conversing with God on that first day? Dear old Dietrich. A good friend . . . gone, like so many of them. Like Gablenz, blown to bits in a collision with a B-24, an hour after telling Ernst that the 24 was easier to knock down than the 17.

Ah, a man on the ground! Two men! Standing, hands on hips, gazing up at the sky, at the oncoming 190s. Suddenly one turns and runs. Has he just realized that the aircraft are German? Is he dashing for a telephone? Or simply for cover?

More wing-waggling from the Ju 88 ahead. It's only a matter of seconds away now. As soon as the target is in view the bomber will turn away and head home, its job done.

You automatically check the instruments on your panel. Gunsight on. Safety off. Bomb fusing selected. You are armed, ready for battle. As if on cue, the emerging light reveals the airfield ahead. A huge field. You know it well. You have studied photographs by the dozen; you know the place as well as you know your own bedroom. Better. You know which buildings house the officers, which house the enlisted men, which contain ammunition, which contain nothing but desks and files. You tend to agree with the Intelligence lads that fuel is stored in the series of cleverly camouflaged mounds along the north-east boundary. A tasty target. But secondary. The principle object of the exercise is the destruction of aircraft. This field has P-51s, according to Intelligence, plus a few other types, samples from the Yanks' bottomless bag of weapons.

Now the bomber banks. You glimpse a raised hand in the cockpit, a comradely farewell. Good luck! Then the Ju is gone, left far behind as the formation thunders in to the attack.

You see the target. Dead ahead. A great open area. Nothing stirring. Tiny aircraft scattered all over the place, just waiting to be demolished.

A glance back. The fighters are close behind, scores of them, bombs clutched tight to their bellies, barrels of cannon jutting from their wings.

It's time for the formation to split, as briefed, into three main sections, one to sweep down the centre of the field, the others to take either side; then, after the first pass, a further breaking up into individual clusters of two and four aircraft for more attacks.

A jeep is motoring along the perimeter track. The driver sees you approaching at zero feet. He hits the brakes so violently that he almost tips his vehicle on to its nose. As you hurtle over him, he dives from the driver's seat, his field cap flying from his head; he has a fat behind.

Now the field is open. It speeds beneath you, seeming to flow like a raging torrent. You see silver P–51s, a cluster of them parked with tarpaulins over their engine cowlings. You fire. The shells bounce on the grass – then explode into the fighters, sending them staggering, shivering. One bursts into flames but it's vanished before you can spare it another glance.

More fighters! Just like the reconnaissance photographs! More hits! One blows up. You graze the fireball, banking to avoid it. A man in a raincoat and peaked cap stares up at you as if he can't believe his eyes.

Main hangars dead ahead. A short burst at a twin-engined Boston parked in front of the main doors. The bomber's transparent nose canopy shatters; the left gear collapses as you sweep overhead. Flame vomits from an engine.

A huddle of huts and small buildings, parked jeeps and trucks. A man, clutching towel and shaving gear, stopping in mid-stride, then running, frantic with fright; a sentry with white helmet and rifle, twisting, unable to decide which way to turn.

The airfield vanishes. You're speeding over a peaceful village, a farm. You bank; the earth rolls obediently; the scene unfolds before you like some living canvas: the airfield, smoke blossoming from a dozen spots; 190s, God only knows how many of them, some still making their initial run, firing.

One fighter ploughs into a hangar. Was the pilot hit – or did he simply not look where he was going? Such things happen.

Another 190 climbs away from the field trailing smoke.

An anti-aircraft gun opens up, pumping shells at the intruders, streaking the air with cotton.

The air is alive with aircraft, turning, diving, firing. Bloody fools! They're going to wipe each other out if they're not careful. The plan was to sweep well past the field before turning back. They've completed their runs too early, most of them. Too damned eager! They're skidding in front of you as you line up for your second attack. . .

Collision! Christ it happens in the corner of your eye! You turn your head. A horrifying tableau. One 190, minus most of its right wing, cartwheels crazily into the ground; the other machine stag-

266

gers, stalls, bursts into flame and tumbles, a confusion of burning
fragments.

Your target hurtles up at you. Your fingers squeeze the firing
buttons. You score hits on a P–51. You streak over the placid
hangars, releasing your bomb. No time to wonder what it hits, if
anything. . . . You rip through a column of dense black smoke
– in time to see a 190 roll on to its back and dive into the ground,
instantly transforming itself into a huge, bursting welter of flame
and smoke and disintegrating metal.

You slam the stick to one side to miss a 190 that suddenly
crosses your path, diving, firing wildly at God only knows what.

On the ground a dozen or more aircraft are burning. A couple
of dozen aircraft perhaps . . . perhaps more. But you can't stop
to count them.

The 190s are like a swarm of insects buzzing around a crippled
victim.

But now the victim is returning the fire. Half a dozen guns are
firing simultaneously. Shells wobble toward you – flecks of light
– then hurtle away behind. You notice a P–51 beginning to move
down there. Madman! He's trying to take off! You bank toward
him. But you're not fast enough. Three 190s are on him already.
The Mustang's rear collapses and he skids to a halt, trailing
flame.

You glance at the ammunition counters at the top centre of
your instrument panel. Only a few rounds left. One last burst.
Your target is a silver P–51, parked between trees. Its propeller
is turning. Another crazy cowboy! He's going to try and get into
the air and fight us all, single-handed! Not this time. . .

The ground sways toward you. A man in overalls points. Then
runs. Flings himself full length on the ground. You open fire.
Cordite fumes waft back into the cockpit. The airframe shivers as
the guns fire their last rounds. Your shells slice through the trees.
Branches shower down, hitting the 51. Did you waste your last
round? No! Explosions on the 51's cowling. A glow. Christ, you're
so bloody close to the thing that you look into the pilot's eyes.
He's sitting in the cockpit, canopy open, goggles pushed up on
his forehead; light brown flying suit; white gloves.

God, you tell yourself, you're as mad as everyone else! You
missed your target by a metre, no more. You damned nearly flew
into him, like one of your fledglings. A fine example for them!
Idiot!

You climb away, banking, seeing the burning airfield rolling away as if it is on hinges. A hell of a mess. Innumerable fires, utter confusion. A pleasing sight; for once it's *them*, not us.

You call your flock on the R/T. Time to head for home. Don't outstay your welcome!

Obediently the 190s reassemble for the trip home.

One last look. Facts for debriefing: at least a hundred aircraft burning on the ground – although some of those fires are the blazing remnants of 190s. How many? Impossible to tell until the head-counting back at base. Several buildings ablaze; half a dozen vehicles of various types. . .

By now the Yanks are wide awake. And angry. Every gun on the place is popping away. But it's too late. You are already out of range.

You grin.

Happy new year, cowboys!

You streak over a village. Soldiers – Americans – run across a street; some fire rifles at you. One slips and falls; his rifle goes slithering on the wet cobblestones. A woman leans out of a second storey window to see what all the noise is about. Her mouth drops open in astonishment as you hurtle by only a few metres above her head.

Gentle pressure on the stick. Time to climb to a safer altitude. The border is only a few moments away; another ten minutes and you'll be circling, lowering flaps and undercarriage; preparing to land. You're looking forward to a second breakfast. You're hungry. Odd, how action can stir your appetite.

You twist in your seat, awkwardly, your movements restricted by the shoulder harness. The 190s are strung out behind you, clusters of them, swaying, swerving in a formation that might unkindly be described as sloppy. But it doesn't matter. The job has been done. Now all that matters is returning to base as rapidly as possible.

You begin to relax. You're pleased; you feel a glow of affection for the pilots who flew with you this morning. They did better than anyone could have expected; they knocked that airfield out of action. The Amis were completely surprised – caught with their pants down, as they themselves would say. But yours was only a part of the total attack. You hope the other formations were as successful. If so, perhaps a crippling blow has indeed been inflicted upon the enemy; perhaps they will be unable to operate effectively for weeks or even months – long enough to permit the Luftwaffe to re-equip with the new jets . . .

Were the planners right after all? Why not? Who the hell are you to criticize? What do you know of grand strategy? Perhaps this operation really does represent the turning point of the air war.

For the umpteenth time in your career you glance at the instruments on the panel before you, the dials and gauges that convey to you the essential data on your aircraft's health: pressures, temperatures, revs . . .

You observe that your artificial horizon needs adjustment. Small wonder, after your frantic gyrations of a few minutes ago . . .

At that moment your world erupts.

Your body collides with an awesome force – crushing, shattering, numbing. Simultaneously the instrument panel disintegrates, dials and gauges popping free, leaving gaping holes like staring, lifeless eyes.

Then fire boils through those holes.

The cockpit is a mass of blinding light.

Curious how calmly, matter-of-factly your mind works.

You've had it. The odds have finally caught up with you. You aren't immortal, after all. You are about to become a statistic.

You sense rather than feel the heat of the flames as they reach for your face and lick at the goggles covering your eyes. How long before the shatterproof panels melt?

No sensation of falling. Yet that is surely what you are doing, for the stick is slack and useless in your hand. You glimpse the airspeed indicator. Incredibly it still functions. Its needle turns steadily clockwise. Velocity, a dim voice intones, is the time rate of change of a body in relation to a specified direction.

Attempt to get out? Pointless – besides, the effort is beyond you. A gigantic weight crushes you into your seat. You were flying at little more than roof-top level. You're in for a brief tumble. At any infinitesimal fraction of an instant it will all be over. You will join all the others – Dietrich, Wolfram, Gablenz and God only knows how many more – in little crisp black pieces: fertilizer for the farmland . . .

You tell Jeanne that you don't mind. It's a sort of relief. No more *trying*; no more hoping, no more wishing or wondering. All questions answered; all files closed.

Quickly. Please . . .

Oberst Wilde's office was busy all that day. At dawn some eight hundred German fighters had attacked Allied airfields in the Netherlands, France and Belgium. And there was no doubt that Operation Bodenplatte was a striking success, particularly so at Eindhoven, Evere and Melsbrock. In all, the Luftwaffe reported destroying approximately three hundred American and British aircraft.

News of the attack was released without delay. Radio broadcasts were interrupted; newspapers published special editions. Bulletin after bulletin flowed from Wilde's office, each more glowing than the last. A major victory had been won! The clean-cut young Aryan pilots of the Luftwaffe had avenged the countless innocent victims of the Allied gangster-flyers. It was something to cheer about in that bleakest of all winters.

What Wilde was careful not to disclose was the aftermath of Bodenplatte. The unhappy truth was that as the Luftwaffe fighters had sped back across the border they were spotted by German anti-aircraft gunners who, because of a regrettable administrative oversight, had not been informed that the operation was to take place. Perhaps understandably, the gunners took the low-level formation to be Allied. They opened fire. Their aim was good. Scores of Luftwaffe fighters fell in flames just as their pilots were congratulating themselves on getting back safely.

The telephone on Wilde's desk rang for the hundredth time that morning. It was one of his assistants, a zealous female named Scheele.

'We've just received a report concerning Major Brehme, sir.'

'Brehme?'

'Unfortunately he was one of our aircraft shot down by . . . accident.'

'By our own flak, you mean.'

'Yes, sir.'

'Is he dead?'

'Not quite.'

'Not *quite*?'

'The report says that he's very badly injured sir. Multiple burns. They're uncertain whether he'll pull through . . . but they do express some hope,' she added as if reading from a press bulletin.

'Disfigured?'

'It sounds like it, sir.'

Shame, thought Wilde as he hung up. Brehme had been quite the best subject in his experience. The boy had possessed a unique quality. Wilde wondered briefly who might be groomed to take Brehme's place. He studied his fingernails as he considered the question; then he shook his head. Perhaps the time had passed for that sort of thing. People didn't care about heroes any more. People cared only about survival.

Wilde reached in his desk drawer and removed a nail file. A corner of the nail on his right forefinger was a trifle jagged. A few deft strokes put the matter to rights. He replaced the file in his drawer. He thought about the Goutard woman. Should she now be released from the camp at Auschwitz? No, on second thoughts, it really wasn't such a good idea. Far better for everyone to continue believing her dead. Safer.

The telephone rang again. Wilde sighed. Was there no peace?

Fiction

☐	**The Island**	Peter Benchley	£1.25p
☐	**Options**	Freda Bright	£1.50p
☐	**Dupe**	Liza Cody	£1.25p
☐	**Chances**	Jackie Collins	£2.25p
☐	**Brain**	Robin Cook	£1.75p
☐	**The Entity**	Frank De Felitta	£1.75p
☐	**Whip Hand**	Dick Francis	£1.50p
☐	**Secrets**	Unity Hall	£1.50p
☐	**Solo**	Jack Higgins	£1.75p
☐	**The Rich are Different**	Susan Howatch	£2.75p
☐	**The Master Sniper**	Stephen Hunter	£1.50p
☐	**Moviola**	Garson Kanin	£1.50p
☐	**The Master Mariner**		
	Book 1: Running Proud	Nicholas Monsarrat	£1.50p
☐	**Platinum Logic**	Tony Parsons	£1.75p
☐	**Fools Die**	Mario Puzo	£1.50p
☐	**The Boys in the Mailroom**	Iris Rainer	£1.50p
☐	**A Married Man**	Piers Paul Read	£1.50p
☐	**Sunflower**	Marilyn Sharp	95p
☐	**The Throwback**	Tom Sharpe	£1.50p
☐	**Wild Justice**	Wilbur Smith	£1.75p
☐	**That Old Gang of Mine**	Leslie Thomas	£1.25p
☐	**Caldo Largo**	Earl Thompson	£1.50p
☐	**Ben Retallick**	E. V. Thompson	£1.75p

All these books are available at your local bookshop or newsagent, or
can be ordered direct from the publisher. Indicate the number of copies
required and fill in the form below   5

....

Name_____

(Block letters please)

Address_____

_____

Send to Pan Books (CS Department), Cavaye Place, London SW10 9PG
Please enclose remittance to the value of the cover price plus:
35p for the first book plus 15p per copy for each additional book ordered
to a maximum charge of £1.25 to cover postage and packing
Applicable only in the UK

While every effort is made to keep prices low, it is sometimes
necessary to increase prices at short notice. Pan Books reserve
the right to show on covers and charge new retail prices which
may differ from those advertised in the text or elsewhere